HOME SWEET HOMICIDE

CRAIG RICE (1908–1957), born Georgiana Ann Randolph Craig, was an American author of mystery novels and short stories. In 1946, she became the first mystery writer to appear on the cover of *Time* magazine. Best known for her character John J. Malone, a rumpled Chicago lawyer, Rice's writing style was unique in its ability to mix gritty, hard-boiled writing with the entertainment of a screwball comedy. She also collaborated with mystery writer Stuart Palmer on screenplays and short stories, and ghost-wrote several titles published under the byline of actor George Sanders.

OTTO PENZLER, the creator of American Mystery Classics, is also the founder of the Mysterious Press (1975), a literary crime imprint now associated with Grove/Atlantic; Mysterious Press. com (2011), an electronic-book publishing company; and New York City's Mysterious Bookshop (1979). He has won a Raven, the Ellery Queen Award, two Edgars (for the *Encyclopedia of Mystery and Detection*, 1977, and *The Lineup*, 2010), and lifetime achievement awards from Noircon and *The Strand Magazine*. He has edited more than 70 anthologies and written extensively about mystery fiction.

HOME SWEET HOMICIDE

CRAIG RICE, *1908 -1957*

Introduction by
OTTO PENZLER

**AMERICAN
MYSTERY
CLASSICS**

Penzler Publishers
New York

38212007101774
Rodman Main Adult Mystery
Rice, C
Rice, Craig, 1908-1957
Home sweet homicide

Published in 2018 by Penzler Publishers
58 Warren Street, New York, NY 10007
penzlerpublishers.com

Cover image: Andy Ross
Cover design: Mauricio Diaz

Paperback ISBN 978-1-61316-103-6
Hardcover ISBN 978-1-61316-112-8

Library of Congress Control Number: 2018947539

Distributed by W. W. Norton

Printed in the United States of America

9 8 7 6 5 4 3 2 1

HOME SWEET HOMICIDE

INTRODUCTION

When I first became involved in publishing mystery fiction, I felt it necessary to educate myself on the business end of the genre that I had previously known only as a reader and a collector. To this end, I read stacks of reference books, each one promising to contain the last word on the subject. And though I learned a lot of valuable information, I also absorbed a good deal of received wisdom that, due to its dogmatic nature, was almost certain to be proved wrong throughout the forty years of experience I've had since. For example, I learned that the private eye story is dead—*so* yesterday; that short story collections and anthologies don't sell; and that humorous detective stories do not appeal to mystery readers.

I'm not sure what these critics were responding to, or what vision they had of the future of mystery fiction, but, from where we now stand, it's clear that they were misled. Of course, the number of outstanding writers of private eye stories has never waned, for which we can all be thankful, else there would have been no Robert B. Parker, no Sue Grafton, no Stephen Greenleaf, no Sara Paretsky, no Robert Crais. If short story collections don't sell, how did Lee Child's Jack Reacher collection, *No Middle Name*, hit number one on the bestseller lists? And why is *The Best American Mystery Stories of the Year* entering its twenty-second year of publication? Why didn't anybody tell Carl Hiaasen, Donald E. Westlake, and Janet Evanovich that they were wasting their time by writing humorous crime fiction?

Fortunately, Craig Rice never read the same reference books that I did, else she might have been discouraged from writing her hilarious novels, many of which featured John J. Malone, the Chicago lawyer whose marginal practice reflects his greatest interest—whiskey.

Born in Chicago in 1908, Georgiana Ann Randolph Craig was raised by various family members after her parents moved to Europe early in her life. Because of her enormous popularity in the 1940s and 1950s, she was often interviewed but was as forthcoming as a deep-cover agent for the Central Intelligence Agency. How her pseudonym was created is a question that remains unanswered sixty years after her premature death. Equally murky is the questions about her marriages, the number of which remain a subject of conjecture. But we do know a number of biographical details with some certainty: She was married a minimum of four times, possibly as many as seven, and is known to have had numerous affairs. She had three children. She started her career working in radio and public relations, and tried her hand at music, poetry, and novel-writing without success before finally turning to writing the detective novels that brought her fame and fortune.

Rice is perhaps best known for the Malone series, though the fictional career of the character began with him being the friend of a madcap couple, press agent Jake Justus and his socially prominent bride-to-be, Helene Brand. Malone's "Personal File" usually contains a bottle of rye. Despite his seeming irresponsibility, Malone inspired great loyalty among his friends, including the Justuses, Maggie Cassidy, his long-suffering and seldom-paid secretary, and Captain Daniel von Flanagan of the Chicago homicide squad. The series began with *Eight Faces at Three* in 1939 and ran for a dozen novels and two short story collections, the second of which, *The People vs. Withers and Malone* (1963), was a collaboration with another giant of the Golden Age of the American detective novel, Stuart Palmer.

Another of Rice's series featured the unlikely crime-solving duo of Bingo Riggs and Handsome Kuzak. Starting out as sidewalk photographers, they graduated to being con men, solving murders out of self-preservation. Typical of their cases is *The Thursday Turkey Murders* (1943), in which they acquire a turkey farm in Iowa where several hundred thousand dollars is reputedly hidden.

Home Sweet Homicide (1944) is arguably Rice's best and most popular novel. It features a woman who is trying to write a mystery novel, struggling to avoid being distracted by her three children— and by the murder next door. Told from the point of view of the children, it recounts their efforts to solve the crime while trying to arrange a romance between their mother and the detective assigned to the case. Given the similarity of the main character to what we know of Rice's home life, the book appears to be at least somewhat autobiographical—presumably sans murders. It inspired a motion picture of the same title, released in 1946, that closely followed its storyline. Directed by Lloyd Bacon with a screenplay by F. Hugh Herbert, the film starred Peggy Ann Gardner, Dean Stockwell, and Connie Marshall as the kids, with Lynn Bari as their eccentric mother and Randolph Scott as Lt. Bill Smith.

Rice had numerous connections to Hollywood in addition to having several of her books and stories filmed, including *Having Wonderful Crime* (1945), with Pat O'Brien, George Murphy, and Carole Landis, and *The Lucky Stiff* (1949), starring Dorothy Lamour, Brian Donlevy, and Claire Trevor. She also wrote the screenplays for two of the sixteen films in the popular series about The Falcon, *The Falcon's Brother* (1942) and *The Falcon in Danger* (1943), the first of which starred George Sanders in the titular role and introduced Tom Conway (Sanders's brother in real life), who then assumed the role of Falcon for the rest of the series.

Rice's association with George Sanders led to her writing a mystery novel, *Crime on My Hands* (1944), under the byline of the actor. Having worked as a press agent for Gypsy Rose Lee, Rice also was long-believed to have ghost-written two novels for the famous burlesque queen, *The G-String Murders* (1941) and *Mother Finds a Body* (1942); however, Jeffrey Marks's recent biography, *Who Was That Lady? Craig Rice: The Queen of Screwball Mystery*, unearthed enough evidence to prove that Lee wrote the books herself. A copy of *Mother Finds a Body* in my own library has a long, warm inscription from Gypsy Rose to Lee Wright, the editor of Simon and Schuster's Inner Sanctum Mystery series, in which she thanks her editor for all her work on the manuscript, lending further credibility to, and evidence of, Lee's authorship.

Though at one time Rice was one of the handful of the most popular and famous mystery writers in America, becoming the first author of detective fiction ever to appear on the cover of *Time* magazine (the issue of January 28, 1946), her work has largely been forgotten today. This is mostly due to the fact that complications concerning the copyrights of her work have left the novels and stories unavailable for quite some time. With this reissue of *Home Sweet Homicide*, I am thrilled to be bringing her most idiosyncratic and hilarious work back to light; stay tuned for more gems from her remarkable career.

—OTTO PENZLER

While the characters and situations in this work are wholly fictional and imaginary; do not portray and are not intended to portray any actual persons or parties, I would like to dedicate it, with my deepest gratitude, to my children: Nancy, Iris, and David. If I had never known them, I would not have had the idea for the story. If they had not given constant help and occasional collaboration, I never could have written it. And, finally, if they had not granted their permission, it could never have been published at all.

—Craig Rice

THE KING TUT ALPHABET

(Note: In King Tut, all words are spelled out.)

A—a	N—nun
B—bub	O—o
C—cash	P—pup
D—dud	Q—q
E—e	R—rur
F—fuf	S—shush
G—gug	T—tut
H—hash	U—u
I—i	V—vuv
J—judge	W—wow
K—kuk	X—x
L—lul	Y—yum
M—mum	Z—zuz

Double letters, as in "well," are followed by the word "squared." Thus, "well" becomes wow-e-lul-squared.

Cast of Characters

Archie Carstairs, aged ten, the financially solvent member of the Carstairs brood

April Carstairs, aged twelve, small, blonde, and seemingly fragile. The cleverest of Mrs. Carstairs' children

Dinah Carstairs, aged fourteen, "the healthy type"

Marian Carstairs, their mother; a successful mystery story writer, whose lack of a "personal life" disturbed April

Polly Walker, an actress, and definitely (as April remarked) "a slick chick"

Flora Sanford, who lived next door to the Carstairs family. Now quite violently deceased

Bill Smith, a police lieutenant who was lonely

Sergeant O'Hare, his assistant, who had "brought up nine kids of his own"

Wallace (Wallie) Sanford, Flora Sanford's young husband, who decided that concealment was the better part of valor

Luke, proprietor of Luke's Place, who dispensed malteds and credits with equal facility

Rupert van Deusen, who started as a figment

of April's imagination, and ended by becoming a startling reality

Mrs. Carleton Cherington III, who evinced a keen interest in the interior of the Sanford home

Henry Holbrook, the Sanford lawyer, whose interest was equally keen

Pierre Desgranges, a man of many parts and many names, who painted nothing but water

Frankie Riley, a bullet-riddled small-time racketeer and blackmailer

Betty LeMoe, a kidnap-murder victim, who had been a burlesque star

"Uncle Herbert," a portrait with one eye shot out

McCafferty, a uniformed policeman, who didn't understand child psychology

Carleton Cherington III, whose photograph belied his name

Armand von Hoehne, an artist, present in the name, but not in the flesh

Slukey, Flashlight juvenile members of "The Mob"

Peter Desmond, whose other names turned out to be purely coincidental

Cleve Callahan, who demonstrated that his alias had been assumed for reasons of love

Chapter 1.

"Don't talk droopy talk," Archie Carstairs said. "Mother can't have lost a twelve-pound turkey."

"Oh, can't she!" his older sister Dinah said scornfully. "She lost a grand piano once."

Archie snorted skeptically.

"She really did," April added. "It was when we moved from Eastgate Avenue. Mother forgot to give the piano movers the new address and they got there after everything else had gone, so they just rode the piano around until she phoned the company. And meanwhile Mother had lost their name and address, so she had to call up all the piano movers in the telephone book to find the right one."

There was a little silence. "Mother isn't really absent-minded," Dinah said at last. Her voice was thoughtful. "She's just busy."

The three young Carstairs sat on the front porch railing, dangling their bare brown legs in the late-afternoon sunshine. From upstairs in the big old stucco house they could hear the faint purr of a typewriter, working at top speed. Marian Carstairs, alias Clark Cameron, alias Andrew Thorpe, alias J. J. Lane, was finishing another mystery novel. When it was done, she would take a day off to have her hair shampooed and to buy presents for the young Carstairs. She would take them extravagantly out to dinner and to the best show in town. Then the next morning she would begin writing another mystery novel.

It was a routine with which the three young Carstairs were thoroughly familiar. Dinah, in fact, claimed that she could remember it as far back as when Archie was in his cradle.

It was a warm, lazy afternoon. In front of the house lay a wooded valley, swimming in a soft haze. Here and there a roof showed through the trees; not many, though. The house had been picked for its quiet seclusion. The only house close by was the pink near-Italian villa of the Wallace Sanfords, a few hundred yards away and set off by a vacant lot, a small grove of trees, and a tall box hedge.

"Archie," April said suddenly, in a dreamy voice, "go look in the sugar bin."

Archie protested, violently. Just because she was twelve and he was only ten, he didn't have to run errands for her. Let her go look in the sugar bin herself. He closed his argument by demanding, "Why?"

April said, "Because I say so."

"Archie," Dinah said firmly, with the full authority of her fourteen years, "shove in your clutch."

Archie grumbled, and went. He was small for his age, with unruly brown hair and a face that managed to look innocent and impudent at the same time. He was always just a trifle soiled, save for the five minutes immediately after his bath. Right now one of his tennis sneakers was untied, and there was a small tear in the knee of his corduroy slacks.

Dinah, at fourteen, was what April called scornfully, "The healthy type." She was tall for fourteen, and well proportioned. She had a lot of fluffy-brown hair, enormous brown eyes, and a pretty face that was filled most of the time with either laughter or elder-sisterly anxiety. She was fashionably dressed in a bright-red skirt, a plaid Okie shirt, green bobby socks, and dirty saddle shoes.

April was small, and looked deceptively fragile. Her smooth hair was blonde, and her eyes—also enormous—were a smoky gray. The chances were that she would grow up to be a beauty; even better that she would grow up to be lazy, and she knew it. Her white sharkskin slacks and shirt were immaculate, she had on red laced sandals, and a red geranium was pinned in her hair.

Archie's returning footsteps sounded like a galloping colt. He let out a loud whoop as he slid through the front door and bounded back up on the railing. "I put the turkey in the icebox," he yelped. "How did you know it was in the sugar bin?"

"Simple deduction," April said. "I found the new sack of sugar in the icebox after Mother put away the groceries this morning."

"Are you a brain!" Dinah said. She sighed. "I wish Mother would get handcuffed again. We need a man around the house."

"Poor Mother," April said. "She doesn't have any personal life. She's all alone in the world."

"She's got *us*," Archie said.

"That isn't what I mean," April said loftily. She gazed dreamily over the valley. "I wish Mother would solve a real life murder," she said. "She'd get a lot of publicity, and then she wouldn't have to write so many books."

Archie kicked his heels against the wall and said, "I wish she'd do both."

Later April declared that Providence obviously had been listening in. Because that was the exact moment when they heard the shots.

There were two of them, close together, and they came from the direction of the Sanford house. April clutched Dinah's arm and gasped, "Listen!"

"Probably Mr. Sanford shooting at birds," Dinah said skeptically.

"He isn't home yet," Archie said.

A car roared past on the road, hidden from the young Carstairs by the shrubbery. Archie slid off the railing and started toward the vacant lot. Dinah grabbed him by the collar of his jersey and hauled him back. A second car went by. Then there was silence, save for the sound of the typewriter from the room upstairs.

"It's a murder!" April said. "Call Mother!"

The three young Carstairs looked at each other. The typewriter was going particularly fast right now.

"You call her," Dinah said. "It's your brain storm."

April shook her head. "Archie, you go."

"Not me," Archie said firmly.

At last the three of them went up the stairs, quietly, like mice. Dinah opened the door to Mother's room a few inches and they peered in.

Mother—J. J. Lane, at this moment—didn't look up. She was half hidden behind a battered brown wood desk which was littered six inches deep with papers, pages of manuscript, notes, reference books, used carbon paper, and empty cigarette packages. Her shoes were off, and her feet were curled around the legs of a small typewriter table which seemed to be fairly dancing as she typed. Her dark hair was pinned up every which way on top of her head, and there was a black smudge on her nose. The room was thick with smoke.

"Not even for a murder," Dinah whispered. She closed the door softly. The three young Carstairs tiptoed down the stairs.

"Never mind," April said confidently. "We'll make the preliminary investigation. I've read all Mother's books, and I know just what to do."

"We ought to call the police," Dinah said.

April shook her head firmly. "Not until we're through investigating. That's the way Don Drexel, in the J. J. Lane books, always does. We may find an important clue to save for Mother." As they started across the lawn she added, "And you, Archie, keep quiet and behave yourself."

Archie jumped up and down and yelled, "I don't hafta."

"Stay home, then," Dinah said.

Archie quieted down and came along.

At the edge of the Sanford grounds, they paused. Beyond the neatly clipped box hedge was a small vine-covered arbor, and, beyond that, a wide, well-kept lawn bordered by a bed of painted daisies. There was gaily colored garden furniture in front of the house, not quite the right color, April reflected, to go well with the pink stucco.

"If there hasn't been a murder," Dinah reflected, "Mrs. Sanford is going to make with a tizzy. She chased us off the lawn once before."

"We heard shots," April said. "Don't back out now." She led the way through the arbor, then paused. "There were two cars," she said speculatively. "Both of them turned into the road from the driveway after the shots. Maybe somebody already knows who the murderer is, and is chasing him." She looked at Archie from the corner of her eye and added, "Maybe the murderer will come back. Maybe he'll think that we were witnesses, and he'll shoot us all."

Archie gave a small squeak. It wasn't a very good job of pretending to be scared. Dinah frowned. "I don't think the murderer would do that."

"Dinah," April said, "you're too literal-minded. Mother always says you are."

They crossed the lawn to the driveway. Its cement was crisscrossed with tire marks.

"We ought to photograph these," April said. "Only we haven't got a camera."

The lawn and garden were deserted. There wasn't a sound or a sign of life from the pink-stucco villa. For a moment the three stood by a corner of the glassed-in sunporch, wondering what the next move should be. Then suddenly a long gray convertible turned into the driveway, and the young Carstairs ducked hastily out of sight, around the corner of the porch.

The young woman who stepped out of the convertible was tall and slender and lovely. Her hair was somewhere between red and gold, and it fell to her shoulders in big, loose curls. She had on a flowered print dress and a wide leghorn hat.

April gasped. "Look!" she whispered. "That's Polly Walker. The actress. Is she a slick chick!"

For a moment the young woman seemed to hesitate, half-way between the car and the house. Then she walked boldly on up to the door and rang the bell. After a long wait, and after pushing the bell several more times, she opened the door and walked in.

The three young Carstairs peered cautiously through the windows of the sunporch, from which they could see dimly into the large living room beyond. Polly Walker came in through the front door, stopped dead just inside, and screamed.

"I told you so," April murmured.

The young woman took a few slow steps into the room and bent down, momentarily out of sight of the watchers. Then she rose, went to the telephone, and picked up the receiver.

"She's calling the cops," Dinah whispered.

"That's okay," April whispered back. "They'll find all the clues and Mother'll interpret them. That's the way Bill Smith works, in the Clark Cameron books."

"That ain't the way Superman works," Archie said, in a shrill, piping voice. "He—"

Dinah clapped a hand over his mouth and hissed fiercely, "Shut up!" Then she said, "In the J. J. Lane books, the detective goes around planting false clues to confuse the police."

"Mother'll do that too," April said. She added prophetically, "And if she doesn't, we will."

Polly Walker, inside the house, put down the telephone, glanced toward the floor, shuddered, and rushed out. A moment later she appeared in the driveway, white-faced and shaken. She ran to her car, ripped off the wide leghorn hat and tossed it onto the front seat, then sat down on the running board, her elbows on her knees, rubbing her hands over her face and through her hair. Then she sat up straight, with a quick little shake of her head, reached in her purse for a cigarette, lit it, took two puffs, and ground it out under her heel. Then she buried her face in her hands.

Dinah said, "Oh!" out loud. It was the same sound she made when Archie fell and skinned his knees and elbows, or April flunked another math exam, or Mother got a letter in the Monday morning mail requesting revisions instead of a check. She ran forward instinctively, almost automatically, plumped down beside the stricken girl on the running board, and put an arm around her shoulders.

Archie's reaction was similar, but it expressed itself in a different way. His big, gray-blue eyes filled with tears, his lip trembled a little, and he said, very softly, "Please don't cry!"

The young actress looked up, her face white. "He killed her. He killed her. She's dead. Oh, why did he do it! It wasn't necessary. He shouldn't have done it. But he killed her." Her voice sounded like a phonograph record running just a little too fast.

"You'd better shut up," April said. "Suppose the police heard you say that. Button your lip, pip."

Polly Walker looked around her and blinked, bewildered. "What on earth—I mean, who are you?"

"We're your friends," Dinah said solemnly.

A small smile moved the corners of Polly Walker's lips. "You'd better run along home. There's been some trouble here."

"Sure," Archie said. "There's been a murder. That's why we're here. Because—" April kicked him savagely on the shin; he yelped once and was silent.

"Who was murdered?" Dinah asked.

"Flora Sanford," Polly Walker breathed. She covered her eyes with her left hand, and moaned, "Oh, Wally, Wally, you stupid fool. How could you!"

"For Pete's sake!" April exploded. "You're going to have to make with fancy answers to the cops practically any minute now, and you can't go into that 'How could you' routine. In the first place, it's corny, and in the second place, *he* didn't do it."

Polly Walker looked up, stared at April, and said, "Oh!" There was a faint and distant sound of sirens, growing louder and nearer. She straightened up and pushed a strand of hair back into place.

"Powder your nose, too," Dinah said sternly. She looked at April and said, "Who's *he?*"

April shrugged her shoulders and said, "How should I know?"

The first police car turned into the driveway with a last little moan of its siren. Polly Walker stood up. She murmured, under her breath, "You'd better go home, you three. This may be unpleasant."

"Not for us," April said.

The police car stopped beside the gray convertible and four men got out, all plain-clothes men. Two of them stood looking at the house, waiting for orders. The other two walked around the car and came over to where Polly Walker was standing. One of them was a slender man, of medium height, with thick, straight, graying hair, a deeply tanned face, and bright-blue eyes. He seemed to be a person of authority. The other was a big man, tall and stout, with a round red face, greasy black hair, and a perpetually skeptical look in his eyes.

"Where's the body?" the big man said.

Polly Walker shuddered slightly, and pointed to the house. The big man nodded, motioned to the waiting two, and led the way. The gray-haired man said, "And who are you?"

"Polly Walker. I phoned the police. I found her." She spoke evenly and calmly, but the skin around her mouth was white.

The police officer wrote it down, looked around, and said, "Are these her kids?"

"We live next door," Dinah said with icy dignity.

The big, red-faced man came hurrying out of the house and said, "The dame's dead, all right. Shot."

"Mrs. Sanford invited me over for tea," Polly Walker said. "I rang the bell when I got here, and nobody answered. I went right in and—found her. Then I called the police."

"The maid's out, Lieutenant," the big man said. "Nobody in the house. Could have been prowlers."

"Possibly," the police lieutenant said. The tone of his voice made it plain he didn't think it was. "You notify the medical examiner, O'Hare. Then try to locate her husband."

"Okay," O'Hare said. He went back into the house.

"Now, Miss Walker." He looked at her thoughtfully, offered her a cigarette and a light. "I know this has been a shock. I'm sorry to bother you with questions right now. But—" He smiled, and his face became disarmingly friendly. "Maybe I'd better introduce myself. I'm Lieutenant Smith of the Homicide Bureau."

Dinah interrupted him with a little gasp. "Oh! What's your first name?"

He glanced at her, slightly annoyed. "Bill." Before he could turn back to Polly Walker, Dinah had gasped again, louder. "Why?" he demanded. "What of it?"

"It's such a coincidence!" Dinah said, excitement in her voice.

"My being named Smith? There's millions of people named Smith."

"Yes," Dinah said. "But *Bill* Smith!"

"All right. There's probably millions of people named Bill Smith, too. What's a coincidence about that?"

Dinah fairly danced up and down. "You're a detective. Mother has a character—" She paused. "Oh, never mind."

He scowled at her. "Listen kid, I've got work to do here. I haven't time to listen to a lot of double talk. Run along now. Beat it."

"I'm sorry," Dinah said contritely. "I didn't mean to bother you. Mr. Smith, are you married?"

"No," he snapped. He opened and shut his mouth two or three times, without making a sound. "Look here. Go on home. Scram. Vamoose. Get the—get out of here."

Not one of the three young Carstairs moved as much as an inch.

Sergeant O'Hare reappeared. "Svenson already called the medical examiner," he reported. "And Mr. Sanford left his office a while ago; he oughta be home soon." He looked from his superior to the three young Carstairs and said, "Never mind, I'll handle 'em. I raised nine kids of my own." He strode up and struck a threatening pose. "What do you think you're doing here?" he roared.

"Don't be rude," April said coldly. She raised herself to a good five foot one, and looked him squarely in the eye. "We came here," she said with magnificent dignity, "because we heard the shots."

Lieutenant Smith and Sergeant O'Hare looked at each other for a long moment. Then the lieutenant said, very gently, "Are you sure they were shots—not backfire?"

April just sniffed, and said nothing.

"I don't suppose," Sergeant O'Hare said, with elaborate casualness, "you happen to know what time it was when you heard the shots?"

"Of course we do," April said. "I'd just gone in to look at the minute-meter to see if it was time to put the potatoes on. We heard the shots. Somebody had been killed." Suddenly her voice rose to a scream. "*Killed!*"

She sank into a limp little heap on the grass, screaming and sobbing. Dinah flung herself down on her knees. "April!"

Polly Walker jumped up from the running board and said, "Get a doctor!"

Police Lieutenant Smith turned pale and said, "What's the matter with her?"

Dinah felt a good hard pinch from the still screaming April. She looked up apologetically. "It's the shock. She isn't very strong."

"Get a *doctor*," Polly Walker repeated. "The poor child—"

Dinah leaned close and heard one fiercely whispered word, "*Home!*" She looked up again. "I'd better take her home. She—she might have a fit."

Archie got into the spirit of the occasion and added, "When she has fits, she breaks things."

"I'll carry her," Bill Smith volunteered.

Dinah caught a signal from April's eyes that said "No!"

"She can walk all right," Dinah said. "In fact, it'll be good for her." She pulled April to her feet and held her with one arm. April continued to sob loudly. "We'll take her home," Dinah said. "Mother'll know what to do."

"Mamma!" April wailed. "I want my mamma!"

"That's the right idea," Lieutenant Smith said, wiping his brow. "Take her home to her mother." He added, almost as an afterthought, "I'll come over and talk to you later." April's moans were fading in the distance by the time he said sympathetically, "The poor little kid!"

Sergeant O'Hare looked at him coldly. "I've raised nine kids of my own," he said again, "and that was the phoniest fit of hysterics I ever saw outside of a courtroom."

Out of sight and hearing of the Sanford villa, April paused and drew a long breath. "Remind me," she said, "to take back everything I've said about the Junior Drama teacher."

"Remind yourself to explain what that was all about," Dinah said sternly.

Archie just looked on, goggle-eyed.

"Don't be moronic," April said. "We're the important witnesses. We can fix the exact time of the crime. But we don't want to fix it yet. Because we might want to give somebody an alibi."

Dinah said, "Oh!" and then, "Who?"

"We don't know yet," April said. "That's why we had to stall for time."

"Tell *me*, tell *me*, tell *me*," Archie yelled. He hopped up and down with impatience. "I don't know what you're talking about."

"You will," April said.

The three stood for a minute just inside the front door, looking at each other and thinking. The typewriter was still going hard upstairs.

"We'll manage it somehow," April said.

A thoughtful look came into Dinah's brown eyes. "I'm going to cook dinner myself tonight," she murmured. "So Mother won't have to cut work. I'm going to bake the slice of ham in a ginger-ale sauce and make candied sweet potatoes and mashed white potatoes, and a big salad with Roquefort dressing, and hot corn muffins."

"You do know how to make corn muffins," Archie said.

"We've got a cookbook," Dinah said. "And I can read. Cream pie, too. She drools for it." She nodded, slowly. "You two had better come on out in the kitchen so we can talk," she finished, "because we have some other plans to make. Important ones."

Chapter 2.

MARIAN CARSTAIRS, alias, at the moment, J. J. Lane, looked around the dinner table and counted her blessings. Three of them, to be exact. She sighed happily.

There was a fresh lace cloth on the candlelit dinner table, and a bowl of yellow roses in the center. The ham was marvelously tender and delicately spiced, the sweet potatoes swam in a thick brown sirup, the corn muffins were scorching hot and light as thistledown. A highly successful experiment had been made in combining the salad.

April, the darling, had brought a glass of sherry upstairs before dinner and said such sweet, such appreciated things! "Mother, you look so much prettier in your blue house coat." "Mother, let me fix your hair tonight." "Mother, put some war paint on. We always like to see you looking schmoozable." And finally, "Oh, Mother, let me put one of the pink roses in your mane!"

Did anyone, ever, have such wonderful children? She gazed at them rapturously. So good, so clever, and so beautiful! Marian smiled at them all, and reproached herself for having had even the faintest and most secret suspicion of them.

Still—there was something familiar about the perfection with which she found herself surrounded. It had happened before. From past experience, she was forced to suspect that some project was shortly to be discussed. She sighed again, not quite so happily.

Such projects were usually commendable and understandable—but also, dangerous, expensive, something that interfered with Work—or, all three.

"O-kuk-a-yum?" Dinah said to April.

"A-bub-shush-o-lul-u-tut-e-lul-yum," April said happily.

"Talk English," Marian Carstairs said, trying to look stern.

"That is English," Archie yelped. "King Tut English. I can tell you what it means!" He beamed. "You take the first letter of every—"

"Shush-u-tut u-pup," April said hastily, kicking him under the table. Archie subsided with a low grumble.

After dinner, when April carried coffee into the living room, and Archie solicitously provided cigarettes, matches, and an ash tray, Marian Carstairs had to conclude that her suspicions were undoubtedly correct. And yet—how could anyone suspect so innocent and wide-eyed a child as April?

"You look tired," Dinah said sympathetically. "Wouldn't you like a footstool?" She brought it without waiting for an answer.

"You hadn't ought to work so hard," Archie said.

"Really," April added, "you ought to have more recreation. Especially, recreation that would help with your work."

Marian stiffened. She remembered the time they had all taken lessons in deep-sea diving, for "atmosphere." True, she had to concede, one of J. J. Lane's most successful mysteries had come from the experience, with the corpse found inexplicably stabbed while in a diving suit. Still—

"Mother," April said brightly, "if a lady was found murdered in her own living room, and if a few minutes later a socko motion-picture star drove up and said she'd been invited to tea, and somebody had heard two shots fired but the lady had only been shot once, and if her husband was missing and didn't have any alibi, but if neither the husband or the motion-picture star had been the person who dood it," she finally ran out of breath, gasped, and finished, "who would you say *did?*"

"For the love of Mike!" Marian said in a startled voice. "Where have you been reading such trash!"

Archie giggled and bounced up and down on the sofa. "It isn't trash!" he said loudly. "And we didn't read it. We saw it!"

"*Archie!*" Dinah said sternly. She turned to Mother and said, "It happened next door. This afternoon."

Marian Carstairs' eyes widened. Then she frowned. "Nonsense. I'm not going to fall for any of your tricks, not this time."

"Honest," April said. "It did happen. It's all in tonight's paper." She turned to Archie. "Get the paper. It's in the kitchen."

"I always have to do everything," Archie complained. He left.

"Mrs. Sanford!" Marian said. "That woman! Who did it?"

"That's just it," April said. "Nobody knows. The police have some loonie-louie theory, but they're all wrong, as usual."

They spread the paper on the coffee table and crowded around. There was a picture of the Sanford villa, pictures of Flora Sanford and of the missing Wallace Sanford. Under a large glamour picture of Polly Walker was the caption FILM STAR DISCOVERS BODY.

"She isn't a star," Marian said. "She's just an actress."

"She's a star now," April said wisely, "in the newspapers."

Wallace Sanford had left his office unusually early and taken the suburban train for home, getting off the train at 4:47. No one had seen him since, and police were searching for him. Polly Walker had discovered the body and phoned the police at five o'clock. There was no indication of robbery or violence.

"Right in our own neighborhood!" Marian murmured.

The three young Carstairs brightened visibly. "Wouldn't it be super," April said to Dinah, "if Mother could get a lot of publicity for her books by finding the murderer and solving the mystery!"

"There's no mystery," Marian said. She folded up the newspaper. "The police will probably pick up Mr. Sanford without any trouble. They're efficient enough in things of this kind."

"But, Mother," Dinah said, "Mr. Sanford didn't do it."

Marian looked at her blankly. "Who did?"

"*That's* the mystery," April said. She drew a long breath and plunged on. "Look. There's always somebody the police suspect of the murder. Like poor Mr. Sanford. But it never turns out that he did it. Somebody else has to find out who really did. Not the police. Somebody like Don Drexel, in the J. J. Lane books."

In one flash, Marian Carstairs understood everything, including the corn muffins and the roses on the table. At least, she thought so. "Now, listen," she said, sternly and positively. "Perfectly obviously, Mr. Sanford shot his wife and he's trying to get away. I don't know that I blame him; she was a thoroughly horrid woman. But this is something for the police department to worry about, not me." She looked at the clock and said, "I've got to get back to work."

"Mother," Dinah said desperately. "Please! Just think of it. You don't realize what a great opportunity this is."

"I realize that I have to earn a living for all of us," Marian Carstairs said. "Right now, I've got to deliver a book by a week from Friday, and it's only two thirds done. I have no time to mix in other people's affairs. And I wouldn't, even if I did have time."

Dinah felt discouraged, but not defeated. If her reasoning failed, they had one weapon left. April would weep. That almost invariably turned the trick. "Mother, think of the publicity. Think of all the books you'd sell. And then—"

The doorbell rang. Archie ran to open the door. It was Police Lieutenant Bill Smith, of the Homicide Squad, and Sergeant O'Hare.

April took a quick look at Mother. Yes, strictly wolf bait. The pink rose in her dark hair successfully hid the streak of gray. The make-up job was still intact. And the blue house coat was definitely tuzzy-wuzzy.

"Pardon the intrusion," Bill Smith said. "We're from the police." He introduced himself and Sergeant O'Hare.

Marian Carstairs' voice as she said "Yes?" indicated that it was not only an intrusion, but a nuisance. She didn't say anything about coming in and sitting down, and she looked again at the clock.

Dinah sighed. When Mother got these working streaks! She flashed her best smile and said, "Won't you have a chair?"

Police Lieutenant Smith said, "Thanks," and sat down. He glanced admiringly around the room.

"Coffee?" April chirped.

Sergeant O'Hare said, "No, thanks," before Bill Smith could open his mouth. "This is an official visit."

Bill Smith cleared his throat and said, "There was a murder next door to you this afternoon. I'm in charge of the case."

"I didn't know anything about it until I read the newspaper a few minutes ago," Marian said. "So I'm afraid I can't help you. I was very busy this afternoon." She added pointedly. "And I'm still very busy."

"Mother writes mystery novels," Dinah said in haste. "*Super*-mystery novels."

"I never read them," Bill Smith said coldly. "I don't like them."

Marian Carstairs' eyebrows rose a fraction of an inch. "Just what is the matter with mystery novels?"

"They're written by people who don't know anything about crime," he said, "and they give the public a lot of mistaken ideas about policemen."

"Is that so!" Marian said icily. "Let me tell you, most of the policemen I've ever met—"

Archie sneezed loudly. Dinah said to Bill Smith, "Are you sure you won't have some coffee?" April finished changing the subject by saying, "But about this particular murder—"

"This particular murder is the police department's business, and not mine," Marian said. "And if you'll excuse me—"

"Your kids heard the shots," O'Hare said. "They're witnesses."

"I'm sure they'll be delighted to testify, when the time comes," Marian told him. "In fact, I don't think you could stop them."

Police Lieutenant Smith cleared his throat for a second time, and reminded himself that a superior's report had once referred to him as "having an ingratiating manner." He smiled amiably. "Mrs. Carstairs," he said, being as ingratiating as he could. "I know all this is very distressing to you. But under the circumstances, I'm sure you'll co-operate."

"I'll co-operate," Marian said. "I'll even buy them all new clothes to wear on the witness stand. And now, if that's all—"

"You listen to me, lady," O'Hare said. He'd never heard about being ingratiating. "These kids of yours seem to be the only people who can fix the time those shots were fired. We want to know."

"We'd just looked at the clock," April said quickly, looking appealingly at Mother, "to see if it was time to put on the potatoes."

Marian Carstairs sighed. "All right. Tell them what time it was, and get it over with."

Archie bounded off the back of a chair. "It was," he began. He broke off with a squeal and began rubbing his arm where April had pinched him.

"I-lul-squared dud-o tut-hash-e tut-a-lul-kuk-i-nun-gug," April said.

"O-kuk-a-yum," Dinah said.

Marian Carstairs' lips tightened. "Talk English," she said.

April looked wistful and a little nervous. She walked over to Police Lieutenant Smith and her lovely eyes threatened to fill with tears. "I'd just looked at the clock to see if it was time to put on the potatoes," she repeated. "They go in to bake at four-forty-five. It was exactly half-past four, so I went out on the porch again."

Bill Smith and Sergeant O'Hare looked at each other, a bit bewildered.

"You never put on the potatoes," Archie said. "Dinah puts on the potatoes."

"I went to see if it was time for Dinah to put on the potatoes," April said.

Dinah gave Archie a *look*, and he shut up fast.

Bill Smith smiled confidingly at April. "I want you to think about this, my dear. Murder is a terrible crime. A man or woman who takes another man or woman's life must be punished. You understand that, don't you?" April nodded, gazing at him trustingly. "This is a very serious affair," he went on, beginning to feel sure of himself. "It's just possible that knowing the time you heard those shots will help us find the person who did this terrible thing. You see how important it is for us to know exactly when it was, don't you? I knew you would. You're a good, sensible, smart little girl. Now tell me, exactly—"

"It was exactly half-past four," April said. "I'd just looked at the clock to see if—Oh, I guess I told you that. If you don't believe me, ask Dinah. Because I came back out on the porch and told her she didn't have to fix the potatoes for fifteen minutes yet."

Bill Smith looked anxiously at Dinah.

"That's right," Dinah said. "I remember. April went in to look at the clock to see if it was time to—"

Archie snorted. "You don't fix the potatoes at four-forty-five. You fix them at five o'clock."

"I did tonight," Dinah said, "because we were going to have baked potatoes. They take longer than boiled potatoes."

"We didn't have baked potatoes tonight," Archie said exultantly. "We had mashed potatoes. So there, you're crazy!"

Dinah sighed. "That's because we heard the shots, and we went over to see what had happened, and when we got back, it was too late to make baked potatoes, so we made mashed potatoes." She dug a forefinger into Archie's back, just below his left shoulder blade. It was a signal he recognized, and he calmed down. "The point is," Dinah said authoritatively, "It was exactly four-thirty when April looked at the clock, and right after that, we heard the shots."

"I'd just gotten back to the porch when we heard them," April added.

"Are you sure?" Bill Smith said feebly.

The three young Carstairs nodded vigorously in unison, presenting a united front.

"Listen," Sergeant O'Hare said. "You lemme handle this. I've raised nine kids of my own." He advanced toward April, shaking a threatening finger under her nose. "Now you tell me the truth," he roared, "or you'll be sorry! What time did you hear them shots?"

"F-f-four-thirty!" April burst into tears, fled across the room, and buried her face in Marian's lap. "Mamma!" she wailed. "He scares me!"

"Stop bullying my child!" Mother said angrily.

"You made April cry," Archie howled. He kicked the sergeant on the ankle.

"I should think you'd be ashamed of yourself," Dinah said disapprovingly. "I thought you'd had children of your own."

Sergeant O'Hare's face turned the shade of an uncooked beet. He said nothing.

"You'd better wait for me in the car," Police Lieutenant Bill Smith said severely.

Sergeant O'Hare strode to the door, his broad face changing from red to purple. He paused for a moment and waved the forefinger toward Marian Carstairs. "You're her mother," he bellowed. "You oughta beat her ears off." He slammed the door and went out.

"I'm so sorry he upset her," Bill Smith apologized. "I can see that she's a delicate child."

"She is not a delicate child," Marian said, stroking April's head. "But this is enough to upset anybody. And if the children say they heard those shots at four-thirty, they heard them at four-thirty, and that's that. Do you think for a minute *my* children would deceive the police?"

Her eyes met his for a long moment. Bill Smith tried to find a polite way to say he thought April was a liar, and gave up. He could picture her on a witness stand, weeping, and swearing that the shots had been heard at four-thirty. He could picture the jury's reaction, too. "All right, it was four-thirty," he said stiffly. "I appreciate the information, and I'm sorry to have troubled you."

"I'm glad we could be of assistance," Marian Carstairs said, just as stiffly. "And I hope it won't be necessary to have any further discussion of the subject. Good night."

Dinah felt a moment's panic. She hurried to the door and held it open for him. "I'm *so* sorry you have to go," she said brightly. "It's been *so* nice, having you here. And *do* come again, soon."

Police Lieutenant Bill Smith looked at her blankly. He felt confused and baffled. And, for some reason he couldn't understand, he hated to go. He was going from here, after a brief report at headquarters, to an expensive, but lonely hotel apartment. Somehow, he wished he could stay just a few minutes longer. "Well," he said, "well, good night." He stumbled on the door sill, blushed, said, "Well, good night" again, and was gone.

April giggled. Marian Carstairs shoved her off her lap and stood, up. "I wish I knew," she said, "whatever gave me the idea I *liked* children." She stalked indignantly to the stairs. "You keep out of this affair," she said firmly, "and keep me out of it." She took two steps up and paused. "Just the same," she demanded, "what were you saying in that heathenish jargon?"

"April said, 'I'll do the talking,'" Archie squealed triumphantly, before either girl could squelch him. "And then Dinah said, 'Okay.' You just take the first letters of—Ow!"

"I'll fix you," April whispered fiercely.

Marian Carstairs sniffed. "I thought so. I didn't believe you, even if that stupid Smith person did. Remember, this is to be the last of it. I have no interest in who murdered Flora Sanford and I *hate* policemen." She turned and went on up the stairs.

The three young Carstairs were silent for sixty stricken seconds. The purr of the typewriter began again from the room above.

"Well," Dinah said wistfully, "it was a good idea, anyway."

"Was, nothing," April said. "You mean *is*. If Mother won't find out who murdered Mrs. Sanford, we will. And we're just the ones who can do it, too. We won't even have to ask her for help, we can just look things up in the J. J. Lane books."

"Oh, *that*," Dinah said. "I mean, *him*." She pointed toward the door through which Bill Smith had gone.

Archie sniffled a little. "I *like* him," he announced.

April said, "There isn't a thing to worry about. As far as Mother and Bill Smith are concerned"—she drew a long breath—"conflict and antagonism on meeting are a sure sign of a successful courtship."

"You read that in a book," Archie said.

April beamed happily. "You're darned right," she told him. "One of Mother's!"

Chapter 3.

WEEKDAY BREAKFASTS at the Carstairs' fell into two classes. There were the mornings when Marian Carstairs was already busy in the kitchen when the three young Carstairs came down. Usually she would have on a gay-printed quilted house coat, with a scarf tied around her head. Once in a while she'd have on her working slacks. Then there were the mornings when the three young Carstairs made their own breakfast and, just before taking off for school, carried a tray with coffee, a cup, and a clean ash tray to a sleepy-eyed and yawning Marian.

They could tell in advance which kind of morning it was going to be. If the typewriter had been clicking, loud and fast, when the last young Carstairs dropped off to sleep, it meant that Dinah would have to scoot downstairs after she turned off the alarm clock and start the oatmeal. This looked like one of those mornings. April and Dinah had stayed awake longer than usual, talking things over. The typewriter had still been going.

The morning started thoroughly badly. Everybody was cross. Absorbed in a discussion of the Sanford murder, Dinah had forgotten to set the alarm clock, and slept fifteen minutes too long. Archie, who'd wakened early, was absorbed in making a cardboard tank, and flatly declined to take any part in starting breakfast. April hung on to the dressing table for thirty minutes, trying four different styles of hairdos. By the time the three young Carstairs reached the kitchen only a half-hour was left before the school bus would go by, and a definitely strained situation existed.

"Archie," Dinah said, "make the toast."

"Oh, boney," Archie said. "Oh, foo." From Archie, that was the last word in profanity. He put on the toaster, though.

"April," Dinah said, "get the milk."

"Oh, barf," April said. But she got the milk.

"And shut up," Dinah said. "You'll wake Mother."

There was silence. When Dinah got That Tone in her voice—

"What's more," Dinah said, picking up a discussion that had been temporarily interrupted, "we are not going to ditch school. You know what happened last time."

April said gloomily, "By the time we get home, the police will have picked up all the clues."

Dinah paid no attention. They'd been over that aspect of the problem before. "And," she added, "we are not going to ask Mother for three excuses. In the first place, she's asleep. In the second place, the superintendent was very difficult about all three of us going to the dentist the day the circus was in town, and if you get Mother in trouble with the superintendent again, it'll waste a lot of her time."

"Oh, all *right*," April grumbled. "But the minute we get home—"

Dinah frowned. "I was supposed to meet Pete and go bowling with him after school."

April put down the milk bottle with a bang. "If you think more of a date with that shot deal than you do of your mother's career—"

"Shushup," Archie said hastily.

"Don't you shushup me." April snapped. She slapped him. He squealed. "You barfer!" and lunged.

April yelled, "Ow! Stop pulling my hair down!"

Dinah made a dive for April, who, in turn, made a dive for Archie. April howled. Archie screeched, and Dinah tried to outyell them. The package of breakfast food landed on the floor with a resounding crash and spilled. Then Dinah said in a low voice, "Hey! Quiet!"

Silence fell.

Marian Carstairs stood in the doorway, pink-cheeked and sleepy-eyed. She had on the quilted house coat and the bright scarf. The three young Carstairs looked at her. She looked at them and at the breakfast food.

"Mother," April said earnestly, "if you dare say 'birds in their little nests agree,' we'll run away from home."

Archie giggled. Dinah began sweeping up the breakfast food. Marian Carstairs yawned and grinned. "I overslept," she said. "What are you eating for breakfast."

"We were going to have that," Dinah said, pointing to the dustpan. "We overslept, too."

"Never mind," Marian said. "It wasn't very good breakfast food, anyway. Tasted like old hay. I can make scrambled eggs in four minutes. And is the morning paper here yet?"

Five minutes later they sat down to breakfast, and Marian Carstairs spread out the paper.

"Have the police found Mr. Sanford?" Dinah asked with elaborate casualness.

Marian Carstairs shook her head. "They're still looking." She sighed. "Who'd have thought a mild-mannered person like Wallie Sanford would have done a thing like that?"

Dinah glanced over her shoulder and read the front-page, column-two story. "You know, Mother," she said, "it's funny. Mrs. Sanford was only shot once. And the police haven't found the other bullet."

"What other bullet?" Marian said.

"There were two shots," April reminded her.

Marian looked up from her coffee. "Are you sure?"

The three young Carstairs nodded in unison.

"That is funny," she said, musing.

They pressed the advantage, fast. "You know, Mother," Dinah said in a rush, "I bet you could figure this out a lot quicker than the police." She remembered Mother's statement of the night before about policemen, and added, "They're all a bunch of dopes."

"I probably could," Marian Carstairs said thoughtfully. "In fact, almost anybody—" She stopped, tried to look stern. "I'm a busy woman," she said, "and you're going to miss the school bus if you don't *flee*."

The three young Carstairs looked at the kitchen clock, and fled. There was a hasty good-by kiss at the front door. April, the last to leave, glanced at the clock again and made a hurried calculation. If she took the short cut and ran all the way, she could spare sixty seconds. She clung to Mother and began to weep.

"For the love of Mike," Marian said in surprise, "what's the matter, baby?"

"I was just thinking," April wailed, "about how awful it will be when we're all grown up and married and gone away, and you're left all alone!" She delivered a quick moist kiss on Mother's cheek, turned, and ran like a rabbit down the hill. That ought to put a few ideas in Mother's head in case she should run into Police Lieutenant Bill Smith while they were away at school.

Marian Carstairs walked slowly back to the kitchen. She picked up the dishes, stacked them in the sink, and let hot water run over them. She put the milk and butter away in the icebox. The house seemed very empty, very quiet now that the three young Carstairs had gone thundering and yelping down the steps. She felt lonely, incredibly lonely, and suddenly bored with everything. April was right. How awful it would be when they'd all grown up and married and gone away.

Upstairs in the typewriter the last line on page 245 read, *Clark*

Cameron rose from examining the still form. "It wasn't a heart attack," he said slowly. "This man was murdered—like all the others." Marian Carstairs knew exactly how the next line was to begin. *There was a frightened gasp from the white-faced girl.* She knew, also, that it was time for her to don the working slacks, and settle down to the next ten pages of *The Seventh Poisoner.*

Instead, she went out into the garden and walked restlessly through its graveled paths. It would be years before she was left alone. Ten, at the very least. But ten years could pass so rapidly. Could it have been ten years now since Jerry—Marian sat down on the bench April and Dinah used for shelling peas, and remembered it all, from the beginning, as she'd remembered it over and over before.

They'd met over the body of a machine-gunned gangster on a Chicago street corner. It was her first assignment of any importance, and she was still only nineteen, though she'd solemnly sworn she was twenty-five when she got the job. She was scared. Jerry Carstairs was tall; he had mussed-up brown hair and a grinning, freckled, homely face. He'd said, "Hello, kid. Forget everything you learned in journalism school? Look—" Ten minutes later he'd said, "How about a date for tomorrow night?"

They didn't keep the date. That was the night of the warehouse fire. They didn't meet again for a year, and then they met in a rowboat being tossed around by the muddy waters of the Mississippi flood. He proposed to her; right then and there in the rowboat. They were married in New York by a justice of the peace, the day Mayor Walker welcomed Charles Lindbergh. He deposited her at the front door of their hotel and went away with a couple of photographers. The next day he showed up, tired and unshaven, and said, "Look, kid, pack fast. We're going to Panama, in about two hours."

Dinah was born in a hot, dusty little Mexican town where there

wasn't any doctor, and where nobody but Marian spoke English—
and she didn't speak anything else. Jerry was thirty miles away,
covering the revolution. April was born in Madrid, on the day
King Alfonso fled. She was born in a Madrid taxi, in which Marian was frantically looking for Jerry. When Marian was completely
awake, the next day, Jerry had gone to Lisbon, leaving a note saying, "Name her Martha for my grandmother." Marian swore tear-
fully into the pillow and named the baby April.

Three weeks later she packed up the two babies and followed
Jerry to Lisbon, to Paris, to Berlin, and finally to Vienna, always
about two trains behind. At Vienna Jerry met her, his arms filled
with all the flowers he'd been able to find, and she forgot that she
was mad at him.

Early in 1932, Archie was born, on a Chinese freighter entering Shanghai harbor the day of the bombardment by the Japanese
fleet. After that, the Carstairs decided to settle down.

There was a job for Jerry on a New York newspaper. There were
a little house on Long Island, a maid named Walda, and furniture that was being paid for at so much per month. For the first
month it was heaven, for the second month it was pleasant, and
then Marian began to be bored. She went around humming *Time
on My Hands* for a week or so, and then she began writing a mystery novel. She wanted to show Jerry the beginning of it, but he was
away, covering the Hauptmann trial. She wanted him to read it;
when it was done, he read it in a Washington hotel room and wired
her, "Good girl!" She wanted him to read the letter from the agent
she'd sent it to but he was down on the Florida Keys. He came
back with a bad cold, and before he'd gotten around to reading the
agent's letter, Dutch Schultz had been murdered over in Newark,
New Jersey. Two days later Jerry went to the hospital; pneumonia,
the doctor said.

He lived five days, and on one of them he was conscious enough to listen to the letter from the publisher, accepting and praising the book, and suggesting another. He'd been pleased. Always. Marian had remembered how pleased he'd been. He'd said, "Nice going kid." Then he'd gone back to sleep.

The contract and the check she found stuffed in her mailbox when she came back from the funeral.

The few years immediately following were a confused blur, as she looked back on them. There wasn't any money. Jerry had always spent his salary the week before he earned it. The check from the publisher paid up the overdue rent on the house on Long Island, and moved the Carstairs family into a tiny Manhattan flat. Walda insisted on going along. Jerry's newspaper offered Marian a job, and she grabbed at it. The next mystery novel was written in her free evenings at home, and on Walda's evenings out, Marian sat typing with one ear cocked toward the nursery, in case one of the young Carstairs woke and cried.

All that seemed very long ago. The years between were vague, half forgotten. Oh, a few things stood out. Walda's being married and, apologetically, leaving them. Her losing her job. Dinah's having the measles. Moving from place to place, and finally finding this house. Ten years at the typewriter.

The three young Carstairs had made it worth it. They'd had a lot of fun together. But it was true, they were growing up. They'd grow up and leave her. They had to live their own lives. And she'd be a lonely middle-aged woman, writing mystery novels on a portable typewriter somewhere in a hotel room.

Marian Carstairs stood up and told herself, "Nonsense!"

She wished she had a date. She wished she was on her way downtown to have a hair-do, a facial, and a manicure. A new dress to wear, and someone ringing the doorbell. She wished she was twenty again. She strolled on down the garden path. "You've got a date," she reminded herself, "with page 245. And you'd better get to it."

Maybe the next line shouldn't be *There was a frightened gasp from the white-faced girl.* Oh, no. Much better, *The police lieutenant turned white and gasped.* Yes, that was right. She began saying it out loud, as she walked. *The police lieutenant turned white and gasped. "I don't understand it," he gulped. "Of course you don't," Clark Cameron said coldly. "No policeman ever understands anything."* No, that wasn't right, that last line. It was too long. It wasn't punchy. She tried a few others, murmuring them. *"Of course you don't. All cops are dopes."* She liked that, and said it again. *"All cops are dopes"*

"I beg your pardon?" Police Lieutenant Bill Smith said, stepping from behind a bush. "What did you say about cops?"

"I said—" With a shock Marian came back from page 245. She glared at him. "What are you doing in my garden?"

"I'm not in your garden," he said mildly. "You're trespassing on property which is temporarily under police jurisdiction. There's been a murder here, remember?"

She remembered. She pulled the rose quilted house coat tighter around her. She said, "I'm very sorry," turned, and stalked up the garden path.

"Wait," Bill Smith said. "Wait, Mrs. Carstairs—"

She turned the corner around the evergreen hedge, and didn't look back.

What would Clark Cameron do in a case like this? There *had* been a murder, and a thoroughly obnoxious—though handsome—police lieutenant was in charge. Of course, if Clark Cameron was a woman—

Marian Carstairs sniffed indignantly, and went a little faster up the walk. Back to page 245, she told herself. *Clark Cameron rose from examining the still form—*

There was a sudden rustling in the bushes beside the path. Marian Carstairs stiffened with terror. There had been a murder, and there was a murderer loose. If anything happened to her, who would look after the three young Carstairs? She opened her mouth to scream, but she was too scared to scream. Maybe Flora Sanford's murderer was hiding there in the bushes, and thought she'd seen him. There would be a shot, or a sudden blow, and then, who would look after Dinah, and April, and Archie? She stood there, paralyzed.

"*Mrs. Carstairs!*" It was a hoarse whisper. Marian turned her head; a haggard, terror-stricken, unshaven face looked out at her from the leaves. A face that had once been handsome, and virile, and admired; that now was scratched and bloody, and dirt-streaked. "For the love of heaven," the hoarse whisper said, "don't call the police. Mrs. Carstairs, you can't believe I murdered my wife!"

It was Wallie Sanford. The man police in three states were searching for. The murderer. She could cry out, and the police would come and get him. There would be newspaper headlines, MYSTERY WRITER CAPTURES KILLER. It would sell a lot of books. But still—

"Believe me," Wallie Sanford gasped. "Believe me."

There were footsteps on the gravel at the bend of the garden path. Heavy footsteps. They were coming nearer.

"Run up through the bushes," Marian Carstairs whispered. "*Run!* I'll keep them from following you."

Wallie Sanford disappeared. The rustling in the bushes died away. The footsteps came closer. Then Marian Carstairs did scream, and loud. Loud and shrill.

Police Lieutenant Bill Smith was at her side in two bounds. He grabbed her arms and said, "What frightened you?"

"It was a mouse," Marian gasped. "There. On the path."

He said, "Oh." There was sudden relief in his voice. "I was afraid—" He gulped. "Look. Mrs. Carstairs. Would you—I mean, will you"—he still hung on to her arm—"I'd like to talk to you. Won't you—dinner—or lunch—or a movie—or, something?"

She looked at him. She said, "I wouldn't dream of it. And take your hand off my arm, please."

He looked at her. He said, "I beg your pardon," turned stiffly, and walked down the path.

Marian Carstairs ran into the house and upstairs to her room. For the first time in ten years, she was afraid she was going to cry.

Wallie Sanford. Hunted. Possibly a murderer. She should have turned him over to the police. But no, not with that look on his face.

A date. She'd been asked for a date. For the first time in—how many years?

She sat down on the bench in front of her dressing table, breathless, and looked in the mirror. Rose-flowered house coat, bright scarf, pink cheeks, bright eyes. "Why," she told the mirror, "I'm still *pretty!*" Suddenly she reached for her working slacks, and said to the mirror, "Nonsense!" Back to page 245. Paragraph two. Line three. Right after *Clark Cameron, et cetera* . . . "*This man was murdered. Like all the others.*"

She began to type, slowly. *The handsome police lieutenant gasped.* No. that was wrong. Police lieutenants didn't gasp. "*I think you're mistaken, Mr. Cameron,*" *the handsome police lieutenant said.* That wasn't right, either. Clark Cameron couldn't make mistakes. She crossed that out, too. Better start a new paragraph.

The handsome police lieutenant said—

"Oh," Marian Carstairs said, "Oh—*nonsense!*"

She xx-ed the whole thing out, and began another new paragraph, typing furiously. "*All cops are dopes.*"

Chapter 4.

"G'WAN, YOU kids, beat it," Sergeant O'Hare said. "Beat it, I told you."

"The nerve of him," April said coolly to Dinah. "Hasn't he ever heard about laws against trespassing?" Archie giggled, loud.

Sergeant O'Hare blushed, retreated two feet from the Carstairs lawn to the Sanford lawn, and repeated, louder, "G'wan, I said. Beat it."

"Why?" Dinah said calmly. "We live here."

"You live in that house," the sergeant said. "That house, there. Beat it, now."

"We live in the front yard, too," April said.

"We live everywhere," Archie squealed, jumping up and down. "Everywhere we are."

Dinah added, "And it's *our* front yard."

"I mean," Sergeant O'Hare said. He gulped. "I mean, beat it away from that there hedge."

"We like that there hedge," April informed him.

Archie, who'd stepped back a few feet, discharged his slingshot into that there hedge. The sergeant jumped, and yelped. "I-said-get-outa-here!" he bellowed. His face turned purple.

"Oh, all *right*," Dinah said. "If you're going to act that way about it."

The three young Carstairs strolled away from the garden gate, without one backward glance.

"We're going to have trouble with him," Dinah said gloomily.

"That's what *you* think," April said, serene and unruffled. "*He's* going to have trouble with *us*." She walked casually up the lawn for a moment or two, until she was sure Sergeant O'Hare had observed the dignified departure. Then she said, "C'mon, kids, there's a gate through the kitchen garden."

The gate through the kitchen garden was watched by a bored young uniformed cop. He shook his head and said, "Uh-uh. Can't come in here."

Dinah looked at him coldly for a minute before she said, "We promised Mrs. Sanford to weed out her turnips."

"Scram, youse." the policeman said pleasantly. "Mrs. Sanford don't care about them turnips. Mrs. Sanford's been murdered. See?"

"We see," April said, raising one eyebrow. "Imagine!" She looked slightly offended. "Murdered! Frightfully bad taste, you know." She raised the other eyebrow at Dinah and Archie and said, "Shall we go now?"

The young policeman looked after them for a long, long minute, his pink face puzzled.

"They've got the whole place guarded," Dinah said unhappily. "Even the garbage gate."

The three young Carstairs paused to consider the problem. "We've got to get in and search, somehow," April said.

"Search for what?" Archie demanded. "Hey! For *what?*"

"How do we know?" Dinah told him crossly. "We just search."

"Oh, boney," Archie said. "For what, for what, for *what?*"

"Archie," April said severely, "this is the scene of a crime. The first thing the detective does when there's been a crime is to search the scene of it. We're the detectives. So, we've got to search."

"Only," Dinah added, "the police are all around the place. See?"

Archie looked about him, and mentally verified Dinah's statement. "Okay, Loonie-Lou," he said. "Why dontcha go up the front driveway? Dopey, dopey, dopey!"

April and Dinah looked at each other. "We might try," April said.

"Y'h, y'h, y'h, y'h," Archie said.

"Shut up, pop-brain," April said pleasantly, "before the posse comes over the hill."

She raced ahead and led the way down toward the driveway, Archie yelping behind her. He caught up with her just at the turn into the front gate.

"Hey," Archie yelled. "Hey, hey, hey. What's a posse?"

April paused and looked scornful. "A posse," she said, "is the plural of poss. You've been to the movies." She struck an attitude, and quoted, "Take the short cut over the hill and head them off at the poss."

Dinah had caught up by then, and she added, "A posse is a little cat with a foreign accent."

April whistled and said, "Here, poss-ee, poss-ee, poss-ee."

"Oh, boney," Archie said, enraged. "Oh, *foo!*"

"Shut up," April said. "You ask too many questions."

Archie plumped himself down on the curbstone. He breathed, and wished he could have been breathing fire and brimstone. He said, "I—hate—girls!" He kicked his heels against the curbstone, and searched his mind for the utmost in profanity, finally exploding with, "Oh, shambles! *Shambles!*"

"For Pete's sake," Dinah said. "Both of you. Be *quiet.*"

"And *come on,*" April said.

She led the way up the driveway. There wasn't a policeman, uniformed or otherwise, in sight. "May be a trap," she whispered dramatically to Dinah. "We'd better duck through the hydrangea bushes. And walk quietly."

As they reached the bushes, they spotted a familiar long gray convertible parked by the house, and two familiar figures standing beside it. They ducked, and fast. They moved closer, walking quietly. Once Dinah caught April's arm. "Remember," she whispered, "what Mother always says about eavesdropping?"

"This isn't eavesdropping," April whispered back. "This is detection. There's a difference. And watch out for the brambles."

They crept up, inch by inch, to within six feet of the convertible, and paused there, hidden by the foliage.

Polly Walker stood by the car. She had on a white linen dress, with bright embroidery around the throat. Her wide brimmed, red straw hat matched the embroidery. Her red gold curls tumbled down over the white shoulders of the dress. She looked extremely young, and completely terrified. Bill Smith was resting one foot on the running board, and one elbow on the window sill. He was trying to look coldly stern, and only managing to look sympathetic and perturbed.

"I tell you," Polly Walker was saying, when they got within hearing distance, "I haven't the faintest *idea* where he is. I haven't heard from him, since—" Her voice broke off in a little gasp.

"Since when?" Police Lieutenant Bill Smith asked calmly. April and Dinah approved his tone and manner. Yes, just like Clark Cameron. Dinah whispered, "I wish Mother could watch this."

"Since the day before yesterday." Polly Walker's lovely mouth opened, and then shut, hard. She drew a breath. Dinah suspected she was mentally counting ten. "Why did you ask me to come out here? Why are you asking all these silly questions?"

"Because," Bill Smith said, "you told us, yesterday, that you hadn't met Wallie Sanford. That you only knew Mrs. Sanford, who'd asked you out to tea." He took his foot off the running board and stood up very straight. "But since you've just admitted you saw Wallie Sanford day before yesterday—" He paused. Polly Walker stood straight as a board, her face white. "When did you first meet Mrs. Sanford?"

"I—" Polly Walker's jaw set. "I don't consider that any of your concern."

April gripped Dinah's hand. "Remember when she said that line in *Strange Meeting?*"

Police Lieutenant Bill Smith drew himself up. He looked thoroughly unhappy. "Isn't it true, Miss Walker," he said, "that you had never met Mrs. Sanford in your life? That you were introduced to Wallace Sanford at a cocktail party on January 16th of this year? That you are known to have seen him frequently since that date, and that Mrs. Sanford, having learned of this—"

"Oh—*no!*" Polly Walker said. "That wasn't it. No, it wasn't that way at all." She bit her lip, straightened her shoulders. "I shan't even attempt to answer your absurd accusations. This is hardly the place for a third degree. If you have any further questions to ask, you may ask them of my lawyers." She opened the door of the convertible.

April suppressed a cheer. Dinah whispered, "That's straight out of her last picture. Remember, we saw it at the Bijou."

This time April said, "Shushup!"

Polly Walker slammed the door shut, and started the motor. Bill Smith grabbed the edge of the door, and said, "Now, you wait—"

"Am I under arrest?" Polly Walker demanded coldly. "Because if I'm not, you'll have to excuse me. I'm dated up to commit a few more murders this afternoon, and I'm behind schedule already."

She backed the car down the driveway in a rush that sent leaves scattering every which way. Lieutenant Smith stared after her for a moment. Then he turned and walked slowly back toward the Sanford villa.

"*That* line, she made up herself," April breathed exultantly. "Is he a dope!"

"Don't talk that way about your future stepfather," Dinah snapped. "And get going. We might be able to catch up with her down by the stoplight. *Move!*"

They shoved through the bushes, ran down the driveway, and raced like rabbits along the road. Ahead of them, the pale-gray convertible slowed up at a turn to let a station wagon drive past. They reached the turn and saw that it had paused by the stoplight. They dived on down the hill. "We'll never make it," April gasped, breathless. "The light—"

The light changed, but the car didn't move. It stood there, one wheel shoved crazily against the curb. A passing car honked indignantly, and then drove slowly around. The light began to change again. The car still didn't move.

"She's got to be all right," April said. She paused and stared at the car. "She's practically all the witness there is. We've got to ask questions—"

There was a white-clad figure sitting bolt upright at the wheel. It might have been molded out of snow.

"What questions?" Dinah demanded. "She's a movie star. She's got lawyers. If she wouldn't answer questions for the police, what makes you think—Oh, April!"

The figure of snow melted, suddenly. The white-clad shoulders shook.

Dinah ran forward. She put a quick, impulsive arm around Polly Walker's shoulders. Polly Walker buried her face against Dinah and sobbed, loud. She didn't seem like a movie star; she seemed like a scared and unhappy little girl. Dinah patted her head, the way she patted Archie's on those rare occasions when the sorrows of life became too much for him. She murmured, "Don't cry. We'll fix everything."

"Oh," Polly Walker wailed. "Oh, Cleve—*Cleve!* I didn't mean—" She choked. She didn't cry gracefully and exquisitely, as she had in

Strange Meeting. Her face got red, her hair came loose, her tears streamed, and she sniffed, loudly and unbeautifully. "Wally!" she sobbed. "He didn't do it. It wasn't necessary. He didn't know. I hate him. But he didn't do it. Oh, these *fools!*"

"There, there," Dinah said, aimlessly and consolingly. Polly Walker sat upright, reached in the dashboard compartment for a handkerchief, and blew her nose. "And I *believed* him," she gasped.

April hopped up on the running board. "Tell us. Who's *Cleve?*"

"He's my—I mean, he was my—" She looked up at them, her face tearstained, her lovely eyes wet. "Well! If it isn't my little friends!"

"Friends is the word," Dinah said solemnly.

"You do turn up at the darnedest times," Polly Walker murmured. She dabbed at her face with a handkerchief.

"And with the darnedest questions," April said coldly. "You'd better powder that map, sap."

Polly Walker reached automatically for her compact. She made one ineffectual stab at her nose with it. "You're such nice kids. If I ever have—I mean, I wish—"

April looked at her critically. "The powder's streaking. Maybe you'd better wash that pan, fran'. And confide in us. Is Mr. Sanford your"—she searched for a word—"gentleman friend?"

It took Polly Walker a moment or two to interpret that. Then she dropped the compact in her lap and began to laugh. "Gosh," she said. "Gosh, no. No, of course not. Whatever—"

"Then why," April said relentlessly, "did he murder his wife?"

"Because," Polly Walker said. "Because of the letter—" She broke off and stared at them. "What are you kids talking about?"

"Would it interest you to know," April said, "that we know he couldn't have murdered his wife. Because he got off the train at 4:47. *We* heard the shots. At 4:30."

Polly Walker stared at them, her mouth open.

"That's right," Dinah said helpfully. "April had just gone to look at the clock—"

"Let's not get into that potato routine again," April said hastily. Then, to Polly Walker, "You see, you haven't a thing to worry about. So don't look so glum, chum."

"But it couldn't have been," Polly Walker said helplessly. "Because at a quarter to five I was—I—"

"Miss Walker," Dinah said, with great dignity. "Would you make perjurers out of us, for a little matter of fifteen minutes?"

Polly Walker looked at them, grinned, and said, "I wouldn't dream of it." The pale-gray convertible roared under her feet, and she said, "You kids better run along and mind your own business."

The convertible raced down the road. April and Dinah stood looking after it for a moment.

"The nerve of her," Dinah said at last, "calling us *kids*. She isn't more than twenty herself."

April sighed. "Whoever *Cleve* is," she said dreamily, "I hope he's worthy of her."

They walked slowly back up the hill. "I feel," April said thoughtfully, "as if we'd learned something very important, only we don't know yet where to fit it in. Like Clark Cameron, in that book of Mother's, where he found the man who kept buying parsley by the ton, and it turned out later the man was the murderer, only he didn't know it at the time. He just knew that something—"

"Keep quiet," Dinah said irritably. "I'm thinking."

"Pardon *me,*" April said.

They took about twenty steps up the hill. Then suddenly Dinah said, "April! Where's Archie?"

April looked at Dinah. She gulped. "He was right there," she said in a faltering voice, "sitting on the curb."

They ran up the hill to the Sanford villa. There wasn't a sign of Archie, not anywhere.

"He's gone home," April said, unconvincingly.

Dinah yelled, "Archie! Arch-*ee!*" a couple of times, and got no response. She turned white. "April," she said. "There couldn't—I mean, nothing could have happened—"

"I don't think so," April said. She spotted a plain-clothes man parked at the stairway gate to the Sanford villa, and approached him amiably. "Have you seen anything of a dirty-faced little boy, with mussed-up hair, holes in the sleeves of his jersey, and his shoes untied?"

The plain-clothes man beamed and said, "Oh, him. Sure. He went up that way," he jerked a thumb, "up the hill, a few minutes ago. Up to Luke's for a malt. With Sergeant O'Hare."

Dinah turned pink with rage, April turned white, and both of them turned speechless.

"Why?" the plain-clothes man asked pleasantly. "Is his mother looking for him?"

"No," Dinah said. "But we are." She muttered one word under her breath. Fortunately, the plain-clothes man didn't hear it. The word was "Judas!"

Chapter 5.

"Not the third degree, psychology," Sergeant O'Hare was fond of saying. "That's what gets 'em every time." When he spotted Archie sitting alone, disconsolate and still raging, at the foot of the driveway, he decided to use a little psychology. After all, he reminded himself, he'd raised nine kids of his own. This ought to be a cinch.

"Hyah, bud," he said agreeably. "Where's your sisters?"

"Who cares?" Archie said gloomily, without looking up.

The sergeant pretended to be shocked. "Hey!" he said. "Is that any way to talk about such nice girls?"

"Nice girls!" Archie muttered. "Oh—shambles!" He looked up. "Y'know what?"

"No," Sergeant O'Hare said. "What?"

"I hate girls!" Archie searched his mind for just the word he wanted. "I—I ab-*dominate* girls!"

"Imagine that!" Sergeant O'Hare said. "Tch-tch-tch!" He paused, and then said with extreme casualness, "I suppose if you should go anywhere, you'd have to tell them."

"I wouldn't tell them anything," Archie said bitterly. "Even their own names, which they're probably too dumb to remember."

"Well, in that case," Sergeant O'Hare said. "I was just about to stroll up to Luke's for a malt, and I wondered if you'd care to join me, bud."

Archie started to say, "Sure!" paused, and said, instead, "Well—"

He sat for a minute, thinking. Sergeant O'Hare was an enemy. On the other hand, he'd been thinking about strolling up to Luke's for a malt. A malt at Luke's cost twenty-five cents, without whipped cream, and not chocolate. A chocolate malt with whipped cream—

Archie stood up, thrust his hands into his pockets. "Okay, pal," he said. "I'm your man."

During the three-block walk to Luke's, listening to Sergeant O'Hare's stories, he began to revise his opinion of the policeman. Capturing nine bank robbers, single-handed! And, unarmed, invading a gangster hangout, where a machine gun was trained on every door and window. And the time two lions escaped from the zoo—

"Of course," Sergeant O'Hare said, "to a policeman that's simply in the line of duty. Besides, they weren't very big lions."

He told his stories modestly. Archie's mouth began to hang open. Finally he said, "Hey. You know what? Did you ever catch a murderer?"

"Oh, sure," Sergeant O'Hare said. "Almost every day. Just routine stuff." He sounded a little bored. "Did I remember to tell you about the time I faced a wild man who'd escaped from the circus, and he was armed with poisoned arrows—"

Archie said, "Uh-uh. Did you?" He looked up at Sergeant O'Hare with worshipful awe. "Tell me, tell me, tell me."

"I will," the sergeant promised. "Give me time." He slid onto a stool in front of the soda fountain and told Luke, "A double chocolate malt with whipped cream for my friend here, and give me a cup of coffee."

Archie said, "Golly!" He felt a sudden qualm. Dinah loved double chocolate malts with whipped cream, and she wasn't here. Then he remembered that he was mad at her.

"As we were saying," Sergeant O'Hare went on, stirring his coffee, "we men understand each other. Now, girls—"

"Y'h, y'h," Archie agreed. "Girls, they don't know nothing." He took a gulp of the malt. It didn't taste as good as he'd expected. He said, "Well, g'wan. About the poisoned arrows."

"Oh, them," Sergeant O'Hare said. "It was like this. I found this man shot full of poisoned arrows. Naturally I had my first-aid kit with me. So what do you think I gave him?"

Archie took the straw from his mouth and said, "An anecdote?"

"You're darned right," Sergeant O'Hare said, pleased. "You and me, we're buddies, yeah?"

"Yeah," Archie said, resuming work with the straw.

"And buddies, they never keep secrets from each other."

Archie performed the interesting feat of shaking his head without taking the straw from his mouth.

"Likewise," the sergeant said, feeling on sure ground now, "likewise, buddies always tell each other the truth. Ain't that right?"

Archie inhaled the last of the malt, with an unpleasantly burbling sound. He withdrew the straw and said, "Yup."

"Say, maybe you can tell me something," Sergeant O'Hare said. "About—Oh, wait, how about another malt?"

Archie gazed into the empty glass. He was having a little private argument with his conscience, which kept whispering "Traitor!" into his ear. On the other hand, he hated girls, and Sergeant O'Hare was a great man, a hero, and likewise his pal. And, a double-chocolate malt, with whipped cream—

"What time *was* it when you kids heard them shots?" the sergeant asked gently.

Archie played for time and said, innocently, "Huh?"

Sergeant O'Hare glanced at Archie, detected the pangs of conscience, and started out in a new direction. "Frankly, I don't believe you know what time it was when you heard them shots."

"Oh, no?" Archie said, challenged. "We do, too."

"Well, your little sister don't know, because she told me wrong."

Archie puffed up a bit at that "*little* sister."

"So I'd be willing to bet you don't know, either," the sergeant said.

"I bet I do," Archie said indignantly. The inner voice that had been whispering "Traitor" retreated to a far place in his brain. Here was his chance to show up April and Dinah, and to show off in front of his new friend. "I do too know."

"Yeah?" the sergeant said skeptically. "When was it at?"

"It—" Archie paused and tried to get a last half drop up through the straw. The sergeant was sitting between him and the window and, beyond the sergeant's massive elbow, Archie could see the street. Out on the sidewalk were Dinah and April, signaling to him frantically. Girls! He hated girls! Then April made a sign that meant family solidarity, and Dinah added one that he'd seen a hundred, a thousand times at the dinner table, that meant "Don't talk." The straw in the malt glass made a repulsive noise. Archie slid off the stool. He said, "It was 'zactly half-past four. Because April had just gone in to see if it was time for Dinah to put on the potatoes. G'by. I gotta go home now."

"Four-thirty?" the sergeant said, half to himself, frowning. Then, "Hey, wait, pal. How about another malt?"

"No, thanks," Archie said. "I know when I got enough."

Dinah and April were waiting for him in the alley beside Luke's. Dinah grabbed him by the arm. April hissed, "What did he want to know?"

"Ouch," Archie said. He wiggled away. "He just wanted to know what time it was when we heard them shots. And I told him."

"*Archie!*" April said.

"I told him it was half-past four. Because you'd gone to see if it was time to put on the potatoes. So there."

Dinah and April looked at each other. "Oh, Archie!" April said. "You super-drooper!" She hugged him. Dinah hugged him from the other side, and planted a kiss on his cheek. Archie squealed and pulled himself loose.

"Hey," he said. "Don't do that! I'm a man now. I got a friend that's a p'liceman."

April looked toward Luke's; her eyes narrowed. "A spy, you mean." She looked at Dinah and said, "You and Archie go on home. I'll fix him."

Dinah said, "I hope!"

Archie protested indignantly. Dinah grabbed him and said, "Come *on*. Your friend that looks like a p'liceman is a spy, so there. And you know it."

"Well," Archie said. He did know it. "Oh, a'right," he said. "I've been duped."

April and Dinah giggled. "Archie," Dinah said earnestly, "I'm going to take the money I've been saving for a compact and buy you the water-pistol you've been wanting. Now, come on home." She looked at April and said, "Fix him *good*. But don't forget, you've got to be home in time to wash the vegetables for dinner."

April shuddered delicately and said, "Don't talk about washing vegetables, at a time like this."

She waited until she was sure Dinah and Archie were out of sight. Then she pushed up her hair, straightened the collar of her blouse, and strolled nonchalantly into Luke's, where Sergeant O'Hare was looking unhappily into an empty cup that had once held coffee. She thought of all the things she'd planned to say to him, about spying scoundrels who took advantage of unsuspecting little boys. They were things of which Dinah—and maybe even Archie—would have approved. Then, looking at the disconsolate sergeant, she had a better idea. Besides, she didn't know yet how much Archie had told him.

She slid onto the stool next to Sergeant O'Hare and said sadly to Luke, "I'd like to have a malt, but I've only got a nickel, so you'd better give me a coke."

"Got no more cokes," Luke said.

April sighed tragically. "O-kuk. A root beer, then."

"I'll look out in back," Luke said. "Maybe I got a bottle of root beer."

April sat still for five seconds. Then she turned her head casually, and her face brightened with pleased surprise. "Why, Sergeant O'Hare! Fancy meeting you here!"

Sergeant O'Hare looked at her and suppressed an impulse to turn her over his knee. He remembered, in time, about psychology. He beamed, and said, "Well, well, well! It's the little lady!"

Luke came back and said, "Sorry, no root beer neither."

"Oh, all right," April said unhappily. "Just give me a glass of water."

"Say," Sergeant O'Hare said, as though the thought had just struck him. "How about having a malt, on me?"

April's eyes widened. She looked surprised and delighted. "Oh, Captain O'Hare! That's so nice of you!"

"Give the little lady a double-chocolate malt," the policeman said purring. "With whipped cream. *Double* whipped cream." He turned back to April and said, "I'm not a captain. Just a sergeant."

"Oh," April said. "You *look* like a captain." She stared at him with wide-open innocent, admiring eyes. "I bet you've solved a lot of murder mysteries."

"Well," Sergeant O'Hare said modestly. "A few—" He wondered if he'd been mistaken in his first estimate of April Carstairs. She seemed like such a nice, well-behaved little girl. Intelligent, too.

"I wish you'd tell me about some of them," April said breathlessly.

He told her about the nine bank robbers, the gangster hideout, the lions from the zoo, and the poisoned arrows. She looked at him, fascinated, all through the first malt, and halfway through the second. Then suddenly tears began to form in her eyes. "Please. Captain—I mean, Sergeant—O'Hare. I've got to ask your advice."

"Why, sure," O'Hare said. "Glad to. Any day."

"I"—she gulped—"I know something about this murder. But I don't dare tell anybody."

Sergeant O'Hare stiffened. "Why not?"

"Because—" She sniffed, and began pawing for a hand kerchief. "Mother. I've never disobeyed her in my life. You don't think a person should ever disobey their—I mean his or her—mother—do you? No matter what?"

"Of course not," Sergeant O'Hare said.

"Well," she said, "that's why I want to ask your advice." She looked around the narrow little drugstore to make sure no one was listening in. Luke was out in front, arguing with a customer over a magazine that hadn't been saved. A man in a gray suit was dozing in the one booth. An old lady in a flowered hat was reading the patent-medicine labels on the shelves in back of the store.

"It's like this," April said. "Do you think a person who had important information that would benefit the police in a murder case ought to give that information to the police, even if that person's mother had strictly forbidden the person to have anything to do with the murder case?"

"That's rather a difficult problem," Sergeant O'Hare said slowly, though he knew the answer he was going to give. "You wouldn't want to disobey your mother. On the other hand, you wouldn't want a murderer to run around loose."

April shivered delicately. "Oh, no! But, you see—I wasn't supposed to be over there, listening. I'd be in a lot of trouble if anyone knew I was there. It was just that Henderson—that's Archie's pet turtle—got loose, and I was chasing him. I didn't mean to listen, really. I just couldn't help hearing. Because she was so frightened, and he was talking so loud."

"Yes?" Sergeant O'Hare said, controlling the excitement in his voice with an effort. "Who was frightened?"

"Why, Mrs. Sanford. Because he threatened—" April broke off and said, "I better finish my malt and get home. I've got to wash the vegetables."

"There's plenty of time," Sergeant O'Hare said soothingly. "Finish your malt, and have another. On me."

"Oh, thanks," April said brightly. She remembered she had a one-malt limit. Still, this was a special case. She finished the malt in two gulps. The next malt arrived, double rich. April took a sip and looked at the rest of it with loathing.

"I wouldn't have remembered it," she said, "if he hadn't threatened to kill her. Of course I didn't know he really meant it. Oh, but no. I shouldn't talk about it. Because Mother told us not to mix up in the trouble next door."

"Well," Sergeant O'Hare said, "I'll tell you. I'm your friend. You can confide in me, confidentially, if you know what I mean. I mean, I won't tell anybody it was you told it to me." He said solicitously, "Is there anything the matter with your malt?"

"Oh, no." April said. "It's swell." She managed to swallow some more of it, and reminded herself that it was in a good cause.

"Go on," the sergeant said gently. "It will be safe with me."

"It was like this," April said. "Henderson—that's the turtle—ate through his rope and got away. We were looking for him. There's a little summerhouse over on the Sanford place and it had a lot of vines around it. I thought Henderson might have gone there, so I was looking there. Then I heard voices in the summerhouse, and I kept quiet because I knew Mrs. Sanford would be terribly cross if she found me over in her yard. I wasn't really eavesdropping, honest I wasn't." She raised wide, moist eyes to the sergeant's. "You know that, don't you?"

"Why, sure, little lady," Sergeant O'Hare said. "You wouldn't intentionally eavesdrop on anybody."

"Oh, thank you," April said. She looked down at the floor and murmured, "Only maybe I hadn't ought to tell anybody. Because he was threatening her. And I wouldn't want to get anybody in trouble." She flashed a wan smile at the sergeant. "Maybe we'd just better skip it."

"Now, listen," he said earnestly. "If this party is innocent, you want him to have a chance to clear himself, don't you? And how is he going to clear himself, if the police don't have all the facts?"

"Well," April said. "Looking at it that way—"

Sergeant O'Hare felt triumphant, but he spoke softly. "What is this party's name, or do you know?"

"Of course I know," April said. She tried to think of a name, fast. The only one that entered her mind was a character from the stories Mother had written for them when they were very little. Persiflage Ashubatabul. That wouldn't do. She said, hastily, "It was like this. They were talking about some letters. He said he didn't have ten thousand dollars. She—I mean, Mrs. Sanford—laughed and said he'd better have. He said"—she squinted up her brow, as though trying to remember—"oh, yes. That before he'd pay her ten thousand dollars for a bunch of letters he'd written when he didn't know his own mind, he'd see her—dead."

April paused for dramatic effect, looked up at the sergeant, and whispered, "I was scared. It still scares me. I'm afraid I'll *dream* about it."

"Oh, no-no-no," Sergeant O'Hare murmured soothingly. "Don't be scared, little lady."

Tears began to roll down her face. She looked about eight years old, and completely helpless. "Captain O'Hare," she said in a tremulous whisper, "He said he'd kill her. And he said it as if he meant it. And she laughed, and said he'd better have the ten thousand dollars there, in cash, at four o'clock. And then he laughed, and said he'd see her at four o'clock, with a gun in his hand, not ten thousand dollars." April pushed her glass away and said in a small, quavering voice, "I *was* scared."

"There, there, there," Sergeant O'Hare said warmly and soothingly. "Just tell me *all* about it, and then—well, just put it right out of your mind." He lowered his voice. "You know, little lady, according to psychology, once you've told something like this, it won't bother you again."

"Oh," April said. "You understand everything so well." She gazed at him with wide, slightly tearful eyes. "I bet you've got children of your own."

"I've raised nine," the sergeant said, trying to sound as though he weren't proud of it. "All turned out well, too. Finish your malt, little lady, it's nourishing. And tell me. Didn't you get a look at this man? Don't you have any description of him?"

April shook her head, and reached for the malt. "I never saw him. I just heard him. I wouldn't even have known his name, if I hadn't overheard it."

"Oh," the sergeant said, "You know his name, then?"

April nodded. "She said—these are her exact words, Captain O'Hare—she said—" She paused. She had to think of a name for this guy. Persiflage Ashubatabul definitely wouldn't do. She searched her mind for names. Mother's new manuscript. She'd read all but the last twenty pages. There was a name. And a couple of lines of dialogue to go with it. April brightened, and smiled up at the anxious O'Hare.

"She said—'Rupert,' she said, 'you'd be afraid to touch a gun, let alone aim and fire one.'"

"Rupert," the sergeant repeated. He wrote it down, "And what did he say?"

"He said"—April hoped she could remember how Mother

phrased it—"he said, 'You think I'm a mouse, but I'll show you I'm a man!' Then"—she had to work the rest of the name in somehow—"then she said, 'Quiet. Someone's coming.' And then there was a pause and then she said, 'Oh, Wally. This is Mr. van Deusen.'"

"Van Deusen," Sergeant O'Hare murmured. He wrote that down, too. "Rupert van Deusen." He beamed at April. "Go on, little lady."

"Well, that's all." April said innocently. "The man—Mr. van Deusen, I mean—said, 'I'm delighted to meet you, sir,' and Mr. Sanford said, 'Won't you come in and have a drink?' And then they all walked away and I didn't hear any more." She smiled at the sergeant. "And after all that, it was Archie who found Henderson. In the laundry hamper."

"Henderson?" The sergeant said, frowning.

"The turtle," April reminded him. "Archie's turtle. I told you. He ate through his rope and got away. We were looking for him, and that's how I happened to hear this."

"Oh, yes," the sergeant said. He snapped his notebook shut and put it into his pocket. "I remember. Henderson. I'm glad you got him back. How about another double-chocolate malt, little lady?"

April concealed a shudder and said, "No, thanks, Captain." She stood up. "I gotta go home and wash the vegetables." A shadow crossed her face. "Promise you won't tell anyone I told you. Because if Mother knew—"

She said it with such passionate vehemence that even the man in the gray suit who'd been dozing in the booth sat up and looked at her. "I'd be in *terrible* trouble if she found out," April said. Her face was pale and worried.

"I promise," the sergeant said.

"Oh," April said, "*thank* you, Captain O'Hare." She made a dramatically dignified exit.

After she'd gone, he took out the notebook and glanced through it again. She was a good, bright little girl. He'd raised nine of his own, and he ought to know. *Captain* O'Hare, she'd called him. Well—maybe—someday—

For instance, if he could just locate that Rupert van Deusen before Lieutenant Bill Smith made any foolish moves! He snapped the notebook shut, stuck it into his pocket, and strode out.

Fifteen seconds after he'd gone, the man in the gray suit bounded out of his booth, wide awake, and said. "Gimme a handful of nickels, Luke."

He shoved nickels frantically into the wall telephone until he got his number. "This is Frank Freeman," he said excitedly. "City Desk." Then, "Hello, Joe? Listen—"

Five minutes later he was still pouring his story into the telephone, and the handful of nickels was almost exhausted. "I said—'reliable witness.' Got it? Okay. And it's van Deusen. Rupert van Deusen. For Pete's sake, why don't you listen? R as in robber, U as in underworld, P as in petrified—Rupert. Got it? Rupert van— Listen. D as in detriment, E as in etymology, U—Don't swear at me or I'll resign. Rupert van Deusen. That's right. Now. It was stated by a reliable witness whose name cannot be revealed—"

Chapter 6.

"WELL, FOR Pete's sake, gosh," Dinah said, "You certainly took time enough getting home." She looked up from the potato she was peeling. "April! What's the matter with you!"

April's face had a definite greenish tinge. "Tell you later," she said, and made a fast exit.

Five minutes later she returned, pale, but not greenish. "One malt is my limit," she reported, "and I hate whipped cream, and chocolate always makes me sick. And three of them—"

Dinah dropped the potato and glared at her. "Well, my gosh. You didn't have to order them."

"It's the most expensive thing on Luke's menu," April said indignantly. "You don't think I'd let that O'Hare dope get away with a nickel root beer, do you?"

Dinah sniffed. She loved whipped cream and chocolate. "All right, Martyr," she said coldly. "Scrub the carrots. And next time—"

"As far as O'Hare is concerned," April said, "I bet there ain't gonna be no next time." She sighed, got out the brush and went to work on the carrots. "I—" She paused. Maybe it wouldn't be wise to confide in Dinah and Archie about the unfortunate and wholly imaginary young man named Rupert van Deusen. Because Sergeant O'Hare might ask questions of them, and they might not be able to keep their faces straight. She was, after all, the only one who'd studied under Miss Grubee in Junior Drama Class.

"You *what?*" Archie demanded, looking up from his job of washing lettuce.

"I am I," April said serenely. "And you are you, and we are we, and they are they, and ours are ours, and twenty-four hours is a day, and three hundred and sixty-five days are a year. Hand me the vegetable brush. Dopey Joe."

"Oh," Archie said, enraged, "Oh—*yammer!*" He pulled himself together and grumbled, "A'right, here's the brush. Loonie-Lou!"

"*Miss* Loonie-Lou to you," April said.

"Shut up, you kids," Dinah said. "Mother's trying to work upstairs." She turned on the stove and put on the potatoes. "Now, listen. It's been twenty-four hours—more than that—and we aren't any farther."

"You mean any nearer," April said, holding a carrot under the faucet.

"Nearer to *what?*" Archie demanded.

Dinah slammed the lid on the potatoes. "Look. Yesterday. Mrs. Sanford was murdered. We're going to find the murderer, remember? So if you two infants will just stop playing and—"

There was a sudden, shrill outcry from next door. April and Dinah looked at each other, and both turned pale. Archie started for the doorway. April dragged him back.

"If it's another murder"—April gasped—"We can catch the murderer on the scene—"

"Wait," Dinah said. "Mother—"

They could hear the typewriter going upstairs.

"We can tell her about it," April said.

"Le's *go,*" Archie said, loud.

They plunged through the bushes of the kitchen garden. Suddenly April grabbed Dinah's arm.

It wasn't another murder. Through the garden hedge they could see a neighbor from down the street, Mrs. Carleton Cherington

III, garbed in violet chiffon and a wide violet hat, trying to pull her wrist away from the grasp of a young policeman, and blushing from her double chin to her plucked eyebrows. She managed to pull loose, and adjusted her hat, trying to adjust her poise at the same time. "I had no idea I was trespassing," she said breathlessly. "I was simply taking a short cut home from a garden party—"

"You were simply trying to get in that house," the young policeman said.

She laughed, not convincingly. "Ridiculous!"

"You're darned right," the policeman said. "Especially when you tried to climb in through that kitchen window."

Mrs. Carleton Cherington III finally got her hat properly adjusted, and caught her breath. "Young man," she said, "I'll confess to you. I *was* trying to climb through that kitchen window."

He wasn't impressed. He said, "Sure. I pulled you out of it."

"Everyone has a weakness," she said confidentially. "I must tell you mine. Unfortunately, it is—souvenirs. I thought, perhaps—a wisp of fringe from a rug—a button from the upholstery. I assure you—"

"Burglary." the policeman said.

"Nothing valuable." she said. "Simply a souvenir." She drew herself up to her full five four. "Young man. *I* am General Cherington's wife. Mrs. Carleton Cherington III."

A disturbance near the house staved off what was obviously going to be a rude remark on the part of the young policeman. He raced toward the source of the disturbance. Mrs. Carleton Cherington III stared after him for a moment and then ran like a rabbit toward the alley gate.

"That fat dame!" April said.

"I like her," Dinah said. "We like her. Remember the time she made us the oatmeal cookies? Maybe she's a puff-puff, but she's nice. And what's more she's worried about something—"

"Pssssst!" Archie hissed. He pointed.

The three young Carstairs moved up through the foliage to the disturbance. They moved fast, and as silently as they could. A violent argument was taking place at the front door of the Sanford villa. Police Lieutenant Bill Smith was taking part in it, so was the young policeman, and a plain-clothes man. Their opponent was a mild-looking little man of sixty-odd, with a frightened, waxy face, white hair, and a neat blue suit. He carried a brief case in one hand.

"But I insist," the man was saying. "I must insist. I am Mr. Holbrook. Henry Holbrook."

"Why were you trying to get in the house?" Bill Smith demanded.

"Well," the little man puffed, "I'm Mr. Holbrook. I am—I should say, I was—Mrs. Sanford—the late Mrs. Sanford's—lawyer. As her lawyer, I felt it my duty—"

"To try and force the lock?" Bill Smith said. "That isn't good enough."

"Why—" He paused.

"Mr. Holbrook, as a lawyer you should know that the house cannot be entered without police permission."

Henry Holbrook turned a shade paler. He mumbled, "Duty to my client—late client."

"I assure you," Bill Smith said, in a gentler tone, "your late client's property is quite safe. These policemen aren't standing around here just to decorate the landscape."

"Is it—customary," Mr. Holbrook stammered, "when there's been a murder—"

"Under these circumstances," Bill Smith said, "quite." He added amiably, "However, if you would like to go through the house—with a policeman accompanying you, of course—"

"I—" Mr. Holbrook gulped. "I don't think it's necessary, really. I'm—quite sure everything is in good shape. I'm—so sorry I—disturbed you." He turned and scuttled down the driveway toward his parked car.

April whispered, "There's something funny about this."

Dinah grabbed April's arm and hissed, "Look! Pierre. Pierre Desgranges. The man who says he's a painter." She pointed.

A short, stocky man with a white beard was moving quietly and surreptitiously up the path on the other side of the driveway, pausing now and then to look around. He had on corduroy pants, a plaid shirt, and a beret. There was an unlighted pipe in his mouth. Suddenly he disappeared behind a bush. The children watched, breathlessly, for five minutes, ten minutes. He didn't reappear.

Archie whispered (it was really what April called a whimsper, half whisper, half whimper), "I wanna go home now."

Dinah grabbed his hand and held it, tight. April murmured, "Don't be scared."

But there was something scary about the scene. The pink villa, where a murder had been committed only the day before. Policemen all around the place. And three people—who couldn't possibly have known each other—trying to break in. The shadow of an old sycamore tree began to throw its shadow over the villa, it looked like the shadow of some enormous hand.

"April." Dinah said, "we really ought to finish with the vegetables."

"We really should," April agreed fast. "Carrots take a long time to cook."

They ran quickly, like mice, along the sidewalk and up their own driveway.

Nobody said a word, not one word, until the carrots were cooking and the lettuce had been washed and put in the icebox. Archie not without protest, began setting the table.

"You know." Dinah said at last, dreamily, "I've been thinking about Mrs. Sanford. And why all those people want to get in her house. They want to look for something. Because Mrs. Cherington certainly isn't any souvenir hunter. And that lawyer, Mr. Holbrook, wouldn't have tried to pick the lock if he'd had a proper reason for being there."

"So?" April said noncommittally. She'd been thinking the same thing.

"And Mr. Desgranges. What would he be doing there?"

"Maybe he wanted to paint a picture," April said.

Dinah snorted. "He doesn't paint houses and trees. Mother said so. He doesn't paint anything but water."

Archie came out into the kitchen for the butter and said, "Paint water! Who ever heard of painting water!"

"Mr. Desgranges does." April said. "He met Mother someplace and he told her he was a painter. Mother asked him, very politely, what he painted, and he said. 'I paint water.'"

"Goony." Archie said. He sniffed, and carried the butter into the dining room.

"I was trying to explain," Dinah said, "that there must be some reason why everybody wants to get into that house." She paused and scowled. "Something hidden in the house, that everybody who tries to get in the house wants to find. April—I think—"

Archie interrupted her, sliding into the kitchen with a whoop. "Y'know what?" he yelped. "Y'know what? People don't paint water. They paint *with* water."

April and Dinah looked at each other resignedly over Archie's head. "Archie," April said, "Mr. Desgranges doesn't paint with water, he paints with oils. He paints with oils."

Archie's round face turned an ominous shade of pink. "Just because I'm littler'n you are—"

"Listen, Archie," Dinah said, sternly and hastily. "And shut up. Mr. Desgranges paints pictures. With oil paints. Understand?"

"Sure, sure, sure," Archie said impatiently.

"Well, he paints pictures *of* water. He goes and sits by the ocean and paints pictures. No beach, no boats, no people."

"No *sky*, even?" Archie demanded incredulously.

"Nothing but water," Dinah said firmly.

Archie snorted. "Why does he go all the way to the ocean?" he said scornfully. "Why doesn't he just sit home and look in a pail?" He gathered a handful of knives and forks and went back to the dining room.

Dinah drew a long breath. "As I was saying." She paused again.

"Well," April said. "Go *on*."

"*I* think Mrs. Sanford was a blackmailer."

For a minute April didn't trust herself to speak. Finally she said, in her most casual tone, "I wouldn't be surprised."

"Why," Dinah said, half surprised, "had you thought of that too?"

April decided to confess. She'd never in her life been able to keep secrets from Dinah, even about Dinah's birthday and Christmas presents. "Listen, Dinah." Dinah wasn't going to approve of this, either. "This afternoon—"

"You know what I think?" Dinah interrupted. "I think we ought to give a party."

April stared at her, aghast. "At a time like this!" she gasped. "You can think about parties?"

Dinah nodded, dreamy-eyed. "Tomorrow night. It's Friday night. You can convince Mother. About ten kids. You invite half and I'll invite half."

"But, Dinah. A party—"

Archie burst into the kitchen. "You gotta let me come, too. Hey. You gotta let me come, too."

"Sure you can," Dinah said, "and invite the Mob."

Archie jumped up and down and said, "*Yipe!*"

April shuddered. The Mob consisted of some ten or twelve

small boys, aged from nine to twelve, all noisy, all dirty, and all disreputable. "Dinah, are you out of your *mind?*"

"A treasure hunt," Dinah said. "That's the idea. It's bound to spill over into the neighbors' yards. Maybe besides searching the grounds, you and I can break into the house."

"I get it," April said happily. "And the Mob—"

"If I know the Mob," Dinah said, "they'll keep the police too busy to bother about us. We'll figure out who to ask, right after dinner. And what were you going to say when I interrupted you?"

"Oh. Oh, yes. Dinah, listen." April moistened her lips. "This afternoon—"

"Well," Marian Carstairs' voice said warmly from the doorway. "You've got dinner all started! I didn't know it was so late."

She still had on her working slacks, her hair was slightly mussed, and there was a smudge on her forehead.

Dinah poked a fork into the potatoes. "Everything's practically done. How's the turkey?"

"Turkey?" Marian Carstairs' face turned white, then red. "I—it's in the icebox. I meant to start roasting it about two o'clock. Then I was thinking of something else. I guess it's too late now."

They all looked at the kitchen clock. Quarter to six.

"That's all right," Dinah said cheerfully. "There's three cans of sardines in the cupboard, and we're all crazy about sardines." She began buttering the potatoes.

"Tomorrow," Marian said. She looked apologetic and miserable. "It's just that I was busy. I love to cook."

"You're the best cook *ever*," Archie said.

"Mother," April said solemnly, "you ought to get married again. Then you could cook all you wanted to."

"Married!" Marian blushed becomingly. "Who'd ever want to marry *me?*"

The doorbell rang. Marian Carstairs fled up the stairway. Half-way up she called, "Dinah, you go. I'll be right down."

She came down in five minutes. She had on the blue house coat, and a fresh make-up job. Her hair was beautifully arranged, and at the last minute she'd tucked one of the pink roses in it.

April whistled and said, "Neat job!"

"Who?" Marian said, looking toward the living room.

"It was just the newspaper boy," Dinah said. "I paid him. You owe me twenty-two cents." She spread the paper out on the table.

"Oh," Marian Carstairs said. Then, very casually, "Anything new on the Sanford murder?"

"For gosh sakes!" Dinah said. "Hey, April."

"Let me see," Archie said, shoving under Dinah's arm.

The four of them crowded around to look.

The words and phrases of the front-page story swam before April's startled eyes. Exclusive story. Rupert van Deusen. Reliable witness whose name cannot be revealed. For a minute she wondered if she was going to faint. No, it was probably just a hangover from the malts.

"Mrs. Sanford!" Marian gasped. "I can't believe it." Then, "Funny. Rupert van Deusen. That name sounds awfully familiar to me. Wonder where I could have met him."

"I betcha the cops will find him easily, with a name like that," Archie said confidently.

"April," Dinah said, slowly. "We were right. She *was* a black-mailer."

But when April was finally able to speak, all she could say was, "Excuse me. I think the carrots are burning."

Chapter 7.

"THE KIDS can bring the food," Dinah said. "We'll buy the cokes." She began thumbing through the phone book.

"With what?" April demanded. "I don't know about you, but I've got twenty cents, and I owe Kitty fifteen."

Dinah scowled. "I've already borrowed next week's allowance from Mother."

"As a matter of fact," April said, "Mother ought to buy the cokes. After all, we're doing all this for her, aren't we?"

"We're doing it for us too," Dinah said. "For the whole family." She thought for a minute. "Maybe Luke would trust us. How many cokes do we need?"

"I doubt it," April said. "And we need—well—twelve kids, not including us—say, about thirty cokes. That's a dollar and a half, not including the bottle deposit. And then, there's the Mob."

"Oh, gosh," Dinah said. "I don't know what to do. I hate to ask Mother, after she's been so nice about letting us have the party. A dollar and a half. And then there's the Mob. There'll be about ten of them, at least, and they'll want two cokes a piece. And we'd better have a few spares. Say, twenty-five altogether. That's another dollar and a quarter. Altogether, it would be two dollars and seventy-five cents. I don't think Luke would trust us for that. Besides, I owe him a quarter already."

April sighed, and sat thinking for a minute. "I guess we'll have to borrow it from Archie. He's got it. He always has money." She added, "Archie's a miser."

Archie came racing down the hall in pursuit of Jenkins, the cat, who'd run off with a leftover sardine. He pulled up short at the sound of his name and decided to let Jenkins have the sardine. "Hey!" he demanded. "What'sa miser?"

Dinah said, "A miser is a rich man, and don't bother us."

April pinched Dinah and said, fast, "A miser is a rich man who is, also, smart and good-looking and fast on his feet and able to lick practically anybody. Like Superman."

"Gosh!" Archie said. "Am I a miser?"

"Darned right you are," April said.

Dinah said, "Sit down, Archie. We want to talk to you."

"*I* want to talk to you," April said, pinching Dinah again. "Listen, Archie. We're not sure you ought to invite the Mob to the party."

"Aw," Archie said. "Please."

"Well," April said, "you see—it's this way—"

Five minutes later, after considerable dickering, a settlement had been reached. A short-term loan of two dollars and seventy-five cents. Archie to have sole rights to all bottle-deposit money not only for the party bottles, but also for a period of seven days. Also, permission to bring the Mob.

Dinah counted the money. Five quarters, eleven dimes, six nickels, and ten pennies. She scooped it into her purse and said, "Well, that's that. Now I'll call up the kids."

"I'm going to ask Joe and Wendy and Lew and Jim and Bunny," April announced.

"Bunny," Dinah said scornfully. "That sad case!" She frowned again. "I'll ask Eddie. He can come with Mag. And Willy."

"Willy's a wolf," April said.

"*Him?*" Dinah said, sniffing. "Are you kidding? He's just a goon that has to be wised up. Anyway, he and Joella are lovelucent, and we've *got* to have Joella."

"Why?" April demanded. "She's such a shot bag."

"Listen," Dinah said. "The kids are going to want to dance. And Joella's the only one we can borrow a lot of phonograph records from." She began counting on her fingers, two at a time. "Eddie and Mag. Willy and Joella."

"Don't forget your O-and-O," April said.

"Well, naturally," Dinah said. "Eddie-and-Mag, Willy-and-Joella, *and*, Pete and Dinah." She looked critically at her sister. "I notice you always invite all the guys that like you, and some dopey girls that nobody likes."

"I'm not a dupe," April said coldly, "and I'm nobody's little mouse. I don't ask for competition."

"Me," said Dinah, "I believe in free enterprise." She reached for the phone.

"And don't call Pete first," April said. "Or by the time you get around to calling anybody else, they'll all be asleep."

It was two hours later when the last call was made. There had, in the meantime, been a lot of phoning back and forth, and weighty discussions between calls. "Well, Mag, you phone Eddie, and then phone me back." "If Joe's mother won't let him go out tomorrow night, how about asking Russell?" "Look. Wendy, it's a treasure hunt. Wear your old clothes." Archie tied up the phone for thirty minutes, calling the Mob. By that time Joe had called up to say he could come, but in the meantime, Russell had been invited. That brought up the problem of finding a girl for Russell. Then Lew called to say he couldn't come, and the problem was solved. "Bunny, most of the kids are bringing hamburgers, why don't you bring a bag of cookies?" "Joella, could you and Willy carry over some phonograph records?"

Finally it was all arranged. Even the call to Pete had been made, beginning with "Hello Pete, this is Dinah. Listen. You know we are going bowling tomorrow night. Well, look—" April timed the call at exactly twenty-two minutes.

Dinah yawned. "I don't know about you, but I want a piece of cake."

"Me too," April said. "Where's Archie?"

He was lying in the middle of the living-room floor, flat on his stomach, deep in the latest issue of *New Comics.* He shook his head and said, "I already hadda piece-a cake."

The kitchen was warm and pleasantly odorous. Dinah got out the cake Mother had baked the day before, three layers, with double-thick maple-fudge frosting. April inspected Jenkins the cat, and Henderson, the turtle, both full of food and comfortably asleep in their respective quarters. Dinah started to cut a generous hunk of cake and then paused, sniffing. "Something's cooking." She looked around. "April, did you leave the oven on?"

"I did not," April said instantly and defensively.

"Well, somebody did," Dinah said. "And it wasn't me."

Before anything more could be said, Marian came into the kitchen. "Does it need basting?" she asked brightly. She had on her old red corduroy slacks, the ones with the acid stains, dating from an experiment she and Archie had carried on with a toy chemistry set. Her tired face was a trifle dirty and innocent of make-up. Her back hair was coming down. Her fingertips were blue-black from carbon paper. "Always hungry," she commented, looking at the hunk of cake. "You're going to end up a big fat slob. I don't suppose it occurred to either of you lazy bums to look at the turkey."

"What turkey?" April demanded.

Marian Carstairs opened the oven door and pulled out the roaster. "I meant to tell you," she said. "I guess I forgot." She took off the lid. The turkey was brown and crisp. It smelled wonderful.

"I thought I'd better cook it tonight," she said, "in case I was busy tomorrow."

April and Dinah glanced at each other. Mother happened to catch the glance. "And," she added acidly, "I'll *moider* the first one of you who says I'd probably forget it tomorrow." She shook the cooking fork at them threateningly. "I am *not* absent-minded," she informed them. "It's simply that I have a lot of assorted things on my mind. Including you." She put down the cooking fork. "And that reminds me. About this party tomorrow night—"

April and Dinah felt a momentary chill. Could Mother have changed her mind? And, after all that telephoning?

"You said the kids would bring the food," Mother said. "But you'd better get in some cokes. And candy and peanuts and stuff." She fumbled through the pockets of her working slacks, fished out a batch of notes, four safety pins, a crumpled and empty cigarette package, six match folders, a grocer's bill, a handful of buttons, a letter from April's math teacher, a box of paper clips, and, finally, three wrinkled one-dollar bills. "There. Will that be enough?"

Dinah gulped. She said, "But, gosh, Mother." April gulped and said, "Honest, we can manage without it."

"G'wan," Mother said. She stuffed the bills into the pocket of Dinah's sweater. "It's my treat." She poked the fork experimentally in the turkey. "It's done," she announced, turning off the oven.

It was done, and a masterpiece. Mother gazed at it proudly, April wistfully. Dinah put the hunk of cake back on the plate. "I don't really want it, after all," she murmured.

Mother sighed. "Maybe I shouldn't have roasted it tonight. It won't be half as good when it's cold."

Archie came tearing in from the living room. "Hey! Whadda I smell?"

Jenkins, the cat, looked up from his sleeping place and said, faintly and sadly, "Mew?"

"Shut up, you liar," Mother said to Jenkins. "You're not hungry."

"But *we* are," Dinah said.

"Well," Mother said, slowly and thoughtfully, "*one* sandwich—"

There was instantaneous activity in the kitchen. Dinah got the bread, April got the butter, and Mother got the carving knife. Archie brought in milk from the icebox. Jenkins asked for (and got) a piece of crisp turkey skin. "Buttermilk for me," Mother said. "One buttermilk," Dinah called. "One buttermilk," April echoed. "One buttermilk coming up," Archie caroled, heading for the icebox. Mother, cutting thick slices of turkey meat, began to sing, happily, and badly offkey.

> *O they gave him his orders, at Monroe Virginia,*
> *Saying, Pete, you're way behind time,*

The three young Carstairs chimed in, even more offkey.

> *This is not eighty-four, this is old ninety-seven—*

Jenkins howled in protest. Henderson crawled as far into his shell as he could get.

"Oh, Mother," Dinah said, "remember how you used to sing Archie to sleep with that?"

"I used to sing you to sleep with it, too," Mother said. "And April. After all, darn it, it's the only song I know." She began stuffing the fat slices of turkey between slices of bread, and went on singing.

> *So he turned around to his fat and greasy fireman,*
> *Said, shovel in a little more coal,*

She paused and pointed the butter knife at Archie. "Bet you ten cents you don't know the next two lines."

"Betcha I do," Archie said, "but show me the ten cents first."

Mother put down the butter knife and began fumbling through her pockets.

"That's all right, Mother," Dinah said. "We understand." She fished a dime out of her pocket and handed it to Mother.

Archie drew a long breath, put down the buttermilk bottle, and warbled:

> *And when we hit that big black mount'in*
> *You jus' watch ole ninety-seven roll.*

"There, I did it. Gimme the dime."

"Catch," Mother said. She smeared the dime with kitchen soap and tossed it into the air. It stuck to the ceiling. Archie said, "Oh, foo!"

"Just wait," Dinah said. "It'll come down."

April said, "Does anybody know the verse that has the line:

> *And they found him in the wreck, with his hand*
> *upon the throttle*"

"Oh, sure," Archie said scornfully. "It begins:

> *O they came downhill making ninety miles an hour.*"

"Sixty miles an hour," Dinah said.

"Ninety."

"Sixty."

"Aw, listen—"

"Shut up," Marian Carstairs said amiably, putting the plate of sandwiches on the table. "And it isn't *came downhill*; it's *came downgrade.*" She turned to put on the coffee, singing loud:

> *O they came downgrade making ninety miles a minute,*

The whistle blew with a scream,
And they found him in the wreck with his hand
upon the throttle.

"Not ninety miles a *minute*," Archie protested. "Ninety miles an *hour*."

"Sixty," Dinah said.

Two sandwiches apiece, a quart of milk, and four verses later they'd agreed on the words, and Dinah had brought the maple cake out again. Archie took one huge bite, said, "Yipes!" and kissed Mother on the nose, leaving a slight smudge of maple frosting. Then he said, "Well, anyway, I betcha I know the whole last verse, all the way through." He sang through a mouthful of cake.

So, ladies, you must take warning—

April and Dinah chimed in, after the first two notes, so did Mother.

From this time on and learn, Never speak harsh words—

There was a sharp official-sounding knock at the back door.

To your true lovin' husband—

The knock came again, louder.

"Never mind," Marian said. "I'll go." She rose and went to the door, while the young Carstairs finished the last line.

He may leave you and never return.

"*Quiet,*" Dinah whispered. The kitchen became instantly silent, and the three young Carstairs turned to stare at the door.

It was Police Lieutenant Bill Smith, accompanied by a uniformed cop.

The three young Carstairs were speechless, first with stunned surprise, then with despair. They looked at Bill Smith, handsome, immaculate, almost dapper. They looked at Mother, at the acid-stained, old red corduroy slacks, the carbon-paper stains on her fingers, the unwashed and unmade-up face. All her back hair had come loose by this time and was collapsing on her neck. The smudge of maple frosting was still on her nose.

"Pardon my coming to the back door," Bill Smith said. "But I saw a light here. Have you been troubled by prowlers?"

"Prowlers?" Mother said coldly. "Not until just now."

April caught the look on Dinah's face and whispered, "Never mind. We didn't really want Mother to marry a policeman, anyway."

Bill Smith stiffened. "I'm sorry to be bothering you," he said. "A Mrs. Harris down the street reports that someone has been stealing food from her back porch. And a Mrs.—" He paused and looked at the uniformed cop.

"Cherington," the cop supplied.

"A Mrs. Cherington reports that someone slept last night in her chickenhouse. Evidently there is a prowler in the neighborhood."

Marian Carstairs felt a sudden panic. "I thought you were in the Homicide division," she said.

"I am," Bill Smith said. "That's why I'm interested in these reports."

"Well, I—" Marian paused. She ought to give what information she could. The haggard, unshaven, terror-stricken face she'd seen only that morning. The hoarse whisper, *For the love of heaven, don't call the police.* She couldn't do it, because, honestly, she didn't believe Wallie Sanford had murdered his wife.

"Yes?" Bill Smith said.

"I—" she smiled wanly and tried ineffectually to pin up the back hair. "I'm so sorry. But I can't help you. We haven't had any prowlers. And I'm sure anyone hiding in the neighborhood would have come here first, because our icebox is on the back porch, and there isn't any lock." She gave up fiddling with the back hair, but the smile grew more cordial. "Don't you think, Lieutenant, that women like Mrs. Harris and Mrs. Cherington are inclined to be a trifle hysterical, when there's been a crime committed in the neighborhood?"

Bill Smith didn't just smile, he grinned. "You're darned right," he said. He turned to the cop and said, "Well, go report we made a routine investigation and didn't find a thing." He turned back and said, "Thanks very much." Then he sniffed. "Certainly smells good in here."

Dinah grabbed at a straw. She jumped up and said, "I bet you're hungry. I bet you haven't had any dinner."

"Well, I had a sandwich," Bill Smith said.

"A sandwich!" April said, with a scornful sniff.

Amazingly—and encouragingly—Bill Smith blushed. He said, "No, really—I must go."

"Nonsense!" Dinah said.

"You'll die of starvation," April said.

Archie added, "It's a awful swell turkey."

Police Lieutenant Bill Smith didn't have a chance. They ganged up on him. Before he knew it, he was sitting at the kitchen table. Before she knew it, Marian was slicing more turkey. April and Dinah hastily found a knife, a fork, and a spoon, a plate, a cup, and a saucer. Archie started the coffee perking. April buttered the bread. Dinah cut a thick wedge of the maple cake.

Bill Smith looked ecstatic. "Maple-fudge frosting!" he said. "My mother used to make maple-fudge frosting. I haven't had any in—years!"

Dinah shoved Mother into one of the kitchen chairs, and April poured her a cup of coffee. Bill Smith bit into the turkey sandwich and said, "Oh, golly!" Jenkins woke up again and complained, faintly. Bill Smith scratched him behind the ears and fed him a piece of turkey skin.

"Do you like cats?" Mother said.

That was when the three young Carstairs tactfully vanished. Save that Archie paused at the door and yelped, "You just try Mother's maple cake. She's the best cook in the whole, whole wide, wide world."

April grabbed the back of his collar and yanked him up the stairs. "There's such a thing as overdoing it," she told him.

There followed the usual nightly battle over whether or not it was Archie's bedtime. As usual, Archie lost. He managed an extra five minutes by pretending he'd forgotten how to say his prayers, and an extra two minutes by pretending he'd forgotten to brush his teeth. Then he dragged out the business of saying good night for an extra ten minutes. Finally he was settled down for the night.

Dinah closed the door of the room she and April shared. "We'd better give Archie back his money," she said.

"Maybe," April said. "I don't know, though." She scowled. "He doesn't know Mother gave us the money for the cokes and stuff."

"That's embezzling," Dinah said severely.

"Could be," April said. "But, Sunday is Mother's Day. We want to give Mother a super present. And if we pay Archie back now, we'll still have to pay him interest. And then if we borrow more money from him to buy her present, he'll charge us more interest. This way"—she looked speculative—"we can tell him we're putting two dollars and seventy-five cents toward Mother's present, and he—"

"Make it three dollars," Dinah said. "We'll keep back a quarter out of the coke money. Then he'd have to put in a dollar and a half."

"And we'll get something really super," April said. "Not candy, it's bad for her complexion, and not flowers. We can get a big bunch of flowers out of Mrs. Cherington's garden. If we tell her it's for a Mother's Day present, she'll give us an armful of her prize roses."

"*Listen!*" Dinah said. She grabbed April's arm.

There was a soft rustling sound from outside. April switched off the light, ran to the window, and looked out. One of the hydrangea bushes moved as though it were alive. Then a dark, furtive figure darted from the shelter of the bush to the old summerhouse.

"The prowler!" Dinah whispered.

"The *murderer!*" April gasped.

"How do you know?"

"A murderer always returns to the scene of the crime. I read that in a book."

"Nonsense," Dinah said. "April, *look.*"

"He's going toward the back porch," April said. She clutched Dinah's hand, hard.

Dinah said, "We'd better yell. We'd better get Bill Smith and Mother."

They went out into the hall and down the stairs. At the foot of the stairs Dinah paused, held April back, and hissed, "Listen!"

There was laughter, friendly laughter, from the kitchen. And Police Lieutenant Bill Smith's voice saying. "Well, maybe I could manage another piece of cake—just a little one, though." And Mother's voice saying, "More coffee? I've just heated it."

April and Dinah looked at each other for a long moment. Then Dinah tiptoed across the living room to the front door, motioning to April to follow. They slipped out the door and closed it behind them soundlessly.

"April, are you scared?" Dinah whispered.

April swallowed hard and said, "Uh-uh!"

"Neither am I," Dinah said. She hoped her teeth weren't chattering. "So, I think *we'll* handle this."

Chapter 8.

"Archie will never forgive us," April whispered. "We should have waked him up and brought him along."

"He's got to go to school tomorrow," Dinah whispered sternly. "Anyway, he never could have gotten out of the house without being heard."

They paused, listening. There wasn't one sound anywhere. The bushes hedging in the moonlit lawn were motionless. They crept quietly along the side of the house.

"If it is the murderer," April murmured, "what do we do?"

"You hold him," Dinah answered, "while I get Mother. Then she can call the police, and she'll get all the credit."

Still there wasn't a sound. They stood for a minute in the shadow of the wall, holding hands, tight. The light from the kitchen window made a big golden rectangle on the lawn. Then, suddenly, there was a sound. A familiar one, that became more frightening because it *was* familiar. The creaking hinge of the back-porch door. Soft, slow, as though whoever had moved the door was being quiet and cautious about it. Two creaks, almost inaudible, that made a minor third, one as the door was opened, one as it closed again, held back from slamming by a careful hand.

April and Dinah thought, secretly and simultaneously, "I mustn't let her know I'm scared."

It might have been a shadow that moved quietly down the

back-porch steps. Except that the quart bottle of milk it carried gleamed brightly in the moonlight for an instant, and a shadow couldn't carry a quart bottle of milk. There was a quick shadowy motion across the corner of the lawn, a soft rustling in the bushes, and then silence.

The two girls moved quietly along the side of the house and through the secret path they'd made through the bushes when they were playing Commandos with Archie.

"If we have to," Dinah breathed reassuringly, "we can always yell for help."

"I'm not scared," April lied.

They snaked up the last few feet of the path to behind the hydrangea bush. Then April grabbed at Dinah's hand. "It's o-kuk-a-yum," she whispered. "It's *him*."

The man hidden behind the hydrangea bush was gulping the milk as though he were starving. April and Dinah sneaked quickly along the last few feet of the path. He looked up, his eyes terrible with fear.

"Don't be afraid," Dinah whispered soothingly, "we aren't going to give you away."

He clutched at the milk bottle and shrank away from them.

April murmured, "Why, *Mr.* Sanford! And with milk at fourteen cents a quart, too! I ought to call the police!"

Wallie Sanford stared at them for a moment. Then he released his grip on the milk bottle. Finally he half smiled.

"Finish your milk," Dinah whispered. "You need it. It's good for you."

Instinctively they realized that he was on the wire-thin edge of hysteria. Just as instinctively, they knew what to do about it.

"Shall we turn him in to the cops?" Dinah said to April.

"Let's not," April said to Dinah. "We like him. He's a good guy."

"He's got a kind face," Dinah said. "No murderer has a kind face."

"Unless it's a deceptively kind face," April said. "Look at him. He couldn't deceive a worm."

"I am looking at him," Dinah said. "He looks hungry." She scowled at the bewildered man and said sternly, "Drink that milk!"

"We can feed him all right," April said, "but where the hash-e-lo-squared can we hide him?"

Wallie Sanford put down the empty milk bottle with a shaky hand. "I did not murder my wife," he said.

"Of course not," Dinah said. "We know that. We're just trying to prove that you didn't."

He stared at them. "I picked up a newspaper this morning. It must have been you kids who told the police the shots were heard at half-past four. But it wasn't half-past four. Because I got off the train at four forty-seven. And I heard the shots, too."

"Don't tell the police that you did," Dinah whispered. "Or they'll ask us a lot of embarrassing questions."

"But why did you tell the police it was four-thirty?" Wallie Sanford asked.

"Because," April said, "we didn't think you murdered your wife. You're not the type."

He groaned, and buried his face in his hands. "Lord only knows," he muttered, "I wanted to."

Dinah and April were tactfully silent for a moment. Then April said, "Look, chum, why are you sticking around here? Why don't you take it on the lam?"

"I've *got* to be here. I've *got* to get into that house." He clenched his left fist, and bit at the second knuckle of his left forefinger. "It was her house, you know. Not mine. She bought it."

He seemed to have forgotten that his companions were the two little girls who lived next door. Dinah and April sensed it. April nudged Dinah and said, "Now, I suppose, you'll marry Polly Walker."

"*Marry!*" he said. "*Her!* Please. It was like this. I didn't—"

Dinah poked April and whispered, "The dam's busted." April nodded. It was an expression they both knew well. There were times when Archie had something to confess and couldn't get past the first few words, until suddenly the confession came out in a rush.

"I met her," he gasped. "I liked her. Maybe I flattered her a little. We had lunch together a lot of times. I shouldn't have done it. But I made her think I knew—important people. I don't, of course. If it weren't for Flora—if it hadn't been for Flora—I'd just have been another real-estate salesman. Now, I'm an estate manager. There's a difference. I suppose now I'll manage Flora's estate, too. Unless they hang me. Oh, no, they don't hang people in this state. But they can't convict me. Because I'm innocent. I didn't murder her. I wanted to— and who didn't want to! But I didn't. Only I'll never be able to prove it. And Polly. She never should have gotten caught up in this—awful thing. She didn't murder Flora either. I'm sure of it. I'm *sure.*"

"Take it easy, bub," Dinah said.

"Believe me," Wallie Sanford said, "you must believe me. I found out that Polly was coming out to the house. I knew why. I was afraid. Look, it happened this way. I left the office early and took the train. It got me here at four-forty-seven. I took a short cut up through the vacant lots. I wanted to head her off—I knew why she wanted to see Polly. I didn't want—" He paused, caught his breath, and said, "I was close to the house. I heard shots. Two shots. Then a car went down the driveway. Then, another car. I ran in the house. She was there, on the floor. Murdered." He jerked up his head and murmured, "I wasn't sorry. She was evil—you couldn't *dream* how evil."

April and Dinah held hands again.

"I ran away," Wallie Sanford whispered. "I knew I'd be the first person they'd look for. Now, they *are* looking for me. I've been hiding. But I'm tired. Oh, I'm so tired." He buried his haggard face in his hands. "Stealing milk and food and newspapers. Maybe I ought to give myself up. But they'd—I mean, I couldn't prove—"

"Calm down," Dinah said, softly and warmly. "What you need is a good night's sleep."

"A good night's sleep," April repeated, "and the wide-open spaces. Wide-open spaces as far away from here as you can get to in a hurry. There *are* trains, you know, and busses. Or maybe you could hitchhike." She looked at Wallie Sanford's white face and added hastily, "If I've said the wrong thing, kick me in the teeth."

"Honest," Dinah said. "Maybe you *ought* to get a long way away from here. You'd be safe."

"Safe," he muttered. "Safe. I could be. But I can't run away, you know. I've got to stick it out. Because I've got to get in that house. She hid the evidence there. If I don't find it, the police will."

"Tell us where it is," April said. "We'll find it."

He stared at her. "If I knew," he said. "If I'd ever known where Flora had hidden it. If I could have found it, and destroyed it, do you think I'd have *married* her?"

"Didn't you marry her for her fatal charm?" April said.

Dinah kicked April and said, "Shut *up!*"

"And then there's Polly," the stricken man said. "I thought I was helping her, and I got her into this. If I should run away, they'd arrest her for Flora's murder. And"—he rubbed his hands nervously over his face—"she didn't murder Flora. I know it. I'm sure of it." He drew in his breath and whispered, "I'm so *sleepy!*"

They stood, watching him, his head resting on his arms, his face hidden in the curve of an elbow. He didn't move.

"He *is* sleepy," Dinah said softly. "And that's no place for him to sleep. Not on that damp grass."

"Maybe we ought to call Mother," April said, "and let her find him. After all, he's the one the police are looking for. She'd get all the credit."

"Are you crazy?" Dinah demanded.

April glanced at the pale, half-asleep face of Wallie Sanford and said, "Only slightly. All right. But where will we hide him?"

That became a serious problem. It would be difficult to hide any-one—particularly a mildly hysterical person accused of murder—in the house without Mother finding out. The basement was no good, because Magnolia was coming tomorrow to do the washing. Archie's tadpole tank made the garage a little too odorous for comfort.

"There isn't any place," Dinah said at last. "He'll just have to stay here. And I'm afraid he'll catch cold."

There was a sudden rustling in the bushes. April and Dinah stiffened. Wallie Sanford looked up, white-faced.

"How 'bout my playhouse?" a small voice said. "Which has got a bunk in it and also a secret tunnel, where the whole fifth grade hid out on ditch-day last year, and the truant ossifer couldn't—"

"Archie!" Dinah said. "You're *asleep!*"

"I ain't neither," Archie said. A small, pajama-clad figure came out from behind the shrubbery. "I'm awake and I heard everything you been talking about. And the playhouse does have a roof on it, and it does have a bunk bed, and it does have a secret tunnel which Wildcat and me dug and in which a person could conceal himself if a person had to conceal himself. It's a *big* tunnel, because we had to hide the whole fifth grade in it."

"Only the guys in the fifth grade," April said scornfully. "And that's about fifteen. And it isn't a tunnel you and Wildcat dug. It's the foundation of a house that was made and then nobody ever built a house on it, and you just built the playhouse right next to it and then kicked a hole through. Secret tunnel. Yah!"

"Well," Archie said, "if it was big enough to hide the fifth grade, it's big enough to hide *him.*"

"We could sneak some blankets out of the storeroom," Dinah

said thoughtfully. "And there's some food in the icebox. And we can bring some coffee out before we go to school in the morning." She scowled at Archie. "Only, what are you doing out of bed, small potatoes?"

"Well, my gosh," Archie said indignantly, "do you think I'd let my own sisters go outdoors at night without me to pertect'em?"

It took a little doing, because the storeroom was locked and Archie had to crawl through the window to get the blankets, because the remains of yesterday's dinner were in the hardest part of the icebox to reach quietly, and because Wallie Sanford was asleep on his feet. But between the three of them, they managed. Fifteen minutes later Wallie Sanford had wolfed down the last of the leftover ham, been shown the entrance to the secret tunnel, and gone dead to sleep in the bunk bed, buried under the blankets.

Now, only the problem of getting back into the house, unseen and unheard, remained. Archie solved it easily for himself. He shinnied up five feet of drainpipe, scrambled up the vine trellis, scampered, barefoot and silent, across the sun-porch roof, and dived in his window. Dinah grabbed April before she could follow him. "Not at your age," she whispered, "and not in those new rayon slacks." April didn't protest. She crept into the house right behind Dinah, not making a sound.

The two girls paused for a moment on the staircase. The typewriter wasn't purring in Mother's room. But the light was still on in the kitchen. And there were voices. Laughing voices.

"I tell you, it's *He came downhill, going—*"

"Down*grade,*" Mother's voice said.

"Oh, all right. *He came downgrade, going ninety miles an hour—*"

"Sixty," Mother's voice said.

"I wouldn't argue with you for the world," Bill Smith said. "You know, Mrs. Carstairs—"

And then April had to go and sneeze.

It wasn't just a sneeze; it was a minor cataclysm. She sneezed, lost her balance on the stair, grabbed at the curtains, which came crashing down, and knocked over the copper bowl on the landing, which bounced to the floor below with a horrendous noise.

"Children," Mother called from the kitchen. "Chil-*dren!*" Dinah moved fast. She was up the stairs in two leaps; she threw April's bathrobe and slippers over the railing. April moved just as fast. She pulled off her shoes and stockings, dived into the bathrobe and slippers, and mussed up her hair.

"*Child*-ren," Mother called.

April wrapped the bathrobe around her and ran through the dining room. She burst in through the kitchen door, pink-faced and sleepy-eyed. Mother and Bill Smith were sitting across from each other at the kitchen table. The turkey was a shambles, and the maple cake was practically gone.

"*Baby!*" Mother said, jumping up, "what's the *matter?*"

"Bad dream," April whimpered.

Mother sat down again, and April climbed into her lap, trying to look about six years old.

"Poor little girl," Bill Smith said. He came around by Mother's chair and began feeding April the remains of the maple frosting. She managed to sneak most of it into her pocket, to share with Dinah later. "She's a very nervous child," Bill Smith said to Mother. April whimpered again, faintly, and Bill Smith said soothingly, "There, there."

"She is not nervous," Mother said indignantly, "and she is not a child." She glanced down and spotted April's blouse showing under the bathrobe. "And what's more—"

The front doorbell rang just in time. Mother shoved April off her lap, said "Excuse me," and went to answer it. Police Lieutenant Bill Smith followed. April took advantage of the diversion to race halfway up the stairs and pause to listen.

"I must apologize for this intrusion," a pleasant masculine voice said. "But I am very anxious to get in touch with the police officer in charge of the case next door. I was informed that I might find him here."

"Why, yes," Mother's voice said. "Won't you come in?"

Then, "I'm Bill Smith. And you—?"

April peeked through the stair rail. She saw a handsome young man, tall and tanned, with smiling blue eyes and curly brown hair. "I've just seen the newspapers," the young man said, "and I understand you've been looking for me."

"Yes?" Bill Smith said.

The young man said, "I'm Rupert van Deusen. I'm quite willing to admit that Mrs. Sanford—the late Mrs. Sanford—was blackmailing me for the possession of certain foolishly written letters. Also I admit that the interview with her took place exactly as reported in the newspapers by some—reliable witness. However, at the time of her death I was having a haircut in a barbershop at least twenty miles from here, and a half-dozen people can testify to that effect."

Bill Smith stared at him for a moment. Then he said, "Would you mind coming down to headquarters with me, so that we can verify your alibi?"

"Delighted to," the young man said. "Glad to do anything that will help."

"Will you excuse us?" Bill Smith said. "And thank you for the supper, Mrs. Carstairs."

"You're quite welcome, I'm sure," Mother said.

The two men went out. April fled up the rest of the stairs, ran into her room, and shut the door, fast.

"For Pete's sake," Dinah said, looking up from her dairy. "You look as if you'd seen a ghost!"

"I have," April said, shivering. "I've seen a man who doesn't exist!"

Chapter 9.

"I DID not join the force for the purpose of giving advice," Sergeant O'Hare said in tones of wounded dignity. "I am not going to be no Dorothy Dix. But you're a pal and if I see you making a bad mistake I can point it out to you, see, as a pal, not officially. You never should of let that van Deusen guy get loose again."

Police Lieutenant Bill Smith sighed, sat down on the bottom front step of the Sanford villa, and lit a cigarette. "At the time Mrs. Sanford was murdered, he was in the Grand Central Barber Shop, in downtown Los Angeles. A dozen people—including the barber—saw him there. Are you suggesting he left the barber chair, traveled seventeen miles, murdered Mrs. Sanford, and traveled seventeen miles back again, without anyone noticing his absence? You've been reading too many comic strips about rocket ships."

"I suppose all these witnesses identified him with his face covered with lather," O'Hare said coldly.

"He was getting a haircut," Bill Smith said, "not a shave."

"Okay, okay," O'Hare agreed. "He's got an alibi. But there's something very fishy about that business. He threatened this Mrs. Sanford. That fine, smart little girl heard him and told me so. He even admits it. Just because he's got an alibi, you let him go. If he didn't have nothing to do with the murder, why did he show up out here?"

"Maybe he's an honest, upright citizen who wants to aid the police," Bill Smith said wearily.

Sergeant O'Hare said one word. It was a very rude one.

"Oh, all right," Bill Smith said. "He murdered Mrs. Sanford and it's a perfect crime, because he has a perfect alibi. So let's turn in a report and stop worrying." He added bitterly, "We've got to make *some* kind of report pretty soon."

Sergeant O'Hare looked at him from the corner of his eye. "Maybe you just need a good night's sleep," he suggested.

Bill Smith sighed, and said no thing. Two days' investigation of the Sanford murder seemed to have left him exactly where he'd come in. For the two hundredth time he let his mind run over the meager assortment of facts he had succeeded in accumulating. A wealthy woman named Flora Sanford—wealthy and domineering—had been murdered. She'd had a husband who—from all Bill Smith had been able to learn about him—was handsome, weak-willed, and somewhat younger than his wife. That husband had been running around with a pretty little actress named Polly Walker. Very pretty, he reflected, but with a sharp temper, a very determined young person who'd probably insist on getting what she wanted.

He'd learned that Mrs. Sanford and Polly Walker had never met, until the day of the murder. But a meeting had been arranged—was it, he wondered, arranged by Flora Sanford or by Polly Walker? They didn't meet, though, because by the time Polly Walker arrived, Flora Sanford had been murdered.

No! Wait! They must have met before. Because Polly Walker's frightened voice over the telephone had said, "—and quick. Mrs. Sanford has been murdered."

"How," he said out loud, "did she know that the dead woman on the floor was Mrs. Sanford, if she'd never seen her before?"

Sergeant O'Hare looked at him anxiously. "Speaking strictly as a pal," he said, "maybe you had better get that good night's sleep. We can come back in the morning and really tear the joint apart. And anyway, if this dame did have any incriminating letters, she would of stuck 'em away in a safety-deposit box under the name of Mrs. John Smith."

Police Lieutenant Bill Smith didn't answer. He lit another cigarette and stared out through the trees. There were too many facts that didn't seem to fit in. The disappearance of Wallace Sanford. Why had he disappeared? He had the most perfect alibi in the world. He'd been on the suburban train at the time the shots were fired. Had he simply run away, or had he been kidnapped—or murdered?

Why had such a curious assortment of people tried to sneak into the Sanford villa after the murder? Mrs. Carleton Cherington III. She didn't look like an ordinary souvenir hunter. That rabbity little lawyer, Holbrook. A lawyer ought to know better than to try to pick the lock of a house where a crime had been committed, even if the victim of the crime had been his client. And that man they'd caught sneaking up through shrubbery, who called himself Pierre Desgranges, and claimed to be a French painter. His accent didn't sound like that of any Frenchman Bill Smith had ever known. And then, this guy, Rupert van Deusen. Where in blazes did he fit in?

Two shots had been heard. One bullet had killed Flora Sanford. *Where* was the other bullet? Certainly not in the chintz-hung living room where the crime had been committed. It had been searched, microscopically. Had there been a *second* murder, and the body carried away? Two cars had roared away from the scene of the crime. Two shots. Two cars. One murder. People with motives and perfect alibis. And a house that had to be searched for a cache of blackmail material. Bill Smith groaned.

"How do you feel, pal?" Sergeant O'Hare said solicitously.

"Confused," Bill Smith muttered. He threw away his cigarette and stood up. Through the trees, he could see the house next door. The kitchen had been warm and pleasant. And not everybody liked railroad songs as much as he did. The turkey sandwiches, and the maple cake—well, Marian—Mrs. Carstairs, he reminded himself—was not only a fine mother, a brilliant woman, and a beauty, but a magnificent cook as well. He walked to the end of the Sanford patio. He could see her, through her lighted window, sitting at her typewriter. She was working hard. What a shame, he thought, that such a charming woman had to work so hard. How sad that she should be all alone in the world, to bring up those handsome and talented children, all by herself!

Suddenly he realized that the entire Carstairs house was brightly lighted, even the porch and front driveway. Was someone ill—one of the children, perhaps? Oh, no, in that case Marian—Mrs. Carstairs—wouldn't be at her typewriter. She'd be at the sick child's bedside, a skillful and soothing nurse. Then, what—?

"Lookahere," Sergeant O'Hare said. "Are we gonna go home, or are we gonna search this place?"

Bill Smith returned—with difficulty—to the world of reality. "Oh, all right," he said crossly. "We'll go home and search."

Sergeant O'Hare regarded him thoughtfully for a long moment. "Pal," he said at last, "you *are* confused."

Suddenly there was a shrill, juvenile scream from the Carstairs house. It was followed by several others, even shriller.

"What the blazes!" Lieutenant Bill Smith gasped. He was down the steps and halfway across the lawn before Sergeant O'Hare caught up with him and slowed him down.

In the meantime there had been more screams. Young, feminine screams. A shrill voice cried, "Eddie! Don't you *dare*!" There was a burst of music from a Harry James record. Then, pure pandemonium.

Bill Smith paused in his race across the lawn and gasped, "O'Hare! Riot call!"

"G'wan," O'Hare said soothingly, catching his superior by the elbow. "It's just them kids over there having a party. I've raised nine of my own, and I know."

Bill Smith caught his breath and said, "Oh!" In the next minute he said, "*Oh!*" as a figure, moving with what seemed to be the speed of a torpedo, shot out of the bushes and butted him in the stomach, sending him sprawling on the lawn.

"Pard'n me, mister." It was a small boy dressed in blue dungarees and a torn jersey, his face not only incredibly dirty, but luridly decorated with red chalk. "I'm one of the Mob. G'by."

He headed back toward the bushes as a young voice hissed, "C'mon back here, Slukey. And keep still. We gotta steal them cokes."

Police Lieutenant Bill Smith picked himself up and brushed himself off. "Maybe," he said, "we had better send in a riot call." He looked up toward the window where Marian Carstairs was still typing furiously. "How does she stand it?" he murmured.

"She's used to it," Sergeant O'Hare assured him. "You should just hear mine sometime." He strode back to the edge of the Sanford property and yelled "*Quiet!*" There was immediate silence. "See?" he reported. "Kids is kids. Now, if you had nine of them—"

"Heaven forbid!" Bill Smith said. He didn't say it with real conviction. There were a lot of times—though he would never have admitted it—when he envied Sergeant O'Hare. Maybe if he'd married that pretty dark-haired girl he'd met in his last year of high school—Her name had been Betty-Lou. She'd had a soft, warm, Southern voice. Definitely the helpless type. He'd worshipped her. The summer after graduation, when he was clerking in Hopner's Drug Store, they'd decided to get married in the fall, if old Mr. Hopner would continue to hire him after the summer season.

But in August, Dad died, after five days in the hospital, from the wound inflicted by a bank robber's bullet. During those five days, he made the arrangements for Bill to enter police school. His last whispered words were, "Take care of your ma, and be a good cop."

Bill started police school. Betty-Lou promised she'd wait for him. Three weeks later she married an automobile salesman from Portland.

He took care of Ma as long as she lived. He was a good cop. He advanced, step by step, from his first assignment as a rookie. Now he was a Lieutenant on the Homicide squad. Dad would have been proud of him. And he hadn't married. Because he didn't have time, because he didn't have money, because the girls he met didn't look like Betty, or didn't have soft Southern voices, or weren't helpless and adoring.

Finally he'd come to the conclusion that he was happier as a bachelor, in a comfortable hotel apartment with excellent maid service and a good restaurant close by.

Lately, though, he'd begun to wonder.

It *was* a comfortable hotel. The service *was* excellent. A skillful maid, for whom he left regular weekly tips, but whose face he'd never seen and whose name he didn't know, hung up his clothes and emptied his ash trays. And it *was* a good restaurant. The waitress didn't bother to bring him a menu any more, she just brought him the evening newspaper and his dinner. He didn't even wonder what she looked like.

Only, he couldn't get maple-fudge cake in the restaurant. And the comfortable hotel apartment was entirely too quiet.

Still—Betty-Lou would never have consented to nine kids. In fact, he reflected, she probably never would have consented to one.

Besides—she would never have developed into a brilliant woman who could write mystery novels. And could sing *The Wreck of the Old Ninety-seven*. And who could look beautiful with a smudge on her nose.

"I'm glad she *didn't* marry me," Police Lieutenant Bill Smith thought out loud.

"Howzat?" Sergeant O'Hare said.

"I was thinking," Bill Smith said. He drew a long breath. "I was thinking we still have to search that house. And I'd much rather—" He didn't finish it.

Dinah and April, meanwhile, were involved in a difficult problem. The party was going well. The cokes were cooling in the icebox. The kids had brought food. Hot dogs, potato chips, popcorn, and cookies. And an enormous chocolate mocha cake had turned up unexpectedly on the kitchen table, with a note reading, "In case your gang gets really hungry. Ma." Joella had brought the records. Eddie and Mag hadn't had a fight, at least not so far. And the Mob wasn't causing any trouble—yet.

But—

The treasure hunt was going well. Wendy found the first clue, under the corner of the sundial. Pete had found the next one, in the goldfish pond, sealed in a bottle. Now, a really enthusiastic search was under way. Pretty soon it would begin to spill over into the Sanford grounds as per schedule.

Only—

They were confident that they looked slick. Dinah in a plaid skirt, a station-wagon sweater, and brown-and-white saddle shoes. April in her pale-blue organdy, with flowers in her hair. Even Archie had washed his face, brushed his hair, and put on his best pants.

However—

The party was a social success, but def. It wasn't even bothering Mother. Dinah and April had sneaked upstairs once to see. She was typing fast, in a white-faced frenzy, evidently close to the last chapter of the current book, and completely oblivious of the racket downstairs.

Except—

The Mob's plan to steal the cokes had been discovered in time, and two strong, reliable guys had been stationed in the back porch to frustrate it. Only one phonograph record had been broken, so far. The crepe-paper decorations in the rumpus room were still intact. Everything was under control.

But—

"How are we going to get away from the kids?" April whispered to Dinah, "and really *search*?"

"I don't *know*," Dinah said in a cross voice. "Pete keeps following me around all the time."

"He's your problem," April said.

"Maybe we ought to explain it to him," Dinah said, "and let him help."

"That lame-brain!" April exclaimed. "Where did you check your mind, or did you just lose it?"

"Well, my gosh," Dinah said defensively. "We've got to do *something*. If only—"

"Hey, *Di*-nah," Pete's voice said, at close hand. April groaned.

"Here I am," Dinah said, resignation in her voice.

Pete stepped from behind the hydrangeas, tastefully attired in dungarees and a plaid Okie shirt. Sixteen years old, five foot ten inches tall, and with a tendency to fall over his own feet. "Hey, April," he said, "Joe's looking for you."

"Let him look," April said serenely.

Dinah had a sudden inspiration. "Oh, Pete. Willya do something for me, willya?"

"Sure," Pete said adoringly. "Anything."

"I forgot to get any paper napkins. Willya ride your bike down to Luke's and get me a dime's worth?"

"Oh, sure," Pete said.

"I'll give you the dime," she said. She felt in her blouse pocket. "April, have you got a dime?"

April shook her head and called "*Archie!*" Archie came up the garden steps, two at a time. "Have you got a dime?"

"Yep," Archie said. "For what?"

"Never mind for what," April said severely. She gave him a meaningful look.

Archie gave the dime to April, who gave it to Dinah, who gave it to Pete. Pete said, "Be right back," and ran off to where he'd parked his bicycle.

"That makes two dollars and eighty-five cents you owe me," Archie said.

"You'll get it," Dinah told him. "And now," she sighed, "we've got to work fast."

They crossed the lawn to the edge of the Sanford grounds. There was a whoop from Joella, who'd found a clue inside a milk bottle floating in the Sanford lily pool. A uniformed cop ran up from the front gate and yelled, "Beat it, you kids!" Eddie shinned down one of the Sanford trees with an exultant cry. He'd found the clue that had been planted in a bird's nest. Another uniformed cop, who'd been on guard inside the house, came racing down the Sanford back steps. And just then Bunny scooted across the Sanford grounds in the direction of the kitchen garden.

"That's working all right," Dinah said. "We've got the run of the grounds. But"—she pointed to Police Lieutenant Bill Smith and Sergeant O'Hare on the Sanford front porch—"what are we going to do about *them?*"

"Why the heck did they have to pick tonight to come over here?" April muttered. She turned to Archie. "Listen. You and the Mob have gotta do something to get them away."

"Oh, corn, corn, corn," Archie swore. "*We* gotta do something. Why don't *you* do something? And whatter *we* gonna do?"

"Well, my gosh," Dinah said, "you can think of something. Go burn down a house."

"Oh, foo!" Archie said. He scampered back down the steps yelling, "Hey, Slukey! Hey, Pinhead! All you guys—"

"They'll manage," April said confidently. "I know the Mob." She went on through the arbor into the Sanford grounds, Dinah close behind her.

The two uniformed cops were thoroughly busy, and Sergeant O'Hare had joined them. But as fast as Wendy was chased away from the rosebeds, Joella turned up by the sundial, and then Willy under the avocado tree. The two cops and Sergeant O'Hare had their hands full. But Bill Smith still stood by the front door of the Sanford villa. "Are you sure you planted enough clues to keep the kids busy?" Dinah whispered.

April nodded. "All over the place. Let's join the—treasure hunt."

They prowled through the shrubbery of the Sanford place while the treasure hunt grew louder. They came on a collection of empty milk bottles, evidently left there by Wallie Sanford. They found a rabbit's nest, a scout knife Archie had lost three weeks before, Mag's handkerchief, and a broken coke bottle. April tore a small snag in the blue organdy, and Dinah skinned her nose on a low-hanging branch.

After fifteen minutes April said, "There's no use hunting around out here. If there'd been anything hidden outside, I'd have found it while I was hiding the clues this afternoon. We've got to get into that house."

"Sure," Dinah said. "But *how?*" Suddenly she grabbed April's wrist and said "*Listen!*"

A siren went screaming down the road. Then another. A third sounded from a long way off.

"Another murder!" April gasped.

"Those weren't police sirens," Dinah said. "Those were—Oh, April, *look!*"

There was a brilliant red glow just around the bend in the road, and great clouds of smoke. An instant later they could see the flames beyond the trees.

"Oh, my gosh," April moaned, "oh, my *gosh!* Archie thought we meant it!"

Chapter 10.

DINAH STARTED to run down the hill toward the road. April grabbed her arm. "Hold everything," she said. "We might just as well take advantage of it."

The Sanford grounds were deserted, except for April and Dinah. Everyone had gone to the fire, including the two uniformed cops, Sergeant O'Hare, and Police Lieutenant Bill Smith. "And the back door is unlocked," April pointed out.

"Archie," Dinah groaned. "Archie! If anyone should find out—"

"We'll see to it they don't," April said. "Come *on!*"

They ran along the edge of the lawn to the back porch. The kitchen door was not only unlocked, but wide open. The kitchen itself was brightly lighted, there was an opened copy of *True Detective Mysteries* on the table, and the uniformed cop had evidently been making himself a ham sandwich.

The rest of the house was dark, frighteningly dark. They tiptoed through the butler's pantry into the dining room, from there into the chintz-hung living room. The living-room floor was covered with paper, covered with wide dark chalk marks. A long oval was drawn on one end of the floor. April shivered.

"It was right *here*," she murmured.

"Don't be scared," Dinah said.

"Scared!" April hissed. "*Me?*" Thank goodness her teeth had stopped chattering. "Have you got your flashlight?"

Dinah nodded. "But I'm not going to use it unless we have to. It would attract attention." She paused. "Maybe this is all a waste of time. The police must have searched the house pretty thoroughly."

April sniffed. "They're men," she said scornfully. "They wouldn't have any idea where a woman would hide things. Just stop and think. Where does Mother hide stuff, like birthday presents, and letters from the school principal, and books she thinks we oughtn't to read?"

"Well," Dinah said, thinking. "In the bottom of the bathroom laundry hamper, and her hatbox, and under her mattress, and behind her dressing-table mirror, and under the dining-room rug, and back of Grandfather's picture, and in the box that has her old evening dress, and behind the old encyclopedia in the upstairs bookshelves. And sometimes under that tapestry thing over the stairs."

"See what I mean?" April said encouragingly. "Imagine the police looking in places like those!"

They crept up the stairs and began going slowly and stealthily through the house. It showed evidences of a police search. Everything had been taken out of the late Flora Sanford's desk, dressing table, and bureau drawers. A little wall safe had been opened.

"Maybe if there was something here, it's been found already," Dinah said.

"Well, we can try, can't we?" April said. She looked under the rug.

"Mrs. Sanford sure must have used plenty of make-up," Dinah commented, examining the dresser. "Just look at all those jars and stuff."

"We're not here looking for beauty hints," April said, moving a picture.

Another siren went by. The red glow from the house down the street brightened the walls of Flora Sanford's dressing room. Dinah glanced wistfully toward the window. "It looks like a really big fire."

"You can go to a fire any time," April said coldly. Suddenly she rose from her investigation of the mattress. "Dinah. The fire. If Mother—"

They ran to the window and looked out. Across the gardens they could see a lighted window, and Mother, bent over her typewriter. They drew a mutual sigh of relief.

"Well, after all, she worked right through an earthquake once," Dinah said. "Remember? When a couple of windows got broken, and the downstairs doors jammed, and a house down the street collapsed. There was an awful noise."

"And we were so scared," April said reminiscently. She giggled. "And we ran upstairs to see if Mother was all right, and she was out in the hall and she said, 'Children! Please stop slamming doors!'"

Dinah giggled. Then she sobered. "April. If Archie gets in any trouble over this."

"He won't," April said. "And get moving. *Search.*"

There was nothing to be found in the dressing room, Flora Sanford's room, or the guest room.

Ten minutes later April said, "We're a couple of dopes. Listen, if she had something incriminating hidden here any place, she wouldn't have hidden it in her own room. She'd have hidden it in *his* room, so that if anything ever happened, he'd get the blame. She was that kind of a babe."

They went into Wallie Sanford's room. It was a sharp contrast to the guest room, lush with rose-printed paper, or Flora Sanford's room, with its gray-and-blue taffeta draperies and full-length mirrors. It was a very ordinary little room, with a cheap maple bedroom set and monk's cloth curtains.

"Not the sort of stuff I'd have imagined he'd pick out," Dinah commented.

"Stupe," April said. "She picked it out. It was her money, remember."

They continued searching. Suddenly Dinah said, "While we're here—Mr. Sanford needs a clean shirt and some, clean socks. I can carry them out under my blouse and slip them to him later."

"Get his razor, too, while you're at it," April said. "We'll get him some soap tomorrow."

Five minutes later April located the big Manila envelope back of the dresser mirror. She gave a low whistle and looked inside. Dinah turned on the flashlight, carefully shielding it from the window. There was a little notebook, there were newspaper clippings, there were odds and ends of letters. April ran through them hurriedly, catching familiar names here and there. Cherington. Walker. Holbrook. Sanford.

"Dinah, I think this is it!"

Dinah looked it over, suddenly gasped. "My gosh! April! That clipping. Something about—Carstairs." She looked closer. "Yes it is, Marian Carstairs."

"Oh, no!" April moaned. She looked. Then she looked up at Dinah, white-faced. "We'll take this home and read it later." She shoved the papers and clippings back and closed the envelope.

Dinah said, between clenched teeth, "Well, anyway, Mother couldn't have—done it. Because when we heard the shots, she was typing—" She broke off and stared at April.

They were remembering the same thing. One of Mother's books, one of the Clark Cameron books. The murderer had a perfect alibi. His landlady and half a dozen other people had heard him operating a typewriter at the time the crime was committed. And then it turned out he'd made records on a home recorder of himself typing, and set them up on an automatic phonograph that played ten records at a time.

"Don't be silly," April said. "We haven't got a recording machine, and our phonograph only plays one record at a time and you have to wind it up in the middle of the record, anyway."

"And when we went upstairs, right after the shots," Dinah said, "she was sitting right there typing."

"Besides," April said firmly, "Mother would never do anything she could be blackmailed for." She looked at the envelope and said, "How are we going to get this out of here, in case we run into anybody?"

"You hide it," Dinah said.

"Under this dress?" April said. "Do I look like a magician?"

"All *right*," Dinah said. She grabbed the envelope and stuffed it into her blouse. "What with this, and Wallie Sanford's shirt and socks and razor—"

April looked at her in mock criticism and said, "You could sneak out a couple of mattresses too, if you really put your mind to it."

"Oh, shut *up*," Dinah said sharply. "And let's get out of here. I'm worried. My gosh, we've got to make sure Archie is all right. And with the kids running around loose and everything—" She switched off the flashlight. "Come *on*, April."

They moved silently along the upstairs hall. Through the windows they could still see a red glow.

"A really swell fire," April muttered bitterly, "and we have to miss it."

"In a good cause," Dinah reminded her. Then, "*Sssh!*"

There were faint sounds from downstairs. Someone moving about, quietly, cautiously. Then there was a sound at the front door, someone working on the lock. Suddenly, a small explosion, and the sound of breaking glass. Dinah and April retreated up the upstairs hall and looked out the window.

A man was running across the lawn, away from the house. He paused, halfway across, looked back, and then went on. His face, in the moonlight, was clearly recognizable. The man who didn't exist. Rupert van Deusen. April smothered a gasp.

"Who's *he?*" Dinah whispered.

"A suspect, no doubt," April whispered back. Her teeth were really chattering now.

They stood for a minute, listening. The soft sounds from downstairs began again. Sounds as of someone searching in the dark. Now and then there was a faint glow from a flashlight.

"Shall we hide?" Dinah breathed.

April shook her head. "No place. If we have to, we'll get out on the roof, and slide down the drainpipe. I hope there *is* a drainpipe."

There was a motion at the foot of the stairs. The two girls stood frozen, staring over the railing. There was a dark figure that paused suddenly, turned, and stood motionless for an instant. They could see his face, lighted by the combination of moonlight and fireglow that came in through the windows. A dark, thin face, under a snap-brim hat. A frightened face, though the moonlight fell on something shiny in his hand. Dinah pulled April back from the stair rail. There was a window, right behind them, that opened on the roof.

Then they heard the shot. A shot, a strange little bumping sound. And silence.

The two girls ran back to the railing. There was what might have been a shadow on the floor at the foot of the stairs. They could see a snap-brim hat rolled a little away from the shadow, and the shiny gun lying on the rug. From somewhere downstairs a door closed, softly.

"We're getting out of here," Dinah gasped hoarsely. "If there isn't a drainpipe, we'll jump."

There was better than a drainpipe, there was a vine trellis. They scrambled down it, half climbing, half sliding, quickly and quietly as kittens, and ran around the corner of the house into the comforting shelter of the shadows.

"Don't—drop—that stuff," April said.

Dinah panted, "Don't worry. I've got it."

They slowed down as they reached the back porch of the Sanford house. It seemed safe here, and normal. Mother by her window, still typing. The moonlight on the Sanford lawn. The red glow on the sky was dimmer now.

"Wait a minute," April whispered. She caught Dinah by the elbow. "*Wait!*"

"For gosh sakes," Dinah hissed. "Let's beat it, quick."

"*No.* There was a murder. We heard it. We almost saw it. Remember that guy in Mother's book who said, 'It is almost impossible to commit a murder successfully without committing, at least, a second one.' Dinah, the murderer is right there in that house, right now."

Dinah said, "If we sneak around the corner here we can look in the sun-room windows. But be careful. Darn this envelope, it's scratching my sunburn. Why did you have to wear that organdy dress, anyway."

"*Quiet,*" April said.

They crept around the corner of the house and moved silently up to the sun-room windows. Moonlight and street light combined to make the Sanford living room as bright as day. They could see the sun room, the living room, and the hall. They could see the curving staircase and the landing. But there wasn't any dark shadow sprawled at the foot of the stairs, nor any snap-brim hat rolled onto the floor, nor any shiny gun on the carpet. There was nothing, nothing at all.

"Dinah," April said, "you're right. Let's beat it. Fast." She choked. "Maybe we dreamed it."

"Nonsense," Dinah said sharply. Too sharply. "He just wasn't murdered, that's all. While we were climbing down the trellis, he just got up and walked off." As though to corroborate her theory, a car that had evidently been parked in the alley back of the Sanford house started its motor and drove away.

"See!" Dinah said triumphantly. "Now, for gosh sakes, let's get this stuff home and hide it, and get back to the gang."

They skirted the deserted lawn and dove through the arbor. There wasn't a soul in sight, there were still excited sounds from the scene of the fire. And the sound of fast, furious typing from upstairs.

"We'll stick it in our laundry bag until the kids have gone home," Dinah began. "Then—"

"Pssst," April whispered.

Police Lieutenant Bill Smith and Sergeant O'Hare were coming up the garden steps. They stopped, looked at the two girls, and Bill Smith broke off in the middle of a sentence, leaving the words "Never should have left the place unguarded" dangling in the air.

April remembered something she'd read about the best defense, and decided to attack. She said indignantly, "Where do you think you're going, across our front yard?"

"Short cut, little lady," O'Hare panted. He wasn't used to climbing steps.

Dinah chimed in quick. "How was the fire? Where was it? How did it start?"

"Under control," O'Hare said. He paused, mopping his brow, glad for the excuse to rest for an instant. "Vacant house on Maple Drive. Somebody set it."

"My gosh," April said. "That's against the law." *Oh, Archie, she thought, how could you!*

"What'll you do to the guy who started it, if you catch him?" Dinah asked.

"Twenty years in Alcatraz," O'Hare said. He finally caught his breath and added, "Don't worry, we'll catch him, all right."

"Oh!" Dinah said. And then, "*Oh!*"

Police Lieutenant Bill Smith's neat gray suit was covered with dust and brambles. There were a few remnants of dead leaves in his hair and a scratch down one cheek. He looked jumping mad.

He glared at the bulge the Manila envelope made under Dinah's blouse and said, "What—"

April looked with startled concern at Bill Smith and said, "Whatever happened to you?"

"One of your brother's little friends tripped me," Bill Smith said. "Deliberately."

"Don't let that worry you," April said, "they do that to us all the time." Something had to be done fast to keep Bill Smith and Sergeant O'Hare from discovering that Dinah was carrying the important evidence under her sweater. "All the time," she repeated, "but only when they stand on their hands and flap their ears."

"Especially every other Thursday," Dinah said, catching on quick.

"But the round corners make it different," April added. "Oh, no, they don't, only when it's raining."

"But you can't get that any more." April began speeding it up. "Besides, the rain makes it turn purple."

"No it doesn't, not if you look at it cross-eyed." Dinah speeded up, too.

"Oh, but if you do that, it'll make the sun go down."

"Not if the next two weeks are going to be Saturdays." "Just a minute," Sergeant O'Hare said. Bill Smith looked bewildered.

April gave Dinah a nudge. They retreated halfway up the front steps. "We're not crazy," April said innocently. She put a forefinger to her lower lip and went, "B-b-b-b-b-b-b-b-b-b-b!"

Sergeant O'Hare chuckled. He couldn't help it. He said, "Take it easy, Smith. I've raised nine of my own, and I know—"

Bill Smith didn't take it easy. He strode into the moonlit rectangle of lawn, glared at Dinah and April and said, "Where's your Mother?"

"She's working," April said icily and with vast dignity, "and she can't be disturbed."

Bill Smith said, "Oh—" He swallowed the last word.

"Shush-cash-rur-a-mum," April whispered.

Dinah fled up the rest of the steps, clutching the Manila envelope and Wallie Sanford's clean shirt and socks. April leaned over the railing, looked at Bill Smith, and said, coldly, "Don't be rude." She moved up a couple of steps and added, "Especially about our Mother. I'm sorry you don't like her, because we do."

Bill Smith pulled a couple of dead leaves from the back of his collar and said, "I do like your mother. She's a fine, brilliant woman. Only, she doesn't know anything about how to bring up children."

"Now," Sergeant O'Hare murmured soothingly. "If you'd raised nine of your own—"

April pressed the advantage. She leaned over the railing and said anxiously, "Oh, Captain O'Hare. Do you really suppose the murderer really set that fire on purpose so he could draw the police away and search the Sanford house? Really?"

Bill Smith and Sergeant O'Hare glanced at each other. Then they shoved through the arbor, quick. The last April saw of them, they were racing across the Sanford lawn.

Dinah was tiptoeing down the stairs. She looked more serene now. She said, "They're in the bag. The laundry bag." She giggled, and then sobered. "We'll take the shirt and socks to poor Mr. Sanford in the morning, with his breakfast."

"And his razor," April said. "And some soap, and a mirror. That's tomorrow. This is now. Let's get the gang together. We're supposed to be having a party, remember?"

Dinah said, "How'd you get rid of—them?"

"Simplest thing in the world," April said. "I just burned down a house."

"Don't joke about that," Dinah said. "Look. We gotta find Archie. He may be in trouble."

April paled, remembering. She ran down the steps beside Dinah, saying, "We'll give him an alibi. He was with us all the time, until the fire broke out."

"Maybe they caught him in the act," Dinah said. "That darned O'Hare guy said somebody set the fire."

"He didn't say who," April panted. "And even if they *have* caught Archie, we'll fix it *somehow*."

"We'll have to," Dinah panted, "he's *our brother*." She added, "Thank goodness he picked a vacant house."

From the foot of the steps they could see the scene of the fire clearly. Red puffs of smoke, a few occasional flames, five fire engines, and a dark ring of spectators. They began running down the sidewalk.

Half a block from the steps, a small, excited, breathless figure ran into them. "Hey," Archie said. "I came back to getcha. You're missing the whole fire. You're gonna miss the whole thing." He jumped up and down. "C'mon, c'mon, c'mon."

"Oh, Archie," Dinah said. "How could you!"

Archie stared at her, looked scared, and almost tearful. He said, "Well, heck."

"Did anybody see you?" Dinah demanded.

"Sure," Archie said, bewildered. "Everybody."

April nudged Dinah. It was no good, she knew, trying to get anything out of Archie by direct questioning. She said calmly, "Say, where were you when the fire started?"

"Well, gosh," Archie said in a hurt voice. "You wanted to get those cops away from that house. So me'n the Mob were down in the bushes, making a trip-trap. We were gonna fix it, and then Goony was gonna yell. That woulda got 'em. Only then the fire engines went by and the whole Mob beat it on me. But that Bill Smith fell in the trip-trap, anyway. And I seen that O'Hare going down the road. So I figured I might as well go, too. Heck, we don't have a fire here every day."

"Oh, gosh," Dinah said to April, with a gasp of relief. "He didn't do it!"

"Praise be," April added.

"Didn't do *what?*" Archie demanded.

"Set that house on fire," Dinah said.

Archie stared at them. "Hey. Me? Are you loony? That would be against the law. That would be arsenic."

April kissed him and Dinah hugged him. Archie wriggled loose and said, "Hey. Hey. You better hurry up, or you won't get there before the roof falls in."

The three of them raced down the hill. Firemen were spraying streams of water on the house that had displayed a FOR RENT sign for the past five years. Other firemen were wetting down the shrubbery and surrounding buildings. Just as the three young Carstairs reached the scene, there was a shrill blast on a whistle, and the firemen fell back. One instant later the roof fell in, with a resounding crash, and sparks flew skyward. A cloud of smoke shot up, like a big balloon. The firemen raced back with their hoses. "See, I tole ya," Archie said. "I tole ya, I tole ya!"

"All right, you told us," April said. "Shush-u-tut u-pup."

"Oh, boney!" Archie said. He ran down among the spectators, calling, "Hey, Slukey! Hey, Goony! Hey, Admiral!"

"The Mob!" Dinah said scornfully. "We missed the whole darn fire. Look, it's almost out now. And where *is* everybody?"

The smoke had changed color, and the flames had died away. A few last sparks shot up from time to time. One of the fire engines pulled itself together and drove away, with a loud motor noise and a mild clanging of its bell. The crowd began to go home.

The kids departed from the crowd and moved toward Dinah and April. Joella said, "Where *were* you?"; Bunny said, "Did you miss any of it?"; Joe said, "Hey, April, I been looking all over for you,"; Pete said, "How did you kids get lost?"; Eddie said, "Didya see the roof fall in?"; and, finally, Mag embraced Dinah and said, "Oh, gosh! That was simply a super fire!"

"We're glad you liked it," Dinah said politely. "We always try to entertain our friends. Next time we give a party, we'll try to arrange an explosion."

Mag giggled, and ran ahead to join Eddie. Bunny called back, "Hey, you kids, let's go on up and dance."

"I'm hungry!" one of the Mob yelled.

The fire chief's red roadster was parked beside the walk. The fire chief himself was standing there talking to a subordinate, as Dinah and April reached the car. "—no doubt about it," he was saying. "Kerosene all over everything. Some kind of time charge, I think. Pure case of—"

"*Di*-nah," Pete called.

"Coming," Dinah called back.

"Ap-*ril!*" Joe called.

"We'll catch up," April called. But she held Dinah back. "Listen. Archie's Mob didn't set that fire."

"Well, gosh no," Dinah said. "Archie can lie, but not that convincingly."

"But the fire did draw the cops away from the Sanford house," April went on.

"For Pete's sake," Dinah said. "I got my eyes open when I was ten days old, too. What of it?"

"Just"—April drew a long breath—"something was planned to happen at the Sanford house tonight. Not by us. We saw some of it. Maybe it went wrong. But that fire was set by somebody."

"Not Archie," Dinah said.

"Sure it wasn't Archie," April said. "But *who was it?*"

A voice ahead of them called, "Hey, *Di*-nah. Hey, April!"

"Hash-e-lul-square with i-tut," Dinah said. "We've done all we can right now. The food's waiting, and there's all those super records we borrowed from Joella. Let's get going. After all, it's our party."

Chapter 11.

It was about two o'clock in the morning when April stirred, half woke, sat up in bed, and said cautiously, "Dinah! *Dinah!*"

Dinah turned over in her twin bed, opened one eye, and said, "Huh?"

"Dinah, I heard a siren."

Dinah raised up on one elbow, blinking, and listened. The world was still, save for a mockingbird that sat in the sycamore tree and repeated, "Purty-purty-purty-purty."

"You had a bad dream," Dinah said. "Go to *sleep.*"

"I *am* asleep," April muttered, burying her face in her pillow.

Dinah listened for another minute. There did seem to be a lot of cars going down the road. And then—yes, there was a siren, not very loud, and very far away. She started to whisper "April!" and then stopped. Maybe it had been her imagination.

The bedroom door opened softly, and a small, pajama-clad figure tiptoed in. "Hey, kids," Archie whispered. "I heard a siren."

Dinah sighed and sat up in bed. "So did I," she told him, "and so did April. Look, we've already been to one fire tonight, and that's enough."

"But this wasn't a fire siren," April said, her voice half muffled in her pillow. "It was a police siren."

"Probably some motorcycle cop chasing a speeder," Dinah said. She didn't say it with conviction, though.

"It was pretty close," April said.

"I wanna go to the murder," Archie said.

"Oh, for gosh sakes," Dinah said crossly. She paused.

"Well," she added thoughtfully, "maybe we had better get dressed and find out what it is."

There were quick, determined steps in the hall, and Mother in the doorway. She still had on her working clothes. "Why haven't you gone to sleep yet?" Mother said.

"We were asleep," Dinah said.

"We woke up," April added.

"We heard a siren," Archie said. "There's been a murder somewhere!"

"Pure imagination," Mother said briskly and cheerfully. "You've been seeing too many of the wrong kind of movies. Now, settle down." She gave Archie a playful slap and said, "Get to bed. Scoot."

Archie scooted down the hall.

"And you two Indians," Mother said, "*go to sleep.*" She closed the door firmly.

"Well," Dinah whispered a moment later, "that settles that!"

She stayed awake for a minute or two, still listening. Yes, it *had* been a siren. What? If the police had found Mr. Sanford, the siren would have been a lot nearer. *Could* it have been another murder? After witnessing the events in the Sanford villa, Dinah was ready to believe that anything could happen. She listened a few seconds more and then whispered, "*April!*"

April was asleep. Dinah murmured, "The heck with it," and went to sleep herself.

It was the smell of bacon frying that woke her the second time. It woke April at the same instant. They sat up in bed, blinking at each other. Dinah looked at the clock. Half-past ten.

"Oh, *April!*" Dinah gasped. "Mother worked late last night! We should have been up to make coffee for her!"

They scrambled out of bed, washed their faces fast, put on bathrobes, and headed for the stairs. Archie raced past them, similarly clad, washed, but slightly tousled. "Hey!" he yelled as he took the last three steps in one jump, "whadda I smell!"

Mother, in the kitchen, was cheerfully whistling *The Wreck of the Old Ninety-seven.* Bacon was turning a crispy brown in the skillet, and pancakes were bubbling on the griddle. The percolator was going "bup-bup-bup-bup" and there was a saucepan of cocoa on the warming plate. The table was set, Henderson was tied out in the back yard contentedly eating dandelion heads, and Jenkins was licking his chops over an empty plate.

"Oh, Mother," Dinah exclaimed. "We meant—"

"Hullo," Mother said. "I was just about to wake you." She had on her working slacks, and her face looked tired.

"How come you're up so early?" April demanded.

"Haven't been to bed yet," Mother said, sliding pancakes onto a warm platter. She added, in a very matter-of-fact voice, "Book's done."

"*Mother!*" Dinah said. "Oh, gosh!"

"Oh, *super,*" April said.

Archie said, "*Yipes!*"

"Stop hugging me," Mother said, pretending to be furious. "You'll upset the cocoa. And get the newspaper, the butter, the maple sirup, and an ash tray. *Git,* now."

Breakfast was on the table in sixty seconds flat.

Halfway through her fourth pancake April looked up critically. "Now I hope you'll get your hair done. Honest, Mother, that upswept hair-do of yours is strictly from cyclone."

"Monday," Mother said. "I've already made the appointment."

"Manicure too," Dinah said firmly.

"Absolutely," Mother said. "Why, I might even blow myself to a facial."

"Glamour girl," Archie said, sneaking a piece of bacon rind to Jenkins, and reaching for his fifth pancake.

At last Mother began the regular postbreakfast procedure, a last cup of coffee, a cigarette, and the newspaper. She started to unfold the paper, and then yawned. "Sleepy," she announced. She rose and went to the stairs. The three young Carstairs followed. She pointed to a fat brown-paper package on the coffee table and said, "When the man from the express company comes, that's it. Good night." Halfway up the stairs she paused. "I'm sorry your party last night wasn't a success."

Dinah blinked, and April said, "Huh?"

"Well," Mother said, "everything was so quiet I was afraid you weren't having a very good time."

"It was a wonderful party," Dinah said.

"Good," Mother said. She went on up the stairs. "See you later."

The three young Carstairs stared at each other. "Either Mother is getting deaf," Dinah said solemnly, "or she certainly was busy last night." She sighed, shaking her head. "Let's get going. We've got to feed Mr. Sanford, wash the dishes, and go downtown and buy a Mother's Day present."

"First," April said, "I want to see what the paper says about our fire." She spread the paper out on the table, looked at it, and gasped, "Hey! Dinah!"

There wasn't anything about the fire on page one. (Later, they found an obscure paragraph about it on page seventeen.) But there was something far more interesting.

"It's *him!*" Dinah said.

It had been dark in the Sanford villa, and the man with the gun had been standing all the way down the stairs. But there wasn't any possible doubt about the dark, thin face under the snap-brim hat.

"Le' *me* see," Archie demanded. He stared at the picture and said, "I know him! He was around here day before yesterday."

"He was!" Dinah exclaimed. "What was he doing here?"

"He was asking how to get to Mrs. Cherington's house," Archie said, "and I told him, and he gave me two bits."

"Oh, Archie," April said. "Why didn't you tell us?"

"Well, heck," Archie said defensively. "I didn't know he was gonna go get murdered."

"No, I don't suppose he mentioned it to you." April said coldly. "But you ought to tell us *everything*."

"Oh, yeah?" Archie yelped indignantly. "I could tell you plenty—"

"Such as?" April taunted him.

"Oh, boney!" Archie said. "Oh, shambles!"

"Shut *up*, you kids," Dinah snapped. "I want to read this.

"Me too, me too," Archie said.

The bullet-riddled body of Frankie Riley, alleged small-time racketeer and petty blackmailer, was discovered early this morning in an abandoned swimming pool at. . .

"We *did* hear sirens," April said. "Dinah, that's the swimming pool at the old Harris place. It's only three blocks from here. The Harrises used to keep ducks in it."

"Let's go see it," Archie said. "Right now!"

"You make too much noise," Dinah said, in an absent-minded tone. She sniffed. "Bullet-riddled! My gosh! There was only one shot!"

"Don't be in such a rush," April said. She pointed to a paragraph halfway down the first column.

. . . appeared at first that Riley, well known to the police and the underworld, had been taken for a ride. The findings of Dr. William Thackleberry, medical examiner, that all but one of the wounds had been inflicted several hours after death, suggested that an attempt might have been made to make the slaying appear to be the work of a gang.

"Sure!" April said. "That's how it was done. He was murdered in the Sanford house, and then he was moved and dumped in the swimming pool."

"Keep *still*" Dinah said. "I'm reading."

The murder was discovered when Mrs. Peter Williamson was awakened by the sound of shots and telephoned a complaint to the police department that neighbors were shooting at her cat. . . .

Dinah giggled. "She would!"

"Hey, I know that cat," Archie said. "Jenkins beat him up last week. Good ol' Jenkins."

"*Quiet,*" April said.

Riley had recently served a term for robbery. At one time he was held for questioning in connection with the kidnap-murder of Bette LeMoe, but was subsequently released for insufficient evidence. . . .

"Wait a minute," April said. "I read about that in *Real Crime Cases.* About two months ago. This guy's picture was in it, too. That's why his face looked familiar!" She, drew a quick breath. "She was a singer—no, a burlesque star, a really important one. She was kidnapped from right in front of the theater and then she sent a note which turned out to be really in her own handwriting, and it said if the ransom money was paid she would be back at the theater at noon Friday, only—"

"Slow down," Dinah said. "You'll blow a fuse."

"Well, the money was paid," April said stiffly. "Fifteen thousand dollars. And she arrived at the theater at noon Friday in a coffin, with a note on top of it that said the kidnapers were sorry they had to murder her, but she could have identified them. And the police never found the kidnapers. The article started to tell about the investigation afterward, but Mother took it away from me before I could finish reading it, and I never could find another copy."

"*Mother* did," Dinah said. "*Why?*"

"I don't know," April said. "She just said it wasn't suitable reading matter and took it away."

"Well, my gosh," Dinah said, "that's darn funny. Because she usually lets us read anything we want to."

"She lets me read all the comic books," Archie said.

"I thought it was funny," April said, "because she never minded before when I read *Real Crime Cases*. Heck, she used to borrow the copies from me and read 'em herself."

"She reads my comic books all the time," Archie said. "And she borrowed all my Oz books and read 'em."

"Archie," Dinah said, "you make too much noise."

Archie sniffed. "Well, if you ask me," he said indignantly, "it was a dirty trick."

"*Archie!*" April said. "You ought to be ashamed of yourself. Mother can borrow your books and comic books any time she wants to, and if she wants to take a magazine away from me—"

Archie jumped up and down and said, "Oh, corn, corn, corn! That ain't what I mean. Those kidnapers. Taking the lady's money and then not letting her go home okay. It was a dirty trick and besides they oughta of known better. Just lookahere. Suppose those kidnapers kidnap some other party. A'right, this party remembers about that lady not getting home okay. He figures out, why should he pay them his money when prob'ly he's gonna be murdered anyhow, so then the kidnapers don't make any profit off him. That's no way to run a business."

"Archie," April said gravely, "you're a brain."

"Oh, sure, sure, sure," Archie said. "And I bet poor Mr. Sanford is just one great big empty stomach by this time."

Dinah and April looked at each other and Dinah said, "Not for long. April, run up and get that razor and stuff while I make some more pancakes."

"Listen, Dinah," April said. "We've got to read that stuff we found in the Sanford house. We couldn't read it last night after the party because it was too late. Maybe we'd better do it right now. For Pete's sake, aren't you even curious?"

"Naturally," Dinah said. "But it's got to wait. My gosh! We've got nine million things to do in the next couple of hours, and that's gotta be the nine million and oneth. C'mon now, April. Get *going*."

April salaamed. "Yes, Master," she said. She ran up the stairs, quietly, in case Mother was already asleep.

"Whaddya mean, nine million things?" Archie demanded. "What nine million things? Count 'em?"

"I'm going to pull nine million hairs out of your head, one at a time, if you don't shush-u-tut-u-pup," Dinah said. "Now go get the laundry pail and fill it with hot water."

"Yes, Master," Archie mocked. He started for the door. "How'd-ya know I have nine million hairs on my head?"

"Count 'em yourself," Dinah said, "and tell me if I'm wrong." She got out a cake of soap, and a fresh towel. April came downstairs with the shirt, socks, and razor just as Archie finished drawing the pail of water. Dinah draped the towel around Archie's neck, stuffed the cake of soap in one pocket, the razor in another, and the socks in a third. She put the neatly folded shirt under his arm and handed him the pail. "Take these over to Mr. Sanford in the playhouse," she said.

"Oh, foo!" Archie said in pretended fury. "I always have to do everything!" He took a firm grip on the pail and went out.

Dinah fried more bacon and made a stack of pancakes. April heated up the coffee and poured it in a thermos bottle. A tray carried across the back lawn might attract attention, so the plate of pancakes and bacon plus a lavish hunk of butter and the sirup jug were put in an old cardboard packing box. A knife, fork, spoon, cup, and napkin were already out in the playhouse.

"Get another package of cigarettes out of Mother's carton," Dinah directed.

"O-kuk-a-yum," April said. "But sooner or later she's going to wonder where all those cigarettes are going. You don't want her to think we're a couple of weed-fiends, do you?"

"I said *get them,*" Dinah said. She sounded cross, and she felt cross.

"Yes, Master," April said meekly. She got the cigarettes.

"And bring along the newspaper," Dinah said, picking up the box.

"Suppose Mother wants to look at it when she wakes up?"

"We'll buy her another one downtown," Dinah said. "Come *on.*"

"Yes, Miss Simon Legree," April said, tucking the paper under her arm. "Did you ever hear about the moron who went to college so he could get his Simon Degree?"

"Did you ever read about the big sister whose little sister made too much noise?" Dinah said. "No? Well, if you live to read about it, you're lucky." She stepped carefully along the walk and said, "This box is darn hard to balance."

"*My* sister," April muttered, as though talking to herself. "The unbalanced type."

They found Wallie Sanford shaved, bathed, and wearing the clean shirt. He was sitting on the edge of the bunk, tying his shoes over the clean socks. He looked up and half smiled at them as they came into the playhouse. His face was very pale, but he was nothing like the frightened, exhausted, and almost hysterical man who had been hiding in the underbrush and living on pilfered bottles of milk.

"How about breakfast, chum?" Dinah said, setting down the box and beginning to lift out its contents.

"Complete with coffee," April added, putting down the thermos bottle. "The service in this hotel is wonderful. Look, the waiter even brings you the morning newspaper with cigarettes."

"If you're as hungry as you look," Dinah added, "we'll turn our backs while you eat."

"I'm so hungry," Wallie Sanford said, buttering the top pancake, "that I don't even care if you *watch* while I eat."

When he got to the last pancake April reached for the thermos bottle and said, "Shall we ply you with more coffee?"

"Ply me with coffee, bury me with roses," Wallie Sanford said. He began to laugh wildly.

"We'll bury you with pleasure," Dinah said sharply, "if you don't stop that."

Wallie Sanford buried his face in his hands. "I'm going to the police. They're looking for me. I'm going to give myself up. I can't stand this any more."

"Just what, specifically, are you complaining about?" April demanded. "The food or the service?"

"The"—he looked up—"the waiting. Hiding. Like a criminal. Suppose they do put me in prison. They can't keep me there, because I'm innocent. They'll find out that I'm innocent. They'll find—whoever really did murder her and then they'll let me go."

"And then you can sue them for false arrest," April said. "Not a bad idea." She paused, and said thoughtfully to Dinah, "You know, I think he's got something there. Maybe he ought to give himself up."

"Huh?" Dinah said. "After all the trouble we've gone to hiding him here?"

"Why don't he grow a beard and go to South America?" Archie said.

"Quiet," April said. "I'm thinking." She scowled. "Look. Suppose he does give himself up. The police figure he committed the murder. Once they get him, they'll be satisfied. We'll be able to go ahead and find the real murderer without any interference."

Dinah said slowly, "Yes, but suppose we don't find the real murderer? Then what happens to *him?*"

"We'd just have to take that chance," April said. She added, "And, anyway. He's got an alibi. He was still on the train when *we* heard the shots."

"That's right," Dinah said. "But it's risky, just the same."

"I've got to do it," Wallie Sanford said. "I've got to."

"Well—maybe—" Dinah began. Suddenly she remembered something. "No. Look. Wait until tomorrow. Tonight, maybe. Will you do that?"

Wallie Sanford stared at her. "Why?"

"Never mind why," Dinah said. "Just trust us. We know what we're doing. Just stay here out of sight until we get back."

"But—" He frowned. "You're just kids. What do you think you can do?"

"We can make sure," Dinah said firmly, "that when you do go to the police, they won't have any motive to pin on you. Any motive. Understand? You'll have an alibi, and you won't have any motive. They'll have to let you go."

"But—can you?" Wallie Sanford said. "*How* can you?"

"Never mind," Dinah said confidently. "It's in the bag." At last he promised to remain in hiding until they returned. Dinah said, "I'll have Archie bring out sandwiches and another thermos of coffee for your lunch. And something to read. Now, *stay put.*"

They went back to the house, where Dinah made the last scraps of turkey into sandwiches and refilled the thermos bottle, and

April collected an armful of magazines. Archie carried it all out to the playhouse while the girls stacked up the breakfast dishes.

"Is he all right?" Dinah asked anxiously when Archie came back.

Archie nodded. "Smoking a cigarette and reading the newspaper."

"He'll be okay," Dinah said. She added, "I hope!" Suddenly she paused in the middle of washing out the coffeepot and said, "It would be awful if it turned out—he *did* do it."

Archie, who'd been mousing in the cake box, said, "Who did what?"

"Stole the dozen doughnuts that were hidden in the flour bin," April said.

"I did not," Archie said in righteous indignation. "And anyway, they weren't in the flour bin, they were in the potato bin, and besides there wasn't a dozen, there was only two, and one of them had a bite took out of it."

"Skip it, you kids," Dinah said. "Look. Suppose it turns out Mr. Sanford did murder Mrs. Sanford."

"But he couldn't of," Archie said. "He's got an alibi. April went in to look at the clock to see if it was time to fix the potatoes—"

"*Archie!*" Dinah said. He shut up.

"Honestly, Dinah," April said, "he couldn't of been acting when he said he didn't do it. And besides—"

"Look," Dinah said. "Suppose it *should* turn out he *did* do it. My gosh! We'd be—accessories."

Archie blinked and said, "You mean like Slukey's father sells?"

April said, "*What?*"

"Automobile accessories," Archie said in a hurt voice.

"Oh, for Pete's sake," Dinah said exasperatedly. "Archie, carry out the wastebasket and dump it."

"*Shambles,*" Archie grumbled. He picked up the waste-basket. "I have to do *everything.*" He banged the screen door as he went out.

Dinah turned around and said, "Honest, April, I'm sort of scared about this."

"Why?" April said, almost too casually.

"Well, my gosh," Dinah said. "We've been hiding him here. And suppose he did murder Mrs. Sanford. And suppose he did murder that other guy last night."

"He didn't," Archie's voice said. He came in and banged the empty wastebasket down on the floor. "On account, of you told him he should stay in the cave while the party was going on. Only some of the mob stayed up by the cave, in case any p'licemen were around." He stuck a finger in the maple-sugar jar and licked it off. "He couldn't of got out of there last night on account of the Mob." He stuck in another finger. "I didn't tell 'em it was account of p'lice-men, either."

"Keep out of that jar," Dinah said. "And how do you know for sure he didn't slip by them?"

"The two best guys in the Mob?" Archie said indignantly. "Wormly and Flashlight? Are you loony?"

"She's only a little loony," April said. "Don't mind her. The thing is, what do we do now? Go downtown and buy a Mother's Day present, wash the dishes, carry out the laundry, or go look over the stuff we got last night?"

Dinah hardly seemed to hear. She frowned, and said, "Do you suppose that gangster really was killed in the Sanford house?"

She and April looked at each other for a long moment. Then they walked to the window and gazed across the wide expanse of lawn. Everything was peaceful and serene at the Sanford villa. Just one policeman on guard, sitting on the back porch, a magazine on his lap.

"We really ought to read that stuff," April said, "after all we went through to get it."

Dinah shook her head. "This has to come first. Because, right now, I don't think we'll have any trouble." She turned to Archie, who was petting Jenkins. "There's a cop on the back porch of the Sanford house. Can you keep him so busy talking that we can climb up the trellis without being noticed?"

Archie gave Jenkins a final pat, shoved him aside, and went to the window. "Is that the only cop around?"

"As far as we know," Dinah said.

"And you wanna get in that house?"

"That's the general idea," April said.

Archie was silent for a moment. "Look," he said, "do I hafta wipe and put away the breakfast dishes?"

"You do not," April said quickly.

"Okuk," Archie said. "An' you might as well go in the back door, because that there cop ain't gonna be there." He paused in the doorway and added, "But 'member, I ain't gonna wipe no breakfast dishes." He vanished around the corner of the back porch.

"Hope for the best," April murmured. The two girls went out and crept up to the very edge of the arbor hedge, as close as they dared to get to the back of the Sanford villa.

There was a shrill, sudden scream. The cop on the back porch dropped his magazine, jumped up, and ran outside. A small figure ran fast across the lawn. The cop intercepted him with an outflung arm. There was a moment's dialogue, which April and Dinah caught only in pantomime. Then the cop began to run down through the Sanford garden, and over the Sanford lawn, in the direction of the shrubbery that hedged the house. Archie, pointing and yelping, led the way.

April and Dinah ran quickly along the edge of the kitchen garden and up the back steps. The back porch was deserted. A copy of *Baffling Detective Mysteries* lay on the floor, face down, beside an overflowing ash tray.

They went into the house. It was empty and still, almost too still. They crept into the living room, from which the staircase ran up to the floor above. Seen now, in daylight, it was a pleasant, sunny, almost friendly room. Expensive English chintz, fine furniture, beautiful rugs, a well-framed aquatint over the sofa, an oil painting—evidently a family portrait—over the fireplace. Nothing about the room now to indicate it had witnessed one murder and possibly two.

April shivered. She took another step into the room and the oil portrait winked at her. She said, "*Dinah!*"

"*Sssssh,*" Dinah whispered. "What's the matter with you?"

"Nothing," April said. "Nothing at all. I just thought I saw Ashabatabul skipping rope."

Any other time, Dinah would have laughed. Ashabatabul was a family tradition. This time, she said, almost angrily, "Don't-jabber-so-talky-much-not."

April took another step into the room. She glanced at her forearms, and reflected that it would be possible to grate carrots on the goose bumps. One more step. The portrait winked at her again.

"If you've got the hiccups," Dinah whispered, "go get a drink of water." She paused at the foot of the stairs, caught April's hand, and said, "There's something wrong here."

"Wrong," April said, shivering, "that's right." She looked in the direction Dinah's eyes were following, and stiffened. "There *is* something wrong. That's where we saw him fall—where we thought we saw him fall."

"Unless we dreamed it," Dinah said. "There's nothing there to show that—some guy—was—" She caught her breath. "Look, he could have been killed somewhere else, and dumped in the swimming pool. Maybe he didn't have anything to do with this case at all."

"Except," April said, "that that scatter rug wasn't at the foot of the stairs where it is now. It was in front of the blue sofa."

Dinah was silent for a moment. "That's right," she said slowly. "Then somebody moved it. Why?"

"Same reason we move scatter rugs in our house," April said coldly. "If something gets spilled on the carpet, we move a little rug or something to cover it up. We *did* over-hear a murder last night. If you want to lift up that rose scatter rug—"

"Never mind," Dinah said hastily. She looked a little greenish. "That's all we wanted to find out. Let's get out of here."

"Just a minute," April said. "Take a look at the picture of Uncle Herbert or whoever he was, over the fireplace."

Dinah protested, but looked. Uncle Herbert was a cross, bearded man, with a politician haircut and a frock coat. There was something strange about his face.

"Funny," Dinah said. "He's got one blue eye, and one yellow eye. You wouldn't think a painter—" April pulled her a few feet toward the sunlight. Dinah gasped. "April! The picture! It winked at me!"

"You're darned right," April said grimly. "It winked at me, too. The way the light fell on it, I guess."

Dinah said tremulously, "April—*gosh*—"

"There were two shots," April said, "but only one murder." She glanced up at Uncle Herbert; he looked, for a moment, almost amiable. "Only one bullet was found." She drew a long breath and smiled up at Uncle Herbert. "And," she finished, "we've found the other one!"

Chapter 12.

"Look," April said excitedly, "Look, Dinah. Whoever shot Uncle Herbert in the eye must have stood over there. It's the only way—"

Dinah looked at the portrait. "It was a darned good shot," she said.

April snorted. "It was a darned poor shot, if you ask me. Look at that portrait of poor old Uncle Herbert. Would you want to shoot at it?" Dinah muffled a giggle and shook her head. "Well," April said, "whoever fired that shot was aiming at something—somebody—else. And probably never had a gun in his—or her—hands before."

"Wait a minute," Dinah said. She glanced at the chalk-drawn oval on the floor and closed her eyes.

"What's the matter?" April demanded anxiously. "Dinah, don't you feel well?"

"Shush-u-tut u-pup," Dinah snapped. "I'm thinking." She opened her eyes. "In that book of Mother's. You know. Where the guy figures out who did the murder because he knows so darn much about geometry or something, and he works out the line of fire—"

"Too bad you flunked second-grade arithmetic," April said. "Or maybe you could find the murderer of Mrs. Sanford with an adding machine!"

"Don't bother me," Dinah said. "There were two shots. Mrs.

Sanford was standing—*there.* From the way she fell, the shot must have come from somewhere over *there.*" She pointed in the direction of the blue sofa at the far end of the room. "Then there was another shot, from the dining room."

"Why?" April asked.

"I don't know," Dinah said. "I'm trying to think. Maybe the murderer missed on the first shot and then tried again."

"Those two shots sounded pretty close together," April reminded her, "and it's a long way from the blue sofa to the dining room. And just as far from the dining-room door to the blue sofa. Of course, if you were on skis—"

Dinah stared at her. "There were two. Two of them."

"We heard two shots," April said. "We heard two cars driving away. So there must have been two murderers. Only, one of them missed." She looked speculatively at the room, her eyes narrowing. "The point is, which one."

Dinah looked puzzled. "I don't get it."

"All right," April said. "You flunked first-grade arithmetic, too. Listen. Two shots, two bullets. One bullet hit Mrs. Sanford, the other one hit Uncle Herbert's picture in the eye. They must have come from two different guns, unless they were fired by Superman and he made it from the blue sofa to the dining room, or vice-reverse, in one bound. So, it works out. See? All you need are the two bullets, and the two guns, and the two angles of fire, and the fingerprints."

"None of which we have," Dinah said gloomily. "And even if we had all that stuff, we wouldn't know who owned the guns, or where they stood, or whose fingerprints they were. Let's go home and wash the dishes."

"Don't be a discouragist," April said. She looked speculatively up at Uncle Herbert's left eye. "Maybe if I stood on a chair—"

There were footsteps, running footsteps, up the driveway. The girls looked at each other, and then looked around for a place to hide.

"The stairway," April breathed.

They dived up it, pausing, listening, on the landing.

"In a pinch," Dinah whispered reassuringly, "there's always the trellis."

"Ssssssssssssh!" April hissed.

The uniformed cop ran quickly into the house, Archie right at his heels. He grabbed the phone, dialed headquarters, and identified himself as "McCafferty speaking." He was a very young, very pink-cheeked, and, at the moment, very excited cop.

"Don' forget to tell 'em about the bushes being all broke down," Archie said, looking around to see where Dinah and April were, "and all the—"

"This is McCafferty," the young cop said desperately, "put me through quick, operator."

"—and the bloodstains all over," Archie said, "and the knife stuck in the tree trunk—"

McCafferty said, "Just a minute," into the phone, put his hand over the mouthpiece, and said to Archie, "What knife?"

"Stuck in the tree trunk," Archie repeated. "Just where the guy must of fell down." He looked small, scared, and pale. "Didn' you *see* it?"

"No," the young cop said, "but—" Just then he connected with headquarters. Slightly breathless, he reported that he'd found the scene of what must have been a homicide. Near the scene of the Sanford murder, and within easy driving distance of the deserted swimming pool where Frankie Riley's body had been found.

While he was telephoning, April managed to catch Archie's eye from their hiding place on the staircase. She gave him a signal that meant, "Get him out of here!" Archie gave back a signal—three fingers against his lower lip—that meant "O-kuk, just watch me!"

McCafferty hung up the phone. April retreated six inches up the stairs. Archie said, innocent-eyed, "Why didn'ya tell 'em about the body?"

"Huh?" the cop said. "What body?"

"Down there," Archie said, pointing vaguely. "In the bushes. Down where I showed you." He drew a long breath and said, "Riddled with bullets."

McCafferty stared at Archie. He picked up the phone again and called for a squad car. Then he fled out through the kitchen and raced across the lawn in the direction Archie pointed out to him.

"Dinah, get me a kitchen knife," April said. She began pulling a chair toward Uncle Herbert's picture. "Skee-make-you-it-appy."

Dinah ran into the kitchen, rummaged through the cutlery drawers, her hands shaking, and came back with the first knife she found. When she returned, April, on a chair, was already prying at the bullet in Uncle Herbert's portrait's eye.

April glanced at the knife and said, "Why didn't you just bring a crowbar?"

"It's—" Dinah gulped. "My gosh. Hurry *up*."

"Don't rush me," April said. "Sometimes these operations take hours." She pried out the bullet, tucked it into her blouse pocket, and anchored it with a crumpled piece of Kleenex. Then she looked critically at the portrait. "He looks awfully silly with only one eye. And besides, maybe we ought to give the police something to worry about."

There was a bowl of slightly faded geraniums on the library table. April selected one, and tucked it neatly into Uncle Herbert's left eye. Then she turned to Dinah. "Let's wash the fingerprints off that knife," she suggested. "And then—well, the police might as well earn their salary doing something."

Dinah stared at her, said, "My gosh, what—Oh, all right!" She washed off the knife while April ran upstairs to find a lipstick.

"Don't touch it with your hands," April said. "Use a kitchen towel. There, that's right." She wrote on the blade, in big red letters: A WARNING! Then, holding it cautiously in the towel, she stood it on the mantel, pointed toward the geranium. "Now," she said, "let's get out of here. *Fast.*"

They went out through the back door and across the kitchen garden. There were sounds of heavy feet tramping through the bushes in front of the Sanford villa. From a great distance came the faint unhappy sound of a siren. The minute they'd crossed into their own territory, April put a finger in her mouth and gave the coyote call. A moment later Archie raced up the steps to join them.

"Archie," April said, "get some of the Mob here. *Quick.*"

"Phone?" Archie asked.

"No. Emergency call."

"O-kuk," Archie said. He put two fingers in his mouth and gave a series of whistles, some long, some short. In a moment there were answering whistles. "They'll be here," Archie reported.

The siren was growing louder. But the Mob arrived ahead of the squad car. Most of it, at least. April looked them over, dirty dungarees, torn jerseys, butch haircuts. They all looked more or less alike, and they all looked like Archie. She explained to them just what they should do.

The Mob caught on quick. They and the young Carstairs moved around to the back of the house, getting there just as the siren died away and the squad car stopped near the front of the house.

Dinah poured soap flakes and hot water into a dishpan, April whisked the dishes from the table to the sink and picked up a dish-towel. Archie and the Mob hastily began a game of marbles in the back yard.

It was about three minutes before heavy footsteps and angry voices were heard on the walk beside the house. "—tell you," Bill

Smith's voice was saying, hot with anger, "that was where I fell over some infernal device rigged up by—"

"But those bushes were all broke down," McCafferty's voice said.

"I broke them down," Bill Smith said. "I fell on them."

The young policeman's voice sounded hurt. "But it looked as if—and this boy said—"

Sergeant O'Hare's heavy baritone said, "Look, McCafferty, when you've raised nine—"

By that time Bill Smith was pounding on the back-porch door. The two girls went out, Dinah with sudsy hands, April holding a plate and a dishtowel.

"Good morning!" April chirruped. "We were just thinking about you. Won't you come in and have a cup of coffee?"

"No, thanks," Bill Smith said. He looked as mad as hops.

"Look. I want you to tell me—"

"Psst." Sergeant O'Hare said, in a perfectly audible whisper. "Let me handle this. After all, I—" He cleared his throat and said, "Well, good morning, little lady!"

"Captain O'Hare!" April said brightly. "How nice! How are you?"

"Just Sergeant," O'Hare said. "I'm fine. How are *you?*"

"Oh, fine," April said. "You're looking well."

"You're looking well yourself," the sergeant said.

"Listen," Bill Smith whispered, "if I wanted to go to a vaudeville show—"

O'Hare gave him a nudge, and said, "Little lady, I have a very important question to ask you, and I know you'll tell me the truth because it won't get anybody in trouble, and it'll help us."

April stared at him, wide-eyed.

"Tell me, little lady," Sergeant O'Hare said in his gentlest voice, "where has your little brother been for the last hour?"

"*Archie?*" April said. She looked surprised and bewildered. She almost dropped the dishtowel. Then she said, innocently, convincingly, and perfectly truthfully, "Helping *us.*" She went on polishing the plate.

Bill Smith shoved the sergeant aside and said, "Helping you *what?*"

Dinah took over, making the most of her sudsy hands and the wet dishcloth she still held. "I know we hadn't ought to ask him to, because he's a boy and shouldn't do housework, but my gosh, there's such a lot to do, with carrying out dishes, and emptying the garbage pail and burning the wastepaper and taking out the tin cans and putting ant powder on the back-porch floor."

Bill Smith glared at her and then at the worried McCafferty. "You couldn't have been having a bad dream," he said coldly.

McCafferty shook his head. "I tell ya," he said unhappily, "I was watching the premises and mindin' my own business, and this kid come up all excited and hollerin' there'd been a murder, and what was I to do?"

"Investigate it, of course," April said.

Bill Smith looked at her and said, "Will you kindly keep out of this?"

"And here were these bushes all broke down and everything. And then while I was telephoning, he tole me about a knife stuck in a tree trunk, and a body riddled wit' bullets. So what was I to do? I done like it tells, in the Manual, I moved fast."

"If you ever fall for anything like this again," Bill Smith said, "you'll move fast back into the traffic squad." He looked at April and Dinah. "Where's your brother?"

The girls looked at him blankly. Dinah looked into the back yard, where the Mob was playing marbles. "He was right around here a minute ago."

April said loudly enough for her voice to be heard in the back yard. "He might be down in the basement cleaning out the fire-place ashes. Or he might have gone down to the store after the potatoes. Or maybe—"

Archie, outside, got the hint. He gave a signal to the Mob, and dived into the basement.

"Never mind," Bill Smith said. "You're sure he's been busy help-ing you?"

"Every minute since breakfast," Dinah said truthfully.

Bill Smith sighed and turned to the anxious McCafferty.

"Maybe it was one of these kids—" He led the way into the back yard, O'Hare and McCafferty right behind him, and Dinah and April watching and listening from the back porch.

McCafferty stood looking for a moment and then said unhap-pily, "They all look alike to me. It might of been him." He pointed to Slukey.

Bill Smith fixed a stern eye on Slukey and said, "Was it you?"

"It wathn't me," Slukey said. He'd recently lost a tooth in hon-orable combat, and the result was a definite lisp. "An' bethideth, th' window wath cracked a'ready before I t'rowed the rock."

"That don't sound like him," McCafferty said. He looked hard at the Admiral.

"Where have you been for the last hour," Bill Smith said.

The Admiral turned white and refused to talk. Finally O'Hare coaxed him into the seclusion of the back porch, where he broke down and confessed. He didn't have no sisters, and his mother didn't have no maid, and somebody had to wash them dishes, only if the Mob should find out—

Sergeant O'Hare promised him solemnly the Mob would never find out.

Goony had been on an errand for his grandmother. Pinhead had been mowing Mrs. Cherington's lawn. Flashlight had been practicing his piano lesson. Wormly had been watering the garden. All the Mob seemed to have good, solid, incontestable alibis. Finally Washboard, youngest and smallest of the Mob, staved off questioning by demanding to know, "Are you really p'licemen? Kin I have yer autographs?"

"They all look alike to me," McCafferty repeated.

"Forget it," Bill Smith said wearily, "and come on. We've got work to do."

They took a few steps along the kitchen walk. Then Archie came puffing up the back cellar stairs, clutching a bushel basket half full of wood ashes. The ashes were blowing out of the basket; his face and hair were covered with them. "H'lo," Archie panted cheerfully. He spotted Sergeant O'Hare, remembered the attempt that had been made to trick him into giving away a secret, and decided to settle an old score. He set the basket down hard just in front of the sergeant. The ashes promptly rose up in a cloud and turned the sergeant's neat blue suit to a dusty gray.

"Yipes!" Archie said. "Awful sorry." He pushed past the sergeant, waved at the Mob, and said, "H'ya!"

Wormly caught the hint. "How much longer you gonna stay down in that there cellar?"

"Aw heck," Archie said, "the whole place is fulla ashes. It's gonna take 'nother coupla hours." He didn't mention that the former couple of hours had been spent a week before. The statement still seemed to him to come within the confines of truth.

"Gug-o-squared-dud gug-u-yum," April called softly from the back porch.

Sergeant O'Hare grabbed Archie by the collar and dragged him over to Policeman McCafferty. "Is this the guy?" he demanded.

McCafferty looked thoughtfully at the ash-smeared face, the mussed-up hair, and the jersey Archie had resurrected from the salvage box in the basement. "No," he said at last. "Don't look the least bit like this guy."

"Well, c'mon," Sergeant O'Hare said. "We got no time to fool around with this stuff. Don't pay no attention to kids' tricks. B'lieve me, I've raised nine of my own, and I know." He led the hapless McCafferty down the path toward the Sanford villa.

"I wonder how the first of the nine turned out," April murmured. "After all—"

Dinah giggled. Then she signaled to the Mob and to Archie. "Hey, you kids. There's a whole quart of ice cream left over from the party, and half a maple cake. Only you have to eat it on the back porch."

The entire Mob was settled on the back porch in five seconds flat.

"It's worth it," Dinah explained to April, after she'd ladled out the ice cream. "Archie would probably have gone to jail or something."

"Good ole Mob," April said, flinging a dishtowel over the rack. "Wow-e-lul-squared, cash-hash-u-mum, let's go up and pry into the late Mrs. Sanford's private life, before more hash-e-lul-squared breaks loose."

Dinah rinsed out the dishcloth and spread it carefully over the edge of the sink. "And," she said thoughtfully, "when the cops happen to look at Uncle Herbert's left eye—it will!"

Chapter 13.

THEY CLOSED the door to their room and dumped the contents of the big Manila envelope on Dinah's bed—letters, papers, documents, newspaper clippings. April picked up one of the clippings at random and glanced at it. "Dinah! Look! This picture—"

It was a picture of a handsome middle-aged man in uniform. A headline above it read

FOUND GUILTY BY
MILITARY COURT

The name under the picture was Colonel Charles Chandler.

"I don't get it," Dinah said. "Who's Colonel Charles Chandler?"

"Look at the picture again," April said. "Imagine it has white hair and a little beard."

Dinah looked and imagined. "My gosh," she said. "It's Mr. Cherington!"

"Carleton Cherington III," April said solemnly.

Dinah stared at her. "That don't make sense. What'd he do?"

April skimmed hastily through the article. "He stole a lot of money. Fifteen thousand dollars. It was five years ago, about, according to the date on the clipping. He managed to make it look at first as if the safe in the quartermaster's office had been burgled, but then they found out it was him, only they never found the money. So the military court run him out of the army."

She turned to another clipping stapled to the first one. "He was arrested and sent to jail. For four years. There's a lot of personal junk about him, how he went to West Point and was a hero in the World War, and his father was an officer in the army, and stuff."

"Four years!" Dinah said. "But they've been living here about three years!"

"Wait a minute, can't you?" April said. She turned to the third and last of the clippings—a very small one. "He got a parole."

"Oh," Dinah said. "And then they came here and changed their names. They certainly picked a nice fancy one."

"Mrs. Carleton Cherington III," April mouthed. "Bet you she picked it out. Just the same," she added, "she stuck with him. Wonder what he did with the money."

"Spent it, I suppose," Dinah said.

"On what?" April said scornfully. "Just use what we like to be polite and call your brain. They came here right after he was paroled. They certainly haven't spent the money. I bet they don't spend two thousand dollars a year. That's a dinky little house, she never buys any new clothes, they don't even have a cleaning woman once a week, and all the entertainment they have is raising prize roses."

"Maybe," Dinah said, "he used it to pay gambling debts."

"*Him!*" April said. "Mr. Cherington? I mean—Colonel Chandler? Does he look as if he'd have that many gambling debts?"

"Well, no," Dinah admitted. "Heck, I don't know what he did with it. But gosh! Mr. Cherington! That nice old guy!"

"He's not so old," April said. "Look at his picture. He must have been just about fifty, five years ago." Her eyes narrowed. "One thing he might have done with the money. Mrs. Sanford was blackmailing him."

"That makes sense," Dinah said. She looked at the collection of papers and said, "Come on, April, we haven't got all day."

Most of the pages of notes, the letters, the pictures and clippings had names written in blue ink across the top, in a small, cramped handwriting. April spotted one labeled "Desgranges" and grabbed at it.

There was quite a little collection on Pierre Desgranges. It consisted of a series of letters signed simply "Joe," addressed to "Dear Flora," and full of such unimportant personal references as "How nice to hear from you again," "How do you like California?" "Remember the wonderful Martinis at Raviel's?" "Are you still happily married?" and "Will you ever forget the night we went to Coney Island?" They were written on the office stationery of a New York newspaper.

It wasn't difficult, though, to pick out the phrases that referred to Pierre Desgranges. Those phrases had been neatly underlined in blue ink.

". . . your mysterious artist answers the description of one Armand von Hoehne, who was smuggled into this country across the border a few years ago and has been looked for ever since. If he should be the man, it would not be surprising if he posed as a Frenchman. His mother was French, and he was brought up in Paris. We have quite a file on him up to the time he disappeared. Let me know what you find out, we might have a story."

In the next letter ". . . if this Desgranges *is* von Hoehne, he isn't hiding out for fear of the FBI. Enemy agents in this country have been looking for him since his disappearance, with orders to shoot him on sight. If this is the man, no wonder he's grown a beard."

Then, ". . . yes von Hoehne would be well supplied with money. It's known that he carried his late mother's jewels with him, when he fled from Europe…."

And ". . . no, there isn't any photograph of von Hoehne. But there's one identifying mark you might be on the watch for. He has a dueling scar on the left arm, a long, diagonal cut from his elbow to his wrist. Look, if it turned out this guy really is von Hoehne, let me know right away. It would be a great break for the paper if we could find him first…."

Finally, ". . . too bad it turns out your Pierre Desgranges isn't Armand von Hoehne. It would have made a nice story. But if he doesn't have the scar, there's no doubt about it…."

April put down the letters and said, "Dinah. He was trying to get into the Sanford house the day after she was murdered. And have you ever seen him with his sleeves rolled up?"

"No," Dinah said, "but—"

"All right," April said. "He *is* this Armand von Hoehne, and he *is* afraid enemy agents are going to murder him. She finds out about it. She finds out he has money."

"And finally he runs out of money," Dinah said. "She says she's going to expose him. So, he kills her."

"Gosh, Dinah," April said. "He'd have known she must have had something in writing that would give him away. Or else he wouldn't have tried to get in the house after the murder. If he'd murdered her, he'd have torn the house apart to find it and destroy it. Or he'd have burned down the house. There wouldn't be any point in murdering her, if he couldn't get rid of the evidence against him."

"I guess that's right," Dinah said thoughtfully. "And, anyway, I can't picture Pierre Desgranges murdering anybody. That nice, gentle little guy!"

"He has a dueling scar from his elbow to his wrist," April reminded her.

"You think he has," Dinah said.

"Leave it to me," April said confidently. "I'll find out."

"How?" Dinah demanded.

"I don't know yet," April said. "But I'll think of something."

Dinah put the Desgranges papers down on the bed. "I guess Mrs. Sanford was a blackmailer, all right."

"And you figured that out all by yourself!" April said. "What a brain!" For a moment she considered confessing to Dinah about her lucky guess, and about Rupert van Deusen. No, better not.

"Well, my gosh," Dinah said, "she's lived right next door to us all this time, and everything."

"She had to live next door to somebody," April said. "And quit getting sorry for her just because she was murdered. People are murdered every day. I looked it up once in the *World Almanac* for Mother, when she needed a statistic. In 1940 there were eight thousand, two hundred, and eight people got murdered in the United States alone, and think of all the rest of the world! Think of how many people that would be every day."

"I could figure it out," Dinah said, "if I had a pencil and paper."

"Don't bother," April said hastily. "Just stop worrying about Mrs. Sanford. Remember what she was like?"

"I do," Dinah said. She shuddered.

"Remember when she chased us off when we went to ask her, very politely, if we could have some of her daffodils to put around Mother's surprise birthday cake?"

Dinah said, "Remember when she threatened to call the police when Archie went over on her lawn to catch Henderson?"

"And she went around in those fancy hostess gowns all the time, and with that lily-look on her face. And Mother always swore that blonde hair was an expensive bleach job."

"Lots of women bleach their hair," Dinah said. "And gosh, she *was* beautiful, even if she was sort of thin and sickly-looking."

"I bet Mr. Desgranges didn't think she was beautiful," April said. "Or Mr. Cherington. Or"—she pawed through the papers—"this guy."

"This guy" proved to be a harmless-appearing manager of a chain shoe store who owned a small bungalow, had a wife and three small children. Unfortunately, he had another wife back in

Rock Island, Illinois. He'd married her when he was twenty-one and she was twenty-nine, they'd stayed married exactly six weeks. Since he hadn't had any money for a divorce, or for alimony, and since she had a good job as waitress in a tavern, he'd simply left town and changed his name.

There was also all the dope on a country doctor, a general practitioner, who'd falsified a death certificate so that the deceased's elderly widow wouldn't lose the tiny income from an insurance policy because of a suicide clause.

There was a fat collection of indiscreet letters from a society matron whose pictures Dinah and April had seen more than once in the special sections of the Sunday *Times*, and who was deeply concerned that no one should ever know that her mother had been a chambermaid in a cheap Cincinnati hotel.

There was information about a near-middle-aged English teacher in a highly proper girls' school, who'd been picked up in a gambling squad raid on what she'd innocently believed to be a perfectly respectable restaurant.

"She worked on the mass-production theory," April said grimly. She turned over a page and said, "Now, here's something!"

It was a letter, in violet ink, on the stationery of an inexpensive Times Square hotel.

DEAR FLO:

You were strictly correct about this tip-off about this Holbrook buzzard. She's his daughter all right, but as I make out the score, he'd suffer a fate worse than death rather than have any of the folks back home know she's a chip off the family tree. He must be some kind of a nut because if I were him, believe me, Flo, I'd be proud of her. When she does that dance with the three peacock feathers and the string of beads, the cash customers rise up in a body and cheer, and if the money she makes every year was laid end to end it would ballast the whole Atlantic fleet. Of course people are funny, Flo, and maybe he objects about her being married three times, but I always say, how is a person going to learn without making mistakes, or maybe he doesn't like all the so-called unfavorable publicity she gets, but the way I feel about it is this, what the heck, if it stands them in line in front of the box office, it's good publicity. Well, Flo, I hope this will fix it up so you can get this Holbrook individual to take care of your legal affairs for free, and believe me, Flo, thanks for the ten-spot, it came in very handy. Hoping you are well,

VIVIENNE

"Mr. Holbrook!" Dinah said. "*Him!* He has a daughter that dances with a bunch of peacock feathers and a string of beads— that respectable guy! Why, he bawled Archie out once for whistling on Sunday, when he was driving down the road from Mrs. Sanford's place."

"You never know!" April said solemnly. She looked at the next letter, also written in violet ink on hotel stationery.

DEAR FLO:

Well, I did like you asked me to, and it worked out all right. I appealed to her because we once worked in the same show in Maryland and at that time she was just in the chorus and I was the star soprano, believe me. So when I got in to see her I said just what you told me, how her poor old daddy was very sick and might not get well, and I had a mutual friend with him who told me about him being sick, and how he pined for some kind of message from her, only it would have to be smuggled in to him and I would see that it would be delivered to him direct, and it didn't have to be more than a few words. She fell for it right off, and bawled even, and she wrote the enclosed, including the envelope addressed to him, which you said had to be part of it. And thanks, Flo, for the C-note, which I really needed because I do have to get my teeth fixed, especially if that Hollywood job you suggested really materializes. Take care of yourself and let me know about the job.

VIVIENNE

Clipped to it there was an envelope addressed to "Mr. Henry Holbrook." Inside, there was a note, written in haste.

DEAREST, DEAREST DAD:

I just heard you were sick. Please get well soon. Forgive me for all the trouble I've caused you. Really, someday I'll make you proud of me. And I've never done anything that would make you ashamed of me and I never will, honest. And get well soon because someday I'll be a star in a real play in a real theater and you'll come on opening night and cheer for me. I love you so much.

B

The next letter in the collection was, again, in violet ink.

DEAR FLO:

I'm sorry about her not signing her right name to the letter, but how was I to know, and once she had put her name on it what was I to do? Don't blame me, Flo, I'm doing the best I can to help out a pal. Well, anyway, I gave her the note you wrote in what looked like her daddy's handwriting, requesting a professional picture of herself and autographed, and she really broke down and cried. So I picked out the picture while she was crying, and gave her the pen, and she signed it with her real name, and I enclose same. And, Flo, if you can help me out with the loan of a few dollars I will appreciate same, on account of I have had a lot of unexpected expenses in the last few weeks. Yrs. always.

VIVIENNE

April turned over the page, looked at the photograph clipped to it, whistled, and said, "What a babe!"

The photograph was signed, "Harriet Holbrook."

"If Mr. Holbrook ever saw this," Dinah gasped, "he'd practically die."

"He must have seen it," April said. She was beginning to look a little mad. "He must have known that Mrs. Sanford had it. That's why he was trying to break in the house, after she was murdered. Because he couldn't let anybody know his daughter was a dancer who wore a few peacock feathers and a handful of glass beads."

"There's more here," Dinah said, lifting up the photograph.

There were a half-dozen notes, the first few in violet ink, all in the same sprawling handwriting. They were all appeals for money.

". . . the dentist says I need a whole upper plate which is going to cost money, and you know I expect to have a job soon, so if you can loan me . . ."

". . . wonder if my last letter to you went astray as I have not had an answer from you. The teeth will have to wait, but I am three months behind in my rent, and the building manager has given me until next Thursday. If you can make me a little loan, Flo, for old time's sake, can you send it airmail special, as this is Saturday . . ."

The letters were uniform in one respect. None of them seemed to have been answered.

The last one was written in pencil, on cheap, ruled paper.

". . . if you can wire me $25, care of the Salvation Army shelter at . . ."

Finally there was one pitifully small clipping. It told of the suicide of Vivienne Dane, former musical-comedy star, in a tiny tenement room.

Dinah slapped the collection down on the bed. She looked good and mad. "That woman! She made this Vivienne person do all her dirty work and stick her neck out, and she sent her"—she thumbed through the letters—"a total of a hundred and ten dollars and the promise of a Hollywood job which was probably phony. And then when she'd found out what she needed, she didn't even answer the poor woman's letters!"

"Don't lose your temper," April said. "You'll wake Mother."

"Well, my gosh!" Dinah said. "When I think about this Vivienne, and Mr. Holbrook, and Mr. Desgranges, and—"

"Calm down," April said. "We've got a lot more stuff here to look over."

Dinah sniffed once, and calmed down.

April picked up the next item in the collection. It was an eight-by-ten shiny photograph that looked like a flashlight picture taken to the surprise of the subjects. Stapled to it were two newspaper clippings. April stared at the photograph and then said, "*Uh*-uh! Look, Dinah!"

Dinah looked, gasped, and said, "Mr. Sanford!"

"And a *gorgeous* girl!" April said.

The scene was a stage-door alley. Wallie Sanford had on evening clothes. The girl had long, dark hair, and a lovely young face. She wore a long, pale formal, and a fur cape. They might have been any good-looking couple going out for an evening, save for the one fact that they both looked not only startled, but scared.

Dinah turned to the clippings.

WAS MYSTERIOUS "MR. SANDERSON"
FINGER MAN IN LEMOE KIDNAPING?
By Marian Ward

Two days ago beautiful Bette LeMoe left the stage of the theater where she was starring to the sound of tumultuous applause. There were curtain calls, and she returned for them. Then she went to her dressing room and made herself beautiful for the young man who was waiting at the stage door.

Her maid testifies she took particular pains with her dress and make-up, and seemed in a particularly happy frame of mind. She went out the stage door, humming happily to herself, and her "escort" greeted her affectionately.

They walked down the alley to the sidewalk. Suddenly a car slid up to the curb. In full sight of a crowd of theater goers, an armed man forced Bette LeMoe into the car. Her "escort" disappeared into the crowd.

Today I interviewed the maid who helped Bette LeMoe don her favorite dress, and the doorman who said "good night" to her when she left the theater, perhaps for the last time. Both of them mentioned the name of "Mr. Sanderson."

A "Mr. Sanderson" had called for Bette LeMoe a number of times, had sent her many gifts, and talked to her frequently on the telephone. There appears to be no doubt that it was this same "Mr. Sanderson" who accompanied her on that last walk down the stage-door alley....

The clipping was torn off there. There was still the second one.

WILLIAM SANDERSON SOUGHT IN BETTE LEMOE SLAYING
By Marian Ward

Police of five states searched today for William Sanderson, young real-estate salesman, believed to be involved in the kidnap-murder of Bette LeMoe.

For several weeks prior to the kidnaping, Sanderson was

known to have been a constant escort of Miss LeMoe, accompanying her to exclusive night spots and sending her costly gifts. Sanderson's employer, Mr. J. L. Barker, when questioned, declared that Sanderson's weekly earnings averaged less than forty dollars, yet there appeared to be no shortages in the Barker accounts. Inspector Joseph Donovan, in charge of the case, stated his belief that the money spent entertaining Miss LeMoe was advanced by the kidnap gang.

Sanderson disappeared the night of the kidnaping and no trace of him has yet...

"William Sanderson," April said thoughtfully. "Wallace Sanford. He didn't show much imagination in picking a name."

"What would you expect him to pick?" Dinah said. "Acidophilus McGillicuddy? Maybe all his clothes and stuff were initialed, and he had to find something to fit. And you aren't showing much sense, if you ask me. Take a look at that by line."

April looked blank and said, "Huh?"

"Marian Ward, you dope," Dinah said.

"Oh, my gosh," April said. "Mother! That was her name when she was a reporter!"

"And there's something in here about her," Dinah said grimly, beginning to paw through the papers.

"Here it is," April said, making a grab for it.

It was another letter from the helpful Joe. Across the top of it was written, in blue ink, *Carstairs.*

DEAR FLO:

Yes, you're right. The Marian Ward who covered the LeMoe kidnap case is the Marian Carstairs you met in California. She used the name Ward (her maiden name) when she went back to reporting after her husband's death. He (Carstairs) was a great guy. I knew him. She was fired off the *Express* for an article she wrote two months after the LeMoe affair, charging the police department with "gross inefficiency" for not having found even a suspect in the case. The chief of police raised such a stink about the article that the paper fired her. Since then she's taken to writing mystery novels under a collection of pen names. I've read a few of them, and they're good stuff. Wonder why she doesn't do one on the LeMoe kidnaping?

When are you going to visit the big town again?

YRS.
JOE

"That guy shows good sense," April said approvingly, putting the letter down. "Too bad he's been doing Flora Sanford's dirty work for her."

"He didn't know that he was," Dinah said. "He thought he was just being friendly. She probably went out with him a few times once, and whenever she wanted to find out something she'd write him a perfectly innocent letter. Like, f'instance, 'I met a charming lady named Marian Carstairs and I wonder if she could be the Marian Ward who—'"

April nodded sagely. "And the way she pried the dope about poor Mr. Desgranges out of him." She drew a long breath. "Maybe that story in *Real Crime Cases* told about Marian Ward and her getting fired and stuff, and that's why Mother didn't want me to read it."

"Seems like," Dinah said. Her eyes narrowed. "Mrs. Sanford's murder has something to do with the Bette LeMoe business. She's saved all this dope about it. She married Wallie Sanford, who used to be William Sanderson. And Frankie Riley was held for questioning after the kidnaping, and he was murdered in her house last night. And she was very anxious to find out if Mother was the reporter who wrote about the case."

"Well?" April said.

"Well," Dinah said. "*Now*, if Mother finds Mrs. Sanford's murderer—I mean, if we do—and maybe solves the LeMoe business at the same time, it'll really be swell for her. Think of the publicity."

"*Miss* Carstairs," April said admiringly, "you really *are* a brain!"

"Thank *you*, Miss Carstairs," Dinah said. "Let's get on with this stuff. There may be some more clues."

There was one letter, on blue dime-store paper, unsigned.

> *Frankie gets out next Tuesday, so watch yourself. He may go to LeMoe's father. Maybe you'd better go on a long trip. Good luck.*

"That *proves* she was mixed up in the kidnaping," Dinah said.

"As if we needed any proof," April sniffed. "Look. She got this Frankie person to do it. Maybe others, too. But he didn't get any of the money, or else he wouldn't have been committing a robbery a year later, and going to jail."

"Fifteen thousand dollars wouldn't go very far, split up among a bunch of people," Dinah pointed out.

April pointed to the letter. "There must be some reason why he was sore at her."

There was a desperate note from the nurse-companion of a wealthy woman, begging Mrs. Sanford not to reveal the fact that she'd gotten the job with forged references, and promising to send "whatever I can spare." There were letters from a worried youth who didn't want his folks back east to know he was working as a bartender. There was an elderly bank clerk who'd once been convicted of forgery in another city, and under another name. And at the very bottom of the pile there was a page torn from a fan magazine—a picture and biography of the new star, Polly Walker—and a couple of letters attached to it.

The biography told about the orphan girl who'd grown up in

exclusive boarding schools and summer camps, only to brave Broadway at eighteen, talk her way into a very minor role, and then go on to stardom.

The first of the letters was written on the engraved paper of an investment trust corporation.

MY DEAR MRS. SANFORD:

You are correct that I was Polly Walker's guardian until she reached the age of twenty-one, a year ago. I am glad you wrote to me regarding these rumors, and I trust you will do what you can to squelch them, since you are such a good friend of Polly's....

"But she wasn't a friend of Polly Walker," Dinah exclaimed. "She was just the opposite. She was—"

"Quiet," April said. "I'm reading."

. . . The rumor does, unfortunately, have its basis in fact, but is wrong in details. Polly's father was not convicted of the murder of Polly's mother. Polly's mother died of pneumonia when Polly was less than a year old, and at that time her father placed her in my charge, not wishing her to grow up with the stigma of being Ben Schwartz's daughter. You will remember him as the gambling and rum-running czar, now serving a life term in Leavenworth. At the time of his conviction he placed what money he had left in my hands, for Polly's education and training.

I do indeed hope that you will do everything possible not only to quell the rumors, but to make sure that the truth will be kept secret. Not only would it be fatal to her career, but it would be a terrible blow to her, after all these years. . .

There were two notes, on thin, pale-gray paper.

DEAR MRS. SANFORD:

I will be delighted to call on you at two o'clock, Monday afternoon.

POLLY WALKER

The second:

DEAR MRS. SANFORD:

I have been able to raise the money and will bring it with me Wednesday.

POLLY WALKER

Dinah and April looked at each other. "Wednesday was the day of the murder," Dinah said. "Polly Walker was out there two days before. Mrs. Sanford showed her this stuff and prob'bly offered to sell it to her. And then—Wednesday—"

"But when Polly Walker got there," April reminded her, "Mrs. Sanford was already murdered."

Dinah sighed and began stuffing the papers back in the big Manila envelope. "It all gets sort of mixed up," she complained. "And there's one awful funny thing. Remember that man we read about in the newspapers?"

"Frankie Riley?" April said.

Dinah shook her head. "The other one. The one who admitted Mrs. Sanford had been blackmailing him, like that reliable witness said, only he had an alibi. Rupert van Deusen. Why isn't there anything about him in this collection?"

"Listen, Dinah," April said. She drew a long breath, and began, slowly, "I want to tell you something—"

Before she could continue, there was a loud pounding at the front door downstairs. Dinah jumped up, stuffed the envelope back in the laundry bag, and headed for the stairs.

"That'll wake Mother," she said.

"Archie's downstairs," April said, close at Dinah's heels.

They heard the front door open. Archie met them at the foot of the stairs. "The cops are here," he reported.

Police Lieutenant Bill Smith and Sergeant O'Hare stood in the doorway. Both of them looked breathless and worried, and the sergeant was a trifle pale. "Where's your mother?"

"She's sleeping," Dinah said. "She worked all night and went to sleep right after breakfast."

Bill Smith looked bewildered, and then said, "Oh!"

"Listen, little ladies," O'Hare said, "have you been home all morning?"

Both girls nodded solemnly, and Archie chimed in, "We ain't been away one minute."

"Have you—" Bill Smith paused, frowned. "We think there may have been someone prowling around the neighborhood. Someone who got into the Sanford house. Have you heard anyone—seen anyone?"

Dinah and April stared at each other and at the cops.

"Not a soul," April said. "We haven't seen anybody or heard anybody, except you."

Bill Smith mopped his brow. "Well, thanks just the same. We were just checking up."

As they turned to go, O'Hare muttered, "I tell you, I'm positive. The whole thing's the work of a maniac. That's the only way I can figure it out."

April looked at Dinah and winked. Dinah hastily smothered a giggle. Archie bounced up and down and demanded, "What'sit? What'sit?"

"Oh, nothing," April said with dignity. "Nothing but Uncle Herbert."

Chapter 14.

"HEY, WHAD'JA get for a mother's day present, hey?" Archie began to chant, meeting them at the door. "Hey, whad'ja get for a Mother's Day present, hey? Hey—"

"You're stuck in a groove," April said.

"Hey," Archie said. "Whad'ja get for a Mother's Day present?"

"Archie," Dinah said. "You make too much noise. Were there any phone calls?"

"Uh-uh," Archie said. "Hey, whad'ja—"

"Listen," Dinah said. "Didn't Pete call?"

"Pete? Uh-uh," Archie said. "Hey—"

Dinah looked stricken. She said, "But this is *Saturday*. He *always* calls me up *Saturday*."

"Hey—" Archie began.

"Weren't there any calls at all?" April said. "Or anything? How about the cops, and everything?"

"No phone calls," Archie said cheerfully. "No cops. No murders. No houses burned down. No nothing. Hey, whad'ja get for a Mother's Day present, hey?"

"All right, Dopey Joe," April said wearily, "we got her a book."

Archie stared. "A *book!* Heck! She *writes* books!"

"She reads them, too," April said.

"And this is a very special book," Dinah added. "We had to go all over town to find it."

"Le' *me* see," Archie demanded.

Dinah took an ornately wrapped package out of a paper bag. "You can't look inside. The lady at Crenshaw's wrapped it up for us special. And we got a very elegant card to go with it."

"Oh, boney," Archie said. "I hafta stay home and listen to the telephone, and you go downtown and pick out some corny book. A'right. I got a very special Mother's Day present, and I ain't gonna show it to nobody until tomorrow, including you."

"That's wonderful," April said. "What is it?"

"Ain't gonna tell."

"It's a bunch of flowers," Dinah guessed.

"It is not neither."

"Something you made," April said. "Maybe a birdhouse, or a desk calendar."

"It is *not*," Archie said, looking happy.

"G'wan," April said. "You're making the whole thing up."

"Oh, I am, huh?" Archie said indignantly. "You c'mon with me and I'll show you—" He paused just in time. "Oh, no, you don't. You don't fool me into making me show you my Mother's Day present ahead of time."

"All right," Dinah said coldly. "We're not even curious. But if it's another turtle, Henderson may not like it."

"And if it's another jar of tadpoles," April said, "*I'm* going to leave home."

"And remember what happened to the white mice you gave Mother for a Valentine," Dinah added, "when Jenkins saw them."

"Oh, foo," Archie said. He sniffed, and said, "This is not a turtle, and it is not tadpoles, and it is not white mice, and what it is nobody knows but me, and I ain't gonna tell."

He looked small, sweaty, dirty, and definitely on the defensive. Dinah reached out a hand and completed the job of mussing up his hair. "Whatever it is," she said affectionately, "Mother's going to love it."

"Darned right," April said with equal warmth, kissing him on his nose.

"Hey, cut it out," Archie said, pretending unsuccessfully to be furious.

Dinah hid the ornately wrapped package under a cushion of the sofa. Then she announced, "I'm hungry. And we got stuff to talk about."

There was a duet of "Me too" after the word "hungry" There was a rush for the kitchen. Dinah got out bread and peanut butter, Archie brought milk and a jar of jam from the icebox, and April dug behind the flour bin for a bag of potato chips she'd been keeping for emergencies. There was cream cheese, and some leftover ham, and three bananas, and a can of olives, and, miraculously, a fat wedge of cake.

"This is just a snack, remember," Dinah said, spreading peanut butter, cream cheese, and jam on a slice of bread. "We're going to have dinner pretty soon. And, April, cut that cake in three *equal* parts."

"I get the biggest piece," Archie announced, peeling a banana and reaching for a handful of olives. "Because I'm the littlest, and I gotta grow."

"Archie," April said severely, licking frosting off her fingers, "you are a swine."

"I am not no swine," Archie said. He spread peanut butter on his bread, dotted it with cream cheese and jam, added a piece of ham, and finally topped it with a wedge of banana. "Because a swine is two or more pigs, and I'm only one pig." He added an olive to his masterpiece by way of garnish, and bit off a good quarter of it.

"A swine can be one pig," April said. "And take your spoon out of the jam jar."

Archie licked off the spoon and said, "Cannot."

"Can too," April said.

"My gosh," Dinah said wearily, "look it up in the dictionary."

Archie went for the dictionary while April went to the ice-box for more milk and discovered that two cokes had been over-looked among the milk bottles. She was dividing the cokes into three equal portions when Archie returned, only slightly crest-fallen, to admit that April had been right and to dispute the pouring of the cokes.

"I'm only a small swine," he stated. "Hey, you're pouring more in Dinah's glass than you are in my glass."

Dinah said, "For Pete's sake." She scooped a remnant of frost-ing off the cake plate and stuffed it into Archie's mouth.

"Shush-u-tut u-pup."

Five minutes later there wasn't so much as a crumb of food on the kitchen table, and Archie was mousing around in the vegetable bin for apples. Dinah carried the dishes over to the sink and began rinsing out the milk bottle. "April," she said slowly, "there's some-thing we've got to do. *You've* got to do."

"I will not carry out the tin cans," April said. "That's Archie's job."

"Our whole family future is at stake," Dinah said to the kitchen window, "and April worries about the tin cans. Listen." She put down the dishcloth with a sudden slap. "You've got to go up to Mrs. Cherington's and ask her for some roses for a Mother's Day bouquet."

April tossed her dishtowel onto the kitchen table. "And while I'm there," she grumbled, "I suppose I'd better ask Mr. Cherington if he murdered Mrs. Sanford because she knew he'd stolen fifteen thousand dollars and been kicked out of the army."

"Well, my gosh," Dinah said, picking up the dishcloth again. "You don't have to be *tactless* about it."

"I'm the tactless type," April said, "but I'll do the best I can. And if Mr. Cherington looks pale and haggard, or if he looks very calm and dignified, what do I do, whistle for a squad car?"

Dinah wheeled around. "You're scared."

"I am not scared," April said. Her cheeks turned pink. "Was I scared when I went up to the Cheringtons' and asked her to make a cake for the PTA Garden Party?"

"That was before you knew Mr. Cherington might have murdered Mrs. Sanford," Dinah said. She wiped her hands on the dishtowel. "Maybe I'd better go."

"Never mind," April said hastily. "I'll come back with roses and evidence. Shall I take along the bullet we found, and see if it fits in Mr. Cherington's gun, if he has one?"

Dinah dropped the dishtowel, said, "April!" caught her breath, and picked up the dishtowel again. "I forgot it—"

"It could be considered a clue," April said. "A bullet fired at the scene of a crime often is. If we could find out what kind of gun it was fired from, and who owned that kind of gun—"

"Betcha *I* can find out," Archie said shrilly. "Betcha and double betcha."

"Triple-triple betcha you can't," April said.

"Gimme the bullet," Archie said. "I'll show you."

"*How* will you?" Dinah demanded.

Archie looked insulted and said, "Heck. I'll just ask a p'liceman. They know all about bullets."

"My brother!" Dinah said bitterly. "What a brain!"

"Wait a minute," April said. "Maybe he's got something there." She looked sternly at Archie. "Do you think you could get away with it?"

"What'dya suppose I'd do?" Archie said, looking even more insulted. "Go tell a p'liceman this here is the bullet you stole outa the picture in Mrs. Sanford's house?"

"Maybe," April said speculatively, "he could get away with it. It's taking a chance, but—"

"Not with me it ain't taking no chance," Archie said.

April and Dinah looked at each other over his head. "Well," Dinah said at last, "he'll be sticking his neck out, not us. Just to be on the safe side, though, maybe I'd better dirty that bullet up a little."

"I'll do it," Archie said. "Just leave everything to me. I know 'xactly what I'm gonna do." He snatched the bullet out of April's hand and said. "And don't worry I'm gonna lose it, neither, because I ain't."

He grabbed a couple of soda crackers out of the box beside the cake bin and dived out the door. A second later he reappeared. "What's more," he declared, "I'm gonna take Slukey an' Flashlight with me. I ain't dumb." He turned and vanished.

Dinah sighed. "Hope it works. If he gets in a jam—"

"He won't," April said confidently. "And if I'm going to promote a bunch of Mother's Day flowers from the Cheringtons, I'd better get started." She didn't look particularly happy at the prospect. For a minute she lingered by the door. "What are you going to be doing?"

Dinah sniffed. "What do you suppose? You and Archie get the easy jobs. All I have to do is finish cleaning up the kitchen, hang out the dishtowels, and get dinner." She looked searchingly at April. "Are you scared to go up there?"

"Don't be insulting." April said coldly. She marched out the kitchen door and across the back lawn.

You're not scared, she told herself grimly. That funny feeling in your stomach comes from combining banana and dill pickle. The idea, suspecting that nice old Mr. Cherington of murder!

But he wasn't old Mr. Cherington! He was middle-aged ex-Colonel Chandler, who'd stolen fifteen thousand dollars, gone to prison, and then changed his name. And Mrs. Sanford had known all about it. April shivered.

Across the wide Sanford lawn she could see Sergeant O'Hare seated on a garden bench, deep in conversation with three small boys who were hanging on his every word. Archie and Flashlight and Slukey. The sergeant seemed to be enjoying himself. April smiled to herself. Good ole Archie!

A narrow, weed-grown path, hidden from view by a thick mass of shrubbery, led up the hill from near the Sanford back gate to the tiny cottage where the Cheringtons lived. There was a longer and more formal way round, but the young Carstairs preferred the more adventurous path on their visits to the Cheringtons'.

It was a small, stucco cottage, two rooms, a kitchen and a bath. Its great attraction was the garden around it—a tiny square of neat and frequently mowed green lawn, and then, a profusion of brilliant roses. April had seen it a dozen, a hundred times before, yet always as she reached the top of the path she stopped and gasped at the riot of color. Roses so dark red they seemed almost purple, great yellow roses, white ones, bright red ones, enormous pink ones. A vine heavy with tiny scarlet blooms ran up one side of the stucco bungalow, and another, with tiny pink blooms, climbed over the arched gate. Mrs. Cherington stood among her flowers, dressed in overalls, her face hidden by a wide straw garden hat. She had a pair of pruning shears in her hand.

Definitely not the type for overalls, April reflected. Not with that figure. She looked almost a little funny. Then she raised her head and called a greeting, and April suddenly realized that Mrs. Cherington was anything but funny. She'd never noticed the deep lines in Mrs. Cherington's forehead and around her once-pretty mouth. She'd never noticed that look in Mrs. Cherington's eyes, that was present even when she smiled. It made her feel a little uncomfortable.

"Hello, April," Mrs. Cherington said. "I just made some molasses cookies. Want some?"

"Oh, gosh!" April said. Mrs. Cherington's cookies were famous, and molasses cookies were April's favorite. Especially with raisins, and Mrs. Cherington always put in lots of raisins. Then suddenly she remembered. She was really here to spy on the Cheringtons, to try and find out something they didn't want her to know. It was distinctly bad etiquette to accept molasses cookies from someone you were spying on. "Well—" she said slowly.

She paused, gulped, and said, "Well, I really came over to ask you a big favor. Tomorrow is Mother's Day. We got her a present but we didn't get any flowers, and—"

"And of course you've got to have flowers," Mrs. Cherington said. "And you shall. All you want." She looked affectionately at April. "Your Mother is a very lucky woman."

"*We're* the lucky ones," April said. Mrs. Cherington's eyes were misty. April looked away and said, "Well, we thought—maybe just a couple of roses—"

"A couple!" Mrs. Cherington sniffed. "A big bouquet! The very best ones we can find. Do you want to pick them out?"

"I'd—rather you did," April said. "You know which ones you can spare."

Mrs. Cherington looked thoughtfully around her garden. "I tell you what. Roses ought to be cut in the early morning, when the dew is still on them. Tomorrow morning I'll make you a bouquet, and you can send Archie up to get it."

"You're swell!" April said.

"I like you, too," Mrs. Cherington said. She resumed her pruning. "And the molasses cookies are on a plate on the kitchen table."

"I—" April stood for a moment, deep in thought. She was making up her mind about something and, she told herself, it wasn't because of the cookies either, or the roses. And it wasn't just because she liked Mr. and Mrs. Carleton Cherington III. It was that—

well, the evidence in Flora Sanford's Manila envelope wasn't suffi-
cient motive for murder. Once, it might have been. But—why, it
was hardly enough to be cause for blackmail. He had already been
dishonorably discharged from the army and had served his term
in prison. If Mrs. Sanford had given away what she knew, they
would simply have moved to another tiny bungalow in another
town, changed their name again, and planted another rose garden.
There was nothing she could have done to them that would have
made it necessary for her to be murdered.

April felt a sense of relief so great that for a minute she was
afraid she might cry. She said, "Golly yes, I'd *love* a cookie." She
started around the side of the house toward the kitchen.

"Not one cookie," Mrs. Cherington called, "take a handful.
They're best when they're still warm."

"Don't tempt me too far," April said.

Mrs. Cherington's warm, friendly laugh echoed across the rose
garden. "Go in the side door and get a paper bag out of the broom
closet, and take some home to Dinah and Archie. If there aren't
enough on the plate, you'll find more in the stone crock on the
pantry shelf."

"Thanks," April called back. "You're *wonderful!*" She darted
in the side door. Dinah and Archie *adored* molasses cookies with
raisins. Tomorrow they'd bring Mrs. Cherington a big bunch of
radishes from their back-yard garden, and the Sunday paper. And
a bowl of the ice cream Dinah was going to make for Mother's
Sunday dinner.

She found a paper bag in the broom closet and started for the
kitchen.

Funny, many times as she'd been in the Cherington cottage
she'd never noticed that photograph at the end of the hall. It had
been there all the time. Seeing it, now, she remembered that it had
been there. But she'd never stared at the face in it before. It was

a beautiful face, framed in a cloud of soft, dark hair. Something hauntingly familiar about it. Where had she seen it before?

Oh, gosh, yes, of course! It was Mrs. Cherington, when she was years and years younger. April stepped closer and looked thoughtfully at the picture. No lines on the forehead or shadows in the dark, almost wistful eyes. The corners of the mouth curved in a faint, shy smile. It was a happy face, a trusting one.

April thought of Mrs. Cherington's plump, rouged face, the plucked eyebrows, and the eyes that could fill so easily with tears. "It's a darn shame," she whispered to the photograph. It smiled back at her. It was signed in the corner, "All my love. Rose." So that was Mrs. Cherington's name. No wonder the Cheringtons raised roses for a hobby.

She went on into the kitchen. There was a plate heaped with cookies on the table. They were warm, and they smelled *lush*. April stared at them ecstatically. Great big fat ones, thick with raisins!

Mrs. Cherington was always making cookies, always ten times as many as she and Mr. Cherington could possibly eat. And all the neighborhood children haunted the Cherington kitchen. She should have had about ten of her own, April reflected.

She reminded herself not to be a pig, and selected exactly nine cookies, three for Dinah, three for Archie, and three for herself. She considered taking one extra, to eat on the way. No, that wouldn't be fair. She took one long sniff instead.

Nobody who made cookies like these could ever, possibly, be guilty of murder!

She put the cookies carefully in the paper bag and went on out the back door. On the back steps she paused suddenly, and gasped. Old Mr. Cherington was sitting on the back-yard garden bench. And he was holding a gun in his hand.

April said, "Oh!", took one more step, and stood still.

He looked up at her, smiled, and said, "Hello there, April."

She forced her face into a smile and said, "Hello, yourself. I've been robbing the kitchen." She hoped her voice wasn't trembling. "But I only stole nine cookies. So don't point that at me."

Mr. Cherington laughed. "I'm not pointing it and it isn't loaded." He admired it as it lay on his palm. "And you could hardly call this a twenty-two—a lady's toy—or maybe, a lady's ornament." He tilted it so that the sunlight reflected on the mother-of-pearl handle. "Pretty, isn't it?"

"Not to me," April said. "Guns scare me." Especially a gun resting in the hand of someone who might still be a murderer, in spite of her reasoning about the motive, in spite of Mrs. Cherington's photograph, in spite of the molasses cookies.

She couldn't help it, she had to stare at Mr. Cherington. He was handsome, he was darn handsome. Tall, and slender and very straight. Military-looking. Well, after all, he'd been Colonel Chandler once, and a war hero. He had gray eyes, beautiful gray eyes. His thin face was tanned. His white hair and neat little white beard were just the right touch. Only, his hair shouldn't have been white. It had been dark in a picture taken just five years ago, and he hadn't had the small beard.

April found herself remembering the poem she'd had to study for English class. "My hair is white, but not with years . . ." Had Mr. Cherington's hair—she couldn't think of him as Colonel Chandler—turned white in prison? Or had it—what was the phrase?—"turned white in a single night"? But Mother had said that was a crazy superstition, and a scientific impossibility. White hair was something that had to do with vitamins. Maybe a person didn't get vitamins in prison. Now, April told herself, you're being silly. Silly, because you're scared. And there wasn't any reason—couldn't be any reason—for being scared of Mr. Cherington.

She swallowed hard, looked at the gun, and said, "Well, it would look cute on a charm bracelet."

"That's about all it's good for," Mr. Cherington said. He laid the little gun down on the table in front of the bench.

April walked over to the bench, sat down beside him, and stared at the gun with fascinated eyes. It was tiny, it was pretty, and it certainly didn't look deadly. She said, "May I touch it?"

"Help yourself," Mr. Cherington said. "I told you it isn't loaded."

April picked it up, and her skin prickled all over. It fitted comfortably into her hand. She pointed it at the top of the pine tree across the street from the Cherington cottage and said, "Bang!"

Mr. Cherington laughed. "If you'd aimed like that, you'd have hit some other tree two blocks away. Look, let me show you. First get the horizontal range, and then—"

"Never mind," April said hastily. She laid the little gun gingerly on the table. "Pretty, isn't it?"

"Couldn't do much damage, though," Mr. Cherington said. "If you really wanted to shoot somebody—" He paused, and said, "But Louise is fond of it. That's why I've been cleaning it for her."

"You know so much about guns," April said admiringly. "You must have been in the army once." She hoped her voice sounded normal, because her stomach had turned into a little ball of ice.

It was a good thirty seconds before Mr. Cherington said, "Oh, you can learn all about guns from reading books in the public library."

But that isn't how *you* learned about them, April thought. She said, "I s'pose so," and kicked her heels against the bottom of the bench. "Say—tell me something." She wished there was a way to sneak the cookies back into the kitchen. It didn't seem quite right to take them, now.

"Delighted," Mr. Cherington said.

"Well—" She gulped. "You know so much about guns, and everything." She paused. Maybe the way she felt was what books described as one's blood running cold. Hers suddenly seemed to be full of ice cubes. "Tell me. Who do *you* think murdered that Mrs. Sanford?"

"Mrs. Sanford?" Mr. Cherington stood up. "Oh, yes." April had a feeling that he was stalling, the way Archie did when Mother wanted to know why he hadn't come straight home from school. "Yes, Mrs. Sanford." Then he smiled at April, warmly, affectionately. "I'm sorry. I'm not a detective."

"Make a guess," April said.

Mr. Cherington looked at her, without seeing her. And without seeing the garden and trees and sky behind her. He said, as though he'd forgotten anyone was there, "Someone—who knew what she deserved."

April smothered a gasp and stood perfectly still, not making a sound.

Suddenly he seemed to remember he had a young guest. He handed her the bag of cookies she'd laid on the table. He smiled at her and made her a courtly bow, as though she were a great lady. He said, "Come over again, soon. Before this batch of cookies is all gone." Then he picked up the gun, turned, and walked—no, marched—into the house, very straight, head held high, shoulders square.

April watched him until the screen door banged shut. Then she scrambled through the kitchen garden, climbed over the picket fence, slid down the grassy hillside to the path, and ran the rest of the way home, down the path, along the alley, across the back lawn.

Dinah was putting away the last dishes in the kitchen. April dumped the paper bag on the table and said, "She'll make a bouquet for us. Archie can get it in the morning." Then she plumped down in a kitchen chair.

Dinah slammed the door to the china cupboard. "Swell," she said. Then she looked in the paper bag. "Oh, gosh! Super!" Then she looked at April. "For Pete's sake!" Dinah said. "You fixed it up about the flowers. You brought home cookies." She reached automatically for a handkerchief. "So what the heck are you bawling about?"

April grabbed the handkerchief, blew her nose loudly, and went on crying. "That's the whole trouble," she said through the handkerchief. "I'm darned if I know!"

Chapter 15.

THROUGH THE gap in the hedge they could see Sergeant O'Hare sitting on a bench in the Sanford garden. Not sleeping, not reading, just sitting.

"I think I better go home," Slukey whispered. "I think Ma's calling me."

"Slu-key!" Archie whispered reprovingly, "you do not neither hear your ma calling you. But if you're too scared to go along with me 'n' Flashlight, maybe you'd *better* run home to your ma."

"*Who's* scared?" Slukey said.

"Not good ol' Slukey," Flashlight said. He peered through the hedge at Sergeant O'Hare. "He does look awful official."

"He's looking for a *murderer*," Archie said. "He ain't even *intr'sted* in the fact that you let Mrs. Johnson's chickens loose onto the club-house lawn. Of course, if you guys don' wanna come along with me, I can always get Admiral an' Wormly."

"*Sure* we're gonna come along," Flashlight said indignantly.

"Well, then," Archie said. "You 'member, now. If you get stuck, you just shuddup, and lemme talk."

"You c'n talk all you wanna," Slukey said. "I ain' gonna talk to no p'liceman."

"You don't *hafta*," Archie said. "All you hafta do is come along an' act like I told you." He drew a long breath, said, "Oke, le's go," and charged through the gap in the hedge, Flashlight and Slukey right behind him. A few feet beyond the gap he pulled up short, stared at Sergeant O'Hare as though surprised to see him, then waved cordially and called, "*H'ya, there!*"

"H'ya, yourself!" Sergeant O'Hare called back. He was glad to see them. For the last half-hour he'd been sitting there on the garden bench, feeling depressed. Bill Smith too had been puzzled over the sprig of geranium that had suddenly appeared in the portrait in the Sanford house, but he'd scoffed unpleasantly at O'Hare's theory that the murder was the work of a maniac. Yes, even in spite of the knife with A WARNING printed on the blade in red letters. When the red had turned out to be lipstick, O'Hare had voiced his belief that the murderer was obviously not only a maniac but a lady maniac. Bill Smith had laughed harshly and told the sergeant to watch the house in case any more lady maniacs turned up, while he went to contact the fingerprint bureau. Since then, O'Hare had been sitting in the garden, depressed and brooding.

"C'mon over," he called to the three small boys who'd appeared at the edge of the lawn.

"He ain't no p'liceman," Slukey said. "He ain't got a uniform."

"He's a detective," Archie said scornfully. "A p'lice detecative, like Dick Tracy. Naturally he ain't got a uniform."

"He don't look like Dick Tracy," Flashlight said.

"Well, naturally he don't look like Dick Tracy," Archie said. "On account of he ain't Dick Tracy. He's Detective Sergeant Mr. O'Hare, and once he captured nine bank robbers all at one time, and he didn't have a gun, neither." He raised his voice. "*Did* you have a gun, Mr. Sergeant O'Hare?"

"Huh?" the sergeant said, startled.

"When you captured all them bank robbers."

"Oh," Sergeant O'Hare said, remembering. "No, I didn't have a gun. Just my bare hands. There were eight of them."

"Nine," Archie reminded him.

"That's right, nine. One of them almost got away, though, after I'd subdued the rest. He was armed with a knife, a revolver, and a submachine gun. I got him just in the nick of time."

"Gosh!" Flashlight breathed.

"And you know," O'Hare said reminiscently, "that very same night was when the mad gorilla escaped from the zoo—"

For a good ten minutes he told of the chase for the mad gorilla, ending with an exciting description of his capture of it in the thirty-fourth floor of a deserted elevator shaft.

"Golly!" Slukey murmured.

Archie kicked Slukey gently on the ankle, by way of prompting. Slukey jumped, remember, and said, "If you're a p'liceman, why ain'tcha got a badge and a gun?"

"I've got a badge," O'Hare said, throwing open his coat. "See? And I've got a gun." He drew it from his underarm holster and laid it on his lap.

"Oh, boy," Flashlight said reverently. "Can I just touch it once? With one finger?"

"Sure," O'Hare said amiably.

"Say," Archie said, "say, y'know what? I read in a comic book about how a cop could look at a bullet and tell what kind of a gun it came out of. Is that the truth?"

"Well," the sergeant said. "Well, yes."

Archie turned triumphantly to Slukey and Flashlight. "See," he said, "I tole you so."

"Aw, I still don't believe it," Flashlight grumbled.

"Show him the bullet," Archie said. "He'll show you."

Flashlight dug into his pocket, unearthed a variety of strange objects, and finally produced the bullet. It was embedded in a wad of chewing gum, and covered with cake crumbs and dirt. "Maybe I oughta clean it off a little," Flashlight said apologetically. He located an almost clean handkerchief in another pocket and went to work.

"Spit on it," Slukey advised.

"Rub some sand on it," Archie said. "That's the only way to get that there gum off of it."

The bullet was reasonably clean by the time it was handed to Sergeant O'Hare. "Betcha he can't tell what kind of a gun it came out of," Slukey said skeptically.

"Double-triple betcha he can too," Archie said. "He's a very smart detective." He looked appealingly at Sergeant O'Hare. "You can too tell what kind of a gun that there bullet came out of, can'tcha?"

Sergeant O'Hare caught the appealing look. He glanced at the bullet, held between his thumb and forefinger, and said, "This bullet was fired from a .32-caliber revolver."

"See?" Archie said triumphantly. "What'd I tell you?"

"I betcha he's just guessing," Slukey said.

"I betcha he is not neither guessing," Archie said. "He *knows*."

"*How?*" Flashlight demanded. "*How* does he know?"

Sergeant O'Hare looked at Flashlight. He said, "If you had a ruler here, I'd show you how I know. You'll just have to take my word for it. Thirty-two caliber means the bullet is thirty-two one-hundredths of an inch in diameter. When you've seen as many bullets as I have, you can tell without measuring them. This came out of a thirty-two."

"Golly!" Slukey said admiringly. "I betcha you've seen a lot of bullets in your life!"

"Millions," Sergeant O'Hare said casually. "Sometime I'll have to tell you about the mad magician who was shot ninety-four times, and the ninety-fourth bullet was the one that killed him. Now, there was a study in ballistics—"

"Tell it *now*," Archie begged.

"Well," O'Hare said. "It happened this way."

They listened to him, breathless and wide-eyed. The story sounded suspiciously like one that had been in a last month's comic book, but they managed to gasp, ask questions, and applaud at the right places.

"And there you are," the sergeant finished. "Ninety-four bullets, and every one of them could be traced to the gun that fired it. Easy, of course," he added, "if you know how." He beamed at the three small boys and wondered if they'd go for the werewolf story. No, anything after his latest invention of the mad magician would be anticlimax. He looked thoughtfully at the bullet he'd been bouncing in his hand. "By the way, where did you get this?"

Archie nudged Flashlight. Flashlight said, "Oh, if you go down by the pistol range at the club you can find lots of 'em." Archie nudged him again, and he said, "Gimme it back, please. It's the only one I got."

Sergeant O'Hare handed it back. "I'll never forget the time," he began reminiscently, "when an enraged tiger escaped from a circus that happened to be in town."

Archie said hastily, "Hey, you know what? You know what? I betcha you know more about guns 'n' bullets than anybody else in the whole world."

"Oh, no," the sergeant said modestly.

"Well," Archie said stoutly, "*a'most.* F'rinstance. Which is the biggest bullet and which is the littlest, and which is the dangerousest and which is the harmlessest?"

The sergeant drew a long breath and said, "It's like this." He launched into a fifteen-minute lecture on ballistics, beginning with the science of projectiles, passing lightly over wounds of entrance, going deeply into identification of bullets, and ending with a story about the murder of a Brooklyn policeman which was solved simply and easily by someone with a knowledge of the subject.

"He's a very smart fella," Flashlight said to Archie.

Archie said, "You betcha my life."

"Gee," Slukey said, "he knows *ever*-a-thing!"

"A policeman has to," Sergeant O'Hare said modestly. "You never know when you'll need a piece of information. Just for an example. There was a wild man, carrying a lot of poisoned arrows he'd brought from Borneo—"

"Hey," Archie said. "Hey, Mr. Sergeant O'Hare." He'd heard about the poisoned arrows before, and he suspected that Slukey and Flashlight were getting bored. A person could depend on those two guys just so far, and that was all. "Hey, tell me sumpin', hey? Hey, tell me—"

"Yes?" Sergeant O'Hare said, breaking off reluctantly. The poisoned-arrow story was one of his favorites.

"Well," Archie said, "what kind of a gun did what kind of a bullet come out of that killed the lady in that there house?" He jerked his head toward the Sanford house and looked hopefully at Sergeant O'Hare.

"Her?" the Sergeant said. "She was shot with a forty-five. A service revolver. That's the kind of a gun that means business."

"Golly!" Archie said. "Is that the kind of a gun you have?" He waited for the Sergeant's nod and said, "Can we see it again?"

"Oh, sure," the sergeant said indulgently. He took out the gun and rested it on the flat of his hand.

"That there is a real gun," Archie said, almost reverently. "What I'd say, a real gun. I betcha, now, you couldn't shoot no dinky little bullet like that one Flashlight's got out a real gun like this, now could'ya?"

"Of course not," Sergeant O'Hare said. He slipped the gun back into his holster. "I don't think you got the idea about the caliber of guns and bullets. Now, it's like this."

He went back into his lecture on ballistics, and the three small boys listened respectfully. He'd gotten as far as "the spiral in the barrel of a gun has a certain pitch which is measurable" when Slukey looked up and said, "Hey—"

There was a long, shrill whistle from somewhere down the road. It had been sounding, by arrangement, at fifteen-minute intervals since the three boys had arrived on the Sanford lawn, but, also by arrangement, no one had noticed it before.

"That's Deadpan whistling." Slukey said apologetically. "It means I gotta go now. Ma wants me. G'by, Mr. Sergeant." He vanished into the bushes.

"Good-by," the sergeant called cordially after him. He cleared his throat and resumed. "By a careful study of the bullet, the number of grooves in the barrel—"

"Hey," Flashlight said. "If Slukey's ma had Deadpan whistle for him, that means I gotta get home quick for supper. G'by, you." He waved, and raced down the path.

Sergeant O'Hare waved back at him and went on.

"So from a knowledge of the caliber of a bullet and the number and direction of the grooves it shows the—"

"'Scuse me," Archie said. "But Dinah's calling. I better go set the table now."

"Go right ahead," the sergeant said. "You're a good boy, to help your sisters. And any time you want to know anything about guns—"

"I'll sure know who to ask," Archie said. "You're *wonnerful!* And I betcha I really am a p'liceman when I grow up." He added, "See y'later—pal." He disappeared through the arbor.

Sergeant O'Hare sighed and gazed after him. He wished he'd had time to tell the story of the nine bank robbers. True, that little Carstairs boy had heard it once, but he could always put in a few variations and improvements. An X-ray machine, for example, that could see into a bank vault.

"Since our guns were trained on him, he had to turn on the

machine. We could see through the walls as though they were glass," he improvised.

Bill Smith's voice, very weary and almost cross, came from behind him. "What are you muttering in your beard about? And who were you talking to?"

Sergeant O'Hare nearly went on about the X-ray machine, and caught himself just in time. "I was questioning some children," he said stiffly, "who might possibly have had some helpful evidence. Sometimes they can be very observant. I've raised nine kids of my own, and I know—"

"I'm getting pretty darn sick and tired of your nine kids," Bill Smith said. "Now, look. The fingerprint man says there's nothing on either the oil painting or the knife."

Down beyond the bushes, Archie paid off to Slukey and Flashlight. Five cents apiece, two cokes, and a copy of *New Comics*. "If I'd hadda listen to one more o' them stories," Flashlight grumbled, "This'da cost ten cents. An' you owe me a stick o' gum for the one I stuck on the bullet."

"That gum had been chewed a'ready," Archie said indignantly.

Flashlight said, "Maybe it had, but it was good yet and I was saving it." He glowered at Archie and said, "Or, you don't get back the bullet back."

"You gimmie back that bullet back," Archie said hotly, "or—" He paused. This was no time for trouble. He fished a slightly battered stick of gum from his pocket and handed it to Flashlight.

Flashlight inspected the gum, said reluctantly, "It'll do, I guess," and handed Archie the bullet.

There was a brief argument over whether to promise to bring back the coke bottles or to pay Archie the two cents apiece. It was settled by the cokes being drunk right then and there, on the spot, and the bottles being delivered back to Archie.

There was another argument going on as Flashlight and Slukey went down the steps to the sidewalk. Slukey was saying, "Maybe it was you as stuck that gum on that bullet, but it was me found it under the stool at Luke's, and b'sides, you'd chewed it twice as long as I had, and so—"

Archie wasn't interested. He walked slowly around to the back of the house, figuring his expenses. "Two cokes, a stick of gum—"

Dinah was washing carrots. April was making butterscotch pudding. Both of them looked up and stopped work when he came in the back door.

"Well?" Dinah said anxiously.

"Five cents apiece," Archie said, "two cokes, that's ten cents, the *New Comics* is ten cents, and a stick of gum—altogether it's thirty-one cents."

April said, "Archie, for Pete's sake—"

"Making a total," Archie said, "of three dollars and sixteen cents which you owe me."

"You'll get it," Dinah said. "Look, about the bullet."

"Oh, sure," Archie said in a lordly manner. "About the bullet." He took it from his pocket and laid it on the kitchen table. "Seems like we got it a little dirty."

"Archie!" April said. "Did you—?"

"Oh, sure, sure, sure," Archie said maddeningly. He looked very casual and unconcerned. "It's a thirty-two-caliber bullet which means it hadda be fired from a thirty-two caliber gun. And the gun which killed Mrs. Sanford was a forty-five service revolver. And in case you're interested"—he drew a long breath—"the science of ballistics is—"

"We're only interested in the fact that this bullet and the bullet that killed Mrs. Sanford didn't come from the same gun," April said coldly.

"And we practically knew that already anyway," Dinah said loftily.

"But," Archie said desperately, "I went to work an' found out the whole thing, all from Mr. Sergeant O'Hare. All about the bullets and stuff. Heck, don't you even *care?*"

Dinah took one quick look at his crestfallen face and said, "April was teasing you. We could hardly wait for you to get back."

"Dinah was teasing you," April said hastily. "Did you honestly ask Sergeant O'Hare and what'd he tell you?"

"Plenty," Archie said. "Now, this here bullet—" He went onto a long and detailed explanation, omitting only the stories of the mad magician, the enraged tiger, and the murdered Brooklyn policeman. "So," he finished, "scientifically speaking, either the murderer had two guns, two diff'rent kind of guns, or else there was two diff'rent murderers, each with his own gun."

"Oh, Archie, you're wonderful," April said. She kissed him on the nose.

"Quit it," Archie growled. "And don't forget now. Three dollars and sixteen cents."

"Don't worry," April said. "You won't let us forget." She began scraping the butterscotch pudding into dessert glasses. "There must have been two of them. We figured that out before. So. Were they both shooting at her, or were they shooting at each other or what?" She shoved the glasses into a neat row on the kitchen table and began licking out the saucepan. Suddenly she put it down and said, "But there's *three* guns mixed up in this!"

Archie grabbed the saucepan quick and reached for a spoon.

Dinah dropped a carrot. "Three?"

"The gun that shot Mrs. Sanford. A—forty-five. The gun that shot the picture. A thirty-two. And the Cherington's gun. He said—'A twenty-two. A lady's toy.'" Suddenly she noticed Archie. "Give me back that saucepan. *I* made the pudding tonight and it's my turn—" She looked into the pan and said, "Oh, *darn* you, Archie Carstairs!"

"Never mind," Archie said consolingly, licking the last drop of butterscotch off his spoon. "Now you won't have to wash the pan."

Dinah put the carrots on to cook. She turned away from the stove and said, "You know—I wonder what kind of a gun shot that man—that Frankie Riley."

April forgot the saucepan. She said, "I wonder too. If it was the same one—"

"Leave it to me," Archie said confidently. "Betcha nine million dollars I can find out tomorrow."

"Betcha the same amount you can't," April said.

Archie looked at her speculatively. "What'll you honestly and genuinely bet?"

"Twenty-five cents," April said promptly.

"Uh-uh," Archie said. "Oh, no. On account of if I win the bet you'll borrow the money from me to pay it. I ain't gonna bet money with you any more."

April sighed. "O-kuk-a-yum. You name it."

"If—" Archie paused, thinking. "If I find out tomorrow what kind of a gun shot that Mr. Frankie Riley, I don't hafta carry down the garbage can for a whole week."

"Make it four days," April said.

"Oh, no. A whole week."

"Well—all right. It's a deal."

"Now, if you children are all through playing," Dinah said severely, "listen to me."

"Yes, Master," April said, salaaming.

"We obey," Archie said very solemnly.

"We know now about the kind of a hold Mrs. Sanford had on poor Mr. Sanford," Dinah said, ignoring their antics. "We know why he ran away after the murder, and why he was hanging around trying to break in the house. Because we got what he was trying to break in after."

"Maybe," April said, "we'd better run out and tell him we got it, and that we'll keep it in a safe place until the real murderer is found and then give it back to him or burn it up. That ought to relieve his mind a little."

Dinah looked superior. "And maybe we ought to ask him what he knows about the Bette LeMoe kidnaping. Maybe he can tell us something that'll give us an important clue."

"Brain!" April said admiringly.

"What if he won't talk?" Archie demanded.

"We'll make him talk," Dinah said. "*We've* got a hold over him, now."

"What if he tells lies?" Archie said insistently.

"Archie," Dinah said, "you make too much noise. Shushu-tut u-pup, if you want to come along with us."

They took one careful look from the back porch to make sure no one was watching. Then they scooted up to the playhouse.

Dinah stopped dead as they rounded the bushes and said, "*Gosh!*"

The playhouse was empty. The blankets were neatly folded up on top of the bunk. The dishes were in an orderly pile on the table, the magazines tidily arranged beside them. The morning newspaper lay on top of the blankets, but the page-one picture of Frankie Riley and the accompanying story had been carefully torn out. And there was no sign of Wallie Sanford, not anywhere.

Chapter 16.

ARCHIE WAS pounding at their door almost at daylight.

"Hey, wake up," he called softly. "Hey, wake up. It's Mother's Day."

April called drowsily, "Come on in."

The door opened quietly and Archie, already dressed and washed, tiptoed in.

Dinah sat up, yawned, rubbed her eyes, and said, "If he did turn himself in to the police, it'll be in the newspaper. If he didn't—"

April yawned and said, "I've got a theory. I was thinking about it just before I went to sleep last night. Suppose that Bette LeMoe had a boy friend."

"She did have," Dinah said. "Wallie Sanford. William Sanderson, he was then." She reached for her bathrobe.

"That isn't what I mean at all," April told her. "I mean a real boy friend. Somebody who was crazy about her. Like Pete is about you."

"Y'h, y'h, y'h," Archie scoffed. "Then why didn't Pete come over last night?"

"Because he had to take his grandmother to the movies," Dinah said with icy dignity. "Go on, April."

"Well," April said half dreamily, "this guy was crazy about her. Prob'bly wanted to marry her. Then she was kidnapped and murdered. The police never find who did it. But this guy devotes his life to finding them and having his revenge."

181

"You got that out of one of Mother's books," Dinah said. "The Clark Cameron one where the guy spends twenty-five years trying to find who murdered his pal, and then—"

"Sure I did," April said. "But it fits. This guy finally locates Mrs. Sanford, and gets the evidence to prove she was mixed up in it. So he kills her. Then Frankie Riley turned up. Same guy kills him. And," she added gravely, "he probably knows about the William Sanderson-Wallie Sanford deal. So—"

Dinah stared at her. "I certainly hope he turned himself in to the police. He'll be safe. Archie, run down and get the paper."

"Oh, boney," Archie grumbled. "I hafta do everything. And I'm *hungry.*"

"Git!" Dinah said. "And I'll make waffles for breakfast."

"Yipes!" Archie said. He opened the door and dived for the stairs.

"You find out if Mother's coming down to breakfast or if she wants it brought up," Dinah directed, washing her face. "And I'll start the waffle batter."

Five minutes later they were down in the kitchen. Mother had announced her intention of coming down to breakfast and had promised to wear her blue house coat. Dinah started beating eggs and April plugged in the waffle iron. Archie came puffing up the steps with the Sunday paper.

"First chance at the comics," he announced.

"*After* breakfast," Dinah said firmly. "You've got to get the flowers. Remember?"

"I hafta do everything," Archie said. "Oh—shambles!" He raced up the path in the direction of the Cherington house.

Dinah spread out the paper. Wallie Sanford had *not* turned himself in to the police. A news item stated that the police were still looking for him.

April said, "Oh!" and sat down on one of the kitchen chairs.

"I hope he's safe," Dinah said. "I hope he isn't—" She gulped.

"At the bottom of some old swimming pool," April said, something close to panic in her voice. "Dinah, if he—if something's happened to him—maybe it's our fault."

"We couldn't exactly have *made* him stay in the playhouse," Dinah said.

"No, but if we'd told the police—he couldn't have been murdered if he was in jail."

"Listen," Dinah said. "We don't know he's been murdered. Chances are he just beat it. So stop worrying. We've got to get breakfast."

April nodded grimly, rose, and began setting the table. Her face was still pale.

"I keep wondering who that guy is," Dinah said, getting out the pancake flour.

April jumped. "What guy?"

"The one who was in love with Bette LeMoe," Dinah said. "You know, there's only one guy mixed up in this that we haven't quite accounted for yet. This Rupert van Deusen."

April said nothing. She'd been thinking the same thing.

"We oughta investigate him," Dinah said, carefully measuring the flour, "before we do anything else."

"Except that we don't know where he lives or anything about him," April said. Or, what his real name is, she thought unhappily.

"We'll find him," Dinah said, serene confidence in her voice.

"Dinah," April said. "Listen. There's something I've got to tell you."

"Just a minute," Dinah said, "the phone's ringing. Watch the bacon—"

April took the frying pan off the burner and followed Dinah to the phone.

"Hello," Dinah said. "Hello."

Over the receiver came the unmistakable sound of coins being dropped into a phone box. Then a familiar voice speaking very low.

"Is this Miss Carstairs?"

"This is Miss Dinah Carstairs," Dinah said, her face puzzled. "Who—"

"This is—this is a friend of yours," the voice said. "I was afraid you'd worry when you found me gone. I just wanted to tell you I'm quite all right."

"Oh!" Dinah gasped. "Mr.—" She bit it off quick.

"Where are you? Why did you go?"

"I'm in a safe place," he said. "Nobody'll find me. I went because—I think I know what happened. So just don't worry about me."

"Wait," Dinah said desperately, "*wait!* We've got to warn you. *We* think we know what happened, too. It was for revenge. He'll be looking for you, too. Because you were mixed up in it. You know who I mean. The man who was in love with—with that girl."

There was a little silence on the other end of the wire. Then, "What the devil are you talking about?"

"Listen," Dinah said. "We found that stuff that Mrs.—that *she* had hidden. You know. We've got it hidden in a good safe place. But we read it. We know everything. The picture of you, going down an alley with—you know. The clippings and stuff."

"Please," he said. "*Please!*" He paused. "I know what you think. It wasn't so. You're such nice kids, and I don't want you to think that. Believe me. I was perfectly innocent. I didn't have any idea what was going to happen. I didn't know I was being used until afterward. And then it was too late. Please believe me."

"We do," Dinah said urgently. "We *do* believe you. But he—the man who—you know what I mean—Mrs. S. and that other man—he doesn't know you're innocent. Maybe he won't believe

you. Maybe he won't even give you a chance to talk. He'll just—
please, be very careful. He's waited a long time for his—revenge."

There was a pause. Then, "Who are you talking about?"

"*The man who was in love with—the girl*," Dinah said.

"Oh, my Lord!" There was almost a laugh over the wire. "There
was only one man in love with—Bette. Me."

Dinah said, "Hey—wait a minute!" She listened for a moment,
jiggled the receiver hook, and finally hung up. "Heck! He hung
up!"

"Well, anyway, he's safe," April said in a relieved voice. "*So* far.
What'd he say?"

Dinah told her. The two girls stared at each other with puzzled
faces. "I'm confused," April said.

"I am too," Dinah admitted. "But I still say, we've got to investigate that Rupert van Deusen. And what were you going to say
when the phone rang?"

"Nothing," April murmured. "Nothing important." She wanted
to tell Dinah, but this wasn't the time. She'd better do some investigating of Rupert van Deusen herself, first. "Hey. Mother'll be
downstairs any minute. We got stuff to do."

Dinah raced into the kitchen. "Let's set the table in the sun
room. It's a very special occasion. And when Archie gets back with
the flowers—"

There was fast and furious activity in the kitchen and the sun
room. In the midst of it Archie returned, carrying one enormous
box and one smaller one. "I shoulda had a truck," he announced,
putting the boxes down on the table.

April opened the biggest box and gasped. "Dinah! Look! Talisman roses, her very best ones! Dozens of them! Golly!"

"Super!" Dinah said joyously. She got down the biggest vase
while April opened the other box and gasped again.

"Oh!" Dinah said. "How darling!"

April lifted the corsage from its box and stared at it with glowing eyes. Tiny Dorothy Perkins rosebuds, sprays of delicate, featherlike fern, all tied together with pale-blue ribbon.

"Well, for Pete's sake," Dinah said, "don't bawl about it."

"Who's bawling?" April sniffed loudly a couple of times. "Mother'll love these. Dinah, she never could have committed the murder."

"*Mother?*" Dinah said.

"Mrs. Cherington," April said.

"My gosh," Dinah said. "I never said she did."

"Loony-Lou," Archie added scornfully.

"All right, Dopey Joe," April said. "You help set the table."

The talisman roses were in the center of the sun-room table when Marian Carstairs came down the stairs. The waffle iron was heated and the batter was in a pitcher at its side. The bacon was perfuming the room from its covered dish, and the percolator was still making a cheerful little noise. The corsage of rosebuds was on Mother's plate. And there wasn't a sign of the three young Carstairs, not anywhere. Mother ran quickly into the sun room and said, "*Oh!*" She looked around. There was a very faint giggle from behind one of the curtains, followed by an even fainter "*Sssh!*" Mother began to talk to herself, in a very loud voice, about what wonderful, wonderful children she had, how beautiful the flowers were, how magnificent the breakfast smelled, and how lucky she was.

They descended on her with loud whoops, and for a minute she was in peril of being hugged to death. Then April pinned the corsage on Mother's shoulder, Archie kissed her wetly on the nose, and Dinah began making the first waffle.

The last drop of batter had been used, the last crumb eaten, and Archie had scraped out the sirup jug when Dinah whispered to April, "You go." April shook her head and said, "No. You." Then Dinah said, "All right, both of us."

They scampered into the living room, lifted up a sofa cushion, and returned with the ornately wrapped package. They laid it in front of Marian with a flourish.

"For *me?*" Mother said in surprise.

"You," April said. "Unless you can find anyone else around here named Mother."

"And a beautiful card," Mother said. "Who made it?"

"April made the flowers," Dinah said, "and I made the letters. Go on, unwrap it!"

They watched happily while Mother peeled off the layers of wrappings, slowly, almost maddeningly. They beamed when she removed the final sheet of tissue paper and laid the book on the table.

HOW TO COPE WITH THE GROWING CHILD:
A SIMPLE EXPLANATION OF CHILD
PSYCHOLOGY, FOR PARENTS
By Elsie Smithton Parsons, Ph.D.

"Look inside," April said. "On the flyleaf."

Inside was written, "To our dear mother, from her loving children. *Dinah. April. Archie.*"

Marian Carstairs swallowed hard and said, "Oh, how wonderful! I love it!"

"And," Dinah said, "we're going to read a chapter of it to you every day. I'll read a chapter one night, and April will read the next night. We figure we can get all the way through the book in twenty-two days, including Sundays."

"That's marvelous!" Marian said. She looked thoughtfully at the title, and then at Dinah and April. "This wouldn't be a delicately implied criticism of the way I'm bringing you up?"

"Oh, gosh, no," Dinah said. "It's just—"

April spoke up quickly before Dinah had a chance to quote Police Lieutenant Bill Smith's remark. "We're *more* than satisfied," she said. "We *like* the way you bring us up. But we thought, just to be on the safe side—well—"

"Do you like it?" Dinah said anxiously. "The book?"

"I'm crazy about it," Marian said. "And I'm crazy about you!"

"We're crazy about you, too," April said.

"I'm crazier about you," Mother said, hugging them both.

"We're crazier about you than you're crazier about us," Dinah yelped.

April finally caught her breath and said, "We're not crazy!" And, with her finger to her lower lip, "B-b-b-b-b-b-b!"

"Say!" Dinah said. "Where's Archie?"

April looked around. "He was right here a couple minutes ago."

"He—" Dinah cupped her hands to call him. Then April nudged her. Dinah stopped in the middle of a breath.

"Listen!" April said. There was a little silence. "He was down in the *basement!*"

There were slow, cautious footsteps on the basement stairs. Then Archie appeared in the doorway, his hair tousled, his face very pink and smiling. He was carrying an enormous box in his arms. He carried it into the sun room, set it on the floor beside Mother's feet, and said, "*There!*"

The huge box was wrapped, lavishly though amateurishly, in gift paper. It was tied with ribbon. There were holes punched in it. A large, crayon-drawn card on the top said, "To Mother. Love. Your child. Archie." And, as they stared at the box, it began to vibrate. April gave a startled yip. The yip was answered by a sound from inside the box. A faint, squeaky sound, but definitely a "Mew!"

"*Archie!*" Mother said.

"Well," Archie said, "Admiral's mother's cat's kittens were big enough to leave home, and these were the very best ones, and they're housebroken and everything, and you *like* kittens."

"I adore kittens," Mother said.

"And they're quite small so they don't eat much," Archie said triumphantly.

He was answered by another faint "Mew!" from the box.

"Oh, Archie!" April said rapturously. "Let's see them!"

"Sure," Archie said. "Only, it's Mother's present. She hasta open up the box."

Mother untied the ribbons and folded back the wrapping paper, while the box continued to vibrate. Then she lifted up the lid. Inside was a saucer of milk, a dish of cat food, a small sandbox, and two tiny, worried-looking kittens, one jet black and one pure white.

"Oh!" Mother said. "The sweet ones!"

"G'wan, pick 'em up," Archie said. "Anytime anybody picks 'em up, they purr."

Mother picked them up and nestled them in her lap. They did purr. April and Dinah petted them very gingerly. They purred louder.

"Their names," Archie announced, "is Inky and Stinky."

April looked up from scratching Stinky under the chin. "Only, Jenkins isn't going to like this."

"Jenkins knows about it a'ready," Archie said. "Lookit!" He went out in the back yard, searched around for Jenkins, spotted him relaxing on the back-yard picnic table, and hauled him into the house. The kittens on Mother's lap stiffened slightly and said, "F-f-f-f!"

"Here," Archie said. "Put 'em down." He picked up the kittens by the scruff of the neck and set them down on the floor. The two kittens promptly arched their backs and laid back their ears. The big, homely gray tomcat, Jenkins, stretched, yawned, and looked bored. He took a couple of steps forward and touched the kittens' noses with his own, first Inky, then Stinky.

"See?" Archie said. "He likes them!"

Jenkins sat down, licked his left front paw, then took a pose and looked dignified, regarding the kittens, who took a couple of sidewise leaps, rolled over, and began to play with his tail. He allowed it for a minute or two, then yawned again, displaying a frightening assortment of teeth, rose, strolled away. The kittens, left alone, sat up, looked after him, and said plaintively, "*Mew?*"

"Oh, the *poor* little *things!*" Dinah said. She scooped them both up and began to pet them. "Oh, they *do* purr!"

"What'd you expect them to do, yodel?" April said. She rubbed Stinky behind the ears and said, "The cuties!"

"They're my present," Mother said in mock indignation. "Give them here!" She gathered them into her lap and stroked them affectionately. The kittens nestled down and purred like a pair of miniature riveting machines.

"And 'member," Archie said, "They're real little and they don't eat much." He added, solemnly and with dignity, "I do hope you like them."

"Of course I like them," Mother said. "I'm crazy about them, and I'm crazy about you."

Archie beamed and said, "I'm crazy about you, too."

"I'm crazier about you," Mother said.

Archie drew a big breath and said, "I'm crazier than crazier than crazier than—"

That dialogue went on for a good five minutes. Then Mother ripped the cellophane off a cigarette package, twisted it into a bow, tied it on the end of a length of wrapping cord, and lured, the kittens into the living room. The three young Carstairs watched ecstatically while the kittens leaped and batted at the new toy. Inky could jump higher, but Stinky could move faster. Mother's cheeks grew pink, and her eyes grew bright.

"Archie!" April breathed. "That was a wonderful idea." She hugged him.

"Hey, cut it out," Archie said, wriggling loose. "I'm a man and I'm gonna be a p'liceman when I grow up."

"I don't care if you are," April said, giving him one more hug. "I'm crazy about you."

"I'm crazy about *you*," Archie said.

"My gosh!" Dinah said. "Let's not get into *that* again!" She jerked a thumb toward the table, "Pssst. The dishes!"

They moved fast. The perishables were stowed away in the icebox. The table was hastily dusted off. The dishes were rinsed and stacked up in the sink for future reference. After all, this was a holiday.

It wasn't more than fifteen minutes before they were all in the living room. Mother was in the middle of the davenport, her dark hair just slightly disheveled, her cheeks matching the Dorothy Perkins roses of her corsage. April and Archie were curled up, one on each side, admiring the kittens, who'd dropped off to sleep on Mother's lap, continuing to purr. Dinah was perched on the ottoman in front of Mother, reading slowly and very soberly out loud.

That was the picture Police Lieutenant Bill Smith saw when he glanced through the glass front door, just as he rang the bell. He felt a pang of envy. He hated to intrude—but by then, he'd already pushed the doorbell. And then he decided he was glad he had an excuse to intrude.

Dinah put down the book and raced to open the door. She welcomed him warmly. "How nice to see you! Have you had breakfast? Can I make you a waffle?"

"I've had breakfast, thanks," Bill Smith said, sniffing the air and wishing he was a liar.

"Coffee, then?" Marian Carstairs said cordially.

"Well—" Bill Smith said. He sat down in the easy chair. "I really shouldn't, but—"

Dinah and April had coffee, cream, and sugar on the end table at his elbow in a record time of one minute and twenty seconds.

"I saw you were reading," Bill Smith said, stirring his coffee. "I was sorry to interrupt, but—"

"Dinah was reading Mother's Mother's Day present out loud," Archie said. "We're going to read her a chapter every day. Here, wanna see it? Dinah and April picked it out because of—" April kicked him hastily in the ankle and he shut up.

Bill Smith looked at the book, at its title, and at the inscription. "Very thoughtful," he said at last.

"*I* thought so," Marian said challengingly.

"And these here are *my* Mother's Day present," Archie said, pointing to Inky and Stinky. "Listen, and you can hear 'em purr, way over there."

Bill Smith listened and agreed that he could, indeed, hear them purr.

"You're sure you couldn't manage just one waffle?" Marian said.

"I wish I could," he said. "I wish I hadn't already had a restaurant breakfast. I love waffles and I hate restaurant breakfasts."

"You ought to have a wife and family," Dinah said solemnly. "A wife who can cook."

Bill Smith turned faintly pink. He cleared his throat. A minute later he said, "Mrs. Carstairs, I must talk to you about something. I know you're very busy, but—"

Dinah pretended to look at the clock. She exclaimed in shocked surprise, "Kids! We've got to get the dishes done quick!"

Archie gulped and said, "We do not neither."

"We do too," Dinah said. "Come on."

"But you said—" Archie protested.

Dinah gave him a Look, and said, "Come *on!*" She herded April and Archie into the kitchen, all but dragging Archie the last few feet. "For Pete's sake!" Dinah whispered to him, "don't you have any tact?"

"Didn't you ever hear about leaving people alone together?" April added.

Archie looked mad, good and mad. He hissed, "But I wanted to hear what Mr. Bill Smith was going to say."

"Well, my gosh," Dinah said. "Who doesn't? And we will." She motioned them to absolute silence, and led them back through the hall to the foot of the stairs. They crept a few feet up the stairs and sat there, very quiet. They were out of sight, but they could hear every word.

There was Mother's laugh, soft, musical, and friendly. Then her voice, saying, "That's very nice of you, Mr. Smith. But I think you're flattering me."

April and Dinah winked at each other.

"Believe me, I meant every word," Bill Smith said.

Archie grinned widely.

"Well, Mr. Smith—"

"I wish you'd call me Bill. Mr. Smith sounds so formal, and you're not really the formal type of woman."

There was Mother's voice, laughing. "Okay—Bill. If I can do anything to help—"

His voice now, suddenly serious. "Frankly, this is the situation, Mrs. Carstairs—"

"I wish you'd call me Marian. Mrs. Carstairs sounds so formal."

This time both voices laughed.

The three young Carstairs, around the corner, beamed happily, crossed their fingers, and listened.

Chapter 17.

I HAVEN'T felt so happy in—ages, Marian Carstairs thought, sitting there stroking Inky and Stinky. The book done, and a few days' rest ahead of me. Those wonderful, wonderful children, with their marvelous, marvelous presents. And now, just relaxing, playing with these precious kittens, and watching Bill Smith over there sipping his coffee.

Funny, what a difference a man in an easy chair can make to a room. A tall, lean man in tweeds that needed pressing badly, sitting—no, sprawled—in the chair, his feet up on the hassock. Lighting his pipe now, a vile, aged pipe that was going to smell up the whole room. Looking for all the world as though he belonged there.

Curtains or no curtains, it was good to smell a dirty old pipe again.

Suddenly she realized he'd been speaking to her, and she hadn't heard a word he'd said. She felt her cheeks growing warm. "A plugged nickel for your thoughts," Bill Smith said.

Oh, Lord! She was actually blushing! She could feel it. "I—" She didn't know what to say. Here she was acting in the inane way Dinah acted when that awful Pete was around. "I was thinking—" *Darn* him! She caught her breath. "I've got to put flea powder for the kittens on my shopping list."

"Don't use flea powder," he said, "unless you brush it right out again. They lick it, and it makes them sick. Besides, how do you know those kittens have fleas?"

"If they don't now," she said, "they will have. All kittens have fleas."

"I know," he said, grinning. "That's how you can tell they're kittens. It's a law of nature." She looked so lovely in that blue, rustly dress, with the pink roses pinned on the shoulder, and her cheeks glowing. He wished with all his heart he had nerve enough to tell her so. "But I didn't come here to talk about kittens."

Inky chose that moment to wake up, sit upright, and scratch vigorously behind his left ear before going back to sleep again. Marian Carstairs blessed him for the diversion, and said very casually, "No?"

"Tell me," he said, "what do you know about the Bette LeMoe kidnap-murder?"

She stared at him, eyes wide. In the shelter of the staircase the three young Carstairs sat bolt upright, listening breathlessly.

"Why?" Marian asked.

"Because—" he paused. "Because I'm really stuck with this case. *Really* stuck. Marian, if you could help me—"

There was another pause, and then her voice said, very low, "I'll do anything I can."

Dinah and April looked at each other. "We might as well turn over the evidence to Mother and retire, right now," April whispered.

"What's that?" Archie whispered.

"Shush!" Dinah whispered.

"But I didn't hear what she said," Archie grumbled under his breath.

Dinah clapped a capable hand over his mouth and hissed, "Quiet! We'll tell you later."

April nudged them both and whispered, "*Listen!*"

"I thought I had this case all sewed up in a neat little bag," Bill Smith said. "Jealous wife, philandering husband, ambitious little actress. Then a man named Frankie Riley is killed. Right in the neighborhood. Might be a coincidence, but the bullet that killed him came from the same gun that shot Mrs. Sanford."

Archie, on the staircase, glared at April and said, "I could of found out by myself, so there."

"Sssh," April said, "bet's off."

"And," Bill Smith was saying, "his fingerprints were all over the downstairs of the Sanford house. And Frankie Riley was involved in the LeMoe case, though nothing could actually be proved on him. And there was a very smart reporter working on that case named Marian Ward, and a telegram to New York confirms my suspicion that Marian Ward is also known as Marian Carstairs."

Marian was silent for a moment, petting Stinky. "Yes," she said. "I covered the case. And I'd met Bette LeMoe, once, at a party, before it happened."

He leaned forward, resting his elbows on his knees. "Yes. Go on. Please go on."

"She was—well, she was lovely. With a very young, and some-how—very *gentle* quality. And with a fine, and very appealing voice. I caught her act once." Her voice grew sober. "Bette LeMoe wasn't her right name, of course, but nobody knew what her right name was, and—afterward—nobody was able to find out. But she definitely *did* have a fine old family somewhere who felt that singing at the Starlight Theater was a fate worse than death. That sounds like a publicity gag, but it isn't. Because there never were any publicity releases about it." Marian frowned. "The family must have been fairly poor. Because she was like a little girl with her first dollar bill. Furs and perfumes and Hattie Carnegie gowns, and terrific excitement over suddenly being a star. There wasn't a dime in her bank account when—it happened."

"Then who paid the ransom?" Bill Smith said quietly.

"Nobody knows. The theater manager—a Mr. Abell—turned it over to the kidnapers, but it wasn't his money, or the theater's."

"He would know where it came from," Bill Smith said.

Marian Carstairs nodded. "Naturally."

Bill Smith took out a little black leather notebook. "Abell. What was his first name?"

"Morris," Marian said.

He wrote that down, too. "Where can I locate him?" "You'll have to ask a spiritualist about that," she said. "Because he died, about two years ago. Not murder, either. Just peritonitis. I suspected it was murder, too, until I found out he'd waited too long to get his bad appendix to the hospital."

Bill Smith tucked the notebook into his pocket and said, "Too bad. You wrote some very nice stories about the case, by the way. I looked them up in one of the newspaper files."

Marian Carstairs lifted her head. "I wrote such nice stories that it cost me my job. I *liked* Bette LeMoe. I cried when I learned how the kidnapers sent her back—in a coffin. The police picked up Frankie Riley. Held him for questioning. Had to let him go. No evidence. They began to cool off about the case. I didn't. I couldn't. I'd *seen* Bette LeMoe when she was alive." Marian Carstairs little fist came down hard on the coffee table. Inky and Stinky woke up, complained, rearranged themselves in her lap and went to sleep again.

"Go on," Bill Smith said quietly.

"I dug them up a suspect, on my own. A good suspect. The— finger man on the job. They followed it up, in a mild way. But they didn't get anywhere because they couldn't get a good enough description of him. And there weren't any pictures of him."

On the staircase, Dinah and April exchanged a long look. There *was* a picture of him. At the bottom of their laundry bag.

"The police," Marian went on, almost savagely, "like the fools they usually are, never found the kidnapers—the murderers. And I lost my temper and wrote a story accusing the police—and quite justifiably—of gross negligence. I had to sneak it past the editor, but it got printed. And then some stuffed shirt in the police department made a loud noise about it, and I was fired. Now, Mr. Smith, are there any more questions you want to ask?"

"Several," he said, "and the name is Bill. Remember? First, I can find this out with a series of wires to New York, but if you can tell me, it'll save a little trouble. What happened to Bette LeMoe's body?"

She stared at him for a moment and then said, "I don't know. That was one of the strangest things about the case. When the police released the body, it was turned over to some theatrical burial society. I followed it up, because I wanted to do a story on Bette LeMoe's burial. But the body was stolen."

"I beg your pardon?" Bill Smith said. "*Stolen?*"

Marian nodded. "From a cut-rate undertaking parlor in Brooklyn, where it had been taken by this theatrical burial society. A car drove up about two A.M. The night attendant was slugged. Bette LeMoe's body, coffin and all, was carried away."

"But—" Bill Smith said in a dazed voice.

"The police let it die on the vine," Marian said angrily. "It would have been a swell story, too. I could have written the headline myself. But by that time I'd been fired for incompetence, and the name of Bette LeMoe was poison to every newspaper in the city. Not only had the chief of police raised Cain, but after all, she was only a burlesque singer, and the ransom had only been fifteen thousand dollars. So, that was the end of it. Now, is there anything else you want to know?"

"Plenty," Bill Smith said. "Including, who murdered Mrs. Sanford, and why? You wouldn't have any ideas about that, would you?"

Marian was silent a moment. "No, I wouldn't."

"Frankie Riley was killed in her house," Bill Smith said; "by the same gun that had killed her. But—it's all mixed up. There's a lot of things I don't understand. The flower stuck in the oil painting, and the knife with 'A Warning' written on it. And Mr. Sanford being missing and a lot of other things. And I've got to find Mrs. Sanford's murderer, it's my job. Marian, you covered the LeMoe case and it's tied up with this, you were a police reporter once, and you're so smart about things—please, Marian, help me."

Up on the stairs, April nudged Dinah. Dinah dropped an eyelid and whispered, "That's sold it!"

But when Marian answered, a good sixty seconds later, it was in a curiously flat, cold voice. She said, "If I did know, or thought I could find out, who murdered Mrs. Sanford, I'd keep the information to myself. Because whoever killed her probably had a very good reason for it. And I hope you never find him."

Bill Smith put down his empty coffee cup and stood up. "That's the trouble with you women. You're emotional. You don't think things through. You'd be willing to see Mrs. Sanford's murderer go free because you disliked Mrs. Sanford."

"I hardly knew Mrs. Sanford," Marian said icily. "How could I dislike her? I simply know that she was an *evil* woman, and deserved to be murdered."

"The laws, both legal and moral, concerning murder," he said just as icily, "don't take into account the objectionable personal characteristics of the victim."

"Oh, go to blazes," Marian said. She stood up too, holding the kittens in her arms.

Bill Smith said, very stiffly, "I'm sorry to have troubled you, Mrs. Carstairs."

"It was no trouble, I assure you, Mr. Smith," Marian said. "I always enjoy being reassured about the stupidity of the police department."

He opened the door, paused, and said, "By the way. I read one of your books last night. *The Kid Glove Murder*, I think it was called."

"I'm glad you liked it," Marian said.

"I didn't like it. I think it's sentimental, wishy-washy, and full of inaccuracies. I think it stinks." He slammed the door behind him. There was a gasp from Marian Carstairs.

April nudged Dinah and Archie. The three of them raced silently up the stairs, and hid behind the door to the girls' room. A minute later Marian Carstairs stalked up the stairs, still holding the kittens in her arms. Her cheeks were scarlet, and her eyes were very bright. She went into her room and shut the door with a bang. Then there was silence.

"Oh, April," Dinah said. "I'm afraid she's going to cry. And on Mother's Day, too."

"G'wan, she wouldn't cry," Archie said. "Why, she's older'n *I* am!" There was an anxious note in his voice just the same.

"Quiet," April said. "Listen! Call that crying?"

They listened, and heard the unmistakable sound of paper being inserted in a typewriter. It was followed by a sudden fury of typing. Then a paper was ripped out and thrown away, and another inserted. The typing began again, still furious. This time, it kept on.

Dinah gasped, went down the hall, and flung open the door to Mother's room. Mother was sitting at the desk, still in the blue house coat, her back hair coming down, and her eyes blazing. The kittens were sitting bolt upright on the desk, looking interested and slightly alarmed.

"*Mother!*" Dinah gasped.

The typewriter paused. The blazing eyes looked up. "I'm so darn mad," Marian Carstairs said, "that I'm starting another book!" She began to bang the typewriter again. Dinah tactfully closed the door.

"Never mind," Dinah said. "We didn't really want a policeman for a stepfather."

"You're full of balloon juice," April said scornfully. "You've been reading the wrong books or something. This is the most encouraging thing that's happened so far." Her eyes narrowed. "Come on! He may still be outside some place."

"But, April," Dinah said, halfway down the stairs. "You can't—"

"Quiet," April said. "I'm having an inspiration."

They paused for breath on the porch. Bill Smith could be seen leaning on the Sanford garden fence, looking thoughtful and melancholy.

"Hey," Archie demanded. "What'sit, what'sit, what'sit?"

"Shush-u-tut u-pup," April said dreamily. "Just remember I'm a genius, and don't bother me. Dinah, when's Mother having her hair done and her manicure?"

"Monday," Dinah said promptly. "Tomorrow."

April was silent a moment, thinking. "Then she won't get home until late afternoon, and her hair never looks really well until it's combed out the second time." She thought for one more minute, then raced down the steps.

Dinah and Archie exchanged a puzzled look, and then followed.

April ran quickly up to Bill Smith and said breathlessly, "Oh, I'm so glad I caught you before you left. Look. Mother wants to know if you can come to dinner Tuesday night. She hopes you can come, and we do, too."

"What?" Bill Smith said, a little dazed. "Dinner? Tuesday night? Why—"

The sound of furious and rapid typing was plainly audible from the house.

"Mother would have come and asked you herself," April said, "but she's terrible busy. You can hear how busy she is."

Bill Smith looked up toward the windows of Mother's room. "She works too hard," he said. "Much too hard. She ought to have someone to look after her."

"She has us," Dinah said with dignity.

"That isn't what I mean," Bill Smith said, still looking at the windows.

April detected a look on Archie's face that indicated he was just about to say exactly the wrong thing. She pinched his elbow lightly and said, hastily, "Then you can come, next Tuesday? Say, about six-thirty?"

"Why—why, yes," Bill Smith said. "I'll be delighted. Tuesday. Six-thirty. Tell your mother I'll be delighted. Tell her"—he gulped—"tell her I'll be here at six-thirty, Tuesday. Tell her—" he paused. "Tuesday. Thanks. G'by, kids." He turned and walked away, almost stumbling into a rosebush.

April repressed a giggle, just in time. He looked exactly like Pete, the first time he'd asked Dinah for a date.

"It isn't funny," Dinah said severely. "How are you going to fix this up with Mother?"

"Oh, that's easy," April said confidently. "Let's see—she'll have her hair done, and a new manicure. We'll promote her into making one of those old-fashioned meat loafs, with gravy. And a lemon meringue pie. All men like lemon meringue pie. And, after dinner—"

Dinah said, "All very fine, but who's going to explain to Mother about him?"

"Nothing to it," April said. "You're my sister, and we share and share alike. All right, I fixed it for him to come to dinner. That's my share. Now, all *you* have to do is tell Mother she invited him!"

Chapter 18.

ARCHIE WENT into the kitchen and brought out a bag of apples, and the three young Carstairs settled down on the front steps to talk things over.

"Instead of getting anywhere when we find out things," Dinah complained, "it seems as if we just get more confused. Like what Mother was telling Bill Smith this morning."

April bit into her apple, and nodded vigorously. "Who would want to steal Bette LeMoe's body? Why?"

"Maybe it was evidence," Archie said, expertly spitting out an apple seed.

"But there'd been a—a autopsy, and an inquest, and everything," April said. "The police had released the body. So—"

"That's pretty easy to figure out," Dinah said. "The man who was in love with her. The man who murdered Mrs. Sanford and Frankie Riley, and is looking for Mr. Sanford."

April picked up the theme. "He loved her, but he couldn't reveal himself, because he still had to have his revenge. So—" She paused, got an inspiration, and went on in a low voice, "Somewhere, in some hidden place, there was a secret burial in the dead of night, while only a lurid moon watched through the gloomy trees. And now, whenever the moon is full—"

"April," Archie said in a small voice, "don't!"

"Stop scaring your brother," Dinah said. "And stop quoting

203

from Mother's first book. She says herself that it wasn't a very good one."

April sniffed indignantly. "Since you're so smart, think this over. Mr. Sanford said *he* was the only man in love with Bette LeMoe."

"I know it," Dinah said. "That's why I get confused." She was silent for a minute. "Or maybe there was someone else in love with her, and he didn't know about it."

"If he was in love with her himself," April said, "he would have known about it."

There wasn't any answer to that. The three young Carstairs sat in silent thought for a while. Suddenly Archie pitched his apple core neatly through the nearest hydrangea bush, and stood up. "Someone's coming up the steps," he announced.

Dinah automatically fluffed out her hair, in case it might be Pete. April just as automatically adjusted her hair bow, regardless of who it might be.

It was little Mr. Holbrook. He was puffing as he climbed the steps; he paused for breath once or twice. He had on a neat gray business suit and a carefully knotted dark-blue tie. His face was pale, and tired, and worried, but his white hair was carefully brushed. The black leather brief case, which seemed to go with him everywhere, was in his hand. April found herself wondering if he took it to bed with him at night. Suddenly she imagined a picture of Mr. Holbrook in an old-fashioned flannel nightshirt and carpet slippers, still holding the brief case, and she hastily smothered a giggle.

Mr. Holbrook climbed the last step, gasped, and said, still breathless, "Good morning, children. Is your mother at home?"

Dinah said, "She's home, but I'm afraid—well, she's busy." Instinctively she looked up toward Mother's windows, and Mr. Holbrook's eyes followed hers. The typewriter was going like a riveting machine.

"Mother writes books," April said. "And when she's working, she just can't be disturbed. You know how writers are."

Mr. Holbrook took out a clean white handkerchief. "Yes, I know your mother is a writer. Very interesting. I have a nephew who occasionally contributes poems to the *Madison State Journal*. No money for them, of course." He mopped his brow with the handkerchief. "I read one of your Mother's books once. Published under the name of J. J. Lane. Enjoyed it very much. Contained a number of legal inaccuracies which I should have liked to discuss with her." He folded the handkerchief neatly and put it into his pocket. He caught his breath again and looked up toward the window. "You're sure—she can't be disturbed?"

"I'm terribly sorry," Dinah said. She looked at him and said impulsively. "It's awfully hot, isn't it? Won't you come in and have a coke, or some ice tea, or something?"

"Thank you," Mr. Holbrook said. "Thank you, yes. Yes, I will. As you say, it *is* hot. And these steps are—rather steep."

They escorted him into the living room. He sank down in the most comfortable chair and looked as though he would like to take off his shoes. He put the brief case in his lap. "I *would* enjoy a glass of water."

"Nonsense," Dinah said. "I'm going to bring you some lemonade. Much better for you than water on a day like this." She fled into the kitchen.

April tried not to stare at him, but she couldn't help it. This was the man whose daughter did a dance attired in three peacock feathers and a string of beads, while the cash customers rose up and cheered, according to the letters the unfortunate Vivienne had written to Mrs. Sanford. It was hard to believe. But it was easy to understand why he'd been willing to handle Mrs. Sanford's legal affairs for nothing, rather than have it known.

Dinah came back with the lemonade, in the biggest glass she

could find. "I didn't put any ice in it," she said, "just very cold water. Ice isn't good for you when you've just come out of the sun."

"Thank you," he said, "thank you. You're very kind." He took a sip of the lemonade and closed his eyes for a moment. Then, "You're absolutely sure your mother is too busy to disturb?"

"I'm afraid so," April said. "But—could we help you?"

"I thought—I wanted—it's really very important," Mr. Holbrook said. He looked a little frightened, and very unhappy. "You see—you live right next door. And once or twice I've seen that police lieutenant—that Bill Smith—coming up to your door. I thought—possibly he might have mentioned something—to your mother—"

Dinah gave April a signal that means, "You handle this." April nodded.

"Oh, he came to see *us*," April said earnestly. "Because we're important witnesses. We heard the shots."

"You—what? Oh, yes, yes, of course. But that isn't exactly—h'm—I thought possibly—he might have talked about the case to—your mother."

"She's been very busy," April said, "but he confides in us. We know all about the case."

Lawyer Henry Holbrook looked at her searchingly, with anxious gray eyes. No one could distrust a face like April's, with its wide, long-lashed eyes, and friendly, innocent smile. He cleared his throat again and said, "Tell me, little girl—"

April stiffened slightly. Little girl! The idea! But she gazed at him, and said, encouragingly, "Yes, Mr. Holbrook?"

"Do you happen to know if—in the course of their investigation—the police happened to find any of—Mrs. Sanford's private papers?"

Dinah opened her mouth to speak, and shut it again. April said hastily, "Why?"

"Because—" He paused. "I was the late Mrs. Sanford's attorney. Naturally, her papers ought to be placed in my hands. The police take a very unfortunate view of the matter. However—quite understandably—I would like to know if the police have succeeded in finding them."

"Succeeded in finding them?" Dinah repeated, curiously. "What do you mean?"

Mr. Holbrook cleared his throat again and took a gulp of the lemonade. "Mrs. Sanford appears to have hidden them," he said.

"Oh," April said. She gazed at him and said very innocently, "Did you look *everywhere?*"

He nodded and said hoarsely, "Everywhere I could think of looking." Suddenly he realized what he'd just admitted, and added hurriedly, "As a lawyer, you understand—my duty to my late client—" He finished off the lemonade, put down the glass, took out the neatly folded handkerchief, and wiped his face again.

Archie said, "Say, how did you get in?"

"There was—it just so happened—Friday evening, I believe—a fire down the street drew the police away from the house. I happened to be in the neighborhood at the time—" He paused again and said stiffly, "I had no intention of breaking the law. I considered that I was quite within my rights, as the late Mrs. Sanford's attorney. The police have been uncooperative, *most* uncooperative." He began folding up his handkerchief.

"And you didn't find anything?" Dinah asked.

"Nothing," he said. "Absolutely nothing."

"Not even any murder victims lying around on the floor?" April asked.

He tucked the handkerchief into his pocket, and glared at her. "Little girl," he said severely, "this is distinctly not a joking matter."

April said nothing. She reflected that the murder of Frankie Riley, on that particular Friday night, hadn't been any joke.

"My little sister has an unfortunate sense of humor," Dinah said smoothly, and trying to sound very grown up. "But if it will make you feel any better, the *police* haven't found Mrs. Sanford's private papers."

"Then—" He stared at her. "Are you *sure?*"

"Absolutely sure," Dinah said.

"Honest," April said. "We *know*"

Mr. Holbrook drew a long breath of relief. "Then they must still be in the house," he said. "And in that case—" Suddenly he looked unhappy and worried again. "In that case, the police may find them any time."

"If they're still there," Dinah said.

He stared at her. "What do you mean?"

April spoke up quick. "I have a theory," she said. "Remember, our mother writes detective novels, and we have a certain amount of knowledge about the science of crime detection." That speech, she thought, ought to impress Lawyer Holbrook, but good!

"Darned right we have!" Archie said.

April pinched him, and he shut up. "Our theory is that Mrs. Sanford might have had something among her private papers which would incriminate somebody, if you know what I mean. So that individual, whoever he or she is, may have snuck into the Sanford house and found those papers, and destroyed them. If that happened, that individual would have had to carry all the papers out, because with the police watching the house, naturally he couldn't stop to sort them out. So then he'd have to burn all of them up, because he couldn't keep the ones that weren't any of his business, because if he did someone might find them, and that would incriminate him, do you see?"

"You're a very bright little girl," Mr. Holbrook said approvingly. He rose, walked to the door, and went through the business of taking out the handkerchief, mopping his brow, folding the handkerchief neatly, and putting it back into his pocket. "Thank you very much for the lemonade. It was very refreshing."

"No trouble at all," Dinah said politely.

They walked out to the porch with him. He paused there, brief case in hand, and looked speculatively at the Sanford villa. "If I could only be *sure*," he said.

"Make another search," April suggested.

"The police," he said. "They've been most uncooperative. The house is being watched. I couldn't—"

"There's a trellis on the north side of the house," April said. "It's really very easy to climb. There's a little roof, and then a window opening into the upstairs hall."

"There is?" Mr. Holbrook said. Suddenly he scowled at her. "I trust you're not suggesting that I climb a trellis and break into the late Mrs. Sanford's house! That would be distinctly against the law!"

"Of course it would," April agreed. "Why, it would actually be illegal!"

"Exactly," Lawyer Holbrook agreed. Then he looked at her suspiciously, and his eyes asked, "Are you making fun of me, by any chance?" One long look at April's face, and his eyes softened. He smiled impartially at them all and said, "Thank you so much for the lemonade. Good-by."

They called good-bys to him. Dinah and Archie started back into the house. April whispered, "Psst! Wait!"

They waited. Mr. Henry Holbrook got halfway down the steps before he paused, looked up, climbed back a few steps, and called, "Oh—you—little girl?"

April leaned over the railing and said in a deceptively sweet voice, "Calling me?"

"Yes. I, I wondered." He hesitated and began to reach for his handkerchief again. "That trellis. Which side of the house did you say—"

"The north side," April said. She practically chirruped it. "Oh. Yes. The north side. Thank you again. And good-by."

This time he went all the way down the steps, stopping just once for a speculative look at the Sanford villa.

Dinah waited until he was out of hearing, and then let go.

"April! Of all things! If he goes and tries to climb up that trellis and get in the house, the police will catch him for sure! They'll *arrest* him."

"I wouldn't be at all surprised," April said.

"But, April. He'll be put in jail!"

"I hope!" April said. "The idea! 'Bright little girl!' 'Hello, little girl!' 'Thank you, little girl.' 'Good-by, little girl.' I'll fix him!"

"H'ya there, little girl," Archie called out mockingly.

April made a dive for him. He ducked quickly behind Dinah.

"Please, kids," Dinah said, "cut it out. In the first place, you'll bother Mother, and she's working, and in the second place, we really have got to stick together."

April said very gravely, "We've got to stick together or we'll all be stuck."

"Apologize to April," Dinah said severely.

Archie called, "Hey, I'm sorry I called you a little girl, little girl."

"Apologize to Archie," Dinah said, still severely.

April said, "I'm sorry I missed you, Archie. Next time, I'll beat your ears off."

"Y'h, y'h, y'h," Archie said.

"Kids," Dinah said. "*Please.*"

"We're still friends," April said. "And while we *are* still friends, let's walk down and see if Luke will trust us for a malt. It's been an hour since breakfast."

"Yipes!" Archie said. He dashed out from behind Dinah and was halfway down the stairs before Dinah could say, "Well—I guess so."

An hour later they strolled leisurely back up the road. Luke had trusted them for two malts apiece, a bag of peanuts, and three candy bars. The market across the street had trusted them for a bunch of grapes, a bag of plums, three peaches, and a package of chewing gum.

There was nothing left now but the chewing gum. There had been the usual argument over the dividing of five sticks of gum into three equal portions. It had ended unusually amiably. After the malts, the peanuts, candy bars, grapes, plums, and peaches, none of the three young Carstairs were in a fighting mood.

Archie was half a block ahead, kicking stones against the trees. Dinah was walking slowly, gracefully, and with great dignity, just in case Pete should happen by. And April was deep in thought.

"There wouldn't be any reason, though," April said suddenly, "for Mr. Holbrook to have murdered Frankie Riley. Mrs. Sanford, yes. But not Frankie Riley."

Dinah started. "Funny," she said. "I was thinking exactly the same thing."

"But just the same," April went on, "we can't dismiss him from our list of suspects. We can't dismiss any suspect, not at this stage. Remember what the detective always says in Mother's Clark Cameron books. He—"

There was a whistle from somewhere up the hill. Archie stopped, listened, and whistled in return. Then he raced back to the two girls. "It's the Mob," he said. "I'll be back soon." He scrambled up the hillside and was out of sight.

April sighed. "As I was saying. Everyone who might be involved is—"

"H'lo there," Dinah called cheerfully.

The familiar figure of Pierre Desgranges was across the street, walking briskly down toward the ocean, carrying easel, camp stool, and painting kit. He paused, made them a courtly bow, wished them a good morning, sent his regards to their mother, and went on.

"To go on," April said. "Everyone who—" She stopped suddenly.

"What's the matter?" Dinah asked anxiously.

"Nothing," April said. "I just thought of something." She turned around and looked back in the direction from which they'd come, knowing that Dinah would turn around too, before she had time to see the roadster parked in front of the driveway, and Rupert van Deusen sitting in it, waiting.

Something had to be done, and quickly. If Dinah walked up there with her, and the man who pretended to be Rupert van Deusen hailed both of them, she'd be in the soup. Oh, if only she'd told Dinah before—but it was too late now.

"Dinah," she said. "I wish—I wonder—I mean, I think—"

"Stop yammering," Dinah said, "and tell me what you think."

"Mr. Desgranges," April said. "He's a very suspicious character. He's gone down by the ocean, to paint. I think you'd better go and talk to him."

"Me?" said Dinah. "Why?"

"Well," April said, "there was all that stuff Mrs. Sanford found out about him. He had plenty of reason for murdering her. And if she told Frankie Riley about him, he'd have had a reason for murdering Frankie Riley."

"Well, sure," Dinah said. "But why *me?*"

"Because," April said, "he likes you. He thinks you're talented. Remember how he praised that poster you made for art class? You can just go and sit by him and ask if he minds you watching him paint, and tactfully engage him in conversation."

Dinah frowned. "Why can't we both go?"

"A person usually talks more freely to one person than to two persons," April said. "I read that somewhere. And you're the one of us he likes best."

"Well," Dinah said hesitantly. "I suppose—but what shall I *ask* him?"

"My gosh," April said. "Don't ask him anything. Just bring the conversation around to the murder, and let him do all the talking, and remember what he says. Be tactful, and maybe you'll find out something."

"Such as?" Dinah asked. Her face was worried.

"Such as, did he murder Mrs. Sanford," April said.

"But—" Dinah paused. "Why don't you come with me, April? I don't know what to say—"

"Positively not," April said. "Investigation is a one-person job. It's your turn. I investigated the Cheringtons, and Archie investigated the bullet. Now this is up to you. Go on now. Don't *you* be scared."

"Don't talk nonsense," Dinah said stiffly. She turned and started down the street. After a few steps, she paused. "Hey, April. Suppose it turns out he did murder Mrs. Sanford. What do I do then?"

April groaned. "Call a p'liceman," she said, "or get him to put it in writing. Or just scream."

Dinah glared at her. "You're a gug-o-squared-fuf!" she said in high indignation. She turned and marched down the street.

April watched until Dinah was safely out of sight around the corner. Then she strolled up the walk, slowly, and with a convincing air of nonchalance.

The man sitting in that car might be the murderer of Mrs. Sanford and Frankie Riley. He might be planning other murders, if he had to destroy any evidence against him. He might be sitting right there with a concealed gun within easy reach, waiting for her to get into range. Maybe she ought to turn around and run. Maybe she ought to yell for Dinah. Maybe she just ought to yell.

But if she did, she'd never find out anything about him!

She walked on up the hill, trying not to look at the roadster, pretending to whistle.

He might take just one shot, with a forty-five. He was a good shot. She wondered if it would hurt. She wondered how Mother and Dinah and Archie would act when the police broke the news to them. It was only about twenty feet to the roadster now, and she could see him watching her.

Would they put her picture in the papers? Not that awful one with the hair ribbons, she hoped. Actually, she didn't have a good picture. This was no time to be murdered.

He was watching her, but not making any move. Maybe he intended to let her walk past the car, and then shoot. Well, she'd walk past the car, pretending not to notice him, and then duck, quick, behind that tree.

"Hello there."

April jumped, gave a small scream, and stood frozen. Then she looked at him. He wasn't going to murder her. He probably hadn't murdered anybody. Not that nice young man, with the tanned face and blue eyes.

She was all over being scared, but she was still mad. She said, "You startled me!"

"I'm sorry," he said. "I really didn't mean to." He was grinning at her.

April determined not to grin back. She looked at him coldly and said, "Quite a coincidence, meeting *you* here!" It was a line she'd once heard Mother use to someone she didn't like.

"It's no coincidence," he said cheerfully. "I came up here to see you. I didn't want to go ring your doorbell, under the circumstances. So I've been parked here, hoping you'd go past."

"How nice of you," April said. She hoped her voice sounded steadier than it felt. She lifted her chin and said, "So you're Rupert van Deusen!"

"Quite right," the young man said, grinning even more broadly. "And so you're the—reliable witness! I suggest—let's be friends!"

Chapter 19.

PIERRE DESGRANGES put down his brush and looked gravely at his young companion. "Something is troubling you, yes?"

"No," Dinah said. "Nothing is troubling me, no." She tried to put conviction into it but she knew, as she heard her own voice, that she'd failed. She felt worried and thoroughly miserable. What the heck was she going to ask nice Mr. Desgranges?

April should have handled this. Or even Archie. Faced with the situation, she suddenly realized that, as Mother had said more than once, she definitely wasn't the tactful type.

She glanced at Mr. Desgranges, who was squinting at his easel. He looked gentle and friendly. Certainly not like a murderer. His funny little brown beard wagged up and down as he looked from his easel to the ocean and back again.

Oh, golly, she didn't know what to say to him! So, she said nothing. She sat, silent and unhappy, and watched him paint.

And Pierre Desgranges glanced at her several times out of the corner of his eye.

Just engage him in conversation, April had said. And bring the subject around to what you want to find out. It sounded easy! April would have known just what to do. Where *was* April, anyway? What was she up to? Dinah opened her mouth, and then closed it again. Oh, darn everything, anyway!

She *had* to say something, and not just sit here like a goof.

"Oh, Mr. Desgranges—"

He went on painting, carefully avoiding looking at her. "Yes, my young friend?"

"Tell me—" she gulped. "Why do you always paint pictures just of the ocean?"

He squinted thoughtfully at his easel. "Why do you make pictures of houses and people and horses?"

"Well," Dinah said, "because I *like* houses and people and horses."

"There you are," he said. "I like the ocean."

"Oh," she said. And then, "Why?" You sound just like Archie, she told herself furiously, only not so bright.

"Because," he said simply, "it is beautiful."

She wanted to get up, say "G'by, I've gotta get home now," and run home fast. And let April finish this. But if she did, April would never stop making fun of her.

She said, "Oh," again, and stopped. Think of *something*, she told herself. "Oh, I thought maybe it was because you wished you were on it."

He put down his brush for a moment. "*On* it?"

Dinah nodded, feeling like a fool. "In a boat."

"Yes, of course, in a boat. Now, why should I wish to be on the ocean, in a boat?"

"Well," she said, "after all, your home is—I mean, well, if you were homesick, and you wished you were on a boat going back to your own country, then you might paint pictures of the ocean." She drew a quick breath.

He looked at her in surprise. "But this *is* my home," he said. "This *is* my country. I have no desire ever to go away."

Dinah said, "Oh" for the third time, and was silent. That hadn't gotten her anywhere.

Engage him in conversation, April had said! She'd fix April, when she got home!

It was a long silence. Finally Dinah said, "Have you been paint-ing pictures a long time?"

He nodded. "A very long time," he said gravely.

Whatever you do, Dinah thought, don't say "Oh" again. She said at last, "Where did you paint pictures before you came here?"

"In Paris," Pierre Desgranges said, picking up another brush.

"But you couldn't paint the ocean there," Dinah said.

"No," he agreed.

"Then what did you paint?"

"Houses and people and horses. And occasionally trees."

She caught back another "Oh" just in time. "But you like the ocean better?"

"Much better," he said.

She darn near asked "Why?" again. The conversation had gone in a complete circle and come back to its starting point. She glanced unhappily at the clock up on the lifeguard station. It had been nearly half an hour, and she hadn't learned anything except that Mr. Desgranges used to live in Paris, and that he painted the ocean because he liked it.

She tried to think of questions. Like, where were you between four and five Wednesday afternoon? Or, did you ever hear of a man named Armand von Hoehne? Maybe, did you know Mrs. Sanford very well? None of them seemed either tactful or partic-ularly useful.

"Mr. Desgranges—"

This time he put down his brush, turned around, and looked at her. "Yes, my child? What is it?" He said it almost sharply, she thought.

"*Did you murder Mrs. Sanford because she'd found out you weren't really Mr. Desgranges, that you were really Armand von Hoehne?*"

Immediately, she realized what she'd done. But those had been the only words that came to her mind. How many times in her life had she heard Mother—and April—say, "Dinah, *don't* say whatever you happen to think." Now, she'd done it again—this time, with probably disastrous results. April would never forgive her for the way she'd muffed this. And—if Mr. Desgranges *was* the murderer—he might—

Pierre Desgranges stared at her, speechless. Then he began, slowly and methodically, to put away his paints and brushes and to fold up his easel. Dinah felt panicked. Not a running-away panic, but a frozen-to-the-spot panic.

Finally he stared at her again. This time he said, "Great God in heaven!" Dinah by then, was too terrified to notice that he'd spoken without the funny little accent the three young Carstairs had admired and tried to imitate.

Maybe he was going to murder her. Maybe there was a gun, a forty-five, in his pocket. Maybe he'd shoot her, and then hide her in an abandoned swimming pool. She couldn't run away, there wasn't any place to run to, on this wide stretch of sand. And there was nobody in sight, in case she should scream. One thought ran crazily through her head, "He mustn't murder me, because there won't be anyone to cook the dinner. Mother's writing, and April doesn't know how to fry chicken, and nobody knows where I hid the watermelon I got for a surprise."

"Please," she said, in a tight little voice, "please don't. Because nobody knows about it but us kids, and we certainly wouldn't tell anybody because we don't care if you are Armand von Hoehne, and Mother says Mrs. Sanford was an evil woman, and so if you did murder her, honest, we don't mind and we won't tell. But if you *do* have to, please call up the house and tell April there's a watermelon hidden behind the potatoes in the cooler, because it won't keep."

"If I do have to *what?*" he said, a trifle dazed.

"Sh-sh-shoot me!" Dinah said closing her eyes tight and screwing up her face.

He dropped the paint kit and began to laugh. He laughed until tears ran down his brown face. "Oh, Lord!" he gasped, "oh, *Lord!*" He sat down hard on the sand, buried his face in his hands, and went on laughing. Then suddenly Dinah began to laugh with him, tremulously at first, then heartily.

"Of all the silly things," Dinah said at last, catching her breath. "But—my *gosh!*"

They looked at each other and burst out laughing again, so loudly that a pair of gulls, circling near by, swooped away hastily and fled, terrified, out to sea.

Finally he wiped his eyes with a bright bandanna handkerchief, blew his nose loudly, and took out his pipe. "So I look like a murderer," he said.

"No, you don't," Dinah said. "That's what makes it so funny that I was so scared."

His face grew very sober. "Dinah, my child," he said, "this is a very serious business."

"You don't have to bother with the accent," Dinah said. "I've heard you without it, now. But I won't give you away."

"I hope you won't," he said. "Because it *is* serious. Tell me—what made you think—"

"Well, heck," Dinah said. "You are Armand von Hoehne. And there were all those letters Mrs. Sanford had. And after all she'd blackmailed away all the money you got from selling the jewels—"

"Dinah," he said, and his voice was very grave. "Where did you get those letters, and where are they now?"

"I—" She paused. "I can't tell. It's a secret between me and April and Archie."

"You'd better count me in on the secret," he said, "if you want me, in return, to tell you about Armand von Hoehne."

"I can't," she said miserably. "Because maybe you wouldn't keep it a secret. Maybe you'd tell the police, or Mother, or somebody."

"You can tell me," he said. "Because if I gave away your secret, you could give away mine. You see, we've got to trust each other."

She looked at him thoughtfully. She did trust him. And yet—

"Well," she said slowly, "it was only because we wanted Mother to solve Mrs. Sanford's murder, for the publicity, so she wouldn't have to work so hard. And so we got in and searched Mrs. Sanford's house, and we found the letters. That's all." The other details, she decided, could be left out of the story.

"You—searched the house—and—found the letters," he said after her, incredulously.

"Sure," Dinah said. "For us, it was easy."

"I have no doubt," he said, puffing at his pipe. "Dinah, where are the letters now?"

"They—" She didn't want to say they were hidden because he might try to find them. She didn't want to say they were destroyed, because that would be an out-and-out lie. She said, "They will never see the light of day again!"

He looked at her closely, recognized the light of truth in her eyes, and said, "Thank heavens!"

"Now," Dinah said, "you will explain to me about being Armand von Hoehne, or I will tell the police, so there." That might not be engaging him tactfully in conversation, but she was willing to bet it would bring results.

"Dinah," he said. "This *is* a serious business. It isn't a game. I'm not talking about Mrs. Sanford now, that has nothing to do with it. You've got me in a corner where I have to explain to you, but if I do—I think you'll understand how important it is never to tell one single solitary soul."

"Except April," Dinah said hastily. "I never could get away with trying to keep something from April. She always finds out."

"All right," he said. "We'll have to include April. Now, pay attention. I'm not Pierre Desgranges, and I'm not Armand von Hoehne. I'm just plain ordinary Peter Desmond, and I was born in Cleveland, Ohio."

Dinah gasped, and stared at him. The beret, the beard, the painting kit, everything. He didn't look like any Peter Desmond from Cleveland. He looked—well, foreign. And even without the little accent, there was something—*different*—about his voice. Besides, he was a painter, and all painters were foreigners.

"My father was in the consular service," he said, "and I was brought up all over the world. I went to school in England, and France, and Switzerland, and Italy, and even Persia. But," he said, "there *was* an Armand von Hoehne. The one who was described in those letters. He lived in Paris, just as I did. He died. At the time, it was considered expedient for me to assume his identity and be smuggled into this country as a refugee from the Gestapo. He would have assumed another name, had it been he who arrived here safely, and so I assumed one. Pierre Desgranges matched the initials on a cigarette case that was the last present my Mother, ever gave me."

"But why?" Dinah demanded. "What are you doing here?"

He sighed. "From where I sit, making very bad paintings of the Pacific Ocean, I can see for miles up and down the beach. There might be enemy agents who would like to arrange signals, from these convenient locations. They might be frightened away, before they could be caught, by someone looking too official. But no one would distrust an eccentric, middle-aged French painter, who"—he grinned—"does not speak it very good, the English."

Dinah said, "Gee!" and gazed at him with awe. Why, he was almost a G-man. Then suddenly her practical nature got the best of her. She remembered how the detective always handled things in Mother's books.

"Just the same," she said severely, "I think you ought to tell me exactly where you were Wednesday, when Mrs. Sanford was being murdered."

He looked at her, smiling. "I was here on the beach, of course, in full view of hundreds of people. It was so warm and pleasant a day that I spread out my blanket and took a nap on the sand." He rose and began unfolding his easel. "The light is still good," he said, "I think I will continue to paint."

Dinah drew a sigh of relief. "I'm glad you didn't murder her," she said. "But I sure wish I knew who did."

"Leave those problems to the police," he advised her, opening his painting box. "They are experienced in these matters. At your age, you should be thinking of other things."

Dinah didn't answer that one. She said, "Well, g'by. I gotta go home and start the dinner now. And thanks."

"You're quite welcome," he said, looking at his painting. "Remember now, not a word—not *one* word."

"Except to April," Dinah said.

"Of course, except to April."

She said good-by again and raced across the beach to the sidewalk. Oh, golly, when she told April *this!* Maybe she wasn't the tactful type, but this time she'd certainly done them both proud!

She was halfway home when suddenly she remembered something. Anyone doing any offshore signaling would certainly do it at night, with lights and stuff. While Mr. Desgranges—Mr. Desmond, she meant—did his painting in the daytime.

She was walking slower, and was about two blocks from the house, when she remembered something else. The real Armand von Hoehne could be identified by a dueling scar on his arm. And Mr. Desgranges-Desmond always kept his sleeves pulled down.

She was walking very slowly and thoughtfully, a block from the house, when she remembered something else. It hadn't been warm and pleasant on the beach that Wednesday and there hadn't been hundreds of people. She remembered very well. Because the three of them had gone down with an idea of spending an hour or two. It was warm and pleasant—almost hot—up on the hillside where they lived, but on the beach it had been damp and chilly and foggy, and there hadn't been a soul in sight. That was how they'd happened to be at home in time to hear the shots that killed Flora Sanford.

Maybe, she thought unhappily, April should have handled this, after all!

Chapter 20.

"WE CAN talk quite freely now," the tanned, good-looking young man said, "because we're friends."

"Purely an optical delusion," April said haughtily. "I never felt less friendly in my life."

He shook his head sadly and said, "St-st-st-st! When we have so much in common. I wouldn't have expected that of you, Miss Reliable Witness."

April stared at him coldly. "If it's any of my business, how did you find out I was the reliable witness?"

"Mm," he said. "Curiosity does rise to the surface, doesn't it? If you must know—and I think you must—it turns out I'd met the reporter who wrote that story. I looked him up and said, quote, who was that reliable witness, unquote. He described you. Quote. A beautiful blonde girl—"

"I admit I'm beautiful," April said, "but I'm not blonde. I'm tawny. Your reporter friend must be color-blind. It's been very nice meeting you, and now if you'll excuse me—" There! That ought to sound dignified enough to squelch him!

"Oh, but I won't excuse you," he said, "until you answer a question that's been bothering me."

"Yes?" April said.

"Where did you find that wonderful, beautiful name, Rupert van Deusen?"

She stared at him. Something Mother had said once came into her mind. *If you ever have to bluff, be sure to bluff first.* She lifted her eyebrows, tried to look unconcerned, and said, "Why, *you* ought to remember. When you were talking to Mrs. Sanford, and she was blackmailing you. You said, 'As sure as my name is Rupert van Deusen—'"

"Uh-uh," he said reprovingly. "You've got it wrong, according to the newspaper account. 'Rupert' was used in one sentence, and 'van Deusen' in another."

April said, "Well, you ought to know."

He grinned at her, and said, "My young friend, I know when I've been outbluffed. Now, let's talk sense. Because I've read all of your mother's books, and admired them, and because I believe in heredity, I think you can talk sense. So, why did you tell poor Sergeant O'Hare that wonderful story about Rupert van Deusen? I bet you a buck you won't tell me the truth."

"Let's see the buck," April said.

He shed a dollar bill out of his pocket. "Go on. Why?"

"Because he's a dope," April said, "who thought he could bribe my little brother into giving him some information about the case. I thought that was a very dirty trick, and I decided to get even with him, and Mother has a character named Rupert van Deusen in a book that hasn't been published yet. There. Give me the buck."

"I lose," he said.

April tucked it into her pocket. "Now," she said, "I bet you won't tell me why you took advantage of that story. I bet—nine million dollars you won't."

"Let's see the nine million dollars," he said.

April fished through her pockets, said, "Darn! I left my wallet in my other suit!"

He didn't laugh. He said, very gravely, "I'll take an I. O. U." Then he said, in a different, serious tone, "I'll tell you why I took advantage of that story. Because I had a very good reason for finding out what really did happen. And I still have that reason, and I still want to find out." He smiled at April. "Look, I have a perfect alibi. I couldn't have murdered Mrs, Sanford. And I'm not a policeman, and I'm not a reporter. I'm just a class-C screen writer on his day off."

April looked skeptical and said, "What pictures have you written?"

"My current one," he said, "is *The Masked Mummy.* Have you seen it?"

"I have," April said. "It was awful." She was disappointed. She'd hoped to find out his real name from remembering screen credits. "Well, just what did you want to find out, Mr.—van Deusen?"

He leaned over the wheel and looked at her, his tanned face serious. "Look, kid. You and your sister and brother were almost witnesses to the murder. You heard the shots. You fixed the time of the crime."

"Dinah had gone into the kitchen to see if it was time to put on the potatoes," April began.

He groaned. "I've been all over that before. I'm getting pretty bored with those potatoes. I read the whole thing in the papers, remember. You saw Polly—you saw the girl who found the body. Didn't you?"

April said, "Oh, you must mean Polly Walker! Yes, we saw her. We were there when she discovered the body."

"You were—*there?*"

"Well," she said, "we were on the premises. We could see through the window."

"Look. Tell me. How did she act? How did she seem to react? Have you seen her since? Had you ever seen her at the Sanford place before? Had you ever seen her there when—Mrs. Sanford was away?"

April's eyes widened. He wasn't smiling now, and there was white under his tan. He looked—frightened. He looked—*desperate.* She leaned on the car, arms folded, and smiled at him. "Take off them long white whiskers," she said. "I know you. You're Cleve, aren't you!"

"Yes," he said automatically. "Cleve Callahan." Then "How do you know my name?"

"Because," April said, "Polly Walker sat in her roadster right on this very street, and bawled like a baby, and said, 'Cleve—*Cleve.*'"

He reached over in a sudden movement and grabbed her wrist. "Are you sure? Sure? It's important—it's—terribly important."

April winced. His fingers were like steel springs. "Of course I'm sure," she said angrily. "None of Mrs. Carstairs' children are deaf." She jerked her wrist away.

"If I could believe it," he said, looking at the steering wheel. "If I *could* believe it. But—Wallace Sanford—"

"Stop muttering in your beard," April said sharply. "Are you in love with Polly Walker?"

"Am I—" He looked up at her. There was something about his face that made her think of Jenkins the cat, when he came in the kitchen just before dinnertime and sat by the kitchen table, looking hungry and sad.

"If you are," April said, "you'd better do something about it. Because she's in love with you."

"Yes," he said, "but you don't seem to understand. Wallace Sanford—"

"Forget Wallace Sanford for a minute," April said sternly, "and listen to me. I know now why you took advantage of that Rupert van Deusen business."

"You couldn't," he said. "How could you?"

"Feminine intuition," April said, hoping to awe him. "Look. If Polly Walker had murdered Mrs. Sanford, what would you do?"

"Protect her," he said unhappily, "of course."

April nodded. "You'd find some way of getting into the case, and you'd do everything you could to keep the police from finding out she'd done it. You'd nose around and ask questions, and you'd try to search the house in case there was any evidence she'd left lying around. What's more, you'd do it without letting her find out—ever. And, since you do think she murdered Mrs. Sanford—"

He stared, up at her and said, "I—"

"Don't just sit there and look silly," April said. Her voice sounded almost cross. "Has Polly Walker got a gun?"

He nodded, dumbly.

"What kind? This is important."

"It's—it's a thirty-two."

April sighed. "It's a cinch your mother wasn't as smart as my mother, or else you're all wrong about that heredity gag. Because Mrs. Sanford was shot with a forty-five."

He stared at her. "Are you—*positive?*"

"Posilutely absotive," April said. "We found that out from the police."

He groaned, leaned over the steering wheel, and said, "Oh—Polly!"

"I'm getting pretty sick of this," April said. "First she sits in her car and says, 'Oh, Cleve,' and then you sit in your car and yap about 'Oh, Polly'! It gives me a pain. You'd better get together with her and tell her what you've been doing, and ask her all the questions you want to ask."

"I want to," he said, "I've tried to. But she won't see me. She won't come to the door when I ring the bell. She won't talk on the telephone when I call her. I sent her letters—telegrams—they came back unopened."

"You don't look like the mouselike type," April said. "And if you'd examined those letters, you'd probably have found out they were opened with a warm knife and then resealed. Now, you listen to me."

She opened the car door, hopped in beside him, and for the next fifteen minutes gave him advice which might have surprised Dorothy Dix. Advice which led to some concrete suggestions, to which he added a few ideas of his own.

Finally he grinned at her and said, "Are *all* your mother's children geniuses?"

"One way or another," April said airily. "And speaking of my mother's children, there's Dinah coming up the street. I'll go and meet her, if you don't mind. And you'd better scram. Because I can keep secrets, but Dinah can't."

He opened the door for her, started the car, waved at her cheerfully, and roared on up the street. April walked slowly down the walk toward Dinah, thinking it over. By the time they met, her face was positively glowing.

"Love," she said. "It's wonderful!"

Dinah glared at her. "What are you talking about? Who are you in love with?"

"Nobody," April said. "But *he's* in love, and how! Rupert van Deusen."

"My gosh," Dinah exploded, "are you crazy, all of a sudden? We figured that out this morning. But Bette LeMoe's dead."

"He probably never even heard of Bette LeMoe," April said dreamily. "He's in love with Polly Walker."

Dinah sat down on the bottom front step. "Maybe I'm crazy. Maybe it's the heat."

"Nobody's crazy," April said. "Except him. He's crazy about her. Isn't it beautiful? And what's more, I won a dollar from him."

"*My* sister," Dinah said, shaking her head sadly.

April sat down beside her. "His real name is Cleve Callahan. He's a screen writer. He wrote that awful picture we saw—*The*

Masked Mummy. He's in love with Polly Walker and, what's more, I bet he gets her."

"Cleve," Dinah murmured reminiscently. "But. But, April. What's this Rupert van Deusen business?"

April drew a long breath. "It turns out that someone, in an attempt to confuse the police, invented that Rupert van Deusen story. There was no Rupert van Deusen. This someone must have gotten the name—out of a book or something. Well, this man is in love with Polly Walker, and he pretended he was Rupert van Deusen, so he could make like a detective. Because he was afraid she might have murdered Mrs. Sanford and he wanted to protect her, but now he knows that she didn't, so now everything's all right, and they'll probably get married." That, she decided, was enough to tell Dinah, right now.

"Gee!" breathed Dinah.

"And I've got a buck I won from him in a bet," April added. "Let's go down to the market and bring back some cokes." She rose and said, "And on the way you can tell me how you made out with Mr. Desgranges."

"Well," Dinah said, "it was like this."

Dinah had a feeling for details. They'd walked the two blocks to the market, bought the cokes, and were almost back to the house before she got to the facts she'd figured out after leaving Pierre Desgranges, Armand von Hoehne, or Peter Desmond, there on the beach.

April started. If she'd been carrying the bag of cokes, instead of Dinah, she probably would have dropped them. "Dinah!" she said, "that's the phoniest-sounding story I ever heard. And you fell for it."

"It sounds phony now," Dinah said. "It didn't, when he was telling it to me."

"There's regular guards on the beach," April said. "All the time.

You should have remembered that." She paused. "Maybe his story was true, in reverse. Maybe it's that the guards wouldn't pay any attention to a funny French painter."

"April!" Dinah said. Then she gasped. "We ought to do something. We ought to do something, right away."

"We will," April said grimly. They carried the cokes into the kitchen, opened two, and put the rest in the icebox. "We could watch him, and maybe catch him spying, or signaling, or something."

"That might take a long time," Dinah objected, "and it wouldn't be easy. One of us would have to be away from the house all the time, and how would we explain to Mother? Besides, there's school and everything." She frowned. "We'll tell Mother. Then she'll tell the police. And she'll get the credit for catching a spy, and all the publicity."

"Not bad," April agreed. "Only. We'll just tell her about him. Not about any of the other things. Unless it turns out he murdered Mrs. Sanford."

They listened for a moment. The typewriter was going hard, upstairs. "I'll make some iced tea," Dinah said, "and we'll take it up to her."

They climbed the stairs a few minutes later with an artfully arranged tray of iced tea and cookies. April tapped on the door and opened it; Dinah carried in the tray. Mother stopped typing for a minute and looked up.

"How nice!" she said brightly. She still had on the house coat, and she hadn't bothered to pin up her back hair. "I was just beginning to get hungry and thirsty."

"Don't forget," Dinah said severely, "you're *between* books, and tomorrow you get your hair done, and a manicure."

"*And* a facial," April added.

"I know it," Mother said, almost apologetically. "I was just putting down a few notes while they were in my mind." She took a big gulp of the iced tea and said, "Delicious." She picked up a cookie, glanced through the last page lying on her desk, glanced at the page still in the typewriter, and added a few words.

"Mother," April said. "Mr. Desgranges, the painter, isn't a painter at all, he's a spy. And his name isn't Desgranges at all, it's Armand von Hoehne, only he claims it's really Peter Desmond, but it probably isn't that either." She caught her breath and said, "So you'd better call the police and tell them he's a spy."

"Of course," Mother said. "Just a minute, dear." She xx-ed out two words, and typed three in their place.

"He told me he was a secret agent, but I don't believe it now," Dinah said, "because there are guards on the beach, and because it was too damp and foggy that day to go swimming."

"Naturally," Mother said. "You mustn't go swimming unless it's warm and sunny." She took the paper out of the typewriter and added, "I'd rather you swam in the club pool, anyway."

"Mother," Dinah said, "you've got to do something about it right away. Call up the FBI" She paused. "Mother! Pay attention!"

Mother put a new piece of paper in the typewriter and typed "page eleven" on the top of it. "I'm listening, dear," she said cheerfully. She turned over the pile of manuscript and began looking at something on about page three.

"He might be sinking a ship or something right this minute," Dinah said.

Mother typed two words, looked up, smiled, and said, "Some other time, kids. Do you mind?"

April drew a long breath and said, "Not a bit." She motioned Dinah to the door. "Sorry we interrupted you."

"No bother," Mother said. "Thanks for the tea." She began to type faster. Just as they opened the door she stopped, looked up, and said, "Did you say you were going to watch Mr. Desgranges paint? How nice!"

"We changed our minds," April said.

Out in the hall, Dinah said, "She didn't hear one word we said."

"She's having an inspiration," April said. "We can't bother her. It's up to us. We'll do the telephoning."

Dinah looked worried. "How are you going to manage without explaining about our finding the letters in Mrs. Sanford's house, and everything?"

"Leave that to me," April said.

There was a slight debate as to whether they could call J. Edgar Hoover, the FBI, the police department, or President Roosevelt. Finally they settled for Bill Smith.

April called the police, was referred to three or four people, and finally was told that Bill Smith was at home. She insisted that the call was important, but the police telephone operator refused to give his private phone number.

"Maybe it's in the phone book," Dinah said hopefully.

There were five William Smiths in the phone book, but none of them turned out to be the right one.

Then April had an inspiration and called Sergeant O'Hare, who was in the phone book. She explained that she had an important message from her mother to give Bill Smith. The good sergeant, scenting possible romance, gave her the phone number.

Finally she got Bill Smith on the phone and told him who she was.

There was immediate anxiety in his pleasant voice. "Is everything all right? Has anything happened? Your mother—"

"Nothing's happened yet," April said, "but we're afraid something will. That's why we called you up. Listen."

She began a carefully expurgated story of Pierre Desgranges, Armand von Hoehne, Pete Desmond. Halfway through it Bill Smith said hastily, "Wait a minute. I want to write this down."

Then she had to begin again, from the beginning. She and Dinah had found out Pierre Desgranges was really named Armand von Hoehne. She related, in detail, the story he had told Dinah when she'd faced him with it. Then she added what she and Dinah had figured out.

"You're a wonder!" Bill Smith said.

April beamed at the telephone. If he'd said, "You're a bright little girl," she'd have hung up on him.

"One thing more," Bill Smith said. "How did you find out his name was really von Hoehne?"

This was the tough one. April answered it carefully and deliberately. "We found out from Mrs. Sanford." There. That wasn't telling a lie; on the other hand, it wasn't giving away anything.

"How did she find out?"

"I don't know," April said. "And now, she can't tell."

There was a brief silence on the other end of the line. Then, "Listen, April. Think very carefully. Did Mrs. Sanford ever tell you anything about anyone else?"

"No," April said. "No, she never did." That was perfectly truthful, too.

"You certainly handled that nicely," Dinah said admiringly, after she'd hung up.

"Nothing to it," April said loftily. "Let's go make a sandwich. I'm hungry."

"Me too," Dinah said. "We'll make a sandwich, and then start fixing the chicken for dinner."

April was spreading jam on top of cream cheese on top of peanut butter when Archie burst through the doorway. He looked breathless, hot, pink-faced, and very dirty. He saw the array of jars on the kitchen table, said, "Yipes!" and grabbed for a knife and a piece of bread.

"Wash your hands first," Dinah said.

"Aw, heck," Archie said. "This is good clean dirt." He washed his hands and went back to inventing a new kind of sandwich. "Hey, y'know what?"

"We know a lot of things," April said, "but we don't know *what*."

"Dinah got a present," Archie said, reaching for a dill pickle. "And I'm a detecative. Are we gonna have chicken for dinner?"

"A present?" Dinah said.

"Yeah. It's out on the back porch, wrapped up in brown paper. An', y'know what?"

Dinah dashed out on the back porch, returned with a large package.

"Y'know what?" Archie repeated.

"Shush-u-tut u-pup," Dinah said, tearing off the paper. "Oh, April!"

It was the painting Mr. Desgranges had been working on that afternoon, still unfinished, and smelling to high heaven of turpentine. But it was signed—initialed, at least—in one corner. P. D. And a card stuck in the back of it said, "To my charming little friend Dinah Carstairs."

Dinah set it on a kitchen chair and stared at it. "April, why on earth—"

"Hey," Archie said. "Hey. Y'know what? I'm a detecative."

"You're practically Dick Tracy," April said, staring at the picture. "Dinah, I wonder—"

"Listen," Archie yelped. "Hey. Hey, listen. This is important!"

"We are listening," Dinah said. "And start with how this got here."

"He brought it here," Archie said. "The guy who paints water. He gave it to me and said it was for you, so I put it on the back porch. Then he got in a car and drove away. Towards downtown. So I thought if you 'n' April could search a house, me'n Admiral could search a house, even if we did have to bust one of the back windows to get in."

"You searched Mr. Desgranges house?" April said.

"Sure," Archie said. "That's what I'm trying to *tell* you."

April put down her sandwich. "What did you find?"

"*Nothing*," Archie said excitedly. "Nothing 'cept the furniture, and that belonged to the house because Goony's sister's husband's aunt lived there once and it was the same furniture."

Dinah and April stared at each other, and then Dinah said, "Archie, you mean he took away all his own stuff?"

"Yeah," Archie said. "That's the whole thing. Kin I have a coke?"

April raced to get one, opened it for him, and said, "*Go on.*"

"That's all," Archie said. "He took away all his stuff like his clothes and his pictures and his books and his razor and everything. I guess he must of had 'em in the car." He stuck a straw in the coke bottle and added, "Looks like he moved away."

"Yes," April said. "It looks like he has."

"Oh, April," Dinah said. "Maybe we ought to call Bill Smith quick and tell him it's too late."

April sighed. "Let's not bother. Any minute now, he'll find out for himself!"

Chapter 21.

"It certainly is worth two dollars," April said. "That three-dollar manicure at Howard's is a hundred times better-looking than the one-dollar manicure Mother always gets. And Bill Smith is coming to dinner tomorrow night, and you know how important beautiful hands are. I wonder what color nail polish he likes."

"But, April," Dinah said. "How are you going to talk Mother into a three-dollar manicure?"

April stopped in the middle of combing her hair and said, "Stupe! I'm going to duck into Howard's during noon period—it's only six blocks, and I can make it if I run, and skip lunch—and fix it up with the girl who always does Mother's manicures. I'll just give her the two dollars and tell her not to say anything about it to Mother, but to give Mother the three-dollar manicure. And Mother won't even notice it."

"Oh," Dinah said. She went on making her bed. Suddenly she paused. "But. We haven't got two dollars. And we don't get our allowance till Saturday."

"I've got forty cents left out of the buck," April said.

"I've got—" Dinah pawed through her purse and the pockets of all the clothes she'd worn lately—"thirty-two cents."

"That makes seventy-two," April said thoughtfully. "And Archie ought to put up a third. How much is a third of two dollars?"

"Sixty something—sixty-six and two thirds. April, hurry up and make your bed. We'll miss the school bus."

"Say, sixty-four," April said. "Sixty-four and seventy-two is—wait a minute—a dollar thirty-six. We'll borrow the rest from Archie."

"*If* he'll lend it," Dinah said. "And *if* he'll agree to contributing sixty-four cents of his own money."

"Well, ask him," April said.

"No. It's your idea. You ask him."

"You're the oldest. You ought to ask him." April paused, and said, "Tell you what. If I ask him, will you make my bed while I'm doing it?"

"Oh, all right," Dinah said. "After last night he's probably still too excited to argue much."

Last night had been exciting. There had been cars going up and down the street. Archie, dispatched to do a little reconnoitering, came back and reported a thorough search of the house Pierre Desgranges had occupied. "Fingerprints 'n' everything," he said.

After dinner Mother had gone back upstairs—"To make a few more notes," she had said. Pete had arrived and wanted Dinah to go for a ride on his bike. April, surprisingly, had urged Dinah to go while it was still daylight. "Let me do the dishes all alone, for once." Dinah had been too amazed to resist. And April had just succeeded in shooing Dinah and Pete out the back door when the front doorbell rang and there stood Bill Smith, with a quiet, determined man in a dark-gray suit.

She was able to say truthfully, and thankfully, that Dinah was out. She invited them out to the kitchen and retold Dinah's story to the quiet man in gray. Somehow the two men found themselves helping with the dishes—Bill Smith washing and the other man wiping—while she told the story. They hadn't quite finished by the time she had, so she added the detail of the picture that had been presented to Dinah. By the time she went to fetch it, the two men were hanging up the last dishtowel.

"As a painting," the man in gray had said, "I can't say much for it. But as an excuse for being out here—yeah. I guess he's the man, all right."

"Did you arrest him?" April said.

"No," Bill Smith said. "He beat it. But we'll find him." He turned back to the man in gray. "Funny, the house being broken into."

April had been tactfully silent. No point in letting Archie be stuck with the price of a new windowpane.

Dinah had returned to find—to her amazement—the dishes done, the kitchen neat, and April listening to the newest Harry James record on the phonograph. Pete had stayed on. He'd wanted to roll up the rug and dance. Then Mag and Joella had dropped in and, five minutes later, Eddie and Willy. Then Archie, Admiral, Goony, and Flashlight had returned from finding Henderson, who'd broken his leash and strayed two blocks from home. Then Inky and Stinky had somehow gotten out on the roof and had to be rescued, and they and Jenkins had had to be fed. And finally Mother had come down the stairs, tired but happy, to announce she had finished her notes and was stopping work for a few days, and how about a lot of food for everybody present.

It had been what seemed like hours later before Dinah could ask April, "Did anything happen while I was out?" and April could answer, very nonchalantly, "Not much. Oh, the FBI was here—"

This was another day. Mother had come down for breakfast and announced her intention of getting not only a hair-do and a manicure, but also a new pair of working slacks. There had been nothing in the paper about the flight of Pierre Desgranges, or Armand von Hoehne, or whatever the hash-e-lul-squared his name really was. Not much, either, about the Sanford murder, save that the police were still searching for Wallace Sanford.

Things were quiet. But, April thought happily, it was the quiet before the big blowup. Tuesday night Bill Smith was coming to dinner, and Mother would have her new hair-do and manicure. Maybe, by that time, the murderer of Mrs. Sanford would have been found. Now, it was just a little matter of talking Archie out of sixty-four cents plus a short-term loan.

She knocked on his door, went in, and said amiably, "I'll help you make your bed."

Archie looked at her sourly and said, "If you're here for what I 'spect you're here for, you can pick up the room, too. And I get all the empty coke bottles for a month, and you carry down the garbage the rest of the month, and I won't loan you more'n a dollar, so there."

April began making the bed, looked at him gravely, and said, "Now, Archie, you love your Mother, don't you?"

Fifteen minutes later she returned with the money, having given a promise to pay back the loan on allowance day, plus the coke-bottle graft for two weeks, and carrying down the garbage for one week.

School, that Monday, seemed dull. April received her first "Unsatisfactory" in Junior Drama Class. Dinah had to be spoken to twice for inattention in Domestic Science, and, after Archie had failed nine simple arithmetic problems in a row, his teacher sent him to the school nurse to see if he was coming down with something. It was a thoroughly exasperating and baffling day for a variety of teachers, and an almost unendurably long one for the three young Carstairs.

Finally they met on the school bus. Dinah was sitting with Pete and Joella, both of whom were trying to talk to her at once; April was surrounded by a number of admirers, aged thirteen to fifteen; and Archie was scuffling around on the floor with Flashlight, to the great discomfort of the already harassed bus driver. But Dinah managed to send April a signal that meant, "Did you fix it?" and April sent back a sign, "Oke."

They finally got together, the three of them, at the bus stop nearest home.

"I fixed up everything," April reported. "Estelle's going to give her the three-dollar manicure, and Mrs. Howard herself is going to give her the facial. I explained to them we were going to give her a surprise party tomorrow night. So—"

"It'll be a surprise, all right," Dinah said gloomily. "How are we going to explain to her about Bill Smith coming to dinner?"

"You're s'posed to tell *her*," Archie said shrilly. "April asked *him*."

April looked at Dinah's worried face and said, "Never mind. I'll do the explaining. I'm good at it. Now let's run down to Luke's before we go home."

"There's still cokes in the icebox," Dinah said.

"I want a newspaper," April said.

Dinah and Archie stared at her. "For what?"

"To read," April said serenely. "So don't ask me any silly questions and I won't have to give you any silly answers." She started down the street toward Luke's. Dinah and Archie followed.

"Hey," Archie said. "We got one paper a'ready. This morning."

"I've seen that one," April said.

"Well, my gosh," Dinah said. "The evening paper gets delivered around dinnertime."

"I can't wait," April said, in her most maddening voice.

"Oh, boney," Archie grumbled. "I'm *hungry*."

April paused and looked at him. "Listen. If I talk Luke into trusting us for three malts, will you pay for them when you get your allowance?"

"Well—" Archie said. April was the only one of the trio who could talk Luke into extending credit. "Oh, a'right!"

"Fine," April said. "Then we can read the paper for free while we're waiting for the malts. That saves us a nickel."

She went in first and conferred with Luke. Then she motioned to Archie and Dinah to come in. Then she picked up the latest edition of the paper, smiled at Luke, and said, "You don't mind, do you?" as she spread it out on the counter.

"Help yourself," Luke said, putting an extra dash of ice cream in the malts.

"It ought to be on page one," April said.

It was. A picture, and a two-column headline.

KEY WITNESS IN SANFORD
MURDER KIDNAPPED

Dinah said, "Oh!" and April hissed "Shush-u-tut u-pup."

"Hey," Archie said. "Le'me see, le'me see, le'me see."

"Well, *look* then," April said crossly, "and don't bother me, I'm reading."

Luke served the malts with a flourish and said, "Don't spill none on that paper or I'll have to charge you for it."

The three young Carstairs automatically moved the malts away from the paper, stuck the straws in their mouths, and went on reading.

Polly Walker, who'd found the body of Mrs. Wallace Sanford, had been kidnapped from her Hollywood apartment, the story read.

"Don't talk here," April whispered to Dinah and Archie, who nodded solemnly.

According to Miss Walker's maid, there had been a telephone call to Miss Walker around twelve-fifteen. A female voice, saying that the message was an urgent one. Miss Walker had taken the telephone call and, after completing it, had appeared greatly distressed. She had dressed immediately, and gone out, after telephoning to the hotel garage, to send around her car.

According to the doorman, Miss Walker had come out on the sidewalk. Then a car that had been parked down the street had suddenly swung out and swung in again into the No Parking zone. A masked man with a gun had forced Miss Walker into the car, which had promptly disappeared down the street.

There followed a résumé of the Sanford murder, stressing Polly Walker's discovery of the body. That was followed by a brief biography of Polly Walker, the finishing-school graduate who'd fought for a bit part on Broadway and risen from it to stardom. The fact that Polly Walker had never had an important part in an important picture didn't matter to the story. She was involved in a murder case, she'd been kidnapped, and, therefore, she was a star.

April drained off the last of her malt, glanced at the clock over Luke's counter, and said, "Hey! We gotta beat it home! Quick!" She shoved away her glass and folded up the paper. "Thanks, Luke." She put the paper back in the rack.

Dinah and Archie finished their malts and followed her out to the street.

"What's the rush?" Dinah said.

"I've got a date," April said joyously. "*We've* got a date."

"Hey, hey, *hey*," Archie called. "Wai' for me!"

"I don't get it," Dinah panted. "Polly Walker's been kidnapped. Was it a gang kidnaping? Like, when Bette LeMoe was kidnapped?"

"No," April said. "This was strictly a one-man job."

"But," Dinah said. "April, wait a minute! It couldn't have been a one-man job."

"Oh, yes it was," April said.

They turned into the street on which the Carstairs lived.

"April," Dinah said, "it was a masked man who forced her into the car. But it was a female voice over the telephone. Evidently giving her some phony message that would lure her out on the street, where she could be kidnapped."

"The female voice," April said, almost out of breath, "was *mine*."

Dinah gasped. Archie said, "Huh?" But before either of them could speak, April was pointing up the street toward the Carstairs' driveway that was never used save by the milkman and the grocery wagon. "And there," April gasped, "is the kidnaper and his victim!"

The three young Carstairs ran like rabbits up the street. Parked in the driveway was a roadster. In it were two people. Cleve Callahan and Polly Walker. And both of them were smiling.

Chapter 22.

"You two can be bridesmaids," Cleve said, "But I don't know what we'll do with your little brother."

"Honest?" April said.

He nodded, and Polly Walker blushed.

"Oh," April said, "Oh—super!" She kissed him on the cheek, and hugged the breath out of Polly Walker. "Archie—my little brother—can be the ring-bearer."

"I'm not little," Archie said angrily, "and I won't. And what is one, anyway?"

"Never mind," Dinah said. "Would somebody mind telling me what goes on here?"

Polly Walker looked up at her and said, "We're going to get *married*." Her hair was loose and there were tearstains on her face. What little lipstick was left was badly smeared. She looked awful. "*Today*."

"You'd better wash your face first," April said. "And make with the make-up. And do with the hair-do."

Polly looked at them, laughed, started to cry again, and said, "I've been such a fool!"

April looked at Cleve and said, "Well, if you want to marry a fool, that's your business!"

"It's your responsibility," he told her. "You fixed it up. You advised me what to do and helped me carry it out. If I have to divorce her after forty or fifty years—"

Polly Walker looked up and said, "She—what?"

"She advised me to kidnap you," he said, "and she called you up this noon and gave you the urgent message that lured you away from the house."

Polly Walker stared at April and said, "*You?* Was that *your* voice?"

"How do you think I get all those A grades in Junior Drama Class?" April said modestly. "And by the way, how did you like my speech?" She struck an attitude and said, "Mees Valker. I haff here zertain documents wheech haff been found een ze Zanford 'ouse. Zey are off no eemportance to me, an' I weel be deelighted to giff zem to you, eef you weel come to—"

"If Miss Grubee could hear that," Dinah said critically, "you'd flunk Junior Drama for the next two years. And will somebody *please* tell me what's going on?"

Cleve Callahan looked at April and said, "You'd better tell her. She's your sister."

April told the whole story, beginning with Rupert van Deusen and ending with the advice she'd given Cleve Callahan.

"And I did kidnap her," Cleve finished for her, "with April's help. And we talked everything over, and we haven't any secrets from each other. And we're going to drive to the airport and fly to Las Vegas and get married, without, I regret, bridesmaids, because you two would look very sweet in organdy dresses."

"I'm sure of it," April said. "Pink for me and blue for Dinah, or vice-reverse, and white broadcloth for Archie."

"By the way," Dinah said anxiously, "where *is* Archie?"

Archie had vanished.

April sighed. "He's probably gone to call the police and tell them a murder suspect is being flown to Las Vegas. So, Miss Walker, you'd better tell all fast, and then get going."

"Tell—what?" Polly Walker gasped.

"That was part of the bargain," Cleve told her. "Remember?"

"A bargain with *me*," April said. "I was to help you kidnap her if you'd bring her out here at four o'clock and she'd tell us exactly what had happened."

"I—can't!" Polly Walker buried her face in her hands. Cleve Callahan said, "Polly—darling!"

"Don't be goony," Dinah said. "You can, too. My gosh! Just because your father was a gangster and he's in a jail some place! I think he must of been a pretty swell guy because of the way he took care of you, and you haven't anything to be ashamed of except maybe acting like this. So, my gosh, quit *bawling*."

"Shush-wow-e-lul-squared," April said under her breath.

Polly Walker borrowed Cleve's handkerchief and blew her nose. "She—that Mrs. Sanford—found out about it, somehow. She kept asking me for money. And I don't make a lot of money. Then I met him—Wallie—at a party. He—well, flattered me—and I found out he was her husband, and I thought—well—maybe—" She blew her nose again. "I didn't really like him, or anything. Cleve knows that."

Cleve held her hand tight and said, "We've been all over that already. Remember?"

She nodded. "Oh, Cleve, I love you so!"

"Tell him about that on the way to Las Vegas," April said. "Tell *us* about Mrs. Sanford."

"Go on," Cleve said quietly. "They deserve to know the whole business. After all, if it hadn't been for them—"

"Well," she said, "he sort of—well, fell for me. I shouldn't have, but I encouraged him. And then—Oh, look, it was like this. I thought, maybe, through him, I could get that stuff—those letters and everything—away from Mrs. Sanford. But he had some ideas of his own. He got—well, matrimonial."

"I don't think that's quite the way to use the word," Cleve said, "but we understand. Quite understandable, on his part. Anybody who took more than one look at you—"

She began crying all over again, and he found a fresh handkerchief. "It wasn't like that. It was because I'm a—I'm a promising young actress and I'll probably make a lot of money some day—I mean I would have made a lot if I hadn't decided to get married and retire and—*Oh, Cleve!*" She buried her face on his shoulder.

"Why don't you just marry Boulder Dam?" April asked him.

Cleve laughed, pushed Polly off his shoulder, wiped off her face, and said, "Go on, baby. Tell all."

"Well. Well, finally, I told Wally about—the stuff she had about my father. He said he'd get it for me if—if he could get a divorce from her and marry me. Then. Then suddenly she wanted me to come out and see her. I did. She wanted a lot more money. I guess—well, I practically know—he must have just told her—everything. She said, for a lot of money she'd give me those letters and give him a divorce and forget everything. So, I said I'd come out Wednesday and bring the money with me."

There was a long, long silence. Finally April said, softly, "We're still listening."

Suddenly Polly Walker sat up straight, no tears in her eyes, though her face was still very pale, and her lovely hair was tumbling over her forehead. "I went there to frighten her," she said. "I had a gun. I meant to—make her give me those letters. Then I could forget her and Wally and everything else. I got there—about—oh, I don't know exactly, but it was between four-thirty and five. I parked my car in the driveway, and I went up to the door. I took out my gun. I wasn't going to shoot her, but—honest, I couldn't shoot anybody, not even her. I just wanted to—oh, you know."

"We know," Dinah said gently.

"I walked into the living room. I rang the bell first, and nobody answered. The door was unlocked, and I walked right in. I had the gun in my hand. She just looked at me, she didn't say a word. I pointed the gun at her and said, 'Mrs. Sanford—'"

"And then?" April prompted.

"Then—everything happened so quickly. I hardly know what—there was a man, came out from—I guess it was the stairs. I just remember he was thin and dark. He had on a snap-brim gray felt hat, I remember that much. He swore, and he ran past me, out the door. Mrs. Sanford didn't even seem to notice him. Then suddenly there was a shot. It came from—the dining-room door. I saw Mrs. Sanford fall. And the gun I was holding—just went off. Not at anything, it just went off. I haven't any idea what it hit but I know it didn't hit—her. And I turned and ran. The man in the gray hat was getting in a car parked farther down in the driveway. He drove off, fast. I got in my car and drove, fast. I don't know where he went. I went down by the ocean, and parked there a few minutes. And I thought. Maybe she—Mrs. Sanford—was just wounded. I ought to go back. I could pretend I'd just arrived there, to have tea with her. So I did drive back. And went up and rang the doorbell, just as if I hadn't been there before." She paused, and pushed the hair back from her forehead.

"Rupert, my friend," April said admiringly, "you're marrying a woman who has *nerve!*"

Polly Walker said, "But she wasn't just wounded. She was murdered. So, I called the police." She looked at Dinah and April, smiled wanly, and said, "And you can take it from there."

He leaned forward and said, "Now look, you two. About this story—"

April looked at him, wide-eyed. "It's a family trait. Heredity. Our mother is very absent-minded, and so are we. I'm sorry, but we've absolutely forgotten every word she said!"

"As for me," Dinah said, "I wasn't even listening." She kissed

Polly Walker on the cheek and said, "Oh, gosh! I'm so darn glad you didn't murder Mrs. Sanford and that you aren't going to marry Wally Sanford even if he is a rather nice person, but that you're going to marry this guy, who, I mean whom, I think is absolutely super!"

"My sister!" April said. "The tactful type!"

"Nun-u-tut-shush!" Dinah said. Tears began to roll down her cheeks.

"Don't mind her," April said. "She always cries at weddings. Just the same, I think it's a dirty trick to go get married in Las Vegas. Because I look Simply Div in organdy. And, anyway, is it legal to take the witness to a murder out of the state even to marry her?"

"I'll ask my lawyer," Cleve Callahan said, "when we get back tomorrow." He looked up and said, suddenly, "Good Lord!"

The Mob was approaching. Most of it, at least. Archie led it, carrying an enormous bunch of hydrangea blossoms. Admiral had an armful of bright purple bougainvillea vine. Goony had a bouquet of his mother's best dahlias, Flashlight had a handful of petunias, and Slukey had a single, carefully held camellia.

"We coulda done better," Archie said breathlessly, "but we hadda work awful fast. Here." He dumped the hydrangea blooms in the car. Slukey handed Polly Walker the camellia, with great solemnity, and the others piled their collection around her.

"I heard you were gonna get married," Archie explained. "And if you get married you gotta have flowers, so I gave the Mob an emergency call."

Polly Walker hugged and kissed him. He would have been embarrassed beyond reason, save that she hugged and kissed the rest of the Mob, too. Then Cleve Callahan started the car and backed down the driveway, calling "Good-by," and Polly Walker started crying all over again.

April beamed at Archie, looked after the roadster, and said, "A swell idea. But unless she turns off Niagara Falls, you'd have done better to have given her about four dozen handkerchiefs!"

The Mob hooted with glee and raced away up the hillside. Dinah and April started up the sidewalk toward home.

"You might have told me," Dinah said, a trifle miffed.

"I wanted it to be a surprise," April said. "And it certainly was. As a matter of fact, it was a surprise to me, too." She scowled, and kicked at a stone on the sidewalk. "Dinah, do you believe Polly Walker's story?"

"Of course I do" Dinah said. "Every word of it. My gosh—"

"So do I," April said. "Dinah, I think we're getting somewhere. The thin, dark man with the gray hat. That was Frankie Riley. He was on the scene of the crime. But he didn't shoot her. Mrs. Sanford, I mean. Polly Walker was there, and she shot Uncle Herbert's picture. *There's* a girl who never ought to be trusted with anything deadlier than a slingshot. And someone fired, from the dining room, and hit Mrs. Sanford. Someone with a forty-five, and darned good aim. Dinah, we've found out a lot!"

"A lot of nothing," Dinah said gloomily. "Don't be so cheerful. Because there's still things we don't know about."

"I'll be cheerful if I want to," April said. "And don't say '*things*,' because there's just one *Thing*." She beamed maddeningly at Dinah. "All we have to do now is find out who stood in the dining room and shot Mrs. Sanford."

Chapter 23.

THE THREE-DOLLAR manicure was a distinct success. So was the hair-do. The three young Carstairs stared rapturously at Mother all through dinner. If Bill Smith could resist *that!*

"Estelle really did beautifully," Mother said, in answer to their compliments. "Especially on my nails. I never knew her to take such pains with them before." She waved them at Dinah and April. "Do you like the color? I never had it before, but she talked me into it."

April and Dinah nodded vigorously. They did indeed like the color. April and Estelle had picked it out. A soft luscious rose-pink.

"And I thought," Mother went on, "since I'm taking a little vacation—suppose we three go into town for dinner tomorrow night, and take in a show?"

April and Dinah looked at each other. Was this the time to break the news that Bill Smith was coming to dinner, Dinah's eyes asked. April shook her head slightly. Dinah's eyes said, well, do *something.*

"Oh, Mother," April said, "that would be *super.* But—oh golly—look, you're usually so busy. And it's so much fun to have an evening at home. Just us four. Honest, I'd a whole lot rather do that, instead."

"I would too," Dinah said vehemently.

Archie chimed in with, "Doggone right!"

"Really?" Marian Carstairs said. The three young Carstairs nodded vigorously. "You blessed kids! All right, home it is. And I'll get a special dinner, to celebrate. What shall it be—steak?"

"I know what I'd rather have," April said. "One of those wonderful old-fashioned meat loafs. With that thick gravy."

"And lemon pie," Dinah said, "with just gobs and gobs of meringue."

"And biscuits," Archie said.

Marian Carstairs shook her head and sighed. "My children! I offer them dinner at the Derby, and seats at the best show in town. They want to stay home and play parchesi. I offer them steak, and they settle for meat loaf."

Dinah giggled. April said, "That's because we know what's good!"

"And—" Archie said.

April kicked him, quick, under the table before he could add, "—and what Bill Smith will like."

"And what?" Mother said.

"And we love you," Archie finished, with a triumphant smile at his sisters.

"And I'll do the dishes tonight," Mother said.

"Not with that manicure," April told her firmly. "You sit in the parlor and make like a lady and read up on child psychology."

"You want to know how to raise us properly," Dinah added.

"Sure," Archie said. "Hey, y'know what? Hey, Mother, y'know what?"

April tried to catch his eye, but he was looking the other way. And he was clear around on the other side of the table, so that she couldn't kick him. She rose and began hastily picking up the unused silverware.

"Y'know what Bill Smith said about you?"

Mother looked interested and said, "No. What?"

By that time April had reached Archie. She stuck a warning finger into his back just below his left shoulder blade and said hastily, "Bill Smith said you were a fine, brilliant woman. As if we didn't know it already. Archie, take out the plates."

"Try and make me," Archie said, insulted. He wriggled away.

April grabbed for his hair with her free hand. He tickled her in the ribs, and the silverware dropped to the floor with a loud clatter. Dinah ran around the table to separate them, tripped over Archie's foot, and the three of them sprawled on the floor.

"Just because you're bigger'n me!" Archie yelled.

"Archie, you *fiend!*" April howled. "My new hair-do!"

"*Children!*" Mother said loudly.

Dinah had hold of Archie by that time, Mother made a dive for April, slipped on a small scatter rug, and sat down hard on the floor. Then the doorbell rang.

There was a sudden and deadly silence. The four Carstairs looked up, aghast. The night was warm, and the front door had been left open during dinner. Bill Smith stood framed in the doorway. There were two men standing out on the front porch.

"I hope we're not disturbing you," Bill Smith said.

Dinah was the first to recover herself. "Not at all," she said politely. She jumped up, helped Mother to her feet, and began patting Mother's back hair into place.

"We always do exercises after dinner," April said serenely. "Good for the digestion."

"Do come in and have coffee," Dinah said. "Archie, bring in the coffee tray." She gave him a warning pinch, and he fled.

One of the two men who came into the room with Bill Smith was the quiet man in gray who'd been there the night before. The other was a stranger. Or was he a stranger? There was something uncannily familiar about him. "I just thought you'd like to know," Bill Smith said, "that your smart daughter Dinah caught a spy."

But he was grinning as he said it. The other two men were grinning, too.

Marian gasped, her eyes wide. "That's not a spy! That's Pat Donovan! *Pat!*" She ran across the floor, hands outstretched.

"Marian!" the smiling brown-eyed man said. He grasped her hands and said, "You're getting to be a terrible dope in your old age. Imagine not recognizing me, all these weeks!"

Bill Smith broke it up by introducing the gray-clad man from the FBI. By that time Marian looked a little dazed. She stared from one to the other.

"Mother," April said earnestly. "He *is* a spy. Dinah caught him."

"Nonsense," Marian said vaguely.

"I did too," Dinah said. "Only he told me he was Peter Desmond and I believed him. But I knew he couldn't be Peter Desmond after I remembered it was cold and foggy that day, because that's how we happened to hear the shots."

"And he paints water," Archie piped up. "He paints water with oils. April said so." He put the coffee tray down on the table.

"And if he isn't Peter Desmond," April said frantically, "who *is* Armand von Hoehne?"

The man in gray laughed and said, "Your children are saner than you think, Mrs. Carstairs."

"They sound saner than I feel," Marian Carstairs said. She sat down and began pouring coffee automatically. "I do wish somebody would tell me what's going on." She added, "I never would have believed Pat Donovan could have fooled me with those fake whiskers."

"They weren't false," Pat Donovan said in a hurt voice. "I grew them."

Dinah had been bewildered. Now she suspected she was being kidded, and she began to get mad. She stood silently watching and listening. Getting mad, with Dinah, was a slow process, but a thorough one.

"You do know this man, Mrs. Carstairs?" the man in gray said.

"Of course I know him. He worked for a newspaper in Chicago at the same time I worked for another newspaper in Chicago. That was years ago. He was best man at my wedding. And I saw him in Paris, and Madrid, and Berlin, and Shanghai. It's been years, now, since I saw him, but I'd have known him anywhere."

"Without the whiskers," Pat Donovan added.

"You might have told me who you were," Marian said, "instead of letting me try to talk French to you, and discuss those awful paintings."

"They weren't so awful," Pat Donovan said. "At least, not as awful as your French."

By now, Dinah was really mad. She rose and said, "My mother speaks good French. And you, Mr. Donovan, or Desmond, or Desgranges, or von Hoehne, or whoever you are, you're a liar!"

"Dinah!" Marian said.

"Hey, Dinah," Archie said. "Y'know what? Y'know what?"

"Shut up," Dinah said to Archie. She glared at Pat Donovan and said, "First you lie to me, and then you criticize my mother's French."

"Y'know what?" Archie yelped. "Dinah, you listen to me. He couldn't be Peter Desmond. Y'know why? Account of Peter Desmond is a guy in the *Gazette* comics. He speaks forty-'leven languages and he can disguise himself any ol' time he wants to."

Dinah remembered. "I read the *Gazette* too," she said coldly. She was good and mad at herself now, too. Falling for a story like that!

"Dinah," Pat Donovan said. "I'll explain it all to you—"

Just in time a line from one of Mother's books came to her. She stood up very straight and said, "I am not interested in your explanations, Mr. Whatever-your-name-is. I have more important matters to attend to." She turned on her heel, strode into the dining room, and began picking up the dishes.

"Oh, Dinah," Marian said. She started after her.

April pulled her down on the sofa. "Remember what the book on child psychology said. Wait till she's through being mad and *then* reason with her." She added, "That always works with Archie and me."

Marian sighed, and sat down. She knew, from long experience, that April was right. "Well, Pat," she said, "just explain to *me*."

Dinah marched back and forth from the dining room to the kitchen, carrying dirty dishes and telling herself that she was not going to listen to what was being said in the dining room. She didn't even care. It was impossible, though, not to overhear fragments of conversation. She began carrying off the dishes one at a time.

"—met this von Hoehne in Paris—"

She put away the salt and pepper cellars.

"—thought there might be a good story—"

She took off the napkins.

"—not much trouble to grow a beard—"

She shook out the tablecloth and replaced it.

"—and this Mrs. Sanford—"

By that time there was no further excuse for being in the dining room. She went out in the kitchen, filled the dishpan with soap and water, and considered running away from home. She'd gotten as far as the silverware when April came out in the kitchen.

"Dinah, he's not a spy, he's a reporter. He writes books. About spies."

"Wipe the glasses," Dinah said.

April picked up the dishtowel. Archie burst into the kitchen and said, "Hey, Dinah! Y'know what?"

"Carry out the wastepaper," Dinah said.

April and Archie tended to their chores in silence. Dinah went on washing dishes and putting away pots and pans. April glanced at her. It was going to be a long, cold day before Dinah asked any questions about Pat Donovan.

Archie came back and banged down the wastebasket. "He paints water!" Archie said. He added a rude noise.

"Archie," Dinah said coldly, "put away the pots and pans. And, April, there's lint in that last glass you wiped."

April and Archie exchanged glances and winks. April rewiped the glass and Archie began putting away the pots and pans.

"You know, Archie," April said, "I bet his book is going to be a best seller. Maybe it'll even be in the movies."

"Yeah," Archie said enthusiastically. "All about how he chased spies all over Europe pretending he worked for a newspaper."

"And how he really did get to know this Armand von Hoehne. Gee! I'd begun to think there wasn't really any such person."

Dinah said nothing.

"It was pretty smart," Archie said, "then letting this—this what's-his-name—"

"Donovan," Dinah said, "and don't talk so fast."

April and Archie exchanged another wink and said, "Why, Dinah, We didn't know you were listening."

"I'm not," Dinah said. "And don't make so much noise."

There was a little silence, and then Archie said, "Well, anyway, it was pretty smart, that's all I gotta say."

"Funny," April said, "what a lot of the story he told Dinah was true. About him knowing all those different languages, and stuff. And how he grew a beard and tried to act like Armand von Hoehne pretending to be somebody else, and always keeping his sleeves rolled down so's nobody'd notice he didn't have a scar on his left arm, and fixing it so this dope in New York would write letters to Mrs. Sanford making it look as if he really was Armand von Hoehne pretending to be somebody else, and—"

"Wait-a-minute!" Dinah said, dropping the dishrag. "Did he do that?"

April and Archie stared at her innocently and said, in unison, "Do what?"

By the time they'd gone through the bread-and-butter-make-a-wish ceremony, Dinah had forgotten all about being mad. "Did he fix it so those letters—"

"Oh, that," April said. "Sure. They figured if there *were* any spies, and if the spies thought he was Mr. von Hoehne, the spies would get in touch with him. All he had to do was grow a beard and paint pictures and be bait."

"Paint *water*," Archie said. "And—and—and—and Mrs. Sanford, they knew she was acquainted with a lot of questioning people—"

"*Questionable*," April said.

"Oh, a'right. Anyway, they figured she'd be as li'ble to know spies as anybody."

Dinah drew a long breath and said, "Is all this on the level?"

"Dinah!" April said. "You don't think we'd kid you!"

That was the wrong thing to say. Dinah glared at her, wrung out the dishcloth, hung it up, and said, "I'm *not* interested." She banged the dishpan into the undersink compartment and marched to the door. There she paused. "Well, why did he run away like he did? And did he actually catch any spies?"

"Sure," Archie said. "That's what we're trying to tell you, only you ain't interested, because you're—"

April kicked Archie and said, "They broke up a reg'lar spy ring, honest. Because you put the FBI on his trail and so he had to beat it, fast. And they—the spies, I mean—were gonna arrange his getaway, but he purposely led the FBI to where they were. And

Mrs. Sanford really didn't have anything to do with it, that was just something he tried and it didn't work."

She paused for breath and said, "And it can't go in the newspapers yet and we have to keep it a secret, but he's going to write a book about all the diff'rent stuff he's done. And he says you deserve all the credit because you were so smart and caught him and that's why he had to run away and everything."

"Me!" Dinah said. Her cheeks turned pink.

"Yeah, you," Archie said excitedly. "He said—he said—he said—"

April went on hastily, "He said the police or the FBI oughta have you working for them, account of you'd make a wonderful detective and you're a wonder at questioning suspects. So there!"

"My sister!" Archie said, with pride.

"Gosh," Dinah said, her cheeks scarlet now. "I didn't do anything!"

"He said you were awful smart not to fall for that Peter Desmond story, but to call up the FBI right away," Archie said.

"Well," Dinah said slowly, "it wasn't exactly that—" She glanced toward the door. "I wonder what they're talking about now!"

The three young Carstairs stole through the dining room and paused at the foot of the stairs, hidden in the shadows.

"—must forgive me for taking you in, Marian. But you were the only person I could use for a—a test case. I felt as long as *you* didn't recognize me, I was safe."

"If I'd known, I'd probably have given you away by accident," Marian said. "It's just as well." She was laughing. Her cheeks were pink. She looked happy.

The quiet man in gray had gone. Pat Donovan sat in the most comfortable chair, sipping a cup of coffee, looking very much at home. Bill Smith sat on the less comfortable chair, holding a cup of coffee that looked cold even from the doorway, his face glum.

"Tell me, Pat," Marian said, "how is Jake? When's the last time you saw him?"

"Jake Justus? I saw him in Chicago about a year ago. He's doing fine. Married a gorgeous blonde girl. Say, will you ever forget the night they had that warehouse fire in Blue Island?"

Marian giggled and said, "Never!"

"And say," Pat Donovan said, "do you ever hear anything from Alma?"

"She's married," Marian said. "Married a man that runs a chain of filling stations in Indiana."

"I'll be darned," Pat Donovan said. "Never will forget the time she got a job as a hotel maid and got an exclusive interview with—"

"Newspaper work must be very interesting," Bill Smith said stiffly.

"You've no idea!" Marian said. "Oh, Pat, remember the time Jim spread that airplane bootlegger story all over the front pages!"

"Forsythe? I sure do! Wonder what's become of him!"

"He's running a newspaper up in Michigan," Marian said. "Doing a marvelous job of it, too. And, Pat—"

"You must meet such interesting people," Bill Smith said, even more stiffly, putting down his coffee cup.

"That's not the half of it," Pat said. "Marian, remember that blonde countess in Havana, that wore a nose ring and led a tame leopard on a leash?"

"I'm sorry," Bill Smith said, rising, "but it's late."

Around the corner, Dinah nudged April. "He's jealous!" she whispered exultantly.

April nudged Archie. "Run up to your room, fast. And then yell! Loud! And keep yelling!"

"Why?" Archie whispered, halfway up the stairs.

"You saw a ghost," April hissed at him.

Down in the living room, Marian rose and said, "Oh, Mr. Smith, must you go?"

"I'm afraid I must," Bill Smith said.

April held her breath.

"But," Bill Smith said, "I'll—"

Archie yelled. April relaxed. A split second more, and Bill Smith would have said, "I'll be here for dinner tomorrow night."

Dinah took the stairs in one leap, while April ducked behind the banister. "Mother!" Dinah called. "Archie's seeing a ghost!"

Mother was halfway up the stairs by then. April headed off Bill Smith and Pat Donovan by emerging calm and smiling, and saying, "That Archie!"

"Marian!" Bill Smith called frantically.

"It's nothing," Mother's voice floated down. "Just a nightmare. Good night, Mr. Smith."

April beamed and said, "Good night. And don't forget we're expecting you for dinner tomorrow." She walked him to the door as she spoke.

"Yes, of course," Bill Smith said, his eyes toward the stairs. April opened the door for him. "You're sure everything's all right upstairs?"

"Oh, sure," April chirruped. "We see ghosts all the time. Or didn't we tell you, this house is haunted? Good ni-i-ght!"

She closed the door just as Marian came down the stairs. "Mr. Smith had to go, Mother."

"I'm so sorry," Marian said. She smoothed her hair, sat down, and said, "Sometimes I think Archie doesn't always tell the truth."

April rounded the corner into the staircase. Dinah and Archie were waiting for her.

"This is all we need," April whispered happily. "A rival. Now it's really in the bag."

"I've got to leave in a few minutes," Pat Donovan was saying.

"Oh. Pat! Look, can't you come to dinner tomorrow night?"

"That would really do it," Dinah whispered. "With her new hair-do and manicure, and the meat loaf—"

The three young Carstairs listened hopefully.

"Sorry," Pat Donovan said. "But I'm catching the midnight plane. Edna and the kids have been parked in Santa Fe for six months, waiting for me to finish this job."

The three young Carstairs looked at each other and tiptoed upstairs.

"Never mind," April said consolingly. "Judging from the way Bill Smith looked tonight, with our brains and Mother's looks I don't think we need to use jealousy!"

Chapter 24.

THE THREE young Carstairs woke early Tuesday morning. There was a feeling of excitement, a sense of great things about to happen, the same feeling that was in the air on the day school was out or the circus was in town. They tiptoed around the house as quietly as kittens, not to wake Mother. An extra hour's sleep now would make her look even prettier at dinnertime.

In the middle of breakfast, April had her idea. She laid her fork down, gasped, and said, "Dinah! Mr. Holbrook's daughter!"

"Huh?" Dinah said. Archie stared.

"We've got to see that picture of her," April said. "*Today.* Because." She paused for a minute. "She's a burlesque star. Or maybe—*was* a burlesque star."

"Was?" Dinah repeated. She looked a little dazed.

"Bette LeMoe was a burlesque star, too," April said dramatically. "And—if she'd been Mr. Holbrook's daughter—"

Dinah choked on her milk. She said, "April! My gosh!" Archie pounded her on the back until she got her breath again.

"Where does Mr. Holbrook live?" April asked.

"Up on Washington Drive." Dinah said. "It's about four blocks from here. He's got a housekeeper. She's cross. Joella and I went up there once to try and sell her a ticket to the PTA garden tea, and she kept us there fifteen minutes telling us why she wouldn't buy one."

"Fine," April said. "Wonderful. That's just what we need." She picked up her fork, returned to the scrambled eggs, and said, "We'll go up there right after school. You and Archie ring the front doorbell and try to sell her a—a magazine subscription. While I sneak in the back and look for the picture."

"Yipes!" Archie said happily.

Dinah frowned. "Suppose you get caught."

"Then I'll get arrested and put in jail," April said serenely. "Don't be a gloomy gus. Suppose I don't get caught and do find the picture."

"If I'm gonna keep her busy while you search," Archie announced, "you won't get caught, don't worry. I know her. She's got a very fine garden, and I'll borrow Flashlight's dog and take him along."

"Archie," April said, "you're a genius. For that you can have my jam."

Archie sniffed, reached for the jam jar, and said. "I just happen to know you don't like this kind of jam."

"But, April," Dinah said. "This is Tuesday."

"So what?" April said. "It usually is."

"Except when it's raining," Archie said. "Then it's Saturday."

"But if you look at it with one eye shut it turns pink," April said.

"Only I like the striped ones best," Archie said.

April said, "But you can't do that, because it's Tuesday."

"Quiet, you kids," Dinah said in exasperation. "It *is* Tuesday."

April and Archie stared at her and said in unison, "Did we say it wasn't?"

There followed the elaborate ceremony that had to be carried out whenever two people said the same thing. Little fingers hooked. "Make a wish." "Bread 'n' butter." Then Archie went on scraping out the jam jar, and April said, "What does Tuesday have to do with it?"

"Tuesday I have after-school gym class," Dinah said. "I don't get out till four-thirty."

"Oh, heck," April said. "You would!" She thought for a minute. "You'll have to cut gym."

"I can't," Dinah said miserably. "I've already cut three times this term. Once when Archie wanted to see that Roy Rogers movie, and once when it was such a nice day to go swimming, and once—"

"Wait a minute," April said. "I know. You've sprained your ankle."

Dinah automatically glanced at her ankles. They seemed perfectly intact.

"Archie," April said, "get the adhesive tape. Thank goodness for those Girl Scout first-aid lessons!"

Dinah looked bewildered, then finally said, "Oh!"

Ten minutes later April had finished a magnificent job of taping the ankle. "Now," she said. "Mother was sleeping when you left for school, so you couldn't ask her for an excuse slip. That gym teacher is such a shot bag that she prob'bly won't remember it by next gym class. If she does, by that time we'll be able to explain all to Mother. Got that straight?"

Dinah nodded.

"We'll invade the Holbrook house at four o'clock on the dot," April said. "And meantime—don't forget to limp!"

At two minutes to four Dinah and Archie walked up to the house on Washington Drive. Dinah was still limping, and Archie was leading Flashlight's big brown mongrel on a tightly held leash. April was going up the alley, parallel to them.

"A subscription to *Farmer's Wife* magazine," Dinah muttered. "What the hash-e-cash-kuk am I going to do if she says she'd *like* to subscribe to it?"

"Tell her you'll come up tomorrow and bring the thing to write out," Archie advised, "and then I'll let Samson loose. That'll keep her busy."

Dinah sighed. They turned in the front walk and she could see April, behind the house, waiting in the shrubbery.

Lawyer Holbrook lived in a medium-sized, unpretentious stucco bungalow with neat, very ordinary grounds, and a carefully arranged garden at one side. A large, cross-looking white cat was dozing by the sundial. Samson growled. Archie jerked on the leash and said, "Shut up." He beamed at Dinah and said, "Oh, boy—if Samson ever gets loose after that cat—"

Dinah rang the doorbell. A minute later a tall, bony, gray-haired woman came to the door and said, "Well?"

"Would you like to take a year's subscription to the *Farmer's Wife* magazine?" Dinah said timidly.

The gray-haired woman glared and said, "Do I look like a farmer's wife? Does this look like a farm?"

"No, ma'am," Dinah said in a small voice. "But—"

"If she sells ten subscriptions she gets a genuine diamond ring," Archie said.

The gray-haired woman's lips tightened. Then she launched into a ten-minute dissertation on why she wouldn't subscribe to the *Farmer's Wife*, what she thought of impudent children going around selling subscriptions and bothering their neighbors, and the bad behavior of modern children in general. She ended by saying, "And you take that dog right out of here!"

Dinah felt sudden panic. April must still be in the house. She was to have signaled to them from a vantage point in the alley the minute she got out, and so far she hadn't been heard from.

Mr. Holbrook's housekeeper started to go into the house and close the door. Archie let go of Samson's leash. Samson promptly went after the cat, who squalled and fled. The housekeeper shrieked, and ran after Samson. Archie and Dinah ran after the housekeeper.

The resulting confusion lasted a good five minutes, and ended in the back yard, with the cat halfway up a telephone pole and Samson raising a terrific row at the bottom of the pole. The housekeeper was screaming at Dinah and Archie. Dinah and Archie were just plain screaming.

In the midst of the excitement April slipped out a side window, raced around the house, and joined the group, exclaiming loudly, "Archie! Aren't you ashamed of yourself, letting that awful dog chase that poor little pussycat!" The poor little pussycat climbed six feet higher up the pole, hurling profanities at Samson.

April grabbed Samson's leash, put it in Archie's hand, and said sternly, "You go right straight home! This minute." Archie beat it fast, dragging a still-barking Samson after him. Dinah ran after him. April lingered just long enough to say sympathetically to the housekeeper, "You'd better call the fire department. That cat'll never get down that pole by herself."

She caught up with Dinah and Archie halfway up the street.

"Well?" Dinah demanded. "Did you find it?"

April nodded. "I found it. It was in his desk drawer, right where I thought it would be. I left it there, because it wasn't evidence."

"Why not?" Dinah said.

April sighed. "The picture of Mr. Holbrook's daughter is pretty lush, what with those beads and peacock feathers. But she's big and blonde and a little on the beefy side. She doesn't look any more like Bette LeMoe than—Archie does."

Dinah stared at her. Archie let go of the leash, and Samson, thoroughly unnerved by now, ran for home.

"Do you mean," Dinah said grimly, "that we went through all this, and chased a cat up a telephone pole, and I went around limping all day, just to find out—nothing?"

"Listen, Goony Gussie," April said. "We found out something

very important. We found out that Bette LeMoe *wasn't* Mr. Holbrook's daughter. That's a big help. Because now we know Mr. Holbrook wouldn't have wanted to murder Mrs. Sanford because she was mixed up in the Bette LeMoe case. All we have to do now is find out who did murder Mrs. Sanford."

Dinah sniffed, and said nothing.

"And," April said, "let's get that bandage off your ankle before we get home and Mother sees it and wants to know what happened to you."

Removing the bandage took a little doing, and considerable debate as to procedure. April borrowed Archie's Boy Scout knife and tried slitting it down the side. That didn't work. Dinah suggested trying to soak it loose with nail-polish remover. April reminded her they didn't have any nail-polish remover. Finally Archie, in exasperation, grabbed one end of the bandage and yanked. Dinah yelped once. The bandage was off.

Dinah put her ankle sock and shoe back on again and they started home.

"Stop limping," April whispered as they crossed the front porch.

"It's a habit now," Dinah said in a melancholy voice. "I'll probably limp all the rest of my life, and it's all your fault."

They went into the house and headed for the kitchen. On the table was a big lemon pie, put there to cool, with a thick, delicately browned meringue. On the stove was the meat loaf, ready to be put into the oven. It smelled—heavenly! There was a casserole of scalloped potatoes waiting beside it and, wonder of wonders, onion soup simmering on the low burner. April sniffed ecstatically and said, "Super!"

Jenkins, Inky, and Stinky were sitting on the kitchen floor, gazing wistfully at the stove. The makings of a magnificent salad were on the rack in the sink. The biscuits were cut out and ready to be baked.

"April," Dinah said happily, "he's as good as handcuffed right now."

April frowned. She said, "Listen! Is that the washing machine?"

They listened. It was the washing machine. And, in the back yard, Mother was whistling *The Wreck of the Old Ninety-seven*, loudly and cheerfully.

With a sudden premonition of disaster, April ran into the back yard, Dinah and Archie close behind her. She stopped just beyond the porch and said, in a scandalized voice, "*Mother!*"

"Oh, hello," Mother said. "It was such a nice day, and I had some spare time, so I decided to wash all the old camp blankets. The last ones are in the washer now. Want to help me hang up?"

"But, Mother," Dinah said. "Your new manicure!"

Mother stared at her. Her jaw dropped. She said, "I forgot all about it."

She looked at her hands, and so did the young Carstairs. The three-dollar manicure was an utter ruin!

Chapter 25.

"It's a good thing Estelle sold you a bottle of matching nail polish," April said sternly. "Honestly, Mother, at your age!"

"I'm still young enough to make mistakes," Mother said very meekly. "And I'm very sorry, and I'll never do it again."

"Hold *still*," April snapped. She squinted critically at her handiwork. "It's going to be as good as new."

"You're an angel to put the new polish on for me," Mother said, "and Dinah's an angel to finish hanging out the blankets. Honest, I just forgot all about having a new manicure. It was such a beautiful day—"

"And you just felt like washing blankets," April said. "I'm just thankful you didn't feel like painting floors or something. Of all the impractical people!"

Marian Carstairs said, "April. Would you kids like me better if I were more practical? Because I *try* to be practical."

April finished the last fingernail. "We couldn't like you better," she said slowly, "no matter *what* you were more of. And now sit there and don't touch anything until that polish is good and dry."

Mother spread out her fingers, sat very still, and said humbly, "Yes, ma'am."

"And don't get inspired and wash any more blankets for at least a week," April said, starting to take the pins out of Mother's hair.

"No, ma'am," Mother said, just as humbly.

"And don't move your head while I'm combing out your new hair-do," April said. "Or I'll be *very* cross." She brushed a strand of hair over her finger and said, "What's more, you've got to wear your very best house coat to dinner tonight. The dusty rose one, with the lace around the neck." How on earth was she going to break the news to Mother that Bill Smith was coming to dinner?

"Well—" Mother said. "But if I'm cooking, I might get spots on it."

"You've finished cooking for the day," April said. "The meat loaf is baking, and the gravy is in the top of the double boiler, and the salad's made, and the soup is ready to serve, and the scalloped potatoes are in the oven, and Archie's setting the table." She put in one last hairpin and stood back to survey her handiwork.

Even in the old pink flannel bathrobe, and with her hands spread out like fans while the nail polish dried, and with her face covered with cold cream, Mother looked—*Div!* April gasped and said, "Oh—*Mother!*"

"Oh, Mother, *what?*" Marian said.

April grinned. "Don't move until those nails are dry. And if you don't do a terrific make-up job to go with that hair-do and that house coat and that manicure and that meat loaf, your children are going to run away from home, so there."

Marian laughed and April, remembering, laughed with her. The time Archie had gotten good and mad and decided to run away from home. And Mother had insisted on helping him. Tying his most precious possessions in a big bandanna, to be carried on a stick over his shoulder. Archie beginning to suspect he was being kidded, and getting stubborn. Finally, Mother and Archie *both* running away from home, ending up at a movie theater that showed a triple-feature Western bill, and arriving home at nine o'clock at night (to the great relief of a worried Dinah and April), full of hamburgers and happiness.

"Don't worry," April said. "If we run away from home, we'll take you. But don't forget now—eye shadow 'n' everything. And I'll go help Dinah with the blankets."

She paused at the door for one last look at Mother. Suddenly she felt all warm and soft inside, as if she were going to cry. If only what they were doing was what Mother would want, if she knew about it! If only Mother would be happy with a handsome husband who was a police lieutenant!

"Something, baby?" Mother said.

"Yes," April said. She gulped. "Mascara, too. And soon's your nails are dry, hold 'em under the cold-water faucet. It makes the polish last longer."

She ran down the stairs and inspected everything. Archie had done a masterpiece of table setting. The centerpiece made from the best of the remaining talisman roses looked gor-gee-super-ous. Fresh candles, and polished candle holders. Bill Smith placed at the other side of the table from Mother, so he'd be seeing her across the roses.

Everything in the kitchen was under control. Dinah was basting the meat loaf, and Archie—protesting loudly about it—was washing radishes.

"Have you told Mother yet?" Dinah demanded.

April shook her head. "I will, though. Right away. And we better get dressed."

There followed a brief debate about what to wear. Dinah favored the pink sweater and plaid skirt combination. April didn't. Finally April said with a flash of inspiration, "Dinah! The white dotted-swiss dresses, with the blue belts and the blue-ribbon bows."

"Oh, gosh," Dinah said, slamming the oven door. "They make us look like—little kids!"

"That's the idea," April said. "Gooney Gussie! you don't want

Bill Smith to look at Mother surrounded by practically grown-up children!"

"Well—" Dinah said. "Oh, all right. This time."

"And you," April said to Archie, "*wash!*"

She went back up the stairs slowly, thinking of ways to tell Mother they were expecting a guest. After all, Mother and Bill Smith hadn't exactly parted friends on their last meeting. It wasn't an easy problem to handle.

A confession of what they'd done, and why? No! That would make Mother self-conscious.

They'd invited him, on their own, because they liked him? *Uh-uh!* That might make Mother mad.

It had been his idea? No good. Very much no good.

She stood, thinking, outside Mother's door for five minutes before an idea came to her.

Mother was taking the rose house coat off its hanger. She spread out her nails proudly and said, "See? All dry, without one nick in them!"

"You're wonderful," April breathed admiringly. "Say, Mother." This had to be handled very carefully. "That cop—Bill Smith—has to be in the neighborhood tonight and there isn't any place he can get anything to eat. So. Is it all right if we give him a sandwich in the kitchen?"

"April!" Mother dropped the house coat. April held her breath. Ages and ages of time went by. "A sandwich in the kitchen," Mother said. "Utterly ridiculous! Ask him to stay to dinner, of course!"

"Yes'm," April said. She fled into the hall and started down the stairs. She'd just reached the landing when the door opened above her and Mother's voice called.

"Oh, April! Put on the lace tablecloth, and get some fresh flowers!"

"Yes'm," April called back. The lace tablecloth was already on the table, and so was the centerpiece of roses.

Once, while she and Dinah were dressing, she opened the door to Mother's room just a crack and peeked in. Mother was sitting in front of the dressing table, doing the most careful job of eyebrow brushing April had ever seen, and smiling while she did it. A flower that matched the rose house coat was artfully pinned in her hair. April closed the door silently and went back to her dressing. "I wish," she said, "I was a kitten."

Dinah said, "My gosh! Why?"

April beamed and said, "So I could purr!"

The timing worked out perfectly. Everything was ready to put on the table when Mother came downstairs, and Bill Smith rang the doorbell at almost exactly that moment.

He had on what looked like a new suit, and he certainly had a brand-new haircut. He was carrying a large box under his arm, and he gave it to Mother. From the watching post behind the dining-room door Archie whispered ecstatically, "Chocolates!"

Then before Mother could mention the business of a sandwich in the kitchen, or he could thank her for the invitation to dinner, Archie let loose Inky, Stinky, Jenkins, and Henderson on the living-room floor. When the resulting excitement was over and there was a danger that the subject might be brought up again, Dinah announced that dinner was ready.

The three young Carstairs had carefully rehearsed dinner conversation in advance.

After everyone had been served, and the biscuits had been passed around the table, Dinah sighed happily and said, "Oh, Mother, you make the most *wonderful* meat loaf!"

"It's delicious," Bill Smith agreed.

Archie caught his cue and said, "You just oughta taste one of her beef-steak pies sometime."

A few minutes later April said, "These biscuits are Div, but Def!"

Bill Smith started buttering his third one and said, "Best biscuits I ever ate."

"And Mother makes the most wonderful corn muffins!" Dinah said.

The three young Carstairs were tactfully silent while Mother and Bill Smith talked about politics, books, and movies. As soon as conversation lagged a little, Archie, on a signal from April, said, "Hey! C'n I have s'more gravy? It's the most wonderful gravy *ever!*"

"How about more for you, too?" April said, passing the dish to Bill Smith. "Mother does make the most *super* gravy!"

"And her steak sauce," Dinah said, "you just ought to taste it once. Gosh!"

One thing about the dinner did worry Marian Carstairs a little. The three young Carstairs were entirely too well behaved. Too well behaved, and too quiet, save for their comments on the cooking. Archie's familiar, "Hey! Y'know what?" was missing, and Dinah remembered to say "Please" when she asked for another biscuit.

But it wasn't until April said, "Mother, did you make this simply super salad dressing yourself?" And Dinah cut in quickly with, "Of course she did. Mother always makes her own salad dressing," that she began to get suspicious. Because not only she, but Dinah and April also, knew that she hadn't made the salad dressing. And she caught the nudge April gave Archie just before he piped up and said, "Mother makes mayonnaise, too, and it's *wonderful* mayonnaise."

Then finally the lemon pie was served, with a flourish. By that time Marian Carstairs had begun to wonder if she was the victim of A Plot. If one of the young Carstairs praised the pie—

But it was Bill Smith who said, "Your mother makes the most super-wonderful lemon pie!"

Marian's eyes met his across the table. His were smiling. She repressed a giggle, and said, "You just ought to taste my gingerbread sometime!"

The three young Carstairs stared, first at him, and then at her.

They made a quick recovery when the pie was finished. (Bill Smith had had three helpings.) "Coffee in the living room," April said. She lighted the candles over the fire-place, while Dinah brought in the coffee tray. There! Coffee, soft lights, and Mother in that lush house coat!

Then she chased Archie into the kitchen while she and Dinah carried off the remaining dishes. Archie protested indignantly. "Hey! I wanna *listen!*"

Dinah folded up the cloth and brushed off the table. Then she complained to April, "We didn't get in that line I was s'posed to say to him—about 'I should think you'd get awful lonely, having to have dinner by yourself every night.'"

"Never mind," April said. "Everything's going all right." She laid a finger to her lips and led the way to the living-room door. Dinah and Archie followed, on tip-toes and listened.

There was soft, friendly laughter. Mother's voice: "Really, Bill—" And his: "Seriously, Marian, I do want to tell you—"

And then the doorbell rang.

"I'll get it," April called. She ran across the living room and opened the door. "Probably the paper boy."

It wasn't the paper boy. It was Sergeant O'Hare. And he looked worried. He looked out of breath. His round face was red. He said, "Hello, little lady. Is—" Then he spotted Bill Smith and said, "Oh, there you are."

April got one look at the tableau before Sergeant O'Hare interrupted it. Mother sitting on the blue sofa, looking lovely. Bill Smith in the big comfortable arm chair, looking at Mother, and with that earnest expression in his eyes. She thought of all the things she'd like to do to Sergeant O'Hare, and none of them were pleasant.

"We found Mr. Sanford," Sergeant O'Hare puffed. "In the bushes near the end of the driveway of his own house. Not been there long. I left Flanagan to watch him."

Bill Smith jumped up, almost overturning his coffee cup. "Murdered?"

"Almost," Sergeant O'Hare said. "Shot. Think he'll live, though. Better get an ambulance, first, and then call headquarters."

Marian jumped up and said, "The telephone's right here."

April raced into the kitchen, hissed "*Come on!*" and led Dinah and Archie into the back yard. On the way to the Sanford driveway she explained what had happened. Then "Archie. There's a cop watching him. Can you get the cop away from there, quick?"

"Sure thing," Archie said. He dived into the bushes. Dinah and April ran on across the Sanford lawn and headed cautiously down the driveway. At the foot of it a policeman stood beside an ominously quiet form covered with a blanket.

Suddenly hideous and terrifying screams came from the bushes. The cop jumped, turned, and ran in the direction of the screams. April and Dinah ran in the direction of the blanket-covered form.

Wallace Sanford's eyes opened and looked at the two girls. His face was very white.

"You're not murdered," April said. "Sergeant O'Hare said so. You're just shot. So don't worry."

"You're *all right*," Dinah whispered.

He tried to speak, failed, closed his eyes, and then opened them again.

"Take it easy," Dinah said.

"Listen," he moaned, "listen. You two. I know, now. The man who murdered Flora—" His eyes closed again.

"Yes?" April breathed. "*Yes!*"

He opened his eyes just the barest slit. "Was—was the man who paid the ransom. He was her—" His eyes closed and didn't open again.

Dinah bent over him. "He's alive," she whispered; "he's just fainted."

There was a rustling in the bushes. "That cop's coming back," April hissed. "*Move!*"

They raced up the driveway. Archie came out from behind a tree just as they reached the gate. Somewhere, down below, the cop blew a whistle. Bill Smith, Sergeant O'Hare, and Mother ran out the front door just as the three young Carstairs reached the back door.

Dinah caught her breath, automatically resumed work on the dishes, and said, "That was close!"

"How'dya like my screaming?" Archie said proudly.

"Fine," Dinah said.

"You just oughta hear my hollering sometime," Archie said. "Hey, April?"

April didn't respond. She sat down on one of the kitchen chairs and leaned her chin on her hands.

"April," Dinah said.

"Shut up, you kids," April said. "And don't bother me." She looked puzzled, and just a little unhappy. "Because. I've got to *think.*"

Chapter 26.

"Flanagan probably heard a hoot owl," Sergeant O'Hare said.

Mother beamed at him and at Bill Smith. "Well, you got your Mr. Sanford, anyway. Now, how about some fresh coffee? I can make some in about two seconds."

"I've made some a'ready," Dinah called from the kitchen. "Bringing it right in."

She carried in the tray. April and Archie came along, ostensibly to carry sugar and cream, but really to look the situation over.

Mother's hair was a trifle disheveled, and the rose in it was sadly askew. But her cheeks were pink, and her eyes were shining. Bill Smith looked breathless and a little worried, Sergeant O'Hare looked perfectly serene. He beamed impartially at the three young Carstairs, looked approvingly at Dinah's and April's aprons, and said, "Helping Mother, eh? That's the way to do." He turned and beamed at Mother. "That's the right way to bring up kids. I've—"

"You've probably raised nine of your own," Mother said, "and you know." She tried to rearrange her hair and only succeeded in making it worse.

Bill Smith grinned. "Either you're psychic," he said, "or he's already told you about them." His face grew sober. "I really should have gone on down to headquarters. As soon as I finish this coffee—"

Sergeant O'Hare took in the candlelit room, Marian Carstairs' rose house coat, and Bill Smith's new haircut. "Forget it," he said. "Let him wait till morning. He ain't hurt bad, and he'll talk better after a good night's sleep. You caught the guy, so you might as well relax and celebrate."

"But—" Bill Smith began, frowning.

Dinah said, "He couldn't have shot Mrs. Sanford. Because, then, who shot *him?*"

"And someone tried to lure the police away from the body," Mother said.

"Those yells," Archie said, with pardonable pride, "didn't sound to me like no hoot owl *I* ever heard, so there."

"Besides, *we* heard the shots," April said. "Dinah had just gone to see if it was time to put the potatoes on—"

Bill Smith said just one word, under his breath. The three young Carstairs didn't hear it and it was probably just as well.

"Come, now," Mother said. "Let's forget about it for the time being. Sergeant O'Hare's right, Bill, you probably will do much better questioning Mr. Sanford after he's had a night's rest. And how about some more coffee? And where did I put that box of chocolates? And, Sergeant O'Hare, I do, think there's one piece of lemon pie left from dinner."

Archie went to get the pie. April poured more coffee. Dinah passed the chocolates. Then the three young Carstairs sat in an ornamental row on the sofa, Archie in the middle.

Sergeant O'Hare praised the pie in lavish terms. It was almost as good, he declared, as Mrs. O'Hare's pie. "But," he added, "you just ought to taste her devil's food cake sometime!"

The three young Carstairs kept their faces straight. Mother and Bill Smith carefully avoided each other's eyes, but Mother's cheeks turned a shade pinker. Sergeant O'Hare rose to go. He looked over the scene, the candlelit room, Dinah and April in their white dresses with the blue sashes, and Marian Carstairs in her rose house coat. He sighed heavily, turned to Bill Smith, and said, "Too bad you haven't got a wife and family. It must be pretty lonely, living in a hotel room. Well, g'night, everybody."

Dinah, April, and Archie silently blessed him.

Bill Smith put down his cup and said, "Marian—"

"April," Dinah said hastily. "We've got to finish the dishes."

They were halfway across the dining room, and Bill Smith's voice could be heard saying, "Marian—I want to tell you—" when the telephone rang.

Dinah and April raced for the phone. It was for Mother. The voice sounded frightened, almost frantic.

Mother took the phone and said, "Yes—*yes*? Oh! Oh, I'm so sorry! Yes, I'll be glad to come right up." A pause, and then, "Smith? It happens that he's here. Yes. Yes, I will. Right away."

By the time she hung up the three young Carstairs and Police Lieutenant Bill Smith were hovering around the phone desk.

"Mr. Cherington," Mother said. "He's had another heart attack, and she's all alone there with him. And for some reason he wants to talk to you, Bill."

"Oh," April said. "Oh, *no!*" She turned white. "It must be true, but I didn't want it to turn out that way."

"April!" Dinah said aghast.

April waved her aside and said, "Mother. You covered the Bette LeMoe kidnaping. Tell me. What was Bette LeMoe's real name?"

Mother looked puzzled. "Why—why, it was—Rose—something. I don't remember."

"I knew it," April wailed. "I knew it! And the ransom money was exactly fifteen thousand dollars, and that's what he embezzled. And he was in the army once, so he probably would have a forty-five revolver. And besides, Mrs. Cherington's eyes aren't brown, they're blue."

"Baby!" Mother said anxiously, feeling April's forehead. "Are you all right? Is your throat sore?"

"My throat isn't sore," April said, "and I haven't got a fever. But Mr. Cherington's name used to be Chandler, and he was an officer in the army. And they had a daughter named Rose, and she went on the stage and changed her name to Bette LeMoe. And she was kidnapped, and he stole fifteen thousand dollars to pay the ransom, and then she was murdered anyway, and he got caught and got kicked out of the army, and went to jail and everything. And I bet you ever since he's been trying to find the kidnapers and that's why he moved out here and rented that house, and—"

"Slow down," Dinah said.

"Well," April said, "it's all mixed up with Frankie Riley getting out of jail. Because he helped with the kidnaping. But she must have gotten all the money because he had to do a robbery, and that's what he went to jail for. Then he got out of jail and came here, and that was prob'bly the proof Mr. Cherington—I mean, Colonel Chandler—was waiting for. So he shot Mrs. Sanford because she'd murdered his daughter and ruined his life, and then he shot Mr. Frankie Riley for the same reason, and he prob'bly was strong enough to cart Mr. Frankie Riley to the old swimming pool, because he wasn't really very old, he was really only in his fifties, and then he trailed Mr. Sanford and tried to shoot him tonight, but he didn't murder him and I'm glad, because Mr. Sanford really wasn't mixed up in the kidnaping, and that's what must of brought on his heart attack, and, anyway that's what happened, and go on up and get his confession." She burst into tears.

Mother gathered April into her arms and said, "My darling child!"

"The picture in the hallway," April sobbed. "It looks like Mrs. Cherington, but it has dark eyes. And it's signed Rose. And it looks like the picture of Bette LeMoe."

Dinah and Archie just looked on, wide-eyed.

Mother stroked April's hair and said, "Don't cry, baby. He did have a bad heart, and—"

"Marian," Bill Smith said hoarsely. "Mrs. Carstairs. Did you know this? Was that why—you wouldn't help, when I—asked you?"

"I guessed it," Marian said. "I saw that picture, too."

April lifted her head and caught the look that passed between Mother and Bill Smith. She stood up and said, "You'd better get up there and talk to—Mr. Cherington."

"She's right," Bill Smith said.

"She's right—about *everything*," Mother said. She kissed April on the forehead.

Chapter 27.

It was four o'clock before the three young Carstairs went to bed, and by then Bill Smith had to carry a soundly-sleeping Archie up the stairs. But Dinah and April were still wide awake.

Mother went into the kitchen and made cocoa. The hair-do was a wreck, her face was tired and pale, but Bill Smith still couldn't keep his eyes away from her face.

Mr. Cherington had confessed, and his confession tallied with April's theory. He'd been taken to the hospital in a police ambulance, and the doctor in charge doubted if he'd ever come to trial. Mrs. Cherington had been brave and, somehow, almost—well, relaxed. She'd told the whole story, now that everything was over.

Yes, he'd stolen the money for his daughter's ransom. Then when she was murdered, it was as though he'd been murdered, too. He hadn't cared much what happened after that, save for burying his daughter where roses could grow around her sleeping place. He couldn't claim her body because to do so would be to reveal his theft. But then the theft was discovered anyway, and he went to prison.

When he was released, he was a sick old man, and he lived for only one thing. He'd accomplished it, and—that was the end.

"Now, he'll die happy," Mrs. Cherington said.

Mother told it to them while she was making the cocoa. Then

she said, "And, you kids. How and why did you get mixed up in this?"

"For you," Dinah said sleepily, "for the publicity."

"We wanted you to solve a real-life murder," April said, nodding over her cocoa. "But you were too busy, so we thought we'd solve it for you. Hey—Archie—"

That was when Bill Smith carried Archie up to bed.

He came downstairs again, looked at Dinah and April, and said, "You go to bed now, before I have to carry you up, too. And—Marian—Mrs. Carstairs—"

"Yes," Mother said.

"It's late now, but—I do want to talk to you about—something important. I know you're very busy but—may I call on you tomorrow night?"

Mother blushed like a schoolgirl and said, "Please do." She walked to the door with him, came back, and told Dinah and April, "Stay home from school tomorrow, and sleep as late as you want to."

They slept till past noon. By that time, reporters were at the door. Bill Smith had let it be known that Marian Carstairs, mystery writer, had solved the Sanford slaying practically singlehanded. The reporters wanted interviews and photographs. Dinah, April, and Archie saw to it that they got them. Marian protested, but the three young Carstairs were firm. After they'd gone to all this trouble, proper advantage was going to be taken of it!

"By this time tomorrow," April said cheerfully, "you'll probably have offers from the movies."

"And think what this is going to do for your new book," Dinah said.

"Perfect nonsense," Mother said. But she didn't have a chance against the three young Carstairs.

They managed everything. April did Mother's hair, and Dinah

cleaned the living room and put fresh flowers everywhere. Archie brushed Jenkins, Inky, and Stinky, and coaxed them into going to sleep on the living-room floor.

Inky and Stinky leaped into Mother's lap just as the *Gazette* photographer was aiming his camera, and that made everything perfect.

April led Dinah and Archie out onto the front porch and left Mother alone with the interviewers.

"April," Dinah said. "All that stuff. You know. The stuff we found at Mrs. Sanford's. We ought to burn it up."

"I know," April said. She scowled. "Let me think."

"Quiet, everybody," Archie said. "April's thinking."

She slapped at him absent-mindedly. "It's serious. All those people. I mean, like the schoolteacher who thought she went to a restaurant and got in a gambling raid, and the guy who don't want his folks to know he works in a saloon, and all the rest of them. They've been worrying plenty since Mrs. Sanford was killed, wondering when somebody would find all that stuff."

"We could mail letters to all of them," Dinah suggested, "and send back the evidence and pictures and everything."

"Too many stamps," April said. "We're broke again." She gazed solemnly at the landscape for a minute and then brightened. "I know what to do! You catch the next reporter that comes out the door."

They waited fifteen minutes or more. A photographer went out. Another photographer went in. Finally a fat man in a gray suit came out, stuffing a folded paper into his pocket.

"Hey, you," April said.

He looked at her, his round face brightened, and he said, "Well! Little Miss Reliable Witness!"

April blinked, stared at him, and said, "I know you! You hide in ice-cream parlors and overhear conversations! How would you like another story from a—a reliable witness whose name cannot be mentioned here?"

"I'd love it," the fat man said. He drew the folded paper out of his pocket.

"Well," April said, "you know already Mrs. Sanford was a blackmailer. So—" She went on and told him at great and convincing length about the fact that a horde of blackmail material had been found in Mrs. Sanford's house. "Including," she said, "innocent people like schoolteachers and—and stuff." The police, she went on, didn't want any of this material to be made public, because it would cause so much unnecessary unhappiness. So, every scrap of it had been burned. "Right here in our own incinerator," she added forcefully.

The fat man made a note and said, "Is this straight goods?"

"It certainly is," Dinah said. "We saw it." She didn't add whether she'd seen the stuff in question or seen it burned.

"You know," April said confidingly, "the police weren't even going to let anybody know it had been found. Because, after all, they got the murderer. But we've been right here watching everything all the time, and we learned about it. So I guess this is what you'd call a real tip, isn't it?"

"You bet," the fat man said happily.

"Only," April said earnestly, "don't tell where you found out about it. Or—or"—what had that character in Mother's last book said?—"we'll deny everything. So there."

"It was stated," the fat man said, grinning, "by a reliable witness whose name cannot be disclosed at this time—" He turned and started down the steps.

"And by the way," April called after him. "You might stop in at Luke's and tell him we'll be in later for a malt apiece. On you."

The fat man stared at her for a minute and finally said, "If you hadn't been correct on that other story, I'd tell you to go to blazes. O. K., a malt apiece."

"Chocolate," April called after him. "With cream."

"You don't like chocolate malts," Archie reminded her in a whisper.

"I can take two comic books and a package of gum instead," April told him.

Dinah frowned. "What other story?"

"Oh, nothing important," April said airily. "Now, I guess we really had better burn up all that stuff. If I know that guy, he'll make a big story of it, and all the people who've been worrying about their reputations are gonna feel a lot better."

"Let's have a bonfire," Archie said. "It's no fun burning stuff in the insinuator."

"The last time we had a bonfire," Dinah reminded him, "Mrs. Williamson's cat got its tail singed, and Mother threatened to send us to reform school."

"She wouldn't, really," April said dreamily. "You know, Dinah. Mr. Holbrook."

"What about Mr. Holbrook?" Dinah asked, remembering the lame ankle and the cat-and-dog chase around the house.

"I think we ought to give his daughter's picture back to him in person. With the letters."

Dinah gasped. "Are you lul-o-cash-o?"

"In the first place," April said, "he'd probably like to have his daughter's picture. In the second place, he might not see the story in the newspapers, and he'd keep on worrying. Yes, I think we ought to deliver it to him."

Before Dinah or Archie could say a word, she'd scooted around the house and gone in the back door.

"Hey," Archie said. "Y'know what? Y'know what?"

"I know, Archie," Dinah said gloomily, "and shut up."

April came back, five minutes later, with an ornately wrapped package in her hand. "We'll tell him it's just a little present," she said. She led the way down to the sidewalk, and added, "And since he'll know we saw the picture and letters, I bet it'll be a long time before he calls me a bright little girl again!"

There was silence all the way to Mr. Holbrook's house. The cross white cat was sitting on the steps. It spit at them and fled.

"Cordial welcome," April muttered. She rang the bell.

A tall, handsome woman with gray-blonde hair came to the door, smiled at them, and said, "Yes?"

April stared at her, turned pale, and said, "Oh!"

A voice from the hall said, "What is it, Harriet?"

"Miss Holbrook—" April gulped.

The woman lifted her eyebrows. "How—"

There was no turning back. "May-we-see-your-father-please?" April said in a very small voice.

Henry Holbrook appeared at the doorway. The pallor seemed to have gone from his face. He was smoking a pipe, and he was smiling.

"Well, well, well," Henry Holbrook said. "My little friends. This is my daughter. Harriet. Better known as Ardena the famous designer."

"Golly!" April gasped. "You mean the one who makes all those super costumes for all those super musicals!" She recovered herself and said, "I bet you're proud of her, Mr. Holbrook!"

"I certainly am," Lawyer Holbrook said, beaming. "She gave me a big surprise. I didn't know anything about it until she came to visit me."

April glanced quickly at the handsome woman. Yes, she was the one who'd worn the three peacock feathers and the string of beads.

"She's a daughter any man would be proud of," Mr. Holbrook said. He put an arm around her shoulders. "What's that you've got, little girl?"

April winced at the "little girl," but this was no time to bother about it. "It's a little hard to explain. Circumstances—well—somehow, we just happened to find this. Which had been hidden in Mrs. Sanford's house. We thought that because—well, we thought perhaps—" For once in her life, she was at a loss for words.

Archie grabbed the package, stuck it in Mr. Holbrook's hands, and said, "Here, you."

Henry Holbrook tore open the wrappings. The picture dropped out. Harriet Holbrook, otherwise Ardena, picked it up and gave a delighted cry.

"Oh, Pops! This is the picture I've been looking *everywhere* for! To use in that publicity spread! How I started out in burlesque and ended up as a—"

But Henry Holbrook had been glancing over the letters. There was a happy, and slightly dazed light in his eyes. "Harriet. Did you—"

"Let's go," Dinah said. The three young Carstairs raced up the walk, unnoticed.

"Well," April said, "I feel like I'd unintentionally done all my good deeds for the next two or three years. Let's stroll down to Luke's and see if we can collect on those malts."

Dinah shook her head. "Home. Fast. Mother has a date tonight, remember? Those reporters must have gone by now."

"I guess you're right," April said with a sigh. "We do have arrangements to make. Home it is. And, Archie, stop throwing stones at Mr. Holbrook's cat. Just because it scratched you!"

Chapter 28.

MOTHER'S DATE tonight was a very important one. What ought she to wear? Blue, Dinah insisted. That was the color men liked best. She'd read it in a fashion magazine once. April held out for rose. Mother looked really wolfbait in rose. They argued about it through two sandwiches apiece and the rest of the cokes. They continued to argue about it while dinner was being prepared. And then when everything was on the table, they realized that a familiar sound had been heard from upstairs all afternoon. So familiar that they hadn't been aware of it.

They ran up the stairs, knocked, and went in. "*Mother!*" Dinah said severely.

Mother didn't look up. The desk was littered six inches deep with papers, pages of manuscripts, notes, reference books, used carbon paper, and empty cigarette packages. Her shoes were off, and her feet were curled around the legs of the small typewriter table, which seemed to be fairly dancing as she typed. Her hair was pinned up every which way on top of her head, and there was a black smudge on her nose. And she had on the *old* working slacks.

"*Hey! Mother!*" April said.

Mother paused between a couple of words and looked up, with an absent-minded smile. "Just starting the new book," she reported. "It's going fine."

Dinah drew a long breath. "Aren't you *hungry?*"

She looked a little blank. "Now that you mention it, I am. I forgot to have lunch. Thanks for reminding me." She got up, slipped her shoes on, picked up a handful of pages, and started down the stairs. Inky and Stinky came out from under her chair and followed her. So did the young Carstairs.

She walked past the dining-room door and into the kitchen. She smiled vaguely at the children and said, "You can fix anything you want for lunch. I'll just scramble me an egg and correct these while I eat."

"But, Mother," Dinah began. "It isn't lunch, it's . . ."

April nudged her. "Quiet! Don't bother her! She's busy!"

They watched in mounting—and horrified—fascination through the procedure that followed. Mother scrambled an egg in the little enameled saucepan. She put a plate, a fork, a piece of bread and butter and a glass of milk on the kitchen table. From time to time she glanced down at the manuscript, pulled a pencil from her pocket, and changed a word. Finally she turned the flame off under the saucepan and sat down at the table, deep in her reading.

"Hey, April," Archie whispered.

"Ssh!" April whispered.

Mother slowly ate the bread and butter and drank the milk as she read. When she finished the last page she picked up her plate and glass, carried them to the sink, washed them, and put them away. Then she went back up the stairs. The egg was still in the saucepan.

Dinah sighed and gave the egg to Inky and Stinky, who began wolfing it down. "Never mind. When she gets hungry, she'll eat. We've been through all this before. We might as well have our dinner."

"But Bill Smith," April said, "and her hair-do. And makeup and everything. And the rose house coat."

"The blue house coat," Dinah said. "Maybe she'll get to a stopping place by that time."

"But hey, y'know what?" Archie said, sliding into his chair. "Y'know what? S'posin' she don't?"

"She's *got* to," Dinah said.

But the sound of the typewriter kept up loudly all during dinner. It was still going when the three young Carstairs carried their dishes into the kitchen and stacked them up to wash. And it was still going when the front doorbell rang.

Dinah and April looked at each other. "Never mind," April said. "We'll just have to handle this ourselves."

Bill Smith had on a new necktie. His hair was sleekly brushed. He looked nervous.

"Hello. Is—your mother home?"

"Sit down," Dinah said.

He blinked at her.

"Sit down," April said severely. "We want to talk to you."

Ten minutes later the three young Carstairs went into Mother's room. She was just putting a new paper in the typewriter.

"Mother," Dinah said. "Bill Smith's here."

Mother left the paper halfway in the roller. She turned pink. She reached for her shoes. "I'll be right down."

"Now wait a minute," April said. "We want to talk to you."

"Yep," Archie said. "Hey! Hey, Mother—"

"You shush," Dinah said. "Mother, listen. Do you like Bill Smith?"

Mother looked surprised. She nodded. "Of course I do."

"Do you"—April drew a long breath—"do you like him well enough to fall in love with him?"

Mother gasped. She stared at them.

Dinah said, "Mother, don't you think you could fall in love with him and *marry* him?"

Mother turned scarlet. She stammered. Then she said, "I—but—he probably doesn't want to marry *me*."

"Oh, yes he does," Dinah and April said simultaneously.

"How—do—you—know?"

"Yipes!" Archie said. "We asked him a'ready!"

Mother gave them one look. Then she jumped up and ran for the stairs.

"Mother!" Dinah called. "Your blue house coat—"

"Mother!" April wailed. "Your hair-do—make-up—"

She didn't hear. She was down the stairs and into the living room. They crept down the stairs behind her, their hearts pounding.

"Marian," Bill Smith said, grinning. "Those kids—" Then, "Oh Marian—you're beautiful!"

And as the three young Carstairs saw her face over his shoulder, she really was! They tiptoed into the kitchen and tactfully closed the door.

A moment later Sergeant O'Hare appeared on the back porch. He was beaming, and he carried a huge box of chocolates under his arm. "Congratulations," he said. "I see you got what you were after."

"How did you know what we were doing?" they said, almost in unison.

His smile broadened. "Oh, I knew it all the time. You can't fool me. Because I've raised nine kids of my own—and I know!"

AMERICAN MYSTERY CLASSICS
from PENZLER PUBLISHERS

Established by Otto Penzler in early 2018, the American
Mystery Classics series is a line of newly-reissued
mystery and detective fiction from the years between
the first and second World Wars, also known as the
genre's Golden Age.

Now Available:

Dorothy B. Hughes, *The So-Blue Marble*

Stuart Palmer, *The Puzzle of the Happy Hooligan*

Clayton Rawson, *Death From a Top Hat*

Ellery Queen, *The Chinese Orange Mystery*

Mary Roberts Rinehart, *The Red Lamp*

Visit penzlerpublishers.com to see more upcoming
authors and titles.